I0820015

THE ANGELS ARE VOYEURS

THE NEXT GREAT DEITY

VOLUME 2

Written by Millard Crow

Cover Artwork by Sara Camponeschi

Edited by David DeRiemacker

Cover Design and Interior Artwork by Millard Crow

ISBN 978-1733557849

"The Angels Are Voyeurs" is a beautiful song by Momus which confronts the uncomfortable truth that, if the gods are watching us at all, it's for their own entertainment.

Last time, on

THE NEXT GREAT DEITY

Thirteen up-and-coming intelligent designers are brought to Heaven to compete in a reality show like no other. Among them, two abducted humans try to rationalize their new supernatural surroundings.

The contestants are split between three rooms. 35-D contains an array of monster men: **Taninim**, an imaginary friend and death metal loving dragon. **The Internet**, an anti-establishment AI in the small body of a snarling werewolf. **Theodore Flores**, a musician, gambler, and one of the abducted humans. And **Zargah**, an insectoid soldier whose language Heaven has trouble translating.

24-C groups the show's women together: **Oshunmare** is a lizard-lady of scant cloth and bubbly, peacenik vibes. **Ishta-Devata** and **Athena** are lovers on the hunt for the truth behind the disappearance of Athena's sister, **Eris**. **Santa Inari** is a CEO looking to expand her public profile. And **Robin Alleyne**, the other abducted human, is a Christian school teacher disgusted by the commodification of Heaven.

The last room is 41-A. These contestants include **Imhotep**, the spirit of Egypt's innovation and pride. **Oksi**, an ancient Ainu god set in his ways. **Csodaszarvas**, the Hungarian deer of wonder and adventure. And **Jarilo**, a juvenile half-goat god of magic and whimsy who, unbeknownst to anyone, grew a half inch in the last challenge.

The contestants are issued their first challenge: create a brand new species worthy to rule over. One contestant will win and receive immunity in the next episode, one contestant will be eliminated from the competition.

After **Theodore** wins the first challenge and **Athena** is eliminated, he learns from **Robin** that **Athena** was not just kicked off the show, but that she was killed. **Robin** wonders why an Atheist would try to win a religious reality TV show and accuses him of being a mole, unaware that behind the scenes, **Theodore** has formed an alliance with the show's interviewer, **Mark Sharkman**, with the express purpose of undermining the show's ulterior motives, whatever they may be.

Here is a compendium of their creations, and their current placements.

CURRENT RANKINGS

THEODORE FLORES

Atheist abducted into Heaven. Musician and poker player. Needs coffee. Own worst enemy.
CREATION: Quartztaphore— large crystal-like species with restrained shape-shifting capabilities
PLACEMENT: WIN

IMHOTEP

Egyptian chancellor and posthumous deity. Mysterious fashion sense. Vegetarian.
CREATION: Reshep—Centipede monstrosities that produce pathogens in self-defense.
PLACEMENT: TOP2

ROBIN ALLEYNE

Christian abducted into Heaven. English teacher in Honduras. Looking for her dead sister, Nala.
CREATION: Humanity—as it currently exists, but under her tutelage.
PLACEMENTS: TOP3

SANTA INARI

CEO of Inari Inc. Loves vodka. Struggles to function without access to her secretary.
CREATION: MindShare—bar-code-faced creatures powered by capitalism.
PLACEMENTS: MID

ISHTA-DEVATA

Hindu goddess. Athena's lover. Creates illusions and sees true desires. Intimidating soft smile.
CREATION: Water Elementals—Colonies of sentient water molecules.
PLACEMENTS: MID

ZARGAH

Alien. Needs a translation collar to understand everyone around him. Moist.
CREATION: Zarganian—Bipedal, fruit loving ant people.
PLACEMENTS: MID

TANINIM

Imaginary friend of an Earth child. Anthropomorphic dragon that plays a golden guitar.
CREATION: Draconus—Musically gifted dragons.
PLACEMENTS: MID

OSHUNMARE

Hippie lizard-lady from Yoruba myths. Has a rainbow tongue and perpetual smile.
CREATION: Feyder—Thin, spindly feline females.
PLACEMENTS: MID

OKSI

Ainu god. A bear of a man. Loves to cook, hates to talk. Despises Imhotep's smug aura.
CREATION: Pewrep—Bigfoot-like brutes in tune with nature.
PLACEMENTS: MID

CSODASZARVAS

A gold-antlered stag from Hungarian myth. Has difficultly telling others 'no.'
CREATION: Váradi—Antler haired elves.
PLACEMENTS: MID

JARILO

Half-goat Slavic deity. Inseparable from Csodaszarvas, but only because he won't let go.

CREATION: Wheatkin—Wheat people with cereal grins.

PLACEMENTS: BTM3

THE INTERNET

Humanity's knowledge shoved into the hard-light form of a small werewolf. Created by Jesus.

CREATION: The Discarded—Robots made from human trash.

PLACEMENTS: BTM2

ATHENA

Goddess from a rich celebrity family. Ishta-Devata's girlfriend. Believes her sister was abducted.

CREATION: Athenians—Greek warriors.

PLACEMENTS: OUT

He only knew three things. Number one: he was stolen.

He didn't know who he was—reasonably so given he was still being formed. Intertwined straw and vines were tightly packed into his wet, fibrous muscles. A layer of leaves wrapped over these weaves and served as a buffer between vulnerable sinew and thick, yellow, ribbed skin. The naked flesh ripened in the paper white void and deepened to a pumpkin orange. He panned around with his hollow eyes and knew this empty place was not his.

This, he worried, *is not where I'm from*. He tapped a creaking finger to his circular head, and drew its tip across his zig-zag mouth. *But, where... am I from?*

He removed his finger and held it in the air in realization. Number two: he was hot.

This was, it must be clarified, in terms of temperature—he hadn't had time to deduce whether the more colloquial term for attractiveness applied to his form. There were no mirrors in the void, but a brief glance across well carved muscles led him to believe the other definition must be true, too. A little leafy in parts, but he could trim that down, when...

When...

When doesn't matter. Where the hell am I?

The previously mentioned muscles ripped apart as the void separated around him. It deposited him into the sky of Heaven. Green flames burned his pumpkin skin from his form.

Ah, that's right, he thought, *I am on fire.*

The third thing Jack knew—his name—seemed the least important fact of them all, and it sat far in the back of his mostly empty head. Jack's ripped body disintegrated in the flames of his comet, and his last thought was that it was a shame he didn't get to see if his face looked as nice as the rest of him.

*****

"We got a live one," the molar-covered demon munched on a cigar at his holographic display. He sat in the lead chair of a roomy hover-van, large enough for several people. The inside was drab, chrome and steel and metal and mirrors, all framed by mounted artillery and communication consoles. "Want me to get this one, Captain? Or..."

Lucifer fussed with a coil of lemon hair. The curls and pins required to keep his Escher-like weaves in place were a work-of-art. If even one coil was out of place, he felt the equilibrium of his presence would falter. The shrill alarm on the demon's console might have startled a less focused beautician, but Lucifer was an expert on balance. With a pin in his mouth and movements as subtle and slow as an acupuncturist, he secured the loose coil among many.

"The roundup for the show is pretty much done," Lucifer checked his reflection briefly in the chrome of his armrest. "I'll get this one then you can start your night shift, András."

András exhaled smoke from his rows of square teeth. "Don't overwork yourself."

Lucifer pushed himself up by the armrests and flipped backwards and cleared the cushioned back of his captain's chair in a single vault. His many metal adornments on his secured baby blue velvet coat—trinkets of glory, medals of honor, and some floral pins of fancy to accent the look—rattled after he stuck the landing. He checked his hair in the chrome.

"If I listened to that advice, you wouldn't be calling me 'Captain' right now."

The demon watched his superior's gymnastics. Just the sight of the effort Lucifer took to get up made him feel exhausted.

"I ain't flexible enough to be no captain," András puffed, "so your job's secure."

A metal platform extended for Lucifer to stand on as he exited the cobby hover-car they used to patrol the outskirts of Heaven. He produced a gaudy pink key-chain made by Inari Inc., and thumbed the cartoon-cat button on its rose-stickered surface. A hover-bike streaked into view, and Lucifer leapt down and mounted it in the middle of its flight.

Lucifer could've taken the hover-car with András if he wanted to. He looked in the reflective blue paint of the hover-bike handle, squinted, and produced a pair of green aviators from a compartment. He flicked them onto his face while swerving around the tree trunks of the Forest of Golden Trees. He gave a quick glance to his reflection in the paint. Hair? Perfect. Uniform? Starched. Medals? Straightened. Glasses? Cool. Skin? Flawless.

Fuck yeah, he revved the hover-bike and blasted off toward the coordinates of the anomaly.

*****

Jack sat up.

"Oh, hey. I'm alive," the pumpkin-man said.

He brought one of his hard orange hands to his face and wriggled the digits. The skin creaked.

"Yup. This sure is life."

He dipped his fingers into the small stream of murky forest water beside him. A gold leaf drifted by his hand and flashed as it caught a leaked beam of light from the forest canopy.

"...why am I alive again?" Jack's gourd head was ill-equipped to grapple with questions of existential weight.

"Hello, stranger," Lucifer used a pointer finger to flick his aviators off his nose. They flew high into the air. He maintained eye contact with the fruit-headed man as he held open a breast pocket on his ornate coat, and the glasses landed perfectly inside. The Captain looked deep into Jack's empty, carved sockets for a reaction to his technique and poise.

"Oh," Jack waved. "Hi."

Lucifer frowned and produced a pen and notepad from a compartment in his hover-bike and readied the metal nib. "Tell me stranger, what's your name?"

Jack tapped his rind. "It's Jack! That was the first thing I knew."

Lucifer typically had many more questions to ask, but Jack's particular bluntness allowed the veteran officer to cut to the point. With a quick rummage through his hover-bike compartment, he replaced his notepad with a small black-and-red scan gun. "Well, Jack," Lucifer smacked the side of the battery compartment till its power light shone. "Let's find out where that knowledge came from."

"Oh, could you?" Jack nodded. His voice rose and peaked with ample joy his zig-zag mouth could not convey, "I don't remember much, and I just got here. I think I have ammonia."

Lucifer stepped to Jack and brought the scan-gun to his well-carved orange pecs. Red lasers danced between valleys of the ribbed surface. "You're... *only* muscle, I take it. 'Amnesia' is the word you're looking for."

Jack shrugged, partially to show off his traps, but mostly because he wasn't sure how else to respond. "Do you want to go on a date?"

Lucifer let go of the scan-gun's trigger. The laser clicked off. "I'm sorry. What?"

"You're pretty and I don't know where I am," Jack's bicep flexed despite its rigid surface. "I thought I'd kill two birds with one stone. Make a friend and learn."

Lucifer's scan gun lowered and his back straightened. He looked into the sockets of Jack's face and searched for the light of intelligence he must've missed. "Do you think I'm a man or woman?"

"I'm a pumpkin," Jack turned his back and demonstrated the beautiful V-shape his thick lats created as they tapered into the small of his back.

Lucifer smiled and sucked in his lips. He considered tact, then settled with: "That you are." The captain brought the scan gun back up and let the lasers swirl up and down Jack's spine. Suddenly, the display flashed red and spat out a wall of text. Lucifer's eyes roamed through the info dump and widened with concern.

"Well, Jack, I have bad news and good news. The good news is that you're cute and stupid, and those are my two favorite things in a man. The bad news is I've already got the best girl in the world. But fret not, a hero's journey has stolen my heart before. You deserve a chance like anyone else. Every Friday after my shift ends, I grab a drink at Purgatory River Pub. If you can make it out of Hell, come find me. I'd love to flirt loudly with you over a pint."

"Hey," Jack pointed a rind-finger at Lucifer. "I mixed up a word. You can't call me stupid. That's rude. Wait... Hell? I don't want to go to Hell! Isn't that a scary place? I think... I've heard of Hell. I think that's a scary place."

"I'm sorry, pumpkin, but you've gotta go to Hell. All strangers have to start at the bottom and work their way up," Lucifer punched some codes into a console on his hover-bike, and a small dot-matrix printer screeched as it spat out a ticket. “You must earn your life, like anyone else.”

Jack shook his head and stammered. “Wh-what? Why am I going to Hell? I just got here, I didn’t do anything wrong!”

Lucifer smiled and handed him the pink slip. “It’s all here, sweetie. Take this to the receptionist and she’ll explain everything.”

“T-this is a ticket?”

Jack brought it up to his carved face.

“I’m being charged with... life?”

“Yes. Congratulations!” Lucifer clapped. “Make the most of it. If you make it back up here, then your drink’s on me, stud.”

“You called me stupid when you don’t know me,” Jack crumpled the ticket in his fist. “I don’t want drinks with you anymore—”

Jack’s complaint was cut short when Lucifer’s eyes started to flash in alternating lights. His luminescent heterochromia of red and blue accompanied a shrill siren that drowned the forest. Birds fled, trees quaked, and Jack fell to the ground. He held his palms against the side of his rind head as the sound rattled in his seed-filled mind and buried him into the dirt.

“The offer of drinks is just to celebrate you making something of yourself,” Lucifer shrugged. “I already told you: I have a girlfriend.”

A vortex of dirt and dust opened up in the ground and swallowed Jack whole. Lucifer exhaled and his eyes drained of light. The sirens died out. He looked to the ground where the pumpkin had been and rubbed a gloved finger against his chin. *He’ll be fine, but... I have to tell András. This is becoming a trend,* the captain thought. He went to the console on his bike and drew his radio receiver to his face, carefully considered his words, and pressed the button.

"It was a bad idea, I'm afraid," he tossed his sunglasses into the air. He stood as still as a shadow as they landed on his face with rehearsed precision. "This one was... unfinished. I think we both know how the chief feels about unfinished creatures."

"Find Eris," Theodore read aloud as he drew his fingers across the scrapes.

He stood with Mark Sharkman in the lemon-painted walls of the Infinite Wine Hallway, surrounded by scattered wine bottles on the ground. They pondered the meaning of the carved words in their own ways: Theodore's stare darted along the length of the shelf, and Mark paced furiously in what once was a white wine coloured ensemble of fine silk. He ripped off his coat and tie, and his oxford shoes and dress slacks were stained in red-wine splatter.

"It shouldn't be possible," the interviewer ran his trembling hands across his head-fin. "If they had carved this recently, the message would disappear. These words... they have to have been here since this place was first made... that's... that's the only thing that can make sense, right?"

Theodore stared at the simple message as if it were a great equation, and tried to work out the variables which led to its creation. It was late at night when Mark dragged him into the Camera World to investigate the cryptic note, and his disheveled appearance reflected that; he squatted against the wall in gray boxer-briefs and a white T-shirt. The bags under his eyes begged for sleep, or coffee, or both. The eyes themselves, brown buttons too tired to reflect light, did not negotiate with his body's demands. Transfixed and perplexed, Theodore could not consider sleep until he solved that which kept him up. He rubbed the stubble on his chin, brittle in its day-old growth. Altogether, he bore closer resemblance to the way he dressed and lived before Cthulhu abducted him, than he did in the lavender suit Heaven forced him into in the first episode.

The healing properties of Heaven's air should cure any damage to anything. Though Theodore's natural inclination was to reject magical explanations for strange phenomena—a trait that brought him into perpetual conflict with Heaven—he at least accepted what Heaven's air *did* even if he had no explanation as to *how.* To have one of Heaven's core qualities defied before he could dissect its mechanism was a troubling development he was unprepared for.

The Infinite Wine Hallway's automatic spell triggered, and the bottles on the middle shelf clinked and shuffled forward with newly generated wine. Theodore watched the slow parade for a moment, honed in on the scuffle of glass against wood, and raised an eyebrow. An idea appeared.

"Have you tried cutting the wall yourself?" Theodore wondered aloud. He brought his mental focus to his eye socket, and to the gift from Heaven that laid underneath. Buried under his skin and organs, his god eye rested—a gold trinket with a cyclops eye that allowed the contestants to create matter with their imagination—but when he called on it, it refused to come out.

"Uh... hey, Mark. I can't... I can't bring it out. Maybe I need coffee?"

Mark stopped pacing. "What?"

"My god eye," Theodore tapped at his cheek. "It's won't respond at all. I was gonna make a knife with it and test the wall, but-"

"Oh, that's by design," Mark stuffed his hands into his trouser pockets. "I figured you'd deduce this sooner or later. I'm the only person 'here' in the Camera World. Your 'presence' here is your mind. Your ego. Your...soul, if you will. You're just a visitor, so your god eye won't work. Even if I gave you coffee—that caffeine buzz won't last once your gone, I'm afraid."

Theodore huffed and returned his gaze to the wall.

"There has to be a check on the contestants to balance a power like this, you know!" Mark insisted.

"I'm not mad," Theodore muttered, then sealed his hand across his mouth. "Just thinking."

The bottles rattled and covered up the wall's message. Theodore removed them from the shelf and set them down in a growing glass pile, an alcoholic shrine to the mystery of the message. As he scrutinized the instructions again, he glanced at the Cabaret in his hand, then smashed it against the shelf. The shattering of the glass startled the shark-man.

"Should have done this in the first place," Theodore stabbed the jagged ends into the wall. "Having a god eye makes you miss the obvious."

He thrust and scraped randomly across the message, tearing at the grooves of the letters. In under a minute, the damage Theodore had done healed from the surface, but the "Find Eris" carving remained.

"Okay, well," Theodore sighed as the bottle reformed in his hand. He leaned his forearm against the shelf, then pressed his head against it. "Fuck."

Mark's shark-mouth, rigid in its nature, curved slightly downwards in the closest approximation of a toothy frown he could muster. "Well, safe to say they didn't use a bottle."

"Not knowing the 'how' or 'with what' is scaring me, because I'm not sure we can figure out the 'why' without it," Theodore pushed himself off the shelf. The skin tugged at his cheekbones as he ground his teeth. "So... what questions are left to ask?"

"I don't have the slightest idea how we'd figure out 'when,' if you even can," Mark clasped at the sides of his rubbery head, "but maybe if we can figure out 'who' wrote this...'"

"'Who...'" Theodore folded his arms. "Well, if our 'who' is someone that knows about Eris, there's a short list of people that *could* have done this, right? Athena, Robin, Ishta-Devata, the judges, or someone else that knows her. If we assume the contestants wouldn't or couldn't, then the judges or an unknown party are most likely. Athena's dead, presumably, so I doubt she wrote it."

"If the judges really killed Athena..." Mark's eyes trailed the wall's bumpy lemon surface, "and if they did so because of her connection to Eris, why would they draw attention to her by doing something like this? Even if they didn't know Athena made the Olympian Tracker, they'd have to think, gosh, Ishta's probably gonna go home at some point and find out Athena's dead. Are they... are they going to kill her too? Are they gonna kill anyone that knows or talks about Eris?"

"I don't know that they would," Theodore said.

Mark looked over to the human, baffled by his confidence. Theodore had grown accustomed to Mark's rigid jaw and coal eyes, and felt he could understand the micro-twist of his expressions, the swivel of confusion in his neck, the nervous grip of rubbery palm against the snap-buttons of his starched shirt.

"My guess is that there's no benefit to the judges to make us more suspicious about what's behind the scenes," Theodore said as he recalled his arrival on the set of the first episode. "Jesus made it clear that the only thing that matters is what happens in front of the cameras. So why kill Athena at all? It certainly isn't good for the show if the contestants found out, or anyone else. With all this in mind, I have to think that Eris is somehow a threat to the very existence of the show itself."

Mark slunk his tailbone to the floor and buried his toothy face in his hands."Th-then... then what do we do?"

Theodore watched the message disappear behind the slow assembly line of wine. He clicked his tongue against the roof of his mouth. “Well. The instructions are right here. We gotta find Eris. And maybe, once we do that, we can find our ‘who.’”

The green morning light spiraled through the windows of 41-A.

His roommates knew when the Hungarian deer entered a room; Csodaszarvas's hooves clacked against the maple floor tiles with a volume natural selection never intended. What his roomies *didn't* know was the annoyance with sounds-that-cannot-be-prevented went both ways.

Csodaszarvas's hearing was exceptional. It was impossible to sneak up on the gold-antlered elder with or without the help of the hardwood flooring in Heaven's Heart Hotel. His giant white ears rotated around his head towards any slight breath, rustle, or creak. As he woke up that morning, he immediately knew Oksi was in the kitchen chopping potatoes and cod. As he wandered out to the hallway, he could hear Imhotep's lips suck off the glass neck of a sweet ale. When he entered the living room, they all exchanged a three-way, wordless glance of contempt and acknowledgement that said: "There you are. I *heard* you."

What Csodaszarvas *didn't* hear was chatter. Oksi and Imhotep said nothing to each other, and the deer assumed by the wall of pressure between the kitchen and living room that the silence was intentionally employed by both parties.

Imhotep reclined in the farthest part of the living room. He allowed the plush couch the honor of his draped, lithe form, barely covered in the twisted liquid silk of his silver robes. The condensation of his morning beer soaked into the coaster on the living room table. Beside it sat his eye shadow and concealer—all ingredients of his morning ritual.

"Well, *someone* should get the goat up," the Egyptian man suggested towards the deer. With slight modesty, Imhotep drew the fallen cuff of his robe back over his pectoral. "You know how reality shows are. It's been seven hours, they'll probably give us a challenge soon."

Csodaszarvas looked at Oksi. The bear of a man, wide and tall and hairy and loosely wrapped in mismatched patterns of orange and black, peeled and chopped potatoes with violent, surgical accuracy. More alarming, he did so while staring at the deer. His pinpoint brown eyes refused to blink from behind his bushy brow, too swallowed in anger at the individual he was forced to share air with: the Egyptian chancellor he denied even a glance towards.

"...right," the deer sighed, and trotted out of the living room. Jarilo, at his most annoying, was still delightful company when compared to these two.

As he crossed the threshold to the opposite apartment hallway, the small, tinny sound of an electronic speaker tickled the finest hairs of Cso's satellite ears. He trotted up to the youth's door and used one of his gold antlers to knock. Though difficult to make out from behind a closed door (and over the kitchen sounds), the wonder-deer believed the sound was from earbuds that played the distorted guitars of sludge metal.

"Jarilo," Cso said. "Oksi is making something resembling breakfast."

"I don't care," a voice croaked from under bed sheets. Csodaszarvas blinked rapidly as he tried to parse the voice—*was that Jarilo?* he thought. *He sounds sick.*

"Are you okay?" Csodaszarvas asked. "You should come out and eat, even if you're sick. You may not get the chance to for a while if a new challenge shows up soon, and given how long it's been, it probably will—"

The bed sheets rustled. Leather boots thumped into the carpet.

Jarilo ripped the door open. He was taller. His goat-legs had thickened with age and his frame had widened with labor, neither of which he could have possibly achieved overnight. He was able to bring his face to the deer's without looking up. Smudged eyeliner dressed his intense glare. He wore a leather jacket half-studded with spikes along the front, and purposefully shredded at the cuffs.

"I'm gonna die anyway, so who gives a shit?" Jarilo chewed on sweet gum like cud. He threw the door shut in the deer's face.

Csodaszarvas circled in place, then buried his nose into the door. "What the hell is going on? Are you Jarilo?"

There was no answer. This wasn't a change of personality or the effects of trauma from his previous performance: the half-goat had *physically* changed overnight. He bore passing traits of Jarilo—the horizontal pupils in blue oceans, the messy blonde hair and tufts of goat fur at his long ears—but it was as if an older sibling bore his name, and stood in his place. An older Jarilo, far older than the passage of time would have allowed.

Csodaszarvas's ear swiveled to the living room, where he heard Imhotep suck down on his beer and Oksi stab at a fish on a cutting board.

"Well, if you need anything, I'm here for you," Csodaszarvas said to the door, and then laid down in the hallway as to avoid the need to cross back into the living room war zone. Though Jarilo was technically on the other side of the door, Csodaszarvas missed him as if he wasn't there at all. He worried.

In the hours after the first challenge, while other contestants slept or partied, Robin and Ishta-Devata locked themselves into their bedroom and began to brainstorm. Robin didn't change her clothes—so focused as she was on her work, she remained in her cyan jeans and navy sweater, the thin sleeves pulled back past her elbows.

They passed notes to each other using their god eyes, and made sure to keep the contents of the notes out of reach of any potential shiqq cameras. Shiqqs, by their gooey nature, could ooze into the corner of a room at any point. It was important to keep their plan to locate Eris—and discover what happened to Athena—a secret.

The shadow of night dulled the room. Ishta-Devata collapsed and twisted among the silk sheets of her bed. She had removed the outer layer of her sari-drape, but remained in the saturated reds and golds of her belly-shirt and regal patterned skirt. The ornate hat she normally wore sat on the nightstand, the glowing numbers of the red alarm clock reflecting off its decorative gold. Her waist-length black hair grew in volume with stress, and each run of her concerned fingers through the coils lifted its frizz more and more. After hours of diligence, Ishta-Devata choked out, "I miss her."

"I know you do," Robin said.

Ishta-Devata had made the ground rule that, once they got back to their dorms, they would not speak aloud so they could eliminate any possibility of their words getting picked up by hidden microphones, should they exist. For Robin to see the blue-skinned princess break her own oath surprised her—perhaps fatigue from hours of concentration had set in. Perhaps she had a change of plans. Or, perhaps—

"You didn't get to know her like I did," Ishta crumpled onto her side, cushioned by the mattress and her curly hair. "I promise you what you saw was Athena at her worst. I'm sorry about that. That's not who I knew."

Perhaps she just needed someone to talk to.

Robin continued to work in a corner of the room away from the window. She had spent hours trying to create a device similar to Athena's Olympian blood tracker. If she could make a tracker that worked with any input given, she surmised she could use it to track one of the judges. However, Athena's tracker was powered by a magic she couldn't convince her god eye to replicate, and the waste basket in their room was full of metal trinkets with no ability attached to them.

Robin, at one point, created a small bird—a sandpiper—out of concern that she had lost her touch in creating any functioning work at all. The white-and-brown orb puffed its feathers and hopped around the room, and with her god eye she programmed within it the simplest of concepts—eat food, stay warm, fly from danger. The sandpiper's voice was insect-like, low and undulating. It was Robin's favorite bird, one that stuck with her long after she learned about it in high-school. She thought this cute thing might bring some levity to the room, but Ishta remained tangled, withdrawn. Robin opened the window, placed a small metal bit underneath some of its head feathers, and allowed it to fly out of the room. As she sealed the window shut again and drew the curtains, she noticed a brown feather on the floor, and picked it up.

"Not that she wasn't normally strong willed," tears welled up in Ishta's eyes, "she was prepared to do anything to find Eris."

An hour passed. Robin worked in silence. Ishta-Devata smiled at fond memories of Athena as they bubbled up in her mind. She remembered the day she met Athena at the exclusive boarding school their families sent them to. She learned more about the world with, and through, Athena than she did anything or anyone else there. They balanced each other, and with Athena's weight gone, Ishta's drive sank to the floor. "Please believe me when I say she pushed me. I'm not naturally outgoing, and she—"

"Ishta."

Ishta-Devata pulled a bed sheet over her head. "Sorry, I'm rambling. I guess we have more important things to focus on."

"That's not it."

Ishta winced, but kept her vision obscured. She followed Robin's blurry form through the thin fibers.

"I have a real soft spot for people that stay true to their loved ones," Robin said. She did not pause to walk over to Ishta, to console her, or to entertain her. Focus possessed her. "I'm sorry that I have to say it like this, but I think you'll see it's for a reason. Even though she was awful towards me, she didn't deserve to die."

Ishta clutched the sheet, and her regrets, closer to her chest.

"I do believe you when you say she was not at her best. Everyone falls at some point, her failure was just... unfortunately public," energy flashed from Robin's god eye and lit the room like an storm cloud. Ishta couldn't make out what was happening through the sheet, but could see that Robin had quickened her pace back and forth between corners of the room. "And that's why I want you to believe me when I say that I had more in common with her than either of you know."

"She was more than a friend to me, Robin," Ishta's voice cracked into a pillow. Another spark zapped from Robin's god eye, and the smell of acrid smoke flirted briefly with the room's air conditioner. Ishta jumped at the sound, scrunched her nose at the smell, and pulled away from the cover.

"I want to find out what they did to her, and I want to stop that from happening to anyone else," Robin said as she waved smoke away from her face. Her back was turned, but something she held to her chest continued to shine—it lit the walls and the edges of her cheek bones and the twist-outs at the lineup of her hair. She looked over her shoulder at Ishta and exhaled, "And that's why... I need you to be honest with me."

Ishta-Devata gripped the sheets. "Honest about what?"

Robin turned. Her left hand held two trackers—Athena's original, which pulsed with the same slow, mysterious blips it usually did, and a new silver tracker which vibrated wildly. It clanked against Athena's tracker and hummed.

"I need you to tell me what your other power is."

Ishta leaned back. "How did you make that? What is it tracking?"

"You told me about the disguise you create when people look at you, but that's not all there is, is it?" Robin said. "When the judges saw you, they didn't react. None of them, on the roof or at judgement time. But *you did* react. You've told me what happens when other people look at you. Now, you need to tell me what happens when *you* look at *them*."

Ishta's eyes trekked from the vibrating metal eggs, to the furrowed brow of the human. From the etched intensity on Robin's face, she understood the depth of her seriousness—Robin's info on the trackers was a ransom for information on Ishta's ability to see the desires of other people.

Ishta-Devata's lips parted into a smile. "My word... you really are from the stars, aren't you?"

The two stared, engaged in a quiet, unblinking war of attrition. There was a knock at the bedroom door. Robin clicked a button on the underside of the metal egg to switch off its power and slipped both trackers into her pocket. For now, they had to settle for a stalemate.

"Hey, are you two awake?" the curious croak of the lizard-lady, Oshunmare, asked from the other side of the door.

"Working towards it," Robin lied.

"You'll have to work faster, I'm afraid," Oshunmare said. "A new challenge appeared in the living room!"

*****

In the living room, Santa Inari stood next to the couch with a gold envelope. With her plump frame dressed in a red-and-white striped pair of pajamas, the CEO of capitalism blinked through sleep-heavy eyes. Her disheveled bed-hair shifted with her slight movements, but didn't impact the perfect shape of the glowing star on the side of her head. Oshunmare slept in the living room after she discovered that Santa's star stays lit even when asleep, an organic night-light the lizard-lady could still see behind her closed, scaled eyelids.

Camera wielding shiqqs oozed into the room from between the slits of the air conditioner, from underneath the refrigerator, and from under the couch. "Cameras are never far away in Heaven, huh?" Santa gave an annoyed side-eye as she moved away from a camera, and its fleshy, gooey appendage, as it snaked out from underneath the couch.

Oshunmare, Ishta, and Robin entered the living room.

"It's in an envelope this time?" Oshunmare took large clumps of her translucent hair between her fingers and drew them up vertically, then used a fine brush to back-comb the white fibers.

They landed in bunches on her head like clouds. "Last time it was just a single sheet of paper..."

"This thing," Santa grumbled as she tapped its gold edge into her palm, "landed on my face while I was asleep."

The Shiqqs oozed their hands in a circular motion and garbled nonsense.

"Guess it's time to open it up," Santa dug press-on nails underneath the glued flap and lifted. The paper erupted in light and shot a firework into the ceiling. Santa screamed in surprise and stumbled backwards onto the couch. The projectile sparked and exploded into the glowing projection of Jesus Christ's head, which giggled down at the girls of 24-C.

"Good morning, contestants!" the head of Jesus beamed. "Sorry I can't gather you all in person; I have business to take care of. Trust me, I *really* am sorry, because I wanted to see your bright and shining faces react to your next challenge!"

"Oh lord," Santa shielded her eyes with her forearm, squinting at Jesus's shining light. "This is way too much to deal with before coffee."

"Yesterday, you made a species for you to rule over! Or, well, hold on, that's not right..." Jesus's head floated around the room. "Hmm. You made... one member of your species. Gods need more than one follower, don't they? Whoever has the envelope, please reach into the light!"

Santa, with a hesitant wince, dug a finger into the light. She blinked with surprise as she fished out another gold envelope in identical dimensions.

"Now open that one and reach in!" Jesus smiled.

Santa handed the original envelope to Oshunmare and opened the new one. It shot light out in all directions, and as she reached into it, she produced a third, identical envelope.

"The fuck?" Santa blinked.

"One more time!"

Like a clown car, the third envelope gave birth to another, identical-sized envelope.

"Good, everyone should have one now. Did you see what the envelopes did? That's your next challenge. Open them up and read the rules. Good luck, everyone!"

The light receded from each envelope and the girls drew out ordinary stationery from within. Robin read the rules. Her eyes widened. She looked at the others. Oshunmare fist pumped. Ishta and Santa shrugged. She looked back down and read again, and started to sweat.

"Oh," Robin gulped. "Oh, no."

THE SECOND CHALLENGE

Be Fruitful and Multiply

Create the reproductive cycle for your species.
Demonstrate reproductive act in up to 10 minute demonstration.
Sentience not required for demonstration, but will be expected in future challenges.
Working Time: 14 hours, with one 2 hour break 8 hours in.

The Angels Are Voyeurs

The **Workroom**

The contestants filed into the muted marble workroom. The free-floating neon lights licked shadows across the dolls of the previous episode's creations, which sat lifeless, crumpled on their ivory work tables. Athena's workspace had been removed and the remaining 12 slabs were rearranged. The distance between the contestants had grown.

Regardless of the clinical verbiage the challenge rules used, there was only one word on the mind of every single contestant. That word meant different things to different souls and painted a full range of emotions across the cast's faces.

Sex.

This was a challenge about sex.

It makes sense, Theodore thought as he leaned his hip into the table. He rubbed his forehead with mild confusion as he stared at his creation—his quartztaphore—and considered his options.

Sex on Earth has a thousand different meanings and interpretations, and many of those perceptions defined one's religion and way of life. All that considered, he was glad he had immunity in this challenge. *I didn't consider I'd have to think about how this thing fucks. I should have, but I didn't.*

Whether or not the contestants considered sexuality during their previous challenge, they were united by a frustrating implication in the current challenge's rules; depending upon how they define sex and reproduction, the contestants would have to create a second model of their species. Perhaps more! Perhaps less. The possibilities of sex and gender and reproduction were far greater than the addition of two extra hours of working time. That extra time, in the minds of contestants working against the clock, read more as an insult than a luxury. After all, Jesus, by some accounts, had seven days to get things right, and the reception of her work is still largely divided.

"What should a quartz dick look like?" Theodore asked aloud. Many snickered, the abrupt absurdity of his question ushered in much needed levity. He knocked his knuckles on his table and sighed an answer to his own question, "like quartz, I guess."

As large as the workload may have been, few faced the mountains that stood before The Internet and Jarilo. Lambasted by the judges in the previous challenge for their aesthetic and execution, the two needed to regroup and redesign their creations before they could approach the topic of sex—unless they believed they could come up with a sex act so thought provoking and extravagant it retroactively made up for their previous poor performance.

Jarilo ripped the wheat arms off of his wheatkin and pushed the fibers into a pile. The Internet smashed apart his creature—a member of the "discarded" species—with a large sledgehammer and collected the parts.

As Jarilo played with different wheat weaves, he cursed under his breath and ripped them apart after only minutes of work. At some points he'd punch his table, toss his new leather jacket across the room, or squeeze his fist around his god eye, which blinked with nervousness in his palm, as if it feared he might crack its gold frame in his grip.

The juxtaposition between Jarilo's juvenile bombast from the episode before and his current teenage cynicism was not unnoticed by the rest of the cast. Both attitudes, loud in theatrics, served as distractions for the other contestants. No one was more bothered by this than Csodaszarvas.

He stared into the empty gaze of his wispy elven creation, which he'd christened the "váradi." Anytime his train of thought chugged towards a new idea, the heavy crumple of Jarilo's studded jacket against the floor would send his inspiration right off its tracks.

Many contestants quietly drafted notes and sketches before they made commitments with their god eye. This was the path of Imhotep, who flourished pen and ink on papyrus. Zargah produced a thin fabric from his home world that he clawed his alien language into; its surface yielded like sand does to a stick. Oshunmare drew directly onto her marble table with a bulky marker and an idle hum. Santa Inari dictated notes via her company cell phone's voice features—despite the poor cell reception of the hotel, a computer is still a computer. Her cell phone served as the database of all her notes for the world she envisioned.

There were a few competitors that had the confidence to jump into the crafting stage without any hint of the need for planning. Taninim, with his god eye wrapped around the head of his golden guitar, improvised a melody of creation and began to build the muscle and scales of a second musical-dragon. Ishta-Devata crafted a glass box with which her god eye poked through, and began to create soft, gray clouds. It was not unlike the glove-equipped boxes used in laboratory studies, though a god eye's magic would likely never find itself under such scrutiny.

Oksi mumbled to himself as he molded the lumpy bear-like monster he called a "pewrep" with the palms of his hands. His god eye slithered out of his mouth and shot small red lasers into the pewrep, which softened its furry frame for Oksi to knead and reshape. The god eye chain squirmed from underneath his tongue and drew tears of pain from the Ainu god's eyes.

And then there was Robin.

Robin looked into her empty-headed clone, which laid flat on its stomach on her worktable. When she originally made her own clone, she never expected it would become a mirror to confront her. Its vacant eyes were full of symbolism and ideology—facets that served her quite well in the first episode—but they had no room for lust or life. She bored a hole into its sockets with her own gaze as she tried to picture it as a vessel for her sexual identity.

She didn't see it.

She didn't see it in the doll. She didn't see it in herself.

Dissension

The salmon colored walls of the hotel's cafeteria flashed with light as Jesus's body kindled into view. Her sudden appearance above the mosaic countertops of the register startled both Cthulhu and the monkfish employee, who was in the process of fulfilling Cthulhu's usual order of mid-afternoon lemon-butter scallops.

"There you are, you son of a bitch," Jesus floated to the ground. Her red ribbon high heels clinked against stone baroque tile, and her white-and-yellow crucifix-covered-sundress settled around her supple form. It was layered, and soft, and stood in stark contrast to her twitching brow and reddened cheeks.

Cthulhu adjusted the cuff of his black-on-black suit. "Um. *Hello.*"

Jesus stomped towards him and pointed her nose up to Cthulhu's mass of face tentacles. The employees behind the counter cowered.

"What's your plan?" she asked.

"Lunch," he replied.

Jesus slapped Cthulhu.

"I," her breast heaved with a staggered hiss, "am not... a FOOL!"

Cthulhu's brow winced around his circular sunglasses. "I... agree?"

She slapped him across the other cheek.

"What is your deal with The Producer?"

"...the same as yours."

Annoyed at the wall of his irreverence, she marched forward. Cthulhu was forced to back-step.

"In every record I can find, when a contestant has to be... dealt with, it's me," Jesus's hair lifted with electric rage. "It's always me. *I am the one* that deals with the problems. Why did The Producer change plans this time? Is this a plot? Are you his voice on the panel Are you here to throw us off the path when we find The Producer's pick?"

She tried to slap him again. Cthulhu caught her wrist mid-trajectory, which twisted the lines of frustration around her face further.

"Is there anyone that you can think of," Cthulhu lowered his voice, "that would willingly ally themselves with The Producer?" A darkness swelled in his green, pupil-less eyes, one that blackened his oil slick sunglasses into a void.

She snatched her arm away and shook with anger. He brought his behind his back and looked down on her, his tentacles relaxed along his face with cool collection. The cafeteria employees retreated.

"I will not be betrayed," she said. "Not by you or anyone else."

"You're paranoid, Jesus," Ocean-Mouth sighed. "It is too early in this season for you to be this unhinged. Get it together. I want to win as much as you do, but the easiest way to go mad is to assume that every little oddity is a conspiracy, or a plant, or what-have-you. The best thing that any of us can do is to play the game, do our best, and hope that we win."

Jesus's hair returned to its normal gravity. As it fell about the corners of her bearded face, she studied Cthulhu's expression with closer scrutiny. There was nary a hint of fear or uncertainty—annoyance, perhaps, at the strikes against his face, but he was nevertheless unshaken.

"You can't believe that anything involving The Producer will be easy," she said.

"Which is why I won't complicate things. I will not allow myself to be distracted," he shook his head. "Now, if you'll excuse me, I'm going to go back to work looking for clues in the show's library. You're welcome to join me, even though you ruined my appetite."

Cthulhu exited the cafeteria with a commanding posture, stiff, controlled. He stood against her rage, and put himself above it. What's worse, what *really* stung Jesus the most, was how effortless he named her weakness. She *was* distracted. Distracted by what she believed was the beginning of The Producer's direct meddling, and distracted by the possibility that she, yet again, will be denied that which was rightfully hers: her kingdom on Earth, her power, and her love.

She bit her bottom lip and paced to the front of the counter, then smacked the register.

"Are any of you back there?!"

An octopus-man whose face tentacles were secured by a hairnet slowly slithered up to the register.

"Y-yes, mam?"

"Red wine. Now."

"Yes, mam."

The Judges

The judgement panel of *The Next Great Deity* is made up of Heaven's highest earning entities. The supernatural realm is based off of the belief of Earth's citizens: the more people believe in them, the more testaments (the currency of the gods) they receive.

The judges have two purposes: to determine the winner of *The Next Great Deity*, and (unbeknownst to the contestants) make sure that the crowned winner is The Producer's favorite. If they succeed in guessing who The Producer's pick is, they will be granted passage to Earth, where each intends to rule.

JESUS CHRIST

The holy host of Heaven. She is the lead judge, but worries that she's losing her grip on the group.

CTHULHU ALLMAN WATERS

Supplier of fish staff, and the abductor of Robin and Theodore. The Producer talks to him psychically.

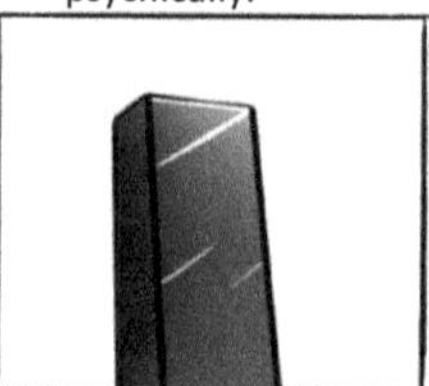

MOHAMMED

Supplier of shiqqs and in charge of security. No one knows what he actually looks like.

Three Coins

The Department of New Souls sat on the continent of Hell, in the country of Kur, in the city of New Meso. It was a stone gray building on a slate gray street with dead glaucous gray bushes and dried taupe gray trees neatly arranged in puce gray gravel, combed and organized under a cadet gray, sunless sky blotted by smoke and haze. Every source of light was artificial; towers with suspended square lights and glowing billboards of heat were guided towards the streets.

Jack sat in the waiting area with his pink slip in one hand and a small numbered paper tab in the other. A depressed eel wormed in the chair beside him. He tried to flex and talk to the eel, but it hissed at him and noodled to a further away seat, which made Jack depressed, too.

"Next!"

The pumpkin-man walked up to the booth, his hard rind feet stomped into soft carpet, and his wide frame barely pushed between the booth's blinder walls. His rind pectorals pressed against the glass divider between the waiting room and the clerk, and not by choice.

"*Hey*," Jack flexed despite the cramped space, and the booth wobbled with his movements. The pumpkin man had a desperate need to make a good first impression everywhere he went, and his consistent failures only made him flex harder with each new interaction. With little more inside his pumpkin head than the knowledge that he looked great, he found himself a slave to certain repetitive behaviors, unaware of a better way.

On the other side of the glass sat an old lady trout in a baby blue polo shirt. Her name—Etta Epaphroditus—sat in Times Old Roman font on a light-bleached name plate. She looked over her bifocals with baggy, unimpressed eyes at Jack's sandwiched form against her glass, then pressed a button on her console. A camera whirred down from the ceiling, placed itself against Jack's face, and flashed.

"Ah!" Jack flinched as bright white light filled his empty cavities.

"Slip please," the trout tapped the open space in the glass. She looked at the monitor in front of her and read Jack's data as it appeared on her screen.

"It just occurred to me," Jack shook his head as the dots in front of his eyes bubbled away. "How did that blind me if I don't have eyes? Actually, wait."

Etta glanced at Jack. He stuck his pumpkin fingers in his triangular, empty sockets.

"How can I see at all?!" Jack gasped.

"Three coins."

Jack removed his fingers from his eye sockets. "Huh?"

"Three coins," the receptionist droned as she slapped copper trinkets onto the counter. "One for every person who believed in you when you arrived. The base of your existence is belief."

"What do I do with these?" Jack's bulging biceps made it difficult for him to scoop the coins off the counter.

"With three coins?" Etta raised a fishy brow. "You can buy a soda on your way to work."

"Work?"

"Yes. Here's your job based off your physical and mental attributes," the old trout pushed through a stack of papers so thick it barely fit through the divider's opening. She took off her glasses, leaned back into her chair, then began to mist herself with a spray bottle. Her gills pulsed with nourishment, "If you discover any special abilities heretofore unknown to the database sheet attached on Page 27 in subsection C, you are instructed to make an appointment at this department with one of our counselors and we can find new placement for you. As it stands, it looks like you'll be working in a warehouse, which, looking at *how much of you* there is, probably makes sense."

"Wha..." Jack flipped through the pages. Each sheet was dense with walls of jargon and rules and policies and numbers and Jack just wanted to flex and make friends.

Etta rattled on. "Before you do that, though, it is advised you spend your first day getting acquainted to your new living space. You'll find the address of your government housing on page 7 subsection Q. If you head out to the left from here, a driver is ready to take you there free of charge. Enjoy it. You won't hear that last part again for as long as you live... well, no, you'll hear it once more on your way to your first day of work, but that's it. Once you enter the rat-race, you'll be runnin' for your life, forever. Work hard, build up belief, and when you reach the threshold as outlined on Page 172 Subsection U, you can move to the suburbs. Do *really* well and you *might* be able to get a starter apartment in Purgatory. Do you have any questions?"

"Wh..." Jack shook as he scanned through spreadsheets and schedules. "What? Why?"

The trout lady spit into her trash can and popped her jaw. "Gonna need some nouns and verbs in there, hon."

Jack's gourd rattled. "Why do I have to do this?"

"It's called 'Hell' for a reason, honey. You got any specific questions?"

Jack slumped. His head-stem tapped against the glass. "Where do I go from here, again...?"

Ol' Saint Smoke

The hallways of Heaven's Heart Hotel were heavily gilded; red carpet and gold miscellany folded into the walls in an infinite spiral of excess. In the center of engravings of angels and demons and heavenly lights, there was a plain green bathroom door, and from within, the sound of running water, hands washing, and heavy sighing could be heard.

The handle clicked open. Santa Inari combed a strand of firetruck hair behind her ear as she entered the hotel hallway. Once the strand settled into a clump of hair, it glowed, as required by the star-shaped luminance that projected from the side of her head.

She rounded a corner on her trek back to the workroom, and found another contestant roaming the halls.

"You lookin' for something, human?" she asked.

Theodore may have appeared to be wandering, but his worried pace was an act. Sure, it wasn't an act far removed from reality; he was the sort of person to stick his hands in his pockets and pace and stare off at nothing in particular. There were plenty of religious murals in the hallways—almost all of which were dedicated to Jesus or Cthulhu—to lose oneself in, too, so it didn't appear terribly odd to see him walking along the long mural of renaissance oil painting. None of those parts were an act, but his positioning was; he had stationed himself specifically so that Santa would have to walk past him in order to get back to the workroom. Since she struck up a conversation with him, the next part of his plan was much easier.

"I'm a pacer," he removed a hand from his pocket and rubbed the back of his neck, "and a coffee drinker. And a smoker. If I'm being honest, I collect vices like they were trading cards. You don't happen to have a cigarette, do you?"

"You got a speech or something for me?" Santa raised an eyebrow.

Theodore tilted his head. "Huh?"

"Is this some sort of stunt like the one you pulled with Athena? You just gonna keep asking strong women to help you get your thing out?"

Theodore held a hand to his chest and pulled his chin downwards. "*Excuse me.*"

"I'm joking," Santa said as she reached into a trouser pocket.

Theodore watched as she withdrew a carton of cigarettes. It was striped red and white like a candy cane, and it had a cartoon of Santa Claus on it, rosy-cheeked and snowy-bearded, quite unlike its owner.

"Santa smokes, huh?" Theodore said.

"I'm an executive," she tapped the top of the carton repeatedly to her palm, "I do a lot of shit to get through the day."

*****

Round the corner from the workroom, there was a small balcony with a steel table and wastebasket. With the glass door propped open, the two smoked underneath a glowing red exit sign—Theodore leaned against the door itself to keep it open, and Santa Inari pressed her back against the frame. The balcony faced the Forest of Golden Trees, which glinted with the same gilded riches as the interior of the hotel, but as it was naturally occurring, it gave the appearance of greater extravagance, as it required the green neon sun of Heaven to shine above it at the right time of day for it to flicker. It was fleeting in its beauty, a marriage of light and material. Theodore admired the view, and wondered what it was like to walk the shimmering paths.

"So you're a CEO?" he asked as he lit his cigarette. He used Santa's lighter, which was adorned in images of snowflakes. "What's your company do?"

"Inari Corp. has its hands in so many industries that I don't even know what we do anymore," she sucked on the candy cane styled cigarette and blew a ring of glittery smoke. "It's all stocks and mergers for me these days. I haven't stepped inside a factory in years, and if I'm lucky, it'll be many years more before I have to."

Theodore inhaled, winced, and exhaled smoke from his cigarette. His face was twisted in mild displeasure, like a dog that's discovered the taste of lemon.

"What the hell is in this?" Theodore watched the glittery ring drift off into the breeze.

"Unicorn horn," Santa rolled her tongue around her bottom teeth, and swayed at the cool, sweet smoke as it danced around her taste buds, "and tobacco."

Theodore gave the cigarette another try. He coughed out his second puff of smoke—the taste did not improve.

"It's like someone set fire to a bowl of fruit loops," he winced, "and stuffed my nose in it."

The two were quiet for a moment. Theodore's eyes trailed down the carefully tailored red business suit that Santa wore. He knew the lifespan of the average cigarette, and decided it was time to act on his plan.

"Hey," Theodore's gaze sat on the square outline in her pocket.

Santa looked to him with lidded eyes.

"I saw that you had a cell phone in the workroom earlier," Theodore said. "Does it have internet? Can I see it?"

"You can see it," she muttered as she drew out her phone. "But the coverage here is absolute ass. Good luck doing anything on the internet. I haven't been able to make calls, stream videos... if a web page had more than two pictures, it was a lost cause waiting for it to load."

Theodore opened the phone and was immediately stunned by familiarity. It was a cold and rigid rectangle secured by a plastic case, slightly transparent and, like everything else Santa seemed to own, Christmas themed. Theodore could take the technology back to Earth and no one would notice. No one would be impressed.

"It's just like a normal cell phone from Earth," Theodore shook his head. "Why is that? Why doesn't Heaven have better magic than technology?

Santa smirked. Theodore typed in some search terms into the phone's internet browser, and looked up at the Christmas CEO in time to catch her lips curl.

"What?" he asked as he waited for a loading bar he was certain would never fill.

"You made such a big deal about not believing in the show, but..." she exhaled a stream of smoke from her nostrils, "I just think it's funny that the thing that may make you a believer in the supernatural is disappointment."

Theodore scrunched his face. "Nobody said nothin' about me believin' anything."

Santa sucked on her cigarette. "Sure."

Theodore glanced towards the screen. The search page staggered across the finish line with text-only results and broken images. Theodore searched for Athena, as he assumed that looking up Eris directly might not be the best way to keep cover. He also assumed that if Athena were really as rich and successful as she claimed, that even with half-loaded entries, Eris's name would appear somewhere, anywhere, on the page. There was a summary of Athena in an entry on the corner of the page, and though her list of relatives appeared with links to their bios, Eris was so unimportant that they didn't even consider her worth mentioning. Athena was at least famous enough for information about her parties, her education, her rich lifestyle. Eris wasn't even a footnote despite being her sister.

"So what are you looking up?"

"Honestly, I just wanted to know more about Heaven," he lied, "and how this place works..."

He trailed off. As he scrolled down the page, a news headline showed up in the results. It read:

CAR CRASH KILLS THREE IN NERAKA, PURGATORY

The text for the article that loaded on the search page did not mention Eris, or Athena, and only seemed to be connected due to the fact it occurred near the Olympian Estate. Of greater significance was the mention of Purgatory itself, which triggered a memory from when Theodore first met Mark Sharkman—how the fishy interviewer claimed he had a vacation home there.

Santa flicked her cigarette to the ground and ground its flame out with a sharp red heel. Theodore heard the familiar sound of sole-to-gravel and closed the search page before handing Santa back her phone.

"Thanks," he said. The two walked back to the workroom. When Theodore got to the double doors, he stood in front of Santa, grabbed the door handle as if to open it, but paused.

"We don't have a computer or internet—well, we have The Internet, but he's different—anywhere in our dorm," Theodore wondered aloud. "Why haven't they confiscated your phone?"

"I may have sponsored one of the judge's fashion lines a couple of years ago," Santa said. Her eyes rolled upwards to the sky as she searched her memory, "maybe *two* of the judges. I can't remember."

Theodore opened the door. "Ah."

The two parted ways towards their own tables. Theodore approached his quartztaphore as it sat quietly on the marble countertop, devoid of life outside of the instructions he programmed into it. Even with immunity in this challenge, the impossibility of balancing his many tasks weighed heavily.

He rubbed the bridge of his nose, and rested his head on a smooth part of the quartztaphore's purple chest. "All I've got is questions," he muttered.

A small movement caught his peripheral vision. He swiveled his head to the left, his forehead pressed against the quartz slab, and caught sight of a shiqq as it oozed up and down in the corner of the room. Theodore looked directly into the camera lens.

Theodore popped into Mark Sharkman's Camera World. His silhouette among the wall of CRT monitors stretched until his back audibly popped. He wondered why he needed to stretch at all if the Camera World only transported his "soul," and why it felt so good to feel the decompression of his upper back.

Since Heaven hadn't provided him with a wardrobe, he crafted a new suit with his god eye the night before—that way, if he ever got to see the show, he could look at the different coloured suits in various interviews and see how his words were edited. Swathed in baby blue pastels from collar to steel-toe, he loosened the yellow tie around his throat and sat down in the stool across from Mark's console.

As he prepared his camera-ready poise, portals of disconnected darkness opened around him, and black cameras whirled out from their depths. Mark no longer needed to guide him through explanations—the blinking red lights, and the hum of electronics, and the whirling camera-arms had become comfortable territory when compared to the rest of Heaven. Theodore was so used to the Camera World, in fact, that it took a moment for him to realize Mark wasn't propped up in his swivel chair. He looked around the light box lit room, then snapped his head towards the console-control when he saw a shark fin rise from behind a monitor, a rubbery crescent from an ocean of light.

"Uh, Mark?" Theodore leaned.

Mark Sharkman popped his head up in surprise. "Hey! Yes. Um," He made a cutting motion across his throat and held up a manila folder. "Sorry, just getting my... *files* ready."

Theodore pursed his lips, took a hint, and forced himself to relax back into the most photogenic pose he could think of.

When Mark rounded the corner, Theodore noticed he had two folders, one in each hand. The shark took his seat opposite of him, played with knobs on the camera-console, placed one folder to the side, opened up the other, then looked into the cameras. With a silent nod, the steel camera-arms and lenses closed in around the human.

"So, tell me about your reaction to the challenge."

"What do I even say?" Theodore melted into the cool demeanor of the reality show star he pretended to be, his smile plastic, the twinkle in his eye a mask for a corroded interior. "It's hilarious. I'm trying to figure out how to turn my quartz dude into a walking J/O crystal. Not *exactly* where I saw my life heading, you know?"

"Have you settled on what you'll make?"

"Absolutely not. I'm glad I have immunity. Last time I started late because I didn't... *understand* the god eye. This time, I'm starting late because I can't think of anything without laughing, which, like, I don't know, maybe that *shouldn't* be your first reaction to sex. If I got in bed with someone and they burst out laughing I'd feel pretty bad."

"Thank you," Mark nodded. He killed the electricity to the camera arms via a switch and watched their steel arms droop. He exchanged folders and exhaled. "Now... for this."

Theodore let his cheerful facade drop. "Hit me. What's up?"

Mark moved to the desk and motioned Theodore over. He spread out the folder's contents across the surface of his desk; all manner of maps and schematics of the hotel crinkled as Mark tried to press them flat.

"Holy shit," Theodore blinked as he drew his finger down the diagrams of many floors. "Where'd you find these?"

"The maps themselves aren't a big deal," Mark sighed. "These are made available for any guest. I get memos every season full of instructions and schedules and diagrams and I've piled them all away. It gets to be a lot after a while, you know? Junk mail. Noise."

"You put these in the infinite wine hallway, I'm guessing?"

"Ah, no! That's just one area."

Theodore looked around for some part of the Camera World he was unfamiliar with. He only knew of the path to the Infinite Wine Hallway, and the safe where Mark had hidden his personal notes. "How many secret doors you got in this place, Mark?"

Mark clicked a tooth. The wooden desk ground against the floor as it slid to the side, along with the wall it was against. A new hallway was revealed, and it was filled with infinitely stretching filing cabinets.

"This place is not inaccurately named when I say it is a 'Camera World,' as opposed to a 'Camera Room.'"

Theodore frowned at the dim lights on gray wallpaper, and the odor of mildew. His nose scrunched as he reached out to a filing cabinet. He lifted a foot and began to walk in. "I think I'd rather be in the wine hallway."

"Most of the stuff in this room is boring, I promise," Mark put a hand on Theodore's shoulder. Theodore stopped, his leather shoe hovering over the dividing line between hallway and interview room. "Before you go digging through all of that, you should look at these maps."

Theodore huffed. He wanted to dig through the files, and the suggestion that the filing room wasn't worth investigation filled him with equal parts suspicion and annoyance. *Still, Mark clearly found something,* he thought as he turned back to study the hotel's schematics again, *let's see what's up.*

"Do you see anything odd?" Mark tapped the more yellowed map.

Theodore shook his head. "Uh. They're different? Looks like they renovate between seasons. Is that unusual?"

"Close. Look at these two, in particular. These two maps paint different pictures of what Heaven's Heart Hotel's layout is, and this one," he tapped a sharkskin finger down on the thin, glossy paper, "is current. What's crazy is... they're both right. Look at this floor that has a pool and nothing else on it. You shouldn't be able to get to this floor from both places, but you can. Look! This floor with the pool used to be M, but it was moved to N. A whole floor, its plan the same as it was before, completely moved! Listen—I see where the shiqqs go on my monitors. I've seen them get to floor N by going up the stairs on both M and O. It doesn't look like they're doing anything unusual, but that's not possible, alphabetically or logistically. Yet, all floors are accounted for."

Theodore flinched. "So we got a phantom floor? Or just a pool that likes to travel?"

Mark leaned against the door frame of the Infinite Filing Cabinet Hallway and rubbed his head.

"It's going to be difficult for you to look for Eris if she's outside of the hotel, but if we theorize that she's inside here, which is what Athena seemed to believe... there's no reason not to at least look around. Even if you don't find her, there's probably *something* there on one of those floors."

Theodore held one of the maps up between calloused fingers and squinted.

The Internet grunted with each swing of the hammer down onto the metal plate of his new creature. His pink dog tongue darted in ragged pants from hours of assembly. Smeared grease muddied the logo of his red Kraftwerk shirt. His flat-brim leopard print hat was turned backwards on his head, and emblazoned in neon pink across the face of the cap was the word "FUCK." The expletive served as a stop sign for anyone that looked towards his table and considered interrupting him. He also hoped that the editing team would be forced to blur out the cap, or remove footage of him altogether; it was a strategic play to reduce his screen time, one informed by the discovery that contestants on reality television are more likely to be eliminated if an episode's editing focuses on them too heavily.

A major part of the feedback the dog-punk received from the last challenge was his weakness in design and finish. The same could not be said of the steel being in front of him—standing at nine feet tall, this metal-organism, while still comprised of miscellaneous parts from a human landfill as per his original concept, showed the designer's hands in its sleek symmetry. Metal and glass and plastic and bottle caps were smashed and polished together into coherent, simplified shapes that, when assembled, melded to a sculpted, sensual humanoid form. Green lights leaked between segments of metal fitted together in the form of biceps, calves, skull-like steel jaws. The square screen of a re-purposed cash register blinked to life above his aluminum-tab teeth. The subtle taper of his plastic groin segmented around V-shaped rubber ligaments and joints. The whole form read of a master sculptor's assembly, which is of no surprise when one learns The Internet had the world of online art courses and video sculpture tutorials in his head for easy access. Now equipped with feedback, he knew which lessons to employ, which artists he should mimic, and whose taste he should cater to. *Never again will my execution be called into question*, he thought.

The Internet's grand plan was to incorporate his old design as a rite of passage for his "discarded" species. The dog-punk took his pain and molded it to visual parable—as these creatures must build themselves into beautiful forms from nothing, he, too, had to survive the last challenge with no experiences to dwell upon. Just as their dog-god had fought in Heaven to make himself better, so, too, must the discarded fight for their best bodies in their new lives.

That this challenge was centered around a specific facet of life—sexuality—allowed The Internet to narrow his focus. Though he complained internally about having twice the amount of work as most of the other contestants, being forced to redesign his robots into more attractive forms was a blatant blessing which addressed both his major failings from the last challenge and positioned him with new creative opportunities in the current. In his electric heart, The Internet did not find it difficult to be confident. (Though there was a nagging cell dog in the back of his mind that reminded him: *I was confident last time, too. Confidence... is only part of this competition.*)

His confidence, however, did not halt his jealously at those who did less work than he did last episode and managed to avoid the bottom anyway.

Contestants like Santa Inari, for example. The CEO's bar-code-faced doll sat with its white mannequin hands neatly placed in its lap. It was a simple and bland creature, and no amount of soul could make its small, black eyes hidden among the bar-code lines appear anything other than lifeless. The Internet was stunned that she received no criticism last episode, and stunned further still that, in this challenge, Santa did not smash the mannequin to bits and start over, but instead wasted time on the creation of small coins. Whatever the purpose of the silver and gold pieces etched with her visage were, The Internet did not care—she had done nothing to tackle the concept that landed her in the middle, and such lack of ambition and inspiration meant, to him, that she deserved to plummet.

And Ishta-Devata! *What is up with the creations of the girl's room?* he thought as he watched her create small, hand-sized storm clouds from her god eye. The small clouds would shoot small bolts of white lightning, only slightly stronger than that of a static discharge into test droplets of water on her table. The lightning sparked the water beads to move around on the table until they spread themselves so thin as to become a singular smear. Was it metaphor? Was it laziness? Was it both?

Yes, he growled, *and what a waste of electricity, too.*

So many of the contestants, to his yellow eyes, seemed to take the easy way out and made Earth-inspired concepts of dual gender creatures, with no sign of original ideas or deeper meaning. *They miss the point,* he thought as he attached wires inside his creature's exposed chest. *You will be judged by someone who authored the* Adam and Eve *story. They will expect symbolism, metaphor, exposition. Anyone who just goes out there and has two creatures fuck without any meaning or purpose deserves to go home.*

His stare shot these thoughts at those he considered the biggest offenders: Oksi, Oshunmare, and Csodaszarvas.

Oksi, in a fashion The Internet started to suspect was typical for the silent bear-of-a-man, floundered. He had started to mold his original character, the lumpy, furry potato he called a pewrep, into a more muscular, defined shape. But with clumsy coordination he would misshape biceps, neck muscles, and lose even the vaguest sense of symmetry in the form. His god eye, which snaked from his mouth, floated dutifully in front of him and softened the flesh of his pewrep for Oksi to knead, but hours of work left him with a confused, lopsided, anthropomorphic pile of flesh that was somehow uglier than the potato-with-fangs he marched out in the first challenge.

Oshunmare had taken her creation—a pale cat-faced humanoid she called a "feyder"—and made an almost identical clone of it. Both were perceptibly female thanks to Oshunmare's insistence on defined breasts, the likes of which The Internet thought looked incongruous with the ghostly, spindly design of the leggy creatures. The only way to tell them apart was via slight color shifts of their pale pastel manes, the difference of shape between their glowing eyes, and a restrained increase of height in the newest model. The Internet hated what she made in the last challenge, and to see her repeat the design incensed him. He wanted to rip apart the translucent dresses they both wore, made of a sturdy yet thin fiber similar to graphene. He calmed himself with the prediction that she'd get ripped up by the judges soon enough.

Csodaszarvas, too, solely relied on yesterday's playbook. He made a female variant of his male elf creature, the 'váradi,' and took her purple horn-hair and blunted its ends into more cubic shapes. There was no exploration of new gender or imagination. The closest the wonder-deer had come in his design to innovation was a small wreath of flowers whose purpose The Internet did not yet know—the deer would guide the female váradi to touch it and the wreath wilted and blossomed with each new contact.

Most of the remaining contestant's work he did not look at with the same level of vitriol. Zargah massaged the palms of his long-fingered ant-man, and as he did so, his god eye hovered over the palm and shot its creation laser into its pores. Green liquid bubbled around the flesh. The Internet knew not what this meant, but found it instantly more interesting than the majority of the work around the room.

He felt the same way about Taninim, who had devoted his time to the creation of new instruments and amplifiers. A blue bass sat disassembled on his work table—the pieces were created with his god eye, but the dragon-god assembled them by hand. They fit together with runes, which activated and fused once Taninim played a particular tune on the golden guitar he forever carried around his neck. The body of the bass was adorned with trinkets of fancy, pearls, and engravings and knobs of gold and silver. The Internet thought it was a logical progression for the dragon-guitarist to build up his world through the layering of instruments—if the dog-punk were totally honest, he was more excited for a concert than anyone else's sex show.

The Internet was not so much annoyed or impressed by what he saw on Theodore's table as he was confused. Theodore's god eye floated in front of his face, and the first thing he used it for was to create a wide array of tissue and bandages. He applied them haphazardly around the side of his head to soak up the blood that erupted from his eye socket when the god eye sprang from it. As far as actual creative content, all Theodore had created was a mound of dirt on his table—he had spent most of his time within the black-blue guts of his quartztaphore. He used the lasers of his god eye to open up its chest and modify aspects of the creature too small for the rest of the room to see. The Internet thought, *whatever he's doing, at least it looks like he's taking a risk. If I had immunity, I'd try to do something weird, too.*

The dog-punk never made the connection that the majority of the contestants he avoided internal criticisms of were his roommates. Nor did he make the connection that the only person he didn't immediately fling vitriol towards that wasn't his roommate was Imhotep—a man who kept to himself, and who received accolades from the judges with challenging, frightening work. Imhotep spent most of his time with his god eye hidden, and instead wrote on papyrus with red and black ink from two small clay pots. His hand waved the quill with sharp, precise movements, and produced a messy short-hand script The Internet could not make out. When The Internet looked at Imhotep, he thought of only two things: his dagger-legged centipede-like monster—the reshep—which sat coiled along the floor, and his tone, which he used to berate The Internet in the waiting room, in his darkest hour during the last challenge. His was the only confidence in the room he respected—and he hoped, after this challenge, he could surpass it.

There was one more person whose work set the most negative parts of his electric anatomy ablaze—Robin.

The Internet sneered. He didn't look at her. He didn't need to. She hadn't made anything yet—all she had done was undressed her clone, laid it on its stomach, and stared into the distance.

All those other fools better be glad she didn't get immunity. He hammered his creature's chest plate closed. *At this rate, she's definitely next to go.*

Sex Type Thing

Robin Alleyne had complicated views on sex.

Raised in a Christian household, she was led to believe in the sanctity and purity of intercourse. The broad summary of her Sunday school teachings was that nothing is more sacred in the eyes of the Lord than saving oneself for marriage—abstinence. The details of this supernatural metaphor, however, were more grounded; the young girl was taught that intimacy and love, true understanding of another human heart, had to come before physical exploration. Sex was an expression of intimacy, but not the means to it. As her family was active in their church-centered community, these lessons were taught to her by her peers and friends. She had no reason to doubt them.

In the early 90s, 16-year-old Robin's youth group went on a canoe trip on the Charles River, an easy enough task since the church was in Brighton, MA, one of the many cities that touched the river's watery line along its 60-mile stretch. When the time came to pair off into groups, Robin positioned herself not-so-subtly next to her boyfriend. An infielder for the high school baseball team, the boy was tall and lean and had started to grow the suggestion of a mustache. Despite his athleticism and nervous charm, his cursed name—Clinton Clinton—made him a target for bullying in school. Clinton went by his middle name of "Chuck" to avoid embarrassment. By choosing his own name, it also helped him identify who his real friends were.

Robin loved Chuck. She loved his awkward gait, his lanky limbs, the elasticity of his wrist as it snapped the ball from 1st to 3rd with refined speed. She loved how hard of a worker he was on the field and how sweet and honest he was off of it. She saw a future in his quiet smile and determination.

The trip itself was intended to be about four hours total, two out to a designated clearing for lunch, then two hours back. The July heat never broke 80, there was no rain in sight, and the thick cotton clouds smoothed the waters to a calm gray. The most saturated color Robin found in the river was the reflection of her neon yellow top and her bright blue jelly bracelets.

"By the way, great job on your win," Chuck said as he shuffled water bottles and aluminum cans around in the small ice cooler that sat in the middle of the boat. His hands neatly palmed each drink in their massive grip. "Officially, your team has a better record than ours."

Robin stared at a Canadian goose as it shuffled their chicks into the foliage. "I wish our team could try to play against some of your opponents."

The two had stopped paddling to cool themselves in the shade. The tall woods curved over the slate waters. The only movement across the surface came from the ripples of their little red canoe.

"I wish you could, too," Chuck said. He frowned as he considered which lie he wanted to tell her. "Maybe someday you'll get to. Want something to drink?"

Robin smiled and turned, secured the ice cooler's handles and lifted it into her lap. "Absolutely. Got a soda?"

"Yeah, I brought some," Chuck leaned in. "Let me see..."

He reached into her box and shuffled its contents. He struggled, but eventually, his finger bumped into the right object.

"There we go."

Two cold red cans, slick from their melting home, clinked together. Chuck met her, drew her in between his legs, and the two guzzled their sugar fizz with the sickening synchronicity of a television commercial. They drifted on calm waters. The carbonation in their cans merged with the squawks of red-eyed black-crowned night herons. A small turtle sat on a rock near the canoe's path, turned, panicked, and flung itself into the river. Robin laid her back against Chuck's chest, the thin fabric of the t-shirt warm from the summer heat. His arm, dew with sweat, wrapped over her collarbone. He protected her.

This is perfect, Robin thought as a cloud drifted by. She adjusted a jelly bracelet that had slid down her forearm.

*****

"Yeah, it's great," Becky chewed off the corner of a turkey sandwich "And it's not, you know... *fucking*."

Not everyone at Robin's school followed their religion's belief's quite as strictly as the Alleyenes. A month prior to the canoe trip, Robin found herself caught between the rules of her church and the sound arguments of her peers.

"It's still sex, though," Robin bit into an apple.

The group of girls were centered in the crowded cafeteria. Amid the loud chatter and clanking trays, you wouldn't have heard the girl's frank conversation unless you walked by them—this particular flock was well versed in keeping their eyes out for roaming teachers, and lowered their voices when any adult approached.

"You're right, Robin," Kelly pushed her huge red-framed glasses up her nose. "I mean, we're gonna be adults in a few years. Marriage isn't that far away. If he loves you, he can wait."

"If you love a guy, though, a blow job is pretty safe and not that difficult," Becky set down her mayo-slathered sandwich and adjusted her fuzzy crop-top. "It's not a big deal. Besides, real sex hurts. This won't. Unless... he's... how big is he?"

Robin boggled at Becky.

"Right..." Becky bit into bread crust, "you haven't seen it, yet."

"'Real sex' doesn't hurt if you do it right," Mallory crumpled her paper bag up. "Don't you remember our sex ed class?"

"Bitch, that was like 4 months ago, you think I remember anything from the *one class* we had?" Becky laughed.

"It's not worth the risk. You could get a STD on your lip or something," Kelly groaned as she stared down at her plastic tub of peas and carrots. She had lost her appetite, and pushed the chopped bits around with her fork. "Besides, it should be his decision."

Mallory squinted. "No, I think Robin *should* get a say in what she does with *her* body."

Kelly's nose scrunched. "And you're wrong. Proverbs 30:20 says 'This is the way of an adulteress: she eats and wipes her mouth and says, 'I have done no wrong.' Chuck has been with you for, what, two years now? Why jeopardize your relationship?"

"Oh my god," Mallory combed her black bangs back and furrowed her brow. "You're why I'm gonna get a theology degree. It also says in the bible that slaves should be pampered. Hey, Robin, is it okay to own slaves as long as you take *real good* care of them?"

All three of the white girls stared at Robin. Robin looked back at the group she had grown up with, and no longer recognized them. She glanced at the core of her apple and shifted in discomfort in her seat.

All she wanted to know was what she should get Chuck for his birthday.

"I guess I'll..." Robin mumbled, "get him a new pair of cleats or something."

She left the table before the bell and tossed the apple core into the trash.

*****

Robin set the empty can of soda outside of Chuck's leg. It slipped from her grip and rolled on the floor of the canoe. She found her hand near his outer thigh, felt the warmth of his skin, exposed as the hem of his shorts slipped down naturally with gravity's cooperation.

She swallowed. Without thinking, her fingertips pressed in and drew across his flesh. She felt the tenseness of his thighs carved from the lengths of the diamond he regularly ran. Chuck shuddered in surprise at Robin's touch—unexplored territory had been breached. Robin could not see his wide eyes, her focus occupied as it was.

*****

Robin and Mallory sat outside the front doors of their high school and eyed the line of cars that clogged the parking lot and busy street.

"Hey, uh," Robin played with a zipper on her bookbag. "You've actually had sex?"

"Yeah."

"Aren't you worried about..."

"Going to hell? No."

Robin sighed. "That's not what I was going to ask."

Mallory combed her bangs back and looked over to Robin.

"I know that we're... not that close anymore," Robin looked up into the eyes of her friend. She needed Mallory to know... "I'm not asking you this from a religious standpoint. I'm asking... aren't you worried it... won't be special if you get married later on to someone else?"

Mallory rolled her head and her vertebrae cracked with thought. She shrugged. "It's still religious."

Robin blinked. "I said..."

"You can say whatever, but I know you, Robin. Come on. You're still thinking about what 'God' thinks. Probably your family, too," Mallory sat down next to her. "Okay, so, like. Listen. Bobby. I gave Bobby a blow job last year."

Robin reeled back. "Bug-Eyed Bobby? The guy that put a tarantula in Mr. Smith's desk?"

"He also plays bass and wants to go to film school," Mallory scrunched her face. "The spider thing was years ago. I wish people would know him for something else. He's cool. He's gonna make movies."

Robin didn't know they had been seeing each other. She once thought she knew everything about Mallory—the reveal made her stare off into the distance as she tried to place where in the timeline of their friendship this could've happened.

"Anyways," Mallory closed her eyes and breathed. "We had fun. I learned a lot. We took it slow. We both researched. We talked about it."

"I don't know if..."

"Robin. Did you know how to throw a fastball the first time that you tried?"

Robin looked down into the granite under her feet. She never felt closer to the ground.

"You make it seem like you're an item on a shelf. Like... as soon as you have sex, that's your expiration date. That's your usefulness. I'm... still here, Robin. I didn't *die* or stop *mattering* because I blew a guy. We're just... people."

"What if Chuck leaves me..." Robin whispered. "What if I disgust him or..."

"Then you work out why he feels that way. You two need to talk about this. Like, *now*. Not when he proposes to you or whatever. Maybe you have to move on if he's not for you. Bobby wants to move to California and, like, I don't. We broke up. We're still friends. It's cool. But we have different lives going in different directions."

Robin tugged the strap of her bookbag to her chest. From her perspective, Mallory and Bobby got together, had oral sex, and broke up in the span of minutes. Clinton kissed her cheek a few times in two years, in comparison.

"If it doesn't work out between you two, then you're more experienced for it. You have your whole life to figure stuff out, Robin. There's a whole world outside of Brighton. Maybe there's a guy in another country for you or something," Mallory squeezed Robin's shoulder. "The most important thing is that if you don't want to do it, then..."

A white Shelby Dakota, helmed by Mallory's father, pulled up next to the girls and honked. Robin jumped. Mallory didn't. She rose to her feet, her black bangs and plaid dress billowed towards the trees.

"...don't."

Every lesson adults had for Robin concerning sex had either been dry lectures or core-shaking horror stories designed to drive her away from pursuit. This was the first encounter Robin had that sounded like what she always thought in her head, but was too afraid to voice to anyone. It was the first conversation that she had that acknowledged her own agency or control.

"C'ya, Robin."

Robin watched the Shelby Dakota disappear behind a right turn into the woods and wondered where their lives had started to diverge. Mallory would avoid the group, mostly due to her strained relationship with Kelly. Robin, too afraid to fracture her inner circle further, did not pursue her. They rarely spoke again.

*****

Everyone else has done it, Robin thought.

Robin brought her face to Chuck's. His handsome face, which had begun to settle into the chiseled skin of the husband she knew he would grow to be, looked at her in wide-eyed surprise. She kissed him hard on the lips, and she tasted him as he was, sweet and shy, yielding like butter, hot as the sun that bore down on her back.

She closed her eyes. He didn't.

It's been two years.

She kissed his neck. A gasp broke free from the prison of his lips.

I know what I want.

She lifted his shirt and sucked the fine point of his chest. He melted into the boards of the boat with a throat-breaking cry.

And after all this time...

She anointed each of his abs with her tongue.

You do too, right?

She freed him from the shackles of his zipper. She opened her mouth and tried to take him to Heaven. She wanted to make his eyes roll so far into the back of his head that they saw God.

After minutes, though, it became clear to Robin that his form was grounded. This angel had no wings, and Robin, despite her efforts, lacked the ability to make them grow.

The future she believed in shriveled away.

Clinton looked around at the waters, disturbed from the motion of their canoe. As he buttoned and zipped himself back up, he coughed with short, staggered embarrassment, "Sorry."

Robin flopped back, bewildered. They rowed with purpose to the designated lunch spot and ate. Silence dominated the rest of their trip.

Eventually, because neither had the guts to talk about what happened, they broke up. Though the words were never spoken aloud, there was a mutual understanding of the palpable incompatibility between them. At first, Robin blamed herself.

Later that year, Clinton started to date Kelly. Robin only knew they were dating because someone else told her, and while part of her thought she should be mad, Clinton and Kelly's relationship was so palpably passionless that, to Robin's own surprise, she didn't mind. There was a certain freedom in the sight of Clinton's slight grip around another girl's hand.

*****

Clinton Clinton ran into Robin again at a grocery store the year before she left for college. They chatted in the spice aisle: the conversation was pleasant, salted by the past but sweetened by their manners and genuine respect they still had for each other.

"You're really leaving the state, huh?" a plastic shaker of paprika clinked into Chuck's cart.

"When I got the letter, oh my god," Robin smiled, "it sent me right out the door."

"That's cool. Nala did the same thing, right?"

"Yeah. She wants to be a botanist."

"What are you gonna do?"

Robin hesitated and adjusted the collar of her white button up blouse. "Well, I enjoyed learning Spanish in school. I think I'd like to expand on that, maybe become a teacher. It'd be handy for mission trips. Maybe I can even lead a few trips for the church."

"Great. I'm not surprised. You'll do fine."

Robin's eyes wandered for the right words. She exhaled, and summoned a smile, "So! Are you still with Kelly?"

Chuck looked at her sideways. Robin also tilted her head, uneasy from the silence.

"I'll take that as a no? Sorry. Kelly and I drifted. Our whole group, really—" she backpedaled.

"Robin. I'm gay."

Robin stared into the floor. Years of her life and romance blew past her mind.

"I came out right before graduation. I thought you heard. Sorry."

"W-wow," Robin held her fingers at her temple. "No, I guess I just... kept my head down. I've been either working on homework or mission trips or college applications."

Chuck shrugged. "Yeah. I mean, I guess it was kind of sudden. I wanted it kept down low, but no one can ever keep a secret, huh? I told Kelly when she wanted to kiss me, and she told everyone. So I guess I didn't 'come out' so much as I was 'dragged out.'"

Robin rubbed her forehead. "O-oh."

"It's fine, though. I'm about to move out of my parents' house. I worked all those part time jobs to save up so that it didn't matter if they kicked me out. They aren't super pleased with me, but I did good in school and I didn't ask for money so I think as long as I don't talk about it, they won't care," he huffed. "That's what it seems like, at least."

"When we were..." she shook her head. "...when we were together, were you..."

"Yes."

"W...when did you find out?"

"I think I knew for a while," he mumbled as he scratched at the side of his beard, a disguise of thick maturity for his young face. Robin studied its even maintenance so that she didn't have to look Chuck in the eyes.

"Why didn't you tell me?"

He looked at her. An eyebrow arched with such height that it may have technically qualified as a scoff despite its lack of sound.

"Okay, but..." she rubbed the sides of her forehead. "Why did you go out with me, then? For so long?"

"I liked you, Robin."

She paused and studied. The eyebrow had returned home. There was no sarcasm there.

"That's not it," she whispered.

"Of course it is!" Chuck protested. "Robin, you kick ass. You always blaze ahead when you find something you want to do, you don't back down from anything, you're a better pitcher than anyone that was on our team, and... I mean, of course I like you. Lots of people like you. But that's not... the same thing... as..."

He looked up. Her face was colored by horror, her eyes darted between spices in the aisle. She covered her mouth until she had words.

"Did I..." she stammered. "Did I..."

Chuck nodded slowly. He understood Robin's expression.

"Robin," he sighed. "You didn't do *anything*. There is nothing for you to have guilt over."

Robin looked at the pepper in her hand. Chuck heard its slight shake, and thought about which lie he wanted to tell her.

"Jesus made me, though. So, there's nothing to worry about, right?" Chuck thought perhaps an appeal to God would comfort her. "We're just some kids trying to figure ourselves out, and we did."

"Jesus had nothing to do with this," Robin jerked. "I forced you into something you didn't want to do, didn't I? I... I want to be mad at you for using me. That's what you did, right? And Kelly. You dated us to keep people from finding out. We were shields, right? Girls that you knew wouldn't try to do anything to you. That's what you looked for."

Chuck nodded and sucked his lips in. "You have every right to be mad."

"NO!" She threw the shaker into her cart, and the sudden clank of plastic on steel grate made them both jump. "I'm the one that stopped because I noticed you weren't into it. What if I didn't? What if I forced you to go through with it? You were going to let me do anything to you if it was to protect yourself, weren't you?"

Chuck blinked. He thought Robin was ready to lay into him, and he believed he deserved it. This is not the direction he expected his comeuppance to go. "Nothing happened. Don't blame yourself for anything."

"Clinton," tears welled in her eyes, "I thought I *knew* you. If I don't blame myself, who am I supposed to blame?" Her breath quickened when she realized that, for the first time since before they started dating, she called him by the name he hated. The name he avoided. The colors of the product labels on the surrounding shelves increased in saturation, and the lights spun. "I have to go. I'm sorry. I'm so sorry that this is how you had to live."

She abandoned her cart and left the store and never saw Clinton Clinton again.

*****

In Heaven, Robin no longer blamed herself.

She frowned at the doll, the mirror of her flesh. *You should've told me to stop if you didn't want it. But you couldn't, could you?*

She didn't blame any of the girls, either. None of them could have known. Their advice was for different people living different lives in different times. For someone, their advice must've been right, but not for her. Not for Clinton. Not for them, in that one confused, hormone-laden moment in a canoe on the Charles River.

How many friends would you have lost, Chuck? How many family members?

She didn't blame Jesus, either. No matter the validity of the game show host's claim to the name of Christ, Robin knew that this particular Jesus did not force anyone in her group into any decisions. There was no predestination for those awkward teenagers, no divine purpose for their embarrassment. Everyone involved made decisions based on who they were and what they thought other people would think of them.

Her god eye slowly snaked out of her clenched fist.

How many people in your life would've left you if you didn't have someone like me at your side?

It blinked with lasers that seared new flesh into existence on the table beside her doll.

If it had been the other way around... If I had someone force themselves on me when I didn't want it... If I had been forced to live with it...

A new form emerged: an ebony pelvis not yet attached to a torso or legs, but fully covered in flesh, smoothed on its ends as if it were a mannequin mid-assembly.

I have to free Earth from fear, she sucked her lips in. *I have to give everyone something to believe in.*

Its penis twitched, powered by blood and cells and heat despite the lack of consciousness attached to it. She reached out with hesitance towards the member and drew a finger around its head. The closer her hand approached, the deeper the red flesh turned, glowing with a phosphorescence of warning.

Upon contact, Robin's hand and arm were blown with a sonic force to shatter her finger and wrist bones. She stumbled backward and bumped into the wall behind her. Heaven fit her ligaments and digits back into place, but the pain was still profound enough to bring tears to her eyes. She bit her bottom lip to prevent a loud cry. Her tooth drew blood. Heaven took care of that, too.

"What was that?" Theodore looked up over his own assembly of quartz. Despite Heaven's air, he felt compelled to ask: "Are you okay?"

She looked to the pelvis. Now that she'd been pushed away, the disembodied flesh drew soft and lost its red glow. Robin popped her neck, wiped the stray blood from her face, and huffed.

"That was progress," she said.

Indecision

In the marble white workroom, Jarilo's eyes glazed over the mulch and petals of his new creature. He tugged on the huge, shiny rhubarb plant leaves that made up its shoulders, and tweaked the soft petals that lined its throat. As he stepped back to study his redesign, a flash of light exploded in the ceiling of the room.

"It's been eight hours, sweeties!" the hologram of Jesus lifted heart-shaped sunglasses, winked to the contestants, and slurped on a swirly straw stuck in a strawberry milkshake. "You know what that means! You don't have to go home, but for the next two hours, you can't stay here!"

The half-goat slung his leather jacket over his shoulders and dragged his bones to the cafeteria. He poked at the pile of greens he was given by the fish-workers and pictured himself in happier times, younger, freer, rolling around in fields of grain, embraced by the sun and the woman he loved.

He jerked back to reality when the loud clop of four hooves landed on the table. His fork and salad bowl rattled. He looked up.

"Boo," Csodaszarvas smiled.

"Hey," Jarilo rested his face on his wrist. His vision wilted down to the salad.

"Last challenge you spooked me when I was down, so I thought I'd return the favor," the wonder-deer hopped down to tile and nuzzled the leather of Jarilo's shoulders. "I see your wheatkin aren't so wheat-y anymore."

"Yeah, well, they didn't like it, so..." Jarilo trailed off.

"Do you?"

Jarilo stabbed a piece of cabbage and shrugged. "It's something."

Csodaszarvas's big nostrils flared. He trotted to the other side of the table and craned his furry-white neck and secured the lip of the salad bowl in his teeth. He dragged it away from Jarilo.

"In case you don't know," the light glittered on Cso's golden horns, "Hungary was founded by two hunters that chased after me. They could never catch me; I'm too nimble and too aware. But through their efforts I taught them that if they work hard and chase their dreams, they can end up in the place they need to be. I led them all the way to a land that would become their new nation."

Jarilo already knew the legend of Csodaszarvas and wasn't in a mental place to be impressed by familiar morals.

"That's what you'd find out if you looked me up, anyway. It's a good parable I try to live by, but it's been years, Jarilo. I don't remember the feeling I had anymore, even though it's my identity. What I do remember: I tried out for this show, and made it on. Me. Few on Earth know about me anymore, and the show still gave me a chance. I could bomb. Statistically speaking, my odds of winning are not great. But as long as I keep up the chase, even if it's not here, I know I'll find where I belong in the end."

The half-goat's lips parted as he scraped his fork against the table. Hearing real implications for the situation he was currently in made the story a bit more meaningful, but still irritating, frustrating, inapplicable. It was advice for someone else—someone with more hope, more potential.

"I think that's true for you, too," he nudged the salad back to Jarilo.

"I'm..." Jarilo exhaled, "sorry for the way I've been today. I tend to live at extremes. I'm pushing, though. I'm always growing, for better or for worse. I'll be done by stage time and I know this design is better than what I had before."

"There you go," a gruff voice said.

A tray of rui-be slid into view beside Jarilo. The half-goat and wonder-deer looked up to see Oksi.

"You looked glum," the Ainu god nodded, "but I see Csodaszarvas beat me to a pep talk. Thought you might like some of these, instead."

Jarilo paused, looked at the salad, then at the tray of glazed fish, then back to the salad. He stabbed some rui-be with a fork and tossed it into his mouth.

"I'll never be so sad that I won't eat these," the half-goat chomped.

Csodaszarvas tilted his head. He had not known Oksi to be particularly warm, or at least he had convinced himself of the bear-of-a-man's standoffishness. Still, it was always he that cooked and looked after Jarilo. Maybe there was goodwill there that his face, covered in wiry, thick hair and frozen with an unblinking stare, couldn't show.

Maybe you're not so bad, Cso thought.

The Staff

No television show can produce content as efficiently and well executed as *The Next Great Deity* without a dedicated and passionate staff. Without the hard behind-the-scenes work of the individuals below, Heaven's favorite reality TV show would surely crumble:

MARK SHARKMAN

The Interviewer. Operates the Camera-World, and serves as a vital link between editing and contestants. Former alcoholic.

RITST

The Editor. Oversees the final cut of the show before it goes on air, and knows where everything is in the hotel. Sucker for salmon bagels.

KÆRAST

Ritst's assistant. Madly in love with his job and his boss, and struggles to differentiate between the two. Excels at multitasking.

"Damn it," Ritst ripped wires and electrodes off his triangular head. "Nothing."

Ritst, the 10-foot-tall fish-man that served as the lead editor of *The Next Great Deity*, had left his conversation with Mark Sharkman hours prior with great unease. Between his orders from The Producer to track down mentions of The Internet on camera, and his own suspicion that Mark had lied to him, Ritst gave up his own work time to scan every contestant's dialogue in the previous episode. Hours and hours of footage thrust into his brain in the span of a few minutes. His occipital and parietal lobes were assaulted with a one-two punch of instant information.

The Overtime Machine was a large metal pod with connecting wires, screens, and levers of all manner of function. It operated as a direct plug-in to the vast library of footage and data for the current season of the show. It allowed the user to quickly parse through any and all footage, but at tremendous cost. Blood poured out of Ritst's earholes, eyes, and mouth. Smoke billowed from the bits of flesh where the electrodes were attached to his once rust colored rubbery skin, now charred black and shriveled, scales turned to ash. In the moments before his vision completely filled with black dots, he saw colors beyond the visible spectrum, brief glimpses of ultraviolet radiation that seeped from the machine. In any place other than Heaven, Ritst would only be able to use this torturous device once.

He collapsed to the floor and let Heaven's air massage him back to health.

"I guess I should be happy I can still trust Mark," he gurgled. One of his razor sharp teeth fell out, stained red like the rest of his mouth. "I suppose The Producer will be comforted, too."

As the tooth reattached under the spell of Heaven, he pulled his shaky long limbs together and rolled back to his full height. His wounds closed and sensation returned to his legs, arms, and angular face. He stumbled over to a touch-pad, leaned against the wall with his claw pressed into the smooth panel, and caught his breath. When he walked out of the room, he stood tall and proud—he refused to be seen damaged by the machine.

One of Ritst's bigger fears was to be pulled from his duties in the editing room. The perfectionist in him had difficulty relinquishing control, and even if he did trust his right hand man, Kærast, to step in while he was gone, he found it impossible to walk away from his desk without the tug of his sense of duty at his back. The high pressure environment of *The Next Great Deity*, along with all the other editing and security details he had worked over the years, had beaten a Pavlovian response into his mind to feel guilt whenever he did anything other than work.

When he sauntered back into the editing room, he saw Kærast seated at his editor's chair. Holographic projections of camera clips whizzed around the room, docked on the user interface in front of the guppy. The small guppy-man waved his fish-scale hand across and sent a holographic file in flight to one of the many other editors in the room. He sensed Ritst's entry into the room shortly thereafter, and looked up, his shimmering powder-blue face aglow with the lights of his console.

"Welcome back, sir!" Kærast's head fins flattened with his squishy smile.

Ritst folded his form, double the size of Kærast's, down to peer over his shoulder.

“Mmm,” Ritst patted the guppy’s shoulder as he eyed the readouts around them, “you’ve really stayed on top of this. Good work.”

Kærast fidgeted with delight as he signed out of the console. “T-thank you sir! I’ll get out of your way...”

As Kærast gathered folders and notebooks and pens from his temporary station, Ritst draped his claws onto the digital display. As the guppy shuffled out of the room, he was stopped in his tracks by Ritst’s rubbery call.

“Kærast,” Ritst said.

The guppy turned back, his head fins fanned out.

“You’re never in the way.”

Kærast hugged his notebooks tight to his chest, and his eyes dilated.

“Come here,” Ritst waved him back to his station. Kærast darted with a sidewinder’s speed.

“Y-yes sir?” Kærast stood stiff, his leather loafers clunked together.

“Kærast, I think after work tonight, I might get a drink. I don’t think we’ve ever gone out before, have we? Would you care to join your boss? No pressure, of course. We can have the whole crew out, but, you know. You stepped up today. You’ve been my number one guy for a while, so I thought you deserved a reward. Drinks on me.”

Kærast’s gills pulsed in panic. He wanted to scream “YES!” but his eyes were pointed down, frozen on the notebooks in his small scaled hands, piles of work he had set aside when Ritst asked him to take the helm. Anger welled at the conflict in his mind as he stood at the border of personal and professional interest.

"Oh, sir! I do want to, but I have this documentation I have to process from the last challenge still. You know how busy everything is!"

Ritst nodded with some disappointment. "Ah, well. I do. I understand. I did throw quite a bit of work at you."

The lightest whimper escaped Kærast's throat. "We can still get drinks... another time, right?"

Ritst smiled, and his razor teeth caught the light of the video console. "Of course. That sounds great. You let me know when."

"A-awesome!" Kærast bounced out the room with a new spring in his step. As he rounded the corner of the metal door, he waved a folder. "I'll hold you to it, boss!"

Ritst laced his claw-fingers and stretched. The tips of his sharp digits touched the metal ceiling. He looked past the flying virtual UI to the team he worked with, several fish-associates all diligent in their compilation of footage for the show's highly efficient release schedule.

I've got a great team by my side, Ritst assured himself as he buried his face in his digital displays. *There's really nothing to worry about at all.*

"Alright, man," the devil-horned driver tapped a screen on his dashboard and waved Jack on without looking at him, "here's your stop."

Jack stepped out of the cab.

"You might want to get some pants, by the way," the demon driver lifted his baby-blue baseball cap, scratched around his horns, then secured it back on his head. His passenger side automatic window slowly rolled up as he muttered, "Doesn't matter how nice an ass you got. You're gonna make people uncomfortable."

The pumpkin man watched the driver disappear around a gray street corner. He looked down at his own body, orange and ripped, once a source of self-love but now a constant reminder of his magnetism to rejection. He noticed its stark contrast with the monochrome pavement under his rind toes, and the rocky steps that led to the slate building in front of him, an unimpressive apartment complex for forgettable people. A small white-and-gray sign draped down the side of the apartment's edge, the least-effort attempt to separate the building's identity from any of the other flats on the street. It read, "New Meso Landing."

"I guess," Jack's voice quaked, "this is where I live now?"

As he waited in chairs and squished black carpet between his toes and rode elevators and clumsily twisted keys into his new apartment door, one emotion dominated his mind: embarrassment. In Heaven, he only knew of confidence and wanted fun. The world of Hell, he began to learn, had no place for either of those notions.

A small card awaited him from the government on his kitchen counter.

"Congratulations on your new apartment," Jack read aloud. The note informed him that his roommate would not be home for roughly one month. The apartment was small in size, but wildly decorated in neon rugs and plants, triangle paint and wavy patterns along the walls. In the corner, a Quaker parrot perched on a pot of fresh fertilizer that bore no growth beyond the soil. The room burst with more color than anywhere else in Hell.

Jack stepped to the windowed balcony and glanced outwards across the gray, sunless sky and litany of rectangular tombs that doubled as apartment buildings. It was the first time he noticed a small, golden split in the sky, a seam of color so thin and distant that it might as well have been a different country, or a different world. He knew not what this golden pillar was, and thought he might not have looked for the contrast of saturation at all were it not for the color of the apartment.

Jack inspected the many flowers and leaves of the living room, bright and blossoming bushes defiant against the gray outside world. All around the room were spiraling *Iris Croatica*, saturated roses, fruity camomile. He inspected the Quaker parrot's dishes in his open cage. There was fresh water and seed filled to the brim of its transparent plastic cup. *Someone's taking care of this place,* he thought. But as he investigated, he only found three other rooms outside of the small living room: his own empty bedroom, a bathroom, and presumably the living quarters of his absent roommate. He peeked in the crevice of the ajar door and saw the shadows of more plants. He knocked lightly on the white wooden frame. There was no response. With respect to privacy, Jack shut the door, and did not investigate further.

The pumpkin man spun in place in the living room and took in the new environment. Waxy leaves and sweet fragrance and gentle nurturing swirled around him. He was overwhelmed at the life and love of this quiet home, a slice of someone's warm personality he had yet to experience. He sobbed. This apartment was evidence that Hell didn't *have* to crush him. There was still someone here that *cared*.

Jack fell to his knees on a pink and cyan rug, curled up, and slept. The Quaker parrot fluttered and sat on the stem of his head and napped with him.

Acceptance

Neon green sunlight rubbed on the crystalline roof of Heaven's Heart Hotel. Robin laid on the floor, light refracted along the sides of her umber skin. Warmed from exposure, she let her palms glide along the smooth surface.

The stairwell door clicked and whined. Robin sat up to her elbows.

"Hey," Theodore pushed the door open with his shoulder. He had a french waffle ice cream sandwich with raspberry sauce in his hand, nestled in delicate paper.

The last time Theodore and Robin had a serious conversation with each other, Robin had given Theodore an ultimatum: abandon your friendship with The Internet, for he poses a threat to humanity. She had, since then, had time to reflect on her stance, and on the ideological differences between Theodore and herself.

At the start of this challenge's break, Robin passed by Theodore's table and delivered a note to him. It read:

We need to talk. Meet me on the roof.

She had wondered why it took Theodore so long to meet her. "What's that?"

"Listen, there's this place called Ralph's in Queens. Best ice cream you can get. If the hotel's cafeteria claims they can make anything, I'm gonna put em' to the test," Theodore bit, chewed, swallowed, and nodded. "They pass."

Robin's eyebrow lifted. Theodore sat cross-legged next to her and nursed the decadent sweet in small, measured nibbles.

"I'm glad you want to talk, though," Theodore said after swallowing a decadent bite. "So. Let's."

Robin eyed him for a bit as she rose to her hips. Theodore had left his powder-blue suit jacket back in the workroom. Now that he was in an untucked, wrinkled white shirt, stubbly and aloof, she couldn't help but think that this version of her fellow human, less made up for the camera, was more approachable than the pressed lavender-suited artifice she assumed him to be in the last challenge.

"I want to apologize," she said. "I hope meeting you here away from any cameras—none that I can find, at least—will indicate my sincerity."

Theodore finished his last bite and crumpled the wrapper in his fists.

"But I'm not gonna take back what I said," she leaned in. "I don't trust The Internet. He doesn't get to threaten humanity like that and get away with it. Not while I'm here."

"I mean, you shouldn't," Theodore shrugged. "Not with what we know right now, at least. I don't blame you for not trusting me, either. Given what's happened thus far, I think a bit of skepticism is healthy. I encourage it."

Robin nodded and brushed her hands across the rough front of her denim jeans. Her tongue drew along the bottom of her teeth, hesitant to reveal her conclusion. "But I can tell how you're playing the game, how you're careful in your alignment. I've thought about it, and I respect it. I think I've made clear what my goal is: I see the other contestants as potential threats to Earth, to humanity as a whole. I want to ensure that whoever wins—even if it's not me—is someone that's good for reality. I would rather assume this place is real and ensure the best possible outcome. And if you think you can lead The Internet towards a more positive creation, I think I can support your alliance with him. Even if I don't share it, and even if I think we have a fundamentally different idea of what Heaven is, I see no reason why we can't support each other. As humans, we should be on the same team."

"If I want to tear the show apart, I can get behind that strategy," Theodore scrunched his mustache and leaned back on his palms. This seemed more in line with Robin as he understood her at the beginning of the show's run. This made her actions at the end of the first episode even more muddled in his mind, so he considered how he could solidify her trust. "I wanted to share something with you. I think it's a crucial bit of information that—"

"No."

Theodore blinked. "It's important—"

"No. *I* want to share something with *you*. I have something to atone for."

Theodore went quiet. The need for atonement was an emotion he could appreciate. "I'm listening."

"When I was in high school, I almost raped a boy," she exhaled.

Theodore's eyes bulged. He tried to rationalize both a younger version of Robin, whom he only knew as a mid-40s English teacher, and a sexually aggressive version of her, whom he only knew as a bit of a religious prude that spent most of this sex-themed challenge in internal conflict.

"I'm pleased..." he stammered, "...to hear the use of the word of 'almost.'"

"I dated him for a few years. We were both in religious families in a religious place, and the church was the backdrop of our lives. I believed he was the one for me; I thought Heaven gave me this beautiful boy that loved baseball as much as I did and I couldn't wait anymore, I wanted to overflow him with every good feeling I had heard about from every single other kid in the school, and he denied me when I tried to go down on him and..." Robin's quickened pace of recollection choked to a halt. She sucked in her lips, and her brow furrowed.

Theodore's eyes darted. He was not terribly used to being someone's emotional support. He patted her on the back with stiff, awkward pause, unsure what else he could offer.

"I felt anger," she shook her head at herself. "The first emotion I had... was anger. How fucked up is that? How entitled was I made to feel? No surprise, we broke up. I couldn't figure out this situation for a long time until I met him again in the grocery store. He admitted he was gay. Apparently, I was the last to find out."

Theodore remembered he hadn't told Robin yet about his own queerness. Given the moment, he wasn't sure if this was the best time.

"But that's not the worst part," Robin straightened her back. "The worst part is how I justified it away. No one ever found out, except for Nala, my sister. After it happened, she was the only person I told. She didn't judge me or estrange me. She prayed with me, and I was lead to believe I was forgiven. She gave me strength and energy in a way only blood can, and you know what? I only got that because she was my family. I was able to be forgiven for something so terrible before I even knew what was going on in Clinton's life. I don't know if Clinton had anyone in his life like that, because back then you could lose everything for just being out. That's not Nala's fault. It's not his. It's not mine. It's... older than that. Older than all of us."

Her hand shook.

"Life moved on. I learned what Clinton was and found myself irrevocably angry at a system of society that would convince him to get into relationships with girls to hide his own truth. Nala died during pregnancy with her first child despite the fact I know she was a virgin until her marriage. It was Arrhythmia. Theodore, there was no purer woman than her. Especially not me. Punishment hit the wrong sibling. It brought chaos to my family. Everywhere I looked, I saw the systems and beliefs my life was built on crumble under the weight of reality, and I watched them bury the good people that just tried to live their life under them."

Theodore nodded and laced his fingers around his knee. "I think... I understand why you want to find Athena's sister so badly."

"I was pumped, for just a minute, when we were first gathered here on the roof and we met Jesus," Robin curled her hands behind her head, "because I thought I could finally find truth about the afterlife. Maybe I'd find Nala, or find a reason to believe there was a better excuse for the type of life Clinton had to lead than 'Shit sucks so bad for a gay kid that he has to pretend to be straight just to live a normal life.' I haven't found either, and learning more and more about how petty people are up here makes me think that I won't."

"It's brave of you to share that," he didn't know what else to say.

Robin exhaled and smiled. "Thank you."

Theodore nodded. Robin bottled this story up for a long time, and he understood the burden of regret held within.

The door that Theodore accessed the roof through started to creak open again. Both looked up: Theodore in surprise, Robin expectantly.

"I'm glad I can tell you that, so you can understand how serious I am," Robin said.

Ishta-Devata pushed the door open. Peeking out from her heavy sari sleeve was a small folded note. Theodore didn't see what it said, but after Robin's next statement, he could guess.

Robin stood up and brushed off her jeans.

"You two both work against the show and create secretive plots away from the cameras," she said, "but both of you are also trying to wrangle me to your side, and I think there are better options."

Theodore and Ishta-Devata looked at each other.

"We're all gonna work together," Robin stood between them. "And we're gonna be honest with each other, starting now."

"What the *fuck*?" The Internet scooted to the edge of his seat when he saw Taninim's plate.

The monster men of 35-D had gathered in the lunch room, as they had in the previous challenge. This time, however, there was a notable absence.

"I hoped Theodore would eat with us again," Taninim frowned. His nose chain glinted in the red, dancing light of his plate.

"Maybe he'll eat with us after you order *actual* food," Internet growled, "you *idiot*."

Taninim's plate was alive with fire. There was nothing else on the surface of porcelain except a magic-bound orb of flames. The only other sustenance he ordered from the cafeteria was a jumbo sized coffee identical to the one Theodore had introduced to him in the last challenge. He was addicted to caffeine, and the jitters it sent through his scales.

"This *is* food," the dragon stared into the flames, transfixed. The Internet looked at his expression and reacted to it, and the drone of his words, with abject horror.

"He mentioned that another contestant wanted to meet with him," Zargah's mandibles whirred around a blue gelatinous cube on his fork, bubbly and covered in sugar. "I wasn't sure it was his choice."

The Internet cut into the rare steak on his own plate, a meal his cell-dogs led him to believe was fit for real adults and real men, sophisticated and efficient and packed with protein, the true definition of masculine excellence. "Your collar sounds like it works," he chewed the bloody meat with his fanged mouth open. Slobber flew.

"Subject I..." Zargah's antennae twitched and bobbed. "I'm... I'm getting the hang of it. It feels close to finished."

"Good. I was gettin' real tired of your shit," the dog-punk swallowed. "Couldn't understand half of what you said, and the other half was worse."

"How does everyone feel about their projects this week?" Taninim said. He opened his maw and his forest of knife teeth separated enough to inhale the flames clean off the plate. The Internet froze at the sight, mouth agape. The bit of steak on his fork fell back to plate.

"It feels like many contestants are uncomfortable with this challenge," Zargah's voice collar clicked. "Please correct my potential errors. I believe I'm starting to pick up on the subtly of the expressions of my opponents."

"They *hella* are," The Internet shook himself free from the distraction of Taninim's fire-eating. Nothing could keep him from participation in his all-time favorite activity: talking shit. "And I love it. The room can easily be divided up into two camps: People that are scared of creating sexually-themed work, and people that are way too excited for it. There's more good in the latter camp than the former, but there isn't a lot of middling work in either."

Taninim gulped down coffee. The smoke of extinguished flames billowed from the gaps in his teeth. "I'm scared I might be in that former group. When I thought of playing 'god,' reinventing sex wasn't the first thing on my mind... or the last."

"The ones who will fail this challenge..." the dog-punk's imagination danced under stage lights. Jesus would applaud his wisdom, he thought, and flowers and cheers would pile up around him from every contestant and shiqq and judge and viewer, "...will be the ones who can't tackle it seriously. If you can't handle the necessity of reproduction with creative maturity, you don't deserve to win. You don't deserve to be a god."

Taninim burped. Flames blew from his teeth and licked across Internet's steak. It ruined its degree of done-ness. The dog-punk snatched his plate in fright and scooted down the cafeteria table.

"And YOU don't deserve to sit next to me during break! Cover your damn mouth! Fuck!"

Ishta-Devata and Theodore were ensnared by the same scrutiny of each other, the narrowing of their eyes animated by curiosity over which one knew more about the other. Robin stepped between them and severed their stares.

"I made a tracker," she said, "which tracks Ishta-Devata."

She withdrew the two compass-like objects—Athena's original gold tracker, and the silver tracker of her own, and held them in each palm. Just as it did during the dawn, Robin's silver compass shook with more violence than the subdued ping of Athena's Olympian tracker.

Ishta-Devata staggered away from the door frame. "W-what?"

Robin guided one locket in the direction of Ishta. It glinted sickly silver-green under the light of Heaven's bizarre sun. "Ishta, what *really* happens when you use your power? What scares you so much about it, even though it's the person looking at you that's being fooled? If you want to continue to work with us, you have to share the full extent of your ability. This tracker is insurance, until then."

"How did you make a tracker for me, specifically?" Ishta's bottom eyelid betrayed her attempt to speak with calm resolve. "You don't know enough about Heaven, or me, to do something like that. I never gave you anything of mine to track—"

Theodore looked between the two. He had no idea there was this much tension in 24-C.

"You cried," Robin said.

Ishta furrowed her brow. "I'm sorry?"

Robin closed her palm. The rattle of the Ishta-tracker muted to a hum.

"You cried over Athena for hours, and I created organisms, bugs as small as specks, flat as sheets of paper, that collected your tears. I know enough about eyes to know they always produce tears to stay moist. As long as you have eyeballs, my tracker will work."

Theodore whistled.

"That's..." Ishta lowered her head, and her golden cylindrical hat slipped an inch before she readjusted it, "...clever. Very clever. You *really* must not trust me to go through all of that."

"At the end of the last challenge, you tried to manipulate me into isolating Theodore, just to see how he'd react."

Theodore raised his eyebrows. "So Robin's speech in the hallway was your idea, huh, Ishta?"

The glare of the two humans bore down on Ishta, who averted her gaze to the floor.

"Right. I guess I have no choice then," Ishta-Devata combed a long strand of black hair back over her shoulder. "My true power... is an exchange of information. Fitting, when you consider this situation we're in. When you see your idea of god, I see your idea of goals. Or more specifically, your dreams. I get to witness what you want more than anything else. Frankly, it's exhausting. I'm so tired of seeing your inner worlds. But I have no choice, so I instead try to act upon the information I receive."

Theodore's shoulders slunk with the weight of this revelation. He didn't like the idea of anyone seeing parts of his mind without his permission. "Well, I'd appreciate it if you stopped."

"Your dream, Theodore," Ishta glowered, "is why I wanted Robin to confront you. To see how you'd react. So many people's dreams are defined. They want money, or a new house, or a specific job. They want to win, or love, or get revenge. Take the judges, for example. When I look at them, I see the depths of their ambition. They want the Earth. They each want to go there and rule, believing it belongs to them. They will do it at the expense of each other. Perhaps this is an unsurprising desire for a god, but one that disturbs me greatly when I consider that if they, the truest of gods, have such a specific desire, then why are they here running this show? I am disturbed by the dreams of their conquests, and the questions they raise. But you know what disturbs me more? You, Theodore. Your desires. When I see you, all I see is a child begging for forgiveness."

Theodore's back straightened. "Is that so?"

"I see blood on your fists. I see rain in your heart. I don't know what you did, but it haunts you. If you did something so bad that it weighs down your soul, then you can't be trusted in times of crisis or moral responsibility."

Theodore's nostrils flared. He put his hands in his pockets and considered how he wanted to respond, then turned to Robin.

"When I was in high school, I beat the absolute piss out of someone that didn't deserve it. Because of who I was and who my parents were, I got away with it without any serious consequences. It pisses me off that I did, and I live with that every day. So, she's right. And however you want to feel about that is also right."

Robin listened. She thought about what Theodore said, considered what aspects he had left out, and then also considered her own mistakes in her youth. She walked across the crystalline floor and brought her face close to Ishta's.

"I believe you've demonstrated your power, so thanks for that," she whispered, barely audible over the loud vibration of the tracker. She pressed it into Ishta's arm, and it shook so violently that the Hindu princess could feel the cold steel shake the bone in her forearm. "but I can't believe you thought *that's* what would make me distrust him over the way you've tried to manipulate people *now.* Is the reason you didn't trust us with this information because we're human? Or is it because were competitors?"

The skin at the back of Ishta's jaw flexed and dented as she bit her teeth down.

"At this point, our alliance is purely because we have the same goal—find Eris, and find out what happened to Athena," Robin returned to her normal tone to ensure Theodore could hear, "anything beyond that, you need to earn *my* trust. You're not going to try to twist my perceptions of people anymore. And I want you to share what you see about the contestants and the judges with us. All of it."

"Okay," Ishta sighed, "we can all relax now."

Robin stepped away from both contestants, and looked out towards the Forrest of Golden Trees. The way they maintained their beautiful hue, a sea of coins from the soil despite the green light above them, she found inspiring.

"Outside of that, I think I have a good framework for our relationship going forward," she walked back between Theodore and Ishta. "Work like you're trying to dissect the show, not like you're trying to win it. That's the promise I want from anyone I can consider an ally from here on out."

Theodore and Ishta, with heavy hesitance, shook hands.

"Good. Now that we got all that out of the way, I can trust you two for a surprise. Theodore, could you move over to Ishta, please? Just in case he flies in, I don't want him to scare you."

"I, uh," Theodore boggled, "alright. How many more surprises you got? Break won't last forever." He stood next to Ishta, and both crossed their arms.

"This wasn't the original plan, but after Athena's death, it occurred to me that I have a way to spy, albeit not so covertly, on the judges," Robin said.

Theodore's eyes widened. He knew exactly what Robin was about to explain, and he kicked himself mentally for not realizing she had this option.

"After her elimination, I used my mind swap on my clone to see if Athena's soldiers were there among the first challenge creations. Both of the Athenians were gone, but I did find a strand of gold hair on the ground. Tell me, Ishta—Athena was the only contestant that achieved sentience during the first challenge. She was also chastised for how closely she resembled her own creations. I think it was Mohammed who said that when the three of them were on stage, they looked like they were a family. What do you think the odds are that he's exactly right?"

Ishta's azure skin blanched to a pallid cloud blue. "You're kidding..."

"If I had to guess, I think Athena's technical success was owed to the usage of herself as a template. I think, in a way, they really *were* family, even if the means of their birth was less than conventional," Robin tapped her finger on her held elbow. "It also explains how real her anger towards me was when I got praised for cloning."

Theodore looked past Robin's shoulder towards an approaching speck. Swallowed in the waning neon light of Heaven's green sun, the silhouette of a bird, a white-and-brown speckled sandpiper, landed on Robin's outstretched palm. From its beak she fetched a single blonde strand of hair. The bird boasted a most unusual ornament; the sandpiper wore a metal bit on the side of its feathered head, as if bolted there by a god.

"The trackers I crafted were all specific in the nature of their goal, and they were centered around Athena. I tried to track her skin cells, fabrics that she wore, even the tracker she made," Robin flipped open the Ishta-Devata tracker and turned it upside down. A single droplet plopped out—Ishta's tear—and she placed the blonde hair in. "But I just couldn't track anything related to Athena at all, even in a broad sense. It's as if the god eye knew what I was really trying to do, and denied me."

She snapped the lid closed on the the silver tracker, and placed it next to Athena's gold one. The silver tracker laid completely dormant, while the Olypmian tracker pinged with feint beats, as it always did.

"I can now say with confidence that looking for Olympians is off limits," Robin nodded. The result of her experiment was exactly what she expected, and confirmed Theodore's suspicions from the previous challenge. "Whoever or whatever decided that looking for Eris is bad has also decided we can't look for Athena, or anyone with Olympian blood. They control our god eyes' output to some degree. Theodore, we discussed in the last challenge how the god eye might interpret our mind's requests, and why it frequently seemed... inaccurate in interpretation. It's as if our creations are collaborative, no? Like we're trying to wrestle with this thing to get it to understand what we want. This experiment seems to prove there's someone with their own intentions molding the god eye's output. When I made this bird, for example, it wasn't with the thought of hunting for this hair—I didn't even have the idea to use its feathers in my tracker until after I made it. Had I had Athena on the mind when I made this bird, I am willing to bet my god eye would have sabotaged the creation."

Theodore covered his mouth, and his brow caved in worry. "So they can read all our thoughts? Or did they just make a blanket rule about the Olympians that gets applied to the god eye automatically?"

"We can't use our god eyes to search for her," Ishta's voice broke. She clenched her fists around her hopes as they bled out of her soul. "Can we even talk about it? All those notes I made to you with my god eye, this means they were probably read. I thought it was enough to stay away from the Shiqqs, but now we know the judges will know what we're doing as long as we have a god eye..."

Theodore raised a finger. "It's not the judges. It can't be."

Robin raised her chin in interest.

"Robin, I wanted to tell you this after the last episode... you aren't the only one that spied," Theodore smiled and pointed to a button on his shirt. "I snuck a microphone into my quartztaphore. I listened in to the judges during their deliberation through my jacket cufflink, and I've decided that every new outfit I wear, I'm going to make with the god eye and attach a similar button to it. If the judges were the ones that controlled the god eye, or if they had bugged it or whatever, they'd have heard me hearing them. They'd know I spied on them. Hell, the god eye shouldn't have let me make a working microphone at all. Remember how mad Jesus got at me when I wanted to go home? They would have confronted me by now. If that's not enough, get this: I took a smoke break with Santa earlier. She has a cell phone, and though it has absolutely awful reception, I was able to use it long enough to at least use a search engine to look up Athena. So it seems the control is limited to just the god eyes' themselves."

Robin and Ishta watched as Theodore held his fingers to his temples.

"In fact... oh man," Theodore started to pace, and his leather dress shoes squeaked on the crystalline floor with each pivot. Theodore remembered the message on the wall of the Infinite Wine Hallway. If Mark Sharkman's control over the hallway was as airtight as he made it seem, then the power needed to break through Mark's Camera World without his knowledge would need to be tremendous. If anyone could have written a message on Mark's wall, it'd be someone with the power of a god eye acting independently of the judges.

"I don't know enough to say anything for certain, but I think I just made a connection," his eyes were wide open with possibility.

"CONTESTANTS!" Jesus's voice bellowed across all the floors of Heaven's Heart Hotel. Lights appeared in mid air, sparkled, and exploded in dazzling fireworks. "I hope you enjoyed your break! It's time to get back to work, I can't wait to see how your creations do the *holiest* of deeds!"

"Damn it!" Theodore ground his teeth and brought the two in a huddle. "Listen, as soon as you get a chance, just ask Mark to see the writing on the wall. He'll understand, and I think you guys will, too."

They exited the roof. The humans were bound in orientation once again, and Ishta-Devata, whether she wanted to trust them or not, was now a part of their crusade.

The blinds were closed. A man sat alone on a king-sized mattress, swathed in shadows and silk and the soft glow of his television set. The small TV played the opening instrumental of Heaven's most popular reality show, *The Next Great Deity*.

*****

Though the walls of the brightly lit workroom were sterile and blank, the contestants within them faced walls of greater complexity. These walls of the mind were covered in colorful, complicated, and heavy decoration. Years of perceptions and doubts built up like grime and dust.

Theodore swallowed. He wanted to believe that, in the last episode, he had smashed through his own mental wall in the exact moment he wrestled out the god eye from his face without giving in to supernatural belief. Theodore had a vivid, mental image-based imagination. Once he was in the right frame mind, it was easy for him to visualize 3D forms and fine details of edge and texture. Even when it came to music, sounds produced landscapes of colors in his mind. The hiss of an air conditioner was gray and brittle, a warm fog across an empty street. A dizi flute swung him into blue-green sky among peppered clouds. Old moogs summoned deep green and pink tubes that clashed against striped walls and shag carpet. He believed it was this quirk of his mind, to bring a palette to the inherently colorless, that allowed him to communicate with the supposedly supernatural device.

Unfortunately, such thinking did nothing to reduce the pain the god eye caused him. To summon the god eye still required considerable physical energy, and more often than not, quite a bit of caffeine. When summoned, it still pushed through organs and erupted from his eye socket. To prepare for this inevitability,

Theodore created a pallet worth of bandages and rags to secure on his face, which he had to change with some regularity as it soaked up blood.

With practice, he felt the god eye had become a new limb; the challenge-winning quartztaphore of episode one was a testament to his control over it. However, as Athena proved in the first episode, mastery of technique is not enough to win the whole show, or even survive whatever darkness awaited afterwards. This was the thought that dominated his mind as he stared at his work for the current challenge.

Three quartz penises of various size and design sat in a row in front of Theodore. He pressed his palms into the table and stared at them. He was sure, had they not been his own work, and had he not lost nearly an hour of work time molding them into existence, that the mere sight of them would have made him laugh.

It wasn't because Theodore found them inherently funny. As a gay man, he thought he'd just start with that which he understood best. He was sure that, as he turned the hills and valleys of that which raised his own heartbeat into beautiful sculptures for a new species, that he'd discover along the way some greater meaning, some thesis with which to elevate and explain his own carnal desire. Instead, once he was done, they looked like little more than what they were: high-difficulty dildos. Theodore attempted to move away from more organic details, and produce abstract shapes, odd tangents of spheres and grooves and ribbing. But with each new attempt, they only looked sillier. He smirked sometimes, with the sort of aware self-deprecation that accompanies a creator that knows he's lost the plot. With the three members in front of him, fine dildos and terrible set-pieces, his smirk turned to a frown. He drew quiet, and tapped the desk.

“This isn’t working,” he mumbled.

He gathered up the members of quartz into a pile. His god eye shot its red creation laser into the rocks, and steam and smoke lifted from them. They glowed as they melted. Theodore folded his arms.

*****

The man shuddered and gripped the gold bedsheet.

*****

Taninim had his own walls, too. Every inch of them were covered in band posters.

On his table sat two dragon-scaled amps—his yellow one from the first challenge, and a new cobalt blue one he had constructed over the past hour. This amp’s glittery-blue coloration and pearl adornments mirrored the aesthetic of the bass that he had spent much of the challenge refining by hand.

The dragon-guitarist set the bass on a stand directly in front of the blue-scaled amp. He strummed his golden guitar, and the runes of connection glowed ocean green across its frame. The amp shook violently and sucked up the bass, and the stand that held it, within itself. Taninim nodded, pleased, his nose-ring chain rattling against his forest of forever-exposed dagger teeth.

Unlike Theodore, Taninim did not believe his walls needed to be torn down or broken through. Perhaps a poster was crooked, and if he found it, he’d straighten it. Otherwise, Taninim was happy with what he was building.

*****

The man ground his silver teeth.

*****

Jarilo was more than willing to break the walls down. He'd take a wrecking ball to the halls of his mind, if he had to.

The half-goat had completely abandoned his wheatkin. His former species laid in ripped apart hay on the side of the table—he didn't *have* to start from scratch, but he found it therapeutic to tear apart his old creature limb from straw-limb. The construction of his new species, made out of shiny green plant leaves and oversized petals, was similarly chaotic and violent. He'd place a stamen here, a stigma there, step back, observe the placement, then rip them off and jab them into another part of the creature. The amount of pacing Jarilo did from flower-mannequin to observation worried Csodaszarvas. By challenge end, the deer-god expected to see a solid black line on the white marble floor from the scraping of Jarilo's hooves.

*****

The man exhaled deeply, and shifted to one side as a deep labor welled within him.

*****

Csodaszarvas was worried that, on the walls of his mind, nothing was hung at all.

The deer-god's god eye struggled to hold its laser up. It possessed the same presence that its user had; a half-lidded eye, and, were its connecting chain a spine, a slumping posture. This same slump was shared by the two váradi the deer-god had made. They were lithe and pale and drowned in satin and, the more the deer-god looked at them, the more he realized they were nearly indistinguishable from humans. Yes, their antler-hair and pointed ears marked them as a different species, but were they different *enough*?

Csodaszarvas chewed on his bottom lip for a while. He had spent a large portion of his challenge orchestrating the copulation itself, a three-act performance he considered at once beautiful and provocative. But, was it? Could you say anything of the sort about the váradi, a species so forgettable that Csodaszarvas was placed in the middle of the first episode's contestants? With this question reverberating in his head, Cso's incisors sunk into the ornate white-and-gold robes that draped on the male váradi. He ripped the robes off, left the male-doll nude on the table, and used his god eye to cut into the fabric. From this single robe, he would create outfits for both his váradi, more titillating fits that exposed skin, and form, and sensuality.

Surely, he thought, *this will get noticed.*

*****

The man's rough, deep breaths grew ragged. He noticed, but what he noticed was not Csodaszarvas's design itself, but the palpitation of the creative mind, the sweat of worry inherent in work, the frustration found in design. He noticed. He scraped his hand along his broad, gold neck. *Oh god*, did he notice.

*****

Some are completely fine with the walls of their mind.

Ishta-Devata laid three plastic pages of three shades of yellow out across her table. The swatches glowed with sparkling energy, and corresponded to a small, finger-sized gray cloud that hovered above her table. The tiny cloud zapped a small petri dish with a single drop of liquid in it. Each time Ishta tapped the swatch, a different color of bolt would spark down. She noted the contrast between canary yellow lightning and blue-green liquid, then compared the contrast to a citrus yellow lightning bolt. She played like this for hours, content with her design, just not yet with its presentation.

*****

Such confidence left the man on edge. His gold toes, segmented and curved into small talons, curled inwards, shimmering in the television light against the pitch-black darkness underneath the bed.

*****

The Internet didn't just break through the walls of his mind. He set them on fire.

His redesigned robot sat on the table with his chest plate open. The dog-punk reached furry digits into the exposed metal rib cage and plugged in wires and screwed in bolts. In response, the blank, black screens of its eyes lit up in neon green. Code flew by on one of the eyes as a start-up sequence installed the intelligence The Internet gifted it: one of his very own cell-dogs.

This challenge is mine, he thought.

*****

"And you're mine!" the man whimpered and fell backwards into the cushions of his bed. "Oh, you've done so good, using those emotions of yours to create something so beautiful and defiant..."

*****

Santa Inari, ever a believer in the power of capitalism, was certain that any structural problem within the walls of her mind could simply be solved by buying a new house.

Santa Inari fit her barcode-faced creature, the mindshare, with a cocktail dress. Two new mindshare laid like corpses ready for autopsy on her work table, nude, absent of genitals, smooth like porcelain, empty of soul and spirit. Once she finished with the cocktail dresses' fit and applique, she would proceed onwards to the red carpet fashion of her lead mindshare's suitors.

After Santa Inari collected a few hours of notes and planning on her phone, she would obsessively plot out her presentation on a clipboard in red ink. The act of writing in ink brought a certain finality and polish to her presentation, she thought. She believed all work, whether it was hers or somebody else's, must be rehearsed and solidified to within an inch of it's life. Otherwise, why bother at all?

Once the red ink hit the paper, there was no room for deviation Always and forever, a good god must have a plan. That is what Santa believed.

*****

"Such a singular vision!" the man moaned, and buried his face into a pillow. As he swiveled his head, the sound of chains clinked against his hard neck.

*****

Robin didn't just want to break through her own walls. She wanted to change all the houses of the world, make every single wall on Earth as sturdy as the richest man's on the planet. Everyone deserved the same security of mind and body.

She affixed a metal bit onto the side of her clone's head. The clone was still dressed in the duplicate sweater and jeans she wore in the last challenge. To the side of her clone sat a neatly folded crop-top and hot pants. Things Robin had never worn, but always wanted to.

"The time's finally come," she whispered to herself. She reached her hands underneath the hem of her clone's sweater, felt the warmth of its stomach on her fingertips, held herself there for a fleeting moment, then drew the fabric up towards the clone's head.

*****

“Such damage! Such will!” the man’s voice drew louder, and were someone outside his bedroom door, they would have mistaken his cry for one of ecstasy. “Oh my, to what depths shall you plunge? To what heights shall you soar? Take me there! High or low! I don’t care! Just fall! Just fly!”

*****

Some will try to break through their walls with the wrong tools. Try as they might, they’ll never pierce wood with a butter knife.

Oksi had spent the entirety of the challenge redesigning his pewrep from scratch. He knew that the lumpy, potato-like beast he sent out in episode one was unacceptable, and he knew it was merely thanks to the sheer number of contestants at the beginning of the show that he had skated through in the middle. His new design breathed with real strength and feral energy. It was a fanged beast with a peeled-back lip, and a quantity of sharp, jagged teeth that made Taninim’s dagger-maw appear constrained in comparison.

Oksi stroked his long beard and for a brief, strange moment in time, felt satisfaction. Eventually, the feeling was replaced: he realized that he had essentially redone the first challenge, and had almost nothing to show for the reproduction challenge everyone else in the room had tackled.

Sweat dribbled down his face. His god eye shot out of his mouth in a panic, and began firing lasers haphazardly. Lumps of flesh burst into bleeding existence, and Oksi’s hands flailed to catch them and smoosh them together into something resembling an idea.

*****

"Such reckless abandon!" The man rolled like an alligator with meat in its jaw, twirling the sheets tight around his hips and thighs. "Oh god, I can feel your ideas all bursting to the surface at once! Such creators that need the threat of time to enter a hyperactive work-state... you are truly special, Oksi!"

*****

Zargah, an alien still growing accustomed to both supernatural and foreign concepts, felt not as if he needed to break through his walls, so much as he needed to understand where his home had ended up. He might have likened his position to Dorthy in Wizard of Oz, had he known of her journey, or who she was.

Still, his confusion did not stop him from remaining focused, or having a good time. He destroyed the pilot's chassis that he used for the first episode and spent the episode's challenge time creating an animal-like sentience for his species, one which he could activate and deactivate at will.

Within the first hour of the challenge, Zargah had, with surgical precision that unnerved his fellow contestants, scalped his ant-man creature and exposed its brain. A white cotton sheet covered the ant-man from the neck down. Zargah wore rubber gloves on each of his four hands, and a clear plastic shield over his face. He created bright, floating lanterns and stationed them around his person. Each lantern had an opaque side, and small shutters that allowed them to focus their beams of light where he needed. He would chatter to the lanterns in his click-based, undulating language, and they would float around his head in response. Each longer burst of clicks from his mouth would get translated by his collar to simple commands: "Move left. Move up slightly. Focus. Widen light."

Over the course of several hours, he used the laser of his god eye directly on to the brain of his creature.

*****

"I don't even know..." the man's form arched. He was a blur of overwhelmed movement in the mixture of shadows and bedsheets and television light, "I don't even know what to feel when you work! What a wild, conflicting concoction of thought you are, alien!"

*****

Oshunmare never had walls in the first place.

The lizard-lady proceeded with the challenge with neither worry nor doubt. There was a certain sexuality already baked into the feyders, her ghost-like cat-girl creations. With their semi-transparent dresses and spindly frames and wide eyes and hips, Oshunmare had nothing but confidence in the sensual and aesthetic side of her species. What she was concerned about now was utilitarian—she believed, perhaps rightfully so, that she was overlooked in the last challenge for leaning more on style than substance.

She pulled at a loose thread on the thin-fabric Feyder dress. It was a material of contradictions—light and stiff, thin and sturdy, graphene in strength and tulle in dexterity. Luckily, utility, too, was something she had already considered. She smiled, and began to unravel the dress with solid tugs.

*****

"Such freedom," the man croaked, and rolled off the bed and to the floor. He landed with a heavy, clanking thud, like a computer knocked off a table. "Such tremendous... spirit..."

*****

And for Imhotep, a man who had spent several lifetimes breaking down walls, there was nothing left for him to break. He stood on the rubble of inhibitions, kicked away the rocks of fear, and left behind the ruin of failure.

The laser of his god eye sizzled at the tip of a golf ball sized egg. It smelled *foul* and *dangerous* yet also distinctly *correct*, like a poorly ventilated bathroom, freshly bleached.

"What color should you be?" he muttered to himself as drew a finger across the egg's slimy surface. No particular expression of pride or displeasure arose in the presence of his own work. Imhotep could have been looking at anyone else's work, and appeared equally as indifferent.

To answer his own question, he scanned other contestants' work. He took mental note of any other egg-like objects on work tables, and of the color, size, and texture they possessed. Whatever everyone else was doing, he would make sure to do the opposite.

*****

The man continued to writhe and roll and moan on the floor from the other contestants' creativity, but seemed to have no particular reaction to the work of Imhotep, himself.

*****

The pile of rocks that were, at one time, destined to be phalli for Theodore's quartztaphore men, had become melded together underneath the god eye laser. Their new shape was splintered, organic, and wild, a bouquet of small semi-transparent rocks of oily sheen. The bunch was no larger than a newborn baby. Theodore looked between the rocks and the much larger, hulking doll of his quartztaphore. He looked for a narrative connection between the two.

He believed that, perhaps, this was the wall he needed to break through.

*****

There was a knock at the door. The writhing man stopped suddenly, his limbs frozen in disarray like a poisoned bug. Then they all fell flat against the dark rug of his shadowy bedroom. He sighed. His self-ministrations disappeared, and a sort of dead coolness took over his gold, segmented body. To look at him now, interrupted, one would never know of the throes he was in moments ago. He rose to his full height, the bedsheets wrapped taught around his broad shoulders, and walked to his bedroom door. He pulled the handle.

A fair-skinned, human-presenting couple, man and woman, stood outside the door. Underneath the floating lights of a brightly lit, gold adorned hallway, they wore loose fitting, flowered-patterned silk robes and slippers. Their exposed calves and forearms and clavicles hinted that the shimmering, loose robes were the only thing between their flesh and the warmth of the lights.

"Oh, I'm so glad you could make it," the man cooed as he cracked open the door. A thin slice of light illuminated the glitter of the gold bedsheet on his shoulders, and one of his gloved fingers rubbed the edge of the door. "You're right on time, and I'm in such a good mood."

Cthulhu's Tower

It's customary that when one enters the pink ivory tower of Cthulhu, that they remove their shoes and jacket and hang them on the purple marble hooks at the entrance.

Few have free access to Cthulhu's Tower—only the judges and a select few of his employees are allowed to roam its stained-glass windowed spirals. Cthulhu never worried about infiltration; his security detail of professional fish-men bodyguards were on every floor, at every door. Even the shadows contained shifting forms of cosmic assassins, ready to pounce on anyone without clearance.

He did, however, worry considerably about loyalty and respect.

Cthulhu's customs were set in place to establish an air of elegance to his living quarters, make clear his social status, and to give the elder god a heads up if someone happened to enter the tower while he wasn't there. The hallway itself was covered in an elaborate fresco from baseboard to ceiling that detailed every excruciating horror of the Cthulhu mythos inflicted upon humanity, the ability to rip limbs from form with tentacles of titan proportion, the rule he had over their inferior human minds, the dreams that he ate, the worlds that he ruled. Painted in purple and green hues, it was beautiful and grotesque and all the things Cthulhu wanted his guests to keep in mind when they trod on his grounds: he was owed, by all, equal parts reverence and fear.

He believed this with all his hearts, despite the fact legend didn't quite match his real capabilities, or size.

He also believed that while Jesus and Mohammed were wealthier in testaments than he was, no god had seen a faster rise in belief on Earth than he. The Producer had told him as much. He could feel that in this season, at long last, his time under the shadow of older gods would come to an end. He could escape his subordinate status to losers that don't know how to adapt to the times, and become the true leader of Heaven.

After one marches down the painted hallway, the next marvel a guest of Cthulhu would be swamped by is the size of his library. Large parts of the tower served as storage for the most important books in Heaven. Many were historical texts (and by proxy, important details on *The Next Great Deity.)* Many others were religious text of all manner of beliefs from across the globe and beyond. Their stories conflicted with each other, just as the denizens of Heaven did.

There were no riches to steal greater than the knowledge within these walls, and no way to navigate it without several lifetimes of study and memorization of each of the millions of books' individual locations. No one could navigate the tower's walkways better than the elder god himself, and even he didn't know where, or what, everything was within its non-euclidean walls.

He wondered if he ever would, or could.

Cthulhu entered the spiral with this thought. His hand twirled face-tentacles with idle concern. He sauntered up Gothic stairs and, once he picked a floor, let his mucus covered fingertips slide across wooden shelves. He discovered that the edge of one shelf was free of dust the others still carried. He realized then that he was not alone in the tower, but he saw no coats at the entrance, no shoes on the floor, and heard not of any check-ins with his staff.

He pointed two fingers upwards. A shadow melted into the form of a barracuda-woman, adorned in a tactical vest, balaclava, and a sub-machine gun. Without a verbal command, she rocketed up the stairs and bounced from banister to banister in arcs that carried little sound beyond the light slap of fin-foot to steel. Cthulhu continued his ascent up the stairwell, with a more heightened alertness than before, and only stopped when he heard his assassin's weapon discharge its volley.

"It's..." the barracuda-woman leaned over the balcony, "it's just Mohammed, sir!"

"God dammit, Mohammed," Ocean-Mouth's eyelid twitched, the drool of annoyance sloshing out of his tentacle mouth.

He reached the 18th floor and saw the obelisk Mohammed hid in, with a book floating in front of its blank obsidian face. Bullet shells littered uselessly about the floor; they failed to dent his obelisk shell.

"How many times have I told you to take off your jacket and shoes, or sign in, or..." Cthulhu removed his oil-slick sunglasses and cleaned them with the untucked part of his button-up shirt, "or let my guards know you'll be here. Something. Anything. Have courtesy. Have class before you come into my tower."

"Bold of you to assume I'm wearing something to take off," the obelisk shifted from side-to-side to emote for the god hidden within its stone, opaque walls.

"Don't... don't. I don't need to know that," Cthulhu slid the round sunglasses back up his slimy, nose-less face. He paused with a sudden realization: Mohammed had been spending more time at his tower ever since the show began. "Why are you here? You have your own mansion."

"I'm bored," a page of the book in front of Mohammed turned without any visible hand's help, "and you have books."

"The legends say you don't know how to read," Cthulhu clicked his contemptuous tongue.

Mohammed's front smooth-wall slid to face Cthulhu, then slid back to its floating book.

"Legends also say you're gigantic," he hissed, "and they're right."

Cthulhu stewed, sighed, and pulled a random tome off the shelf. He joined Mohammed in flipping idly through the pages of *The Next Great Deity* records.

"Another weight joke," the elder god said, "I'd be angrier if I hadn't lead."

"What percentage of the individual season's records have you actually read, Cthulhu?" Mohammed wondered.

Cthulhu sighed. "I have no idea. Considering that records for the show span up to at least the 75th floor, not enough. And that's just in this dimension."

"So the stats we've been referencing?"

"Compilation books on the 27th floor. Probably assembled by some intern."

"Are you sure?"

Cthulhu clapped the book close, a cloud of dusty powder puffed into the air. "Of course not. Why even ask something like that? We're in Heaven. Anything can happen."

"Geeze, settle down, Ocean-Mouth."

"Don't call me that."

"I'm asking because... well, look."

Cthulhu leaned near Mohammed's book and saw the description of a challenge from a past season.

"It's the same," Mohammed said.

Though the episode took place at a different part of that past season, the challenge itself—create the sexuality of your invented species—was identical.

"There are often many different challenges between each season, but this one seems to show up in every book I've opened since I've been here," Mohammed's stone form wobbled with concern. "What does this mean? Is it a clue to help us figure out *the one*?"

*****

If the winner of *The Next Great Deity* was the same as The Producer's favorite contestant, each of the judges would be free to travel to Earth, free of their hosting duties, free of the constraints imposed on them by Heaven. Mohammed was motivated, more so than he ever had been by anything before, by this prize.

In recent years, Heaven's news had inflated his ego—the entertainment press constantly reported on his massive hoard of testaments and surging Earth popularity. He was Heavenly Body #2, and with his many butlers and personal chefs, he had grown accustomed to a certain level of respect and notoriety. He had climbed far enough in Heaven that he believed he could leave it and go to Earth—and he was wrong. There was no transportation to the mortal realm. No one knew how to get there, and everyone he met simply assumed that the next wealthiest deity up in Heaven would know. Such inaccessibility left him with a sense of emptiness he had not known before. He dreamed of Earth's food, their rainwater, and their women. The ease of his life became difficulty when he considered that there was an even easier world, a place that loved and worshiped him even more than he already was, forever out of reach. He knew Earth had to be his, and yet, for the first time in his life, there was something that his testaments could not purchase. The secret of Heaven that no one talks about is that it has a ceiling that not even the gods can break.

One day, The Producer sought him out. He appeared in Mohammed's bedroom without alerting his security system. He had slid into the room from strange perspectives, as if

Mohammed's vision could not comprehend the methods of his transportation. Even when he stood directly in front of Mohammed—who was laying in bed with grapes while watching replays of the 2016 Cricket World Cup grand finals between England and the West Indies on a wall-sized TV—Mohammed found it impossible to make sense of his appearance. He was segmented, shattered, reforming, so close to incorporeal that Mohammed believed this might have not been The Producer at all, but a transmission. The only reason Mohammed believed this might have actually been The Producer was that the sound that he made when he moved—a rattling of metallic chains—perfectly mimicked his movements. It synced with his position in the room. It was no recording or slight of hand—this sound, whatever it was, was in the room with Mohammed. The Producer said, "I've seen your dreams. And I know others that share them, too." And it took little convincing to raise Mohammed out of bed, to get him to confess to his desires, his dreams, his hunger for more than this reality was capable of giving him.

*****

Cthulhu stared hard at Mohammed. He slapped the book out of Mohammed's mental grip, and it slid across red-and-gold embroidered rugs.

It annoyed Mohammed that he could be so loved by a planet of people, to the extent that he became filthy rich in Heaven through little effort of his own, and yet he was treated so poorly by his peers when he actually tried to work.

"What the hell?" Mohammed balked.

"What do you think it means, you idiot?" Cthulhu waved his hands in disbelief. "It means The Producer likes sex. It's a reality show, what did you expect?"

The **Pumpkin** Goes to **Work**

A series of sirens blared, their Doppler screams bounced between each potted plant and wall. The parrot panicked and rapped its beak against its cage. Jack jerked awake from his sleep in the middle of his apartment and rubbed the pumpkin seeds from the corner of his triangular eyes.

"EMPLOYEE," an authoritative male voice bellowed from ceiling speakers hidden behind potted foliage, "THIS IS YOUR TEN MINUTE ALARM."

"...What?" Jack sat on the floor. His pumpkin head bobbled, still clawing back to the surface of his new reality.

"YOUR DESTINATION," the man over the speakers bellowed. Mid-sentence, he switched to a porn actress's exaggerated coo, "*Beelzebub Boxing,*" then switched back to the terror-inducing baritone, "IS 6 MINUTES AWAY. YOUR RIDE WILL BE HERE SHORTLY. PLEASE COMPLETE ALL REST ACTIVITIES AND PROCEED TO THE PICK-UP ZONE."

"I..." Jack whimpered, "I don't want to."

Red lights flooded the apartment.

"THIS INNOVATIVE MORNING IS MADE POSSIBLE BY THE INARI CONGLOMERATE," the speaker screamed, "PLEASE ENJOY YOUR ALARMS AND HAVE A BLESSED HELL-DAY."

A panel opened up from the ceiling and a hose lowered down. It launched a baby-blue colored polo-shirt and khaki shorts at Jack with cannonball speed.

"*Get dressed,*" the sultry actress-speaker cooed, barely audible over the alarms, "*get dressed, get dressed, get dressed, get dressed...*"

Jack, entangled in panic and cotton, squirmed his muscular limbs into the entirely-too-tight company uniform.

"*Thank you,*" the porn-voice moaned. The sirens continued to scream.

Jack threw himself into an elevator and sprinted out of the apartment's entrance doors and tumbled down the outside stairs. The alarms didn't stop until he reached the sidewalk, where the same ride-share devil-driver pulled up in synchronous timing.

"I can hear them all the way from down here!" Jack panted as he crawled into the backseat. "Why are they so loud?"

"The alarms?" the driver looked at him from his rear-view mirror. "Everyone can hear them. That's how sound works."

Jack shivered and stuck his rind thumb into his carved smile. The slight sounds of fear betrayed his carved expression.

"Hey," the driver furrowed his brow into the mirror, "sit up and buckle up. If you lay down, I'm not legally allowed to drive. It's not safe."

"Good," Jack cried and remained horizontal.

The devil-driver stared, sighed, and reached into his glove compartment.

"Every fuckin' newbie is like this," he said.

Jack watched as the devil-driver pulled a wooden object out of the compartment. From the tapered wood stretched a long, black metal double-barrel. It was grooved, segmented and cold. The devil-driver cocked his shotgun, leaned, turned his upper body backwards, and aimed at Jack's head.

"If you don't buckle up in 1 minute and 12 seconds, we both get in trouble," the devil-driver's tone was despondent, so heavy and bored with the world as it was. "I am authorized to kill you if you obstruct my job, and I am one year away from buying a home in Purgatory. You are *not* going to ruin this for me."

Jack slowly removed his thumb from his carved mouth and sat up in a stiff, seated position. He buckled up for safety.

"Okay," Jack whispered and shivered.

They drove to Beelzebub Boxing in silence. Only the gravel, ground underneath the cruelty of government tires, could be heard between them.

Foreplay

Mark Sharkman whirled around, clacked pen against clipboard, and flashed pyramid teeth at each contestant that materialized in the canvas director's chair across from him. The whirring camera arm behind him blinked its red recording eye and captured their thoughts during this most intimate challenge.

"So, it's almost time for judgement," the finned interviewer readied his pen, "how do you feel about your work for this *sexy* episode?"

*****

"Today went better than yesterday," Oksi muttered with such slight volume that his thick black beard appeared frozen. He offered no more words, no twitching emotions, no unnecessary movement.

Mark leaned in and waited for more, his coal-black eyes widened with suggestion. Oksi either deliberately ignored, or didn't pick up on, the social cue.

"Oh... kay," Mark blinked, "tell me about your work! What can you share with us about how the pewreps *get down*?"

"They are powerful," Oksi muttered. Mark leaned in again. Oksi folded his arms across his chest.

"Right. Good luck!" Mark sent the wall-of-a-man away with the click of a tooth.

*****

"Subject Sex..." Zargah began. His antenna bobbed; he shook his head with a spasm, and then scratched at the translation collar around his neck. "Apologies. Still adjusting. Sex is... universal concept. No trouble understanding the challenge."

Mark brightened. This was the most straightforward speech he had heard from the alien. "Do you think you'll win?"

“I feel powerless to say,” Zargah looked at the floor, “when culture divides me. But I like the world in my mind. I believe my creation will perform a sexual act of the most meaning and beauty.”

“You’re not controlling it? Last time you had the...” Mark pantomimed the vague shape of Zargah’s chassis, “I believe it was similar to an airplane pilot’s steering column around your body. Does this mean you managed to give your creature sentience?”

“The judges desired sentience,” Zargah nodded, “and I believe I’m understanding this world well enough to give it a try. Do you have an expression like... ‘I removed the training belt?’”

Mark scribbled down in his notes. “Yes. Well, *close.* Wheels.”

*****

Oshunmare shifted in her seat. She opened her mouth to talk, hesitated, and replaced the words loaded in their chamber.

“Last challenge, I don’t think I expressed my love of color quite so well,” she nodded her head as she looked at the workroom through one of the monitors at Mark’s desk. Her bouffant white hair, filled with pink flowers arranged with delicate precision, bobbed along with her nod.

“Your feyders are rather ghostly and pale,” Mark quipped, “I wouldn’t have guessed your intention was colorful.”

“Yeah, and that’s on me. I had an idea and though I still like it, maybe it wasn’t 100%... I dunno, on brand?” the lizard woman’s rainbow tongue darted. “But I’ll correct that today. It’s important to me, because I made a promise with border patrol.”

Mark froze. “Border patrol?”

“Yeah.”

“What do you mean?”

Oshunmare tilted her head. "The god-police. The uniformed people that capture the divine births. Doesn't everyone know of them?"

Mark didn't, but realized, as an interviewer, this wasn't about him. It was more important to get Oshunmare to connect as a character with the audience, so he seized the opportunity. "Would you mind sharing your promise?"

Oshunmare smiled, her yellow eyes lidded, the slit of her speckled pupils obscured by a tear. "When I was born in the wilds of Heaven, they told me I wouldn't be there for long. I dunno, it's just... the officer that found me was so beautiful, and they saw beauty in me. I didn't know who I was yet, and that little compliment set me off on the right path. 'Look at all the colors you were born with. You wear them all so well,' they said to me." She fidgeted with the neon laces on the side of her pink shorts.

Mark scribbled notes. Some were for the show, some were for himself.

"I told the officer," Oshunmare held her arms to her body and hugged her memory close, "'I'll fill the world with color, if it needs it.' I had so little in my head then, so those words came from the purest part of my being. It was my 'start.' That officer also helped me connect with my family, my *Orisha*, who were already in Purgatory, so I didn't have to start in Hell with no connections. And now... I'm here. I'm gonna fill the world with color."

*****

Taninim twisted the machine-heads of his golden instrument. "The hardest part about this challenge was seeing everyone else's work."

"You were intimidated?" Mark blinked. He had trouble picturing the horn-crowned dragon rocker as the sort of lizard-man who'd second-guess himself.

Taninim shook his head, his nose-chain rattled with the motion "No. Embarrassed. There's just... dicks and boobs everywhere. I'm uncomfortable."

"Oh."

"But it's okay. Whenever there's something I'm uncomfortable around, I have a way to deal with it—the only true way to deal with fear in life."

"What's that?"

Taninim strummed a power chord of dirty, unabashed distortion.

"What else could it be? What else can I do but ROCK," he slashed his hands downwards across the glowing pickup, "THE FUCK," his rebound brought his claw high in the air, and the momentum from the strum lifted his nose-chain in suspended animation, "OUT!?"

Mark stared at Taninim as he crumpled onto his knees and let the distortion of his chord fill the room and die into silence.

"...Right," Mark agreed, and pressed no further.

*****

Santa Inari adjusted a stray shoulder pad on her pine-green power suit, combed her red hair back to its star-splaying side, and smiled into the camera with a full row of saleswoman teeth.

"Today, I'll present a new way of integrating sexual activity with modern concepts of religion and societal progress," she recited with plastic perfection.

"You don't have to hit me with your full presentation," Mark waved his sharkskin hand, "just tell me... how do you *feel* about it?"

Santa Inari reached deep into the lessons she had learned from her million-testament public speaking classes. Unfortunately, those lessons were centered on connecting with an audience of suits, and not a camera.

"I feel energized and engaged," her fire-hydrant lipstick burst in saturation, but its vibrancy was not enough to color her gray delivery, "I'm ready to get the ball rolling on my sexual proposal."

*****

Csodaszarvas chewed the bottom of his muzzle-lip. "I have a massive gold coat rack on top of my head, and my fur glows and sparkles in strong enough light."

Mark squinted.

The wonder-deer shook his head, and his golden horns came dangerously close to camera-arm collision, "I never thought I'd be in jeopardy of not standing out on a TV show. But last challenge I was in the middle, and I fear I might be there again, too, now that I've seen everyone else's work. I have classic tastes and I feel I'm not as... *out there* as some of the other people in this competition. I can't believe that's even possible for me. Look at me."

"Do you believe it's enough to win this competition to just be yourself?"

Csodaszarvas's nostrils flared.

"See," he clopped a hoof on the floor, "when you say it like that, I sound like an ass. I'm not an ass. I'm a deer."

The two stared. They waited for something from the other.

"That's a joke," Csodaszarvas sighed.

"That's a joke!" Mark scribbled.

*****

"So, I got bodied last week," The Internet dug his crossed arms deep into his pits, and found it difficult to look into the camera. He thought for a moment, then willed himself to look into the glass eye of the camera, his wolf-brow furrowed with a spark that flickered across his whole form, down into the clenched fists out of frame, "But I understand how this stuff works now. This is a new Internet. This is my redemption arc."

"An entire redemption arc in two episodes, huh?" Mark smiled. "You must be *very* confident."

Internet bit back the urge to insult Mark, to mock him, to chastise him for trying to get sound clips out of him that could be used to paint him in a negative light. He closed eyes, breathed deep, and had his cell-dogs chant:

The story, the story, the story is what matters.

"I know what went wrong last challenge," The Internet's eyes opened back up. They were emeralds of resolve. "I've addressed the design shortcomings and done something with today's performance I know no one else will do. I'm going to finish on time. I'm not just ready; I *can't wait* to show everyone what I've done."

*****

"I got immunity," Theodore folded his arms across his chest. He tried to batten the corners of his creeping smile, "I'm still going to try my best, of course, but considering how weird a... sex-invention challenge is going to get, I'm glad I don't have to worry too much about the results."

"Thank you," Mark said.

The poker player watched the cameras around him power down.

"Hey," Theodore adjusted the cuffs of his sky-blue suit, "you haven't talked to Robin and Ishta yet, have you?"

Mark glanced up from his clipboard. "No...?"

"They're gonna ask you about the writing on the wall."

Mark dropped the clipboard down to the safety of his lap and adjusted his posture. His spine popped audibly with concern.

"And... why?" The shark's voice was colored with annoyance, but he was attentive, and ready to hear a rational explanation. "You were just fighting with Robin earlier, and I hope I needn't underline how risky it is to talk about something like that outside of the Camera World."

Theodore glanced over to a monitor. The grainy footage stuttered with lines of distortion as each contestant touched up their final creations. Theodore wondered, for a moment, why the reception on Mark's monitors, despite their supernatural abilities, was so bad. He thought studio technology straight from Heaven should, under no circumstance, appear to have worse quality than the broadcast capabilities he could find on his cell phone. He considered this thought a distraction, and turned his eyes back to Mark. "We talked on the roof, and I kept details to a minimum. They don't know what's written there, they don't know anything about you and I. As for 'why,' well—Robin has been doing a lot of work on her own. She created a tracker to follow another contestant. She told me she spied on the judges. She works with the same distrust of the staff we do, even if she hasn't quite admitted it yet to herself."

Mark rubbed the crinkled, rubbery skin between his eyes. "In short, she's clever and you want someone like her on our side."

"Yeah."

"And Ishta?"

Theodore cleared his throat. "They're a package deal. I trust her about as far as I can throw her. I did play football, though, so maybe my bench press record isn't the best unit of measurement here."

Mark sighed. "Theodore..."

"Well, there's also her relationship with Athena," Theodore raised his palm and brushed away the worry he saw condense in the air between them, "and it seems Robin has blackmailed her into submission. Ishta has a power that allows her to see the vision of someone's intention. It's vague and annoying, but to my mind, useful."

The glint of Mark's triangular teeth peeked out in thought. "She... if she's telling the truth, she can use that power on the judges!"

Theodore smiled. "If she's telling the truth, there's no way she hasn't already. When she asks to see the wall, make her pay for it. Information for information. If her relationship with Athena is half as meaningful as it seems, and if Robin has any influence on her, I think she'll be more than happy to share."

*****

"I hate it," Jarilo lit a cigarette and sucked the smoke in with greedy need.

Mark wasn't sure when Jarilo started smoking. "Why do you hate your work?"

"Well, I've completely changed up my idea. It's not a wheatkin anymore, and I hate that, because it's no longer what I wanted to make," Jarilo's nose crinkled. The child-like innocence of the goat-boy from the first episode was completely gone, reduced to the cinders that drifted from each tap to his cancer-stick.

Mark scribbled down Jarilo's response, and the camera angles which captured his soured expression best. Jarilo slumped forward to rest his elbows on his knees.

"But I'm also being hard on myself," Jarilo lowered his chin to his chest, and his voice softened, "and I know I'm being over-dramatic."

Mark raised an eyebrow. A camera-arm inched towards the side of the half-goat's face.

"I know that being challenged is the best thing for my work," Jarilo admitted. "I've completely redesigned what I've made based off their suggestions. I can step outside myself enough to see that it's objectively better work. Even if it's not what I set out to make... I see myself in it. I know I can take this new plant man to the place it needs to go."

Jarilo puffed out a ring of smoke, leaned back in his chair, and slapped his forehead. "Though... shit, man," the ragged goat-boy sighed, "I still haven't named this thing."

*****

"I walked away from the last challenge with one of the strongest presentations," Imhotep managed to recline across the canvas chair's arms, his legs crossed over the edge and dangled, "and today will be no exception. I know what the judges want."

Mark shifted in his seat. The smoky confidence of Imhotep's words, coupled with the way his form hung on the chair like honey from a spoon, had such an inherent eroticism that Mark wondered if Imhotep had planned this pose out just for this interview. Sharkman made sure to keep the Egyptian god a little bit longer than most, and let the cameras linger on his lithe frame from creative angles. Sex sells, after all.

*****

Robin stared at the message on the wall.

"'Find Eris', huh," she said. She bit her thumb in thought, "So this just... appeared?"

Mark Sharkman's rubbery fingertips jabbed into each other. He wasn't sure how to measure himself around Robin, as he had not developed trust for her yet. "I don't know how long its been there."

"But who is it for?" Robin muttered.

Mark blinked and rubbed his head-fin. "Eh?"

"Am I supposed to assume this is for us? Or someone else?" Robin paced the lemon-painted infinite wine hallway. "Is it a message for you, Mark? If you're the only person consistently here..."

"Why would anyone working against the show leave this message for me?" Mark protested, "I work for them!"

Robin looked at him.

"T-technically. You know what I mean. I'm *employed* by them."

Robin grunted and wandered out of the hallway. "Ugh, I need to think about this. You can send me back."

The shark-interviewer trotted after her, his wine-collared coat billowing behind him. "Wait!" he said, "I haven't asked you about the chall-"

"I have nothing to say."

Mark's leather loafers squeaked as he halted. He stared at her, silhouetted by the wall of static-filled monitors, her hand on her chin, the details of her form turned to confused, obscured shadows. Her mind was everywhere except there in the room.

*****

Ishta-Devata put her hand out. She touched the lemon wall, and drew her finger tips across the carvings of the letters.

"I will," she whispered. She spoke directly to it, as if Athena herself were talking to her. A tear fell down her cheek, "I promise."

Mark shifted with some discomfort as he leaned against the wall. "I'm sorry," Mark said, "I think it's safe to say you knew Athena and Eris well."

"Athena? Yes. Eris? Not terribly well, believe it or not," Ishta's chuckle sounded pained. She wiped the tear from her cheek and smiled through it, "but this sounds like something Athena would've said. She was a pretty straight forward girl. It's what I liked about her."

Mark pushed himself from the wall. "But you have met her? Eris, I mean."

"Yes, of course. She's an Olympian. They're money, so what is there to say?" Ishta shrugged. "They were well-off and happy. I suppose Eris was a little bit more wild than Athena, if you can believe that. I remember when we were all in middle school, she punched another girl in the mouth at a party the Olympians had thrown. I think it was our classmate, Bia. They bickered over something which is much less important to my memory than the image I have of Eris turning over a table full of pastries on top of her. Bia pushed the wood and mounds of pitarakia off and rose up and those two stared at each other and I thought for sure they'd start brawling from one end of the ballroom to the other. Then, they just... started laughing. We all took a shot. That was a great party."

Mark blinked. "Do all Olympians like to fight?"

Ishta-Devata smiled. "All the ones I've loved, yes."

Time Is Up

As contestants polished new entries of their species and fine-tuned their most intimate anatomy, the image of Jesus flickered to life in the middle of the workroom, transparent but present, saturated beyond reality. She wore heart-shaped sunglasses lined with blinking LEDs and she sipped a novelty sized mixed drink from a winding curly straw.

"Time is up, everyone!" she sang after a swig of liquid delight. "Let's make this honeymoon *official*."

As in the previous challenge, the contestants shuffled their creations into respective portals. The scandalous nature of this episode led eyes to wander longer and with more curiosity than before—they tried to work out the anatomy of their opponent's creations, their purpose, and the greater meaning behind each hormonal design. Never before in the history of creation has such sexual scrutiny been so academic.

As the contestants piled into the starless void of the showroom, Jesus greeted them with a gentle wave and a painted smile. Her antebellum dress, modernized by the bare suggestion of a sweetheart neckline, swayed side to side with her coy hips. She laughed during her swirl, her paid-for perfect grin catching the lights. Every camera angle found her cream-colored hoop skirt in its wild rotation, the swirl of its slapdash ribbons, and the flash of red, blood-like splatter on the back of her billboard bustle. The crimson paint read: *Do You Believe?*

The orchestra of the contestants' single file march of shoes and heels and talon-tips on the transparent glass floor echoed far into the eternal blackness of the showroom's ceiling, if it had one at all. Across the stage from their illuminated chairs, now numbering 12 in Athena's absence, sat the three judges' seats, leather and posh.

"Welcome back, gods-in-training, to *The Next Great Deity*!" Jesus clapped her hands together. "You remember our judges, of course. To my right is *The Shape of Water*'s biggest critic, Cthulhu!"

Cthulhu, with his shirt unbuttoned down to exposed the middle part of his chest, swirled a neon cocktail in his wet hands. "It had unrealistic beauty standards for Deep Ones, that's all. Hopefully you'll do better, contestants."

"And to my left is the Mecca-Man himself, Mohammed!"

Mohammed preferred a frosted milkshake, whose 1950's style glass floated by his rectangular walls. Whip cream disappeared with each glass-on-obsidian clink. A small party hat sat precariously on the apex of the obelisk.

"Let's see them BOOBS," he screeched and vibrated in his chair. His party hat fell off.

Jesus's smile, ever professional, sucked her lips inwards. "You sure that's the take you want to go with?" she muttered out the side of her mouth.

Mohammed cleared his throat. "Contestants, I can't wait to see your work for this... *exciting* challenge." The rectangle leaned back in his chair.

Jesus's red nails glinted at the tips as she held her hands out. From her palms snaked out her god eye, which winced and shot lasers into the air above the contestants. Candle jars landed in each of their laps, and upon thigh contact, the wicks lit.

"This week's challenge was about the reproductive cycle of your species, and how it relates to the religion you'll create," she said in a tone that was as seductive as it was aggressive. "Is it beautiful? Is it ugly? Is it *kinky*? Let's find out how you think about sex... *right now*!"

Jarilo, unsure of when his time would come, chose to light a cigarette with the candle flame. The flame flared upwards and turned the end to glowing ash. From this, the candle went out, and the smoke from the wick twisted into the shape of numbers: "01."

"*Great*," Jarilo muttered as he stuffed the filter into the side of his mouth. He readjusted his leather jacket, hoofed his hooves over to the tape-marked starting position for contestants, and waited patiently for the camera-wielding shiqq to signal him.

Their boneless arms wiggled in his general direction, and he turned his head towards the creature portal. As he did so, glowing spheres of light twinkled into existence around his waist.

"Jarilo, All-Mighty, knows your seeds
Knows your time, knows your deeds
Your true purpose is to be harnessed
For the *True God's Harvest*!"

If Jarilo's motions were that of a conductor's in the first episode, then this challenge's summon could be more accurately attributed to the technique of a disc jockey. He held his hands at waist level and seized the glowing orbs of light between his fingertips, turned and twisted the top of the light-spheres, maestro of the growing star field circling him.

Two bipedal, light-skinned creatures crawled out of the portal. The creatures were not meat, but made of plant fiber, their flesh of slight transparency, with the toughness of banana skin. Orchid petals and short, stringy hair weaved into a mess of chaos along their shoulders and chest. The germinating parts of a flower sprung from each of their faces: a bright yellow stigma bobbed prominently from the center as red, fuzzy stamen drooped underneath.

“Wheatkin no more,” Cthulhu adjusted his oil-like sunglasses.

Jarilo’s hoof scratched against the floor when he heard Cthulhu’s whisper. “I’ve pivoted. Now they’re called *raskos*.”

Jarilo used the tweaks and twists of his star-field to remote-control the two raskos to center-stage. The genderless plant-creatures pressed their faces together, their large off-white petals wrapped and intertwined with each other. A soft luminescence burned between the petals, and silhouettes of their stigma and stamen shone through. They pulsed and prodded and parried, and over the next ten minutes, the yellow dust of their pollinating love leaked through their flower-faced seal. The romance brought them both to their knees, their long, curly stem-fingers gripped each other hard. They made no sound other than the subtle shift of plant-skin and leaves as they rubbed like sandpaper against the grain.

The judges wrote on their note cards, their heads bobbed up and down between paper and the pollination in front of them. Jarilo was annoyed to see no stares of wonderment or rapture, no flushed cheeks of embarrassment. He eased his anxiety with a reminder: the judges were professionals. Their expressions would give him no reprieve, and he should not expect them to. He had to remain confident.

With twenty seconds left, the raskos separated their faces in a sudden pop. Glittery pollen drifted between them, and dispersed into the air.

“Ugh, I’m never going outside again,” Theodore whispered to The Internet.

“Why’s that?” the dog-punk turned his head.

"I've never wanted to think of pollen as plant-ejaculate, even if that's what it is," Theodore lowered his voice as much as he could. The Internet bit his fangs down hard to prevent laughter.

As the challenge-ending buzzer sounded, a flower began to bud and blossom on the glass surface between the raskos. One picked up the fledgling in its vine-fingers and held it to their chest. Jarilo wiped sweat away from his blonde bangs, and dragged his hooves back to his seat.

Taninim's Entry

The dragon-rocker's candle flickered and died, the smoke trail from the wick curved into the numbers: "02."

"Hang on, Jeremy," Taninim muttered to himself as he rose to his feet. Every song, every note, and every breath, they were all for Jeremy, but Taninim needed to remind himself as often as possible what his goal was.

The impossibly-toothed guitarist strode to his mark and nodded to the shiqqs. His summoning-arpeggio wheeled out his dragon scaled amp from the creature portal. Attached to its side was a new accessory not present in the previous challenge: a small, gold distortion pedal. Once the amp bumped into his ankle, he lifted his talon-toed boot, placed it on the amp's top, and snarled into the camera.

"Let's rock!"

He slashed downwards. His guitar pick crossed the silver strings of his golden guitar and the amp screeched octave chords.

Taninim's creation, a shoulder-mounted-speaker dragon, flipped out of the amp in a blaze of streaking flames. The grills of his circular shoulders vibrated with a slashed chord. With his own jet-black V-guitar in his reflector-yellow claws, the truck-sized lizard started to play a riff that climbed and fell in schizophrenic streaks along the neck of his guitar.

Taninim strummed again, and another burst of light and fire spewed from his amp. A similarly sized speaker-dragon spiraled out, blue-scaled, thick in the hips and lithe in her clawed hands. She held a six-string bass of iridescent pearls which plugged into her shoulders, and her claws plucked a thick, heavy bass-line for the lead guitar.

Taninim kicked the distortion pedal off of the side of his scaled amp and anchored the speaker-dragons' melodies with his rhythm guitar. "When two of my draconus find harmony with each other, I'll bless them...."

He leapt and stamped down on the gold distortion pedal. All of their tempos doubled. A whirlwind of sound and pressure spun around them, and whipped at the garments of the spectator-contestants and judges.

"...with a full band!"

The two draconus, mid-rapturous crescendo, arched their backs and drew their scaled fingers across the frets. Sparks burst from their instruments, and an arc of lightning flew back and forth between their pickups.

That burning passion, the melody of their music, formed an egg of lightning between them. It cracked and exploded and two small dragons, gold and purple, rolled out. They were clearly children; their horn-crown height only reached five feet.

The gold child's shoulders were mounted with cymbals, and a kick-drum sat in her belly. She set up a snare as she landed from her tumble. Without hesitation, she slapped down a high-energy gallop in 3/5ths time.

The purple child was born with a pearl-encrusted microphone, and he sang two words, which he held in a beautiful falsetto, high and smooth: "LAUDE DRACONUS!" He slid several feet on his scaley knees and collapsed in front of the judges. He panted. His new family struck their final chord. The gold child attacked across her cymbals, and all four killed their held notes in unison with her kick-drum.

The challenge siren signaled the end of Taninim's time. The dragons bowed, the judges laughed, and Jesus wiped a tear from her eye.

"Thank you, Taninim," she choked out, "that was beautiful."

Csodaszarvas's Entry

Csodaszarvas's candle puffed into the numbers: "03." The wonder-deer rose to his hooves with a heavy sigh and dearly wondered why the show bothered to have a chair-for-bipeds on set when they knew he couldn't sit in it. He trotted over to the mark.

In the last episode, Jarilo cheered Csodaszarvas on with violent disregard for the seriousness of the proceedings. Today, his half-goat roommate stared away from the stage, buried in a leather jacket too big for his scrawny shoulders, his face swathed by cigarette smoke. He looked older and disenchanted in ways Csodaszarvas never could have anticipated. When the deer saw Jarilo's withered face, he felt it was a reflection; the grind and time constraints of the competition had sucked the joy out of them both.

This is so much more work than just leading humans to Levedia, he thought. His god eye slithered out from the tip of one of his shimmering antlers. Then, he whistled.

The whistle summoned his creations, the hair-antlered váradi, to dance from the creature portal. Their pointed ears twitched in sync with their ballet. The elven male was dressed in scant gold-and-white silk, the suggestion of tassels and ribbons around his neck and wrists and groin flowed with his movements. A female váradi of gold hair-antlers tip-toed out of the portal thereafter, her own bare suggestion of satin floated around her bosom and ankles. They locked hands, and their shadows glowed purple.

They waltzed. The male lifted the female by her hips, revolved, then dropped her to the tips of her toes. In a fluid motion, they traded places; the female now swung her partner above her, and they spun, and he landed, and they revolved again, twirling and twisting.

The pair's tornado-like dance stuttered their shadows to life. The dark forms broke free of the chains of mimicry, their orbits separate, their expressive twirls and poise owned by themselves alone. The four forms, shadow and váradi, became distinct in their art; they groped, they laughed, they carried themselves with jolly disregard for the world and tumbled into splits and twined limbs. The shadows kissed the váradi, and the váradi kissed the shadows. They all swapped spit and energy and tongues and the fluids of their holiest passion until the shadows and light that swirled between them coalesced into one bright, burning form that erupted into purple cinders.

The shadows were gone, dissipated within purple smoke. The váradi remained; they cradled a new child, whose hair-antlers were but stubs on his forehead. The alarm for the performance sounded.

Csodaszarvas banked his competition lifeline on lithe ballet and erotic magic. In the process, he was so lost in his place on the show that he had no idea what to think of his own work, much less what the judges might think. He hoped that his spectacle would carry him through.

As they always did, the judges buried themselves in note-taking, and didn't seem particularly compelled to look up and study the new family in front of them.

The wonder-deer returned to lay in front of his seat, and stared off into the void of the showroom.

The flame on Theodore's candle sparked and, had he not pulled his face away, would have singed the tip of his nose.

"Jesus," he jerked back in his seat.

"Over here, honey," Jesus wiggled her fingers in a wave. The smoke of Theodore's candle, "04", seemed to circle around her before disappearing. Theodore, ruffled, took his mark.

His time began. The quartztaphore from the previous challenge wandered out of the portal, its crystal, oil-slicked purple skin shimmered in the spotlights. Jeweled feet clinked against the glass as it reached center stage. In its hand was an orange pouch, from which it dumped dirt onto the floor.

"I've decided the quartztaphores need to feel a bond with each other," he explained, "which must be inherently difficult when every member of your species can change shape. This fertilizer here is meant to simulate any dirt from their home world. Please forgive me, I haven't quite had the time to make a whole planet yet."

The judges did not respond. He cleared his throat.

The quartztaphore held up one of its long, jagged rock arms. The creature's form began to wobble and morph, and its purple skin dulled to a sharp gray blade.

"So, this is how their family is made."

The quartztaphore held up its other hand, still in its original form. The blade hand sliced downwards and sliced it off at the elbow. Black blood spilled from its body and covered the dismembered rock-limb on the floor, which twitched for a moment before slender fingers curled like a poisoned roach, rigid in death.

Cthulhu looked on with intent, his mucus-coated fingers trailed along the edges of his note cards. Theodore noticed this, and carried on with renewed confidence.

The blade-arm morphed again. It maintained its gray color but flattened and thickened near the end. The blade was now a hammer.

“With sacrifice.”

The quartztaphore smashed the limb with a single heavy blow, and its pieces shattered into the dirt.

“Over the course of several months, the letting of blood of the quartztaphore will nourish these crystals and allow them to grow. This is accelerated for demonstration purposes.”

The quartztaphore parent, hunched over the blossoming crystals, re-opened its stub-wound and spilled another waterfall of blood onto the dirt. The crystals drank the blood and grew, its shattered shape, in artificial time-lapse, straightened into a more humanoid form.

“It’s painful and difficult and the crystals will only grow with the particular combination of proteins and enzymes found in quartztaphore blood. To raise a crystal child requires a real part of yourself.”

The alarm went off, and Theodore winced, as he still had more that he wanted to say—he’d hardly covered how he’d incorporate the creature’s birth in the context of his religion. The quartztaphore picked up its new jewel-child and cradled it in its remaining arm.

“I feel that’s the way should be,” Theodore punctuated his performance after the buzzer, in some haphazard attempt to convince the panel this was all he intended to show.

The judges buried themselves in their notes. Theodore stuffed his hands into the pockets of his blue suit. He was thankful for his immunity.

Ishta-Devata's candle flame puffed out with the scent of rose petals and ginger. The sweet smoke curled into the shape of "05", and with some hesitance, she stood to her feet. The world-conquering ambitions of the judges, through Ishta's mind's eye, played behind them in horrific clarity. Every day she would stand on this runway, she knew she'd have to face them, face the darkest parts of their hearts, the cruelest arrogance of gods at the top of heavenly society.

She took her spot.

"I'm..."

She considered drawing her god eye out and attacking the judges, but knew that the ensuing chaos would not benefit her or prove the guilt of their actions or the horrors of their intentions. She was up against an ancient system that surely had stood against stronger attacks of passion than she, currently without a plan, could provide.

"...ready."

For the moment, she played their game. Her time began, and she produced her diamond-cut wine glass and laid it on the showroom floor.

"I established in the last challenge that my water elementals are a colony. As I began to construct an answer to today's brief, a different question arose in my mind."

In the last challenge, her water elemental splashed out of the creature portal and joined the judges. Today, there was already water in the glass, dormant save from the slight ripples created when Istha set it down.

"So what separates a normal water molecule, and the molecules of my elementals?"

Ishta's god eye snaked out of her hand and shot a thin, red laser beam which puffed gray vapor into existence. It clumped into a cloud and drifted high above the stage, and a deep rumble shook within.

"Love, I would say. A little bit of love from god is the spark they need for life."

Lightning struck from the cloud and into the glass, which shattered into a mist of shards. Even the glass floor underneath cracked from the impact, but was, as all things are, smoothed over by Heaven's Air. The judges and contestants and shiqqs all shrieked and flinched. Except, of course, Ishta-Devata—her half-smile remained, unflinching in calm as a projectile shard stuck in her nest of black hair. She picked it out and flicked it aside.

"Water evaporates and returns to the clouds and rains its children back down to the planet. If the custodians of my world are tied to its cyclical atmosphere, I think it stands to reason that lightning, the snap of my fingers, should help give them depth."

The water from the glass crawled back to the center of the smoking floor. Beads bled into each other, built on top of their liquid frame, and rose into a humanoid shape. It stretched its liquid limbs and blinked its whirlpool eye sockets at the judges.

Cthulhu went to write furiously on his card, but then realized that there was a shard of glass stabbed through its center.

"I yield the rest of my time," Ishta-Devata smiled. "Thank you."

Zargah's candle flared out, and left a smoke trail in the shape of: "06." The alien only knew it was his turn because he observed the actions of others when their candles went out: he had no clue that the smoke patterns were numbers, as the Arabic numerals were but vague foreign shapes to his eyes.

He pushed aside his intricate military shawl and strode to his mark. The insectoid popped the knuckles on each of his four hands. In the last challenge he had created a complicated chassis to pilot his creature. Today, he rolled up his ornate military sleeves and revealed the bristled forearms of his four arms. He rubbed them together in a progressive rhythm, which stridulated a cricket-like chorus of chirps.

These scrapes summoned his original zargan creature from the portal. Two toned black-and-red, four feet in height, and porous like a strawberry, the ant-man came, hand in hand, with a friend—a second zargan of purple-and-green coloration, shorter stature and more squat, well-fed proportions.

These two ant-bipeds plodded with regal movements towards Zargah's song. They blinked their coal-black eyes with the most basic sense of curiosity, but they were dense and barely aware of themselves and their surroundings.

Zargah changed the position of his four-armed forearm percussion, and modulated the tone down to a low baritone. The zargans locked hands and a green lather foamed between them.

"I feel like I'm watching something that needs David Attenborough narration," Robin whispered to Oshunmare. She had, as she did through many of the day's presentations, struggled to keep her hands in her lap. Her entire being told her to cover her eyes.

Theodore remembered that when he first met and shook hands with Zargah, the alien soldier's hands were covered in a fine mucus. He made the decision to remain ignorant of this fact for the rest of this presentation, in case there was any correlation.

The zargans, after several minutes of gentle exploration of each others palms and long fingers, pulled their hands apart. The purple-and-green zargan, whose hands had received the majority of the lather, slapped all four of their palms together and kneaded and balled the slime into an egg shape.

"The egg would take approximately 10 hours to form after intercourse," Zargah crossed his forearms. He played new stridulations with slow tenor, "if I am to understand your terminology for time correctly. We have 10 minutes, though, so..."

The slime-ball hardened and deepened from green foam to a semi-transparent purple shell. Theodore closed his eyes—he found it difficult to stomach live births in nature documentaries, and was certain that hatching was about to occur. The baby ant-creature, whose eyes took up almost the entirety of its bulbous head, could be seen through the semi-soft shell.

"...once the egg is formed, the parents will provide nutrients to the egg with applications of juices from fruit and meat, incubating it until it is ready to hatch after 5 months."

The siren went off. Theodore waited to open his eyes only after he heard the crackling sound of Zargah's creations enter the creature portal. Zargah had returned to his seat by then.

"...my hands are not the same as theirs," Zargah clicked as he leaned over Theodore's shoulder.

Theodore bristled. He felt *known*, as if in that moment Zargah's awareness of him as a individual person transcended language and expression and all other boundaries one must normally cross to get to a person's inner thoughts. All the poker players Theodore had ever faced, all the opponents and obstacles he'd encountered in his life, and no one had ever called him out in so few words. Theodore uncrossed his arms and stared at Zargah, whose antennae bobbed with vague curiosity, but betrayed no animosity or malcontent. If Zargah could peer into Theodore and read him like he had known him his whole life, then this knowing, intimate observance was a one-way street. Theodore had not yet found such a confident reading of the alien or his intentions, and knew not what thoughts lay behind those dual-pupil, wasp-yellow eyes.

But Theodore was calm, for he knew that in time, he can read anyone; perhaps, even aliens.

Robin's Entry

The flame of Robin's candle died out and the smoke formed the shape of "07."

If you were uncomfortable during Zargah's presentation, Robin's thoughts were directed towards herself in snide rebuke of her hands, which rotated and rubbed around each other until the skin was hot from friction, *wait till you see this.*

Shiqqs readied their camera arms as Robin walked to her mark.

"Ready?" Jesus asked.

"Let's go," she nodded.

Robin accepted that, as a god, you will have to make decisions you don't like. It's not dissimilar from any other decision one has to make in order to grow.

She tapped the metal bit on her temple and she swapped to her clone's body. She piloted her copy through the creature portal, identical in form to her own body, yet it was as if she was in someone else's car, someone who owned the same model of vehicle, but painted it in a different colored coat.

Robin's clone wore intentionally skimpy clothing: black hot pants and a striped crop top under a white leather jacket, neon-yellow sneakers and chunky leather purse of purple painted faux-alligator skin. Her eyes were obscured by mirrored sunglasses.

"I had an additional challenge today, since human reproduction and sexuality already exists, and has many different fragments and cultures stemming from how it works," Robin spoke from her clone's mouth. This was a Robin ready to go out to a club for the evening. She was a completely unrecognizable creature from the conservatively dressed teacher that the contestants—and the most of the people in Robin's life, for that matter—knew. She was a pastiche of everything Robin knew she wasn't and, on rare occasion, wished she could be.

With a tap on her metal bit, Robin switched back to her main body, "...and I have no intention of changing that, for the most part."

She pulled a second metal bit from her pocket and attached it to the other side of her head, tapped it, and brought another human out of the creature portal. An umber-skinned man in head-to-toe denim, Robin's male invention was built like a construction worker in form but gifted with the soft, bearded face of an immaculately trimmed magazine model. It was clear from his pinpoint fade and treated skin that there was more than a little bit of Robin's fantasy in the mould of this man.

Which made the next part difficult for Robin. Difficult, but necessary.

"But I've decided that if there's any area of human physiology I'd like to change," she clenched her fist, "then I'd like to equip the modern human with the ability to protect the most intimate parts of their anatomy, without the need of weaponry or trust."

The male-model approached the clone-Robin. Clone-Robin clutched her purse close and pretended to be oblivious.

"The measures we've taken thus far..." Robin considered how on-the-nose she wanted to be in presentation, and banished her hesitation, "...education, guns, systematic changes... none of it has completely worked, for we are flawed at the physical level. There will always be predators. There is no certainty of safety in the world of humans, no matter what."

Jesus's eye winced.

"So..."

The male-model grabbed clone-Robin and started to kiss her neck and grope her breast and ass.

"I don't consent," clone-Robin growled at her assailant and tried to push the male-model away, but she was weaker in strength and lacked leverage.

"I figure if I just add one more natural defense to humanity..." Robin's eyes winced in pain as she tried to control both creatures at once, her mind split between the two in nausea-inducing rhythm.

Clone-Robin's breasts began to glow red where the male-model's hands were. Robin performed now as the male, and had him pull his hand away when a new warmth below the skin surprised him.

She switched back to her main body. Her breath was ragged, but she persisted. "It's not a perfect solution, but it'll make assholes think twice about trying to take advantage of someone else's body."

The male-model tried to grab clone-Robin again despite the verbal and physical warnings he was given. Upon touch, he was blown backwards by a sonic force that shook the glass floor and startled judges and contestants alike. The male-model's hand was shattered and spat blood from his broken fingers. Clone-Robin brushed her striped top to smooth out wrinkles, hiked her purse strap over her shoulder, and walked past the male-model as he screamed and cried in pain. She disappeared into the creature portal.

The judges wrote furiously on their cards; they had plenty of thoughts. Jesus's face was cross with opinion, whereas Cthulhu seemed more reflective; he took long moments to lean back and ponder before scribbling on his card. Mohammed was impossible to read beyond the wall of obsidian.

“I yield the rest of my time,” Robin said. The male-model stopped screaming; Heaven’s Air healed his hand, and she guided the puppet back into the portal.

The "08"-shaped puff of smoke twitched The Internet's cold nose enough to flash one of his fangs in the stage-lights. The dog-punk fought back a sneeze, set the candle down, and marched to the tape mark, his hands clutched behind his back in professional confidence. He clapped his heels together and stared into the camera, his yellow eyes burning with focus. "Today, we discuss the assembly of the discarded," he proclaimed as his network of cell-dogs summoned his creation.

With grinding gears and steam and the clink of steel on the glass floor, The Internet's redesigned metal organism appeared from the creature portal. Gone was the concept of haphazard, patchwork design—though still made of the same discarded remnants of human technology, The Internet's new vision for his android was streamlined into perfect symmetry. The seams of metal plates curled around trim waistlines. Bolts and plastic and screens emulated the seductive shape of humanoid pectorals and biceps and calves, and at its massive frame towered over all in the room. It moved with a knowing carnality in its accentuated hips that contradicted the cold scroll of endless numbers and code on its flat-screen face.

"Without humanity to impede them, the discarded will take these preexisting designs and infrastructure and put them together in a such a way as to reject the idea that they are trash, that they are remnants of another species. They will be new."

The discarded dragged behind it a large net full of broken bottles and steel beams and monitors and all manner of metal and plastic. It ripped the net apart, chose its favorite parts from the spill of metal, then welded the odds and ends together with torches and saws and other attachments hidden within its frame.

"Every new member of the discarded..."

Sparks flew. Metal melted. Wires crossed.

"...is a chance to improve."

The new discarded stood in front of its creator, similar in shape but made of new parts, new paint. It was a little bit sleeker, a little bit taller, a little bit more intimidating. The creator-discarded dragged a cable out from its chest and plugged it into an opening in its creation. The created hummed to life, its flat screen face lit with new code.

In just 10 minutes, the discarded made a new creature in its image. The siren sang. The Internet bowed.

"Thank you," he hid a fist pump from the camera lens on his way to his seat.

Oksi's Entry

When Oksi's candle puffed out and formed the numerals "09" in its smoky wake, he wondered what would happen if he relit the flame. Would the judges laugh? What about the contestants? Would he be punished? Would there be ensuing drama that delayed the proceedings, and allowed him to sneak in some extra work time on his project? Would any of these possible results work in his favor enough to justify his continued participation in the show?

These were the thoughts that constantly poisoned Oksi's mind.

He ignored them, rose with a glazed-eye grunt and dragged himself to the mark. Behind the crossed arms and disheveled mounds of beard and hair, beyond the mumbles and cold stares, Oksi's mind was focused not on victory, but survival.

He produced his wooden-segment scroll and nodded to the judges. His time began, and he whispered to the oak; ink symbols stirred to life and summoned his pewreps to the stage.

The fanged pewrep, which in the last challenge had a comical potato-shape due to Oksi's poor sculpt, had been improved; its head was smaller, elongated to that of a racoon's maw, its lips peeled back to show off and enhance its many jagged teeth. The form was now more humanoid; though its gorilla-arms were still quite long, and its legs proportionally quite short, the added definition of muscle on the torso and neck gave the pewrep the air of a proper wild animal.

Emerging behind the brown pewrep was an albino variant, similar in all manner of shape and size and construction, but covered in pale fur with a pink triangular nose and sandstone eyes. Saliva trailed from its maw as it scrambled to catch up with the lead pewrep.

The two took center stage, created distance of about 15 feet between themselves, then faced each other.

"There are four sexes in the spectrum of the pewrep," Oksi explained, "one is capable of childbirth, one is capable of impregnation, and two of them are capable of both."

The pewreps huffed and growled, kicked at the ground, snorted vile liquid of anger from their jagged teeth and flared nostrils.

"I've created something of a rock-paper-scissor diagram with their sexual organs. The *suma* can impregnate the *kupapa*. The *kupapa* can impregnate the *shire*. The *shire* can impregnate the *suma* and the *cikap*. The *cikap* can impregnate the *suma* and *kupapa*, but cannot impregnate the *shire*. They all can impregnate themselves, except the *cikap*."

The judges whispered to each other.

"I like the idea of sexual game theory," Cthulhu whispered behind the cover of his note cards.

"...but why are there only two on stage, then?" Jesus whispered back, her brow twisted.

The actual answer to Jesus's question was that Oksi ran out of time, just as he had in the last challenge, and had to cut corners. But Oksi is nothing if not aware of his own shortcomings, and how to persevere despite them.

"On stage in front of you are two *suma*," Oksi gestured to the beasts.

And he's showing us only one of his proposed four sexes? Jesus's brow twisted in cursive confusion.

"They love each other very much," he said before he whispered to his control-scroll.

The albino pewrep leapt through the air and struck the brown pewrep with its laced fingers like a club. The victim staggered, and its stout legs wobbled.

"...and now they must decide who will carry the child."

The brown pewrep appeared as if it would topple, but it was a ruse: its wobble turned into a sprint, and it clothes-lined the albino pewrep across the throat. It mounted its lover and opponent and wailed at its head with its boulder-breaking fists, which the prone albino tried to block with its slab-like forearms.

The judges stared wide-eyed. It was quite the contrast to the previous entries.

"The pewrep species settles their most important decisions with no pretension and no pretense. Strength is their most important, and most honorable, quality," Oksi drew his arms into the sleeves of his loose robes.

After one too many blows to the head, the albino pewrep let out a squeak of submission. Its vision blurred from the battering it took, and red defeat slobbered out of the corners of its fanged maw. It spread its legs and the victor positioned and gripped its claim with strength that would surely bruise its opponents flesh. The transition between battle and copulation, and the normalcy with which both creatures found the blur of the two acts, was frightening to all in attendance. There were those that enjoyed a good fright, though; Cthulhu, in particular, found himself quite entranced by the spectacle. The spell on the elder god was only broken as the siren signaled the end of the challenge, and at the same time, both beasts roared in violent climax. The glass of the floor cracked under their thrusts.

"...Thank you, Oksi," Jesus blinked rapidly as she tried to parse what she had witnessed.

Oksi knew sex and violence struck the core of all livings things. He wasn't sure if it would win, but he figured it didn't matter: there's still a large number of contestants in the field.

For now... he thought, *all I have to do is keep them curious.*

Santa Inari's Entry

The tenth candle belonged to Santa Inari. As it extinguished itself, she smoothed a wrinkle out of the fabric of her pine green pencil skirt and approached the mark with a clipboard in her hand.

"Thank you for joining me today, esteemed judges of T*he Next Great Deity*," she said as she hooked a pair of red rimmed reading glasses on the bridge of her small nose. "Let us begin."

She wrote on her clipboard, and the authoritative scribble of pen to paper summoned four representatives of her mindshare species. The barcode-face leader of the pack was a porcelain skinned living mannequin who wore a black cocktail dress that glittered under the studio lights. The three mindshare that followed were of similarly fancy dress: two masculine presenting mannequins wore black business suits with differing colored ties—one red, one green—and the final mindshare wore a crimson silk evening gown fit for a starlet's Hollywood walk.

"The mindshare values 'value' above all else," Santa Inari peered over her glasses' rim. The lead mindshare turned on a dime to face the three that trailed behind her. "They find freedom in the free market; every aspect of their life and worship is woven through quantifiable demand."

The mindshare species had, up until this point, not appeared to have facial features or orifices of any kind. But when the lead cocktail dress mannequin turned and posed on the spot of the catwalk that made her sequin-drowned hip catch the most light, her three followers all opened new mouths from their smooth faces. These pits were wide and sharp and filled with razor thin teeth. Dollar bills and coins and checks jettisoned from the depths, and formed piles in front of each suitor. Eventually, Green-Tie, out of money, fell to his knees and hacked the last bit of cents from his body. When he saw that he was far out financed by the competition, he vacuumed his vomit-dollars back in and staggered away despondently. Cthulhu's face tentacles twisted and tangled themselves in some desperate attempt to suppress his laughter.

"Build yourself up, and sell yourself for the betterment of your species," Santa tilted her head with pride. "That is the way of the mindshare."

As the last few coins clunked from the evening-gowned mannequin's face hole, she, too, collapsed to hands and knees and accepted defeat.

Red-Tie cleared his throat in coin crunching hacks. A thousand dollar bill with Santa Inari's face printed on its red paper slid out of his last voluntary cash cough. He straightened his tie and sauntered up to Cocktail-Dress and swept her into her arms. The two collapsed into the pile of vomit money and their porcelain hands roamed and explored the intimate zones between their legs. They rubbed and prodded and the tussle of their bodies loudly disturbed the mounds of coins and paper they laid upon.

As the siren signaled the end of the challenge, Cthulhu realized that the sounds he heard during the mindshare's head-swiveling kiss were not moans of pleasure, nor the suction or dampening of tongues. It was silver. Gold. Coins rattled between the empty vessels, passed back and forth with reckless abandon.

"This concludes my presentation," Santa Inari removed her glasses, bowed, and tucked her clipboard under her arm. She returned to her seat with her red lips stretched wide, certain she'd remain on the stage during deliberations.

Oshunmare's candle went out, and the "11" shaped smoke tickled the tip of her scaled snout. She did a blind check to make sure her bouffanted hair was in place and slithered to the stage mark.

"Since religious beliefs tend to inform a society's perception of sex," the lizard-lady explained as she uncoiled puppet strings from her claw tips, "I thought it was important to show you the opposite. Today, I want you to see how the feyders' unique biology shapes the fabric of their world."

With marionette motions, Oshunmare summoned two feyders from her portal. The cat-faced creatures were various shades of ghost gray, and their pearl eyes fluttered as they silently stepped, hand-in-hand, in front of the judges. Their near transparent dresses billowed around them.

"In the last challenge, I introduced you to my graphene-inspired material for their dresses. I told you before that it was an invention, but I've given that some thought and decided that there's a more important place for it in my narrative."

The feyders faced each other and looped finger tips underneath the spaghetti straps on their thin collar bones. In unison, they peeled themselves out of each other's dresses, but never did their pearl eyes stray from each other. Their slender claw tips trailed across the fur of their shoulders and forearms. The sheer fabrics had done little to hide the slight hump of their chests or the curves of their hips, but now there was nothing between the two at all. With their naked bodies exposed to Heaven, they stepped together. Their whiskered, twitching noses bumped, their fronts pressed inwards, and their hands roamed over their backs, lower and lower until they figured out how to tease the slightest squeak from each other's throats.

Oshunmare swallowed. *Well, no turning back now.*

"The fabric of their clothes is the result of their orgasm," she finally said after nervously fiddling with her claws.

Purple strands crawled their way to the floor from one set of legs, and cerulean from the other. The feyders' voices wept like a violin, beautiful and shrill and lost. By the time they were through, two mounds of shiny strands of fibers laid in piles between them.

"Spiders make webs, albeit in a less emotionally invested way," Oshunmare swayed as she talked, the rotation of her shoulders spoke with more confidence than her downcast eyes. "Because of the sturdiness of the material, it can serve as a cocoon for newborns, whose early forms are a larval gelatin. This material helps incubate life, keeps them warm in the wild, and as they gain sentience, influences their concepts of design and creativity."

The aforementioned gelatin dripped safely onto a bed of tulle-like, freshly born fabric. The two feyders, free of the throes of their ecstasy, reached down and scooped up the gelatin and fabric. They swaddled the gelatin within the folds and strands, and the gelatin dampened the fabric and hardened it in the simulation of incubation. A small, hairless paw cracked through the fabric-egg, and a kitten's maw poked out. It mewed, its bulging white eyes lit with surprise at the impossibility of its own frail life.

The sirens signaled the end of Oshunmare's presentation. She bowed, clumps of her bouffant fell out of their place, and she guided her feyders away with the motions of her puppet strings. She felt she could talk at length about the themes and thoughts of her work—finitc time to express herself was her biggest frustration as a creator.

Imhotep's candle went out. Before the smoke could shape into the numerals of "12," he breathed it in, the scent and exhaust from the wick consumed by his nostrils. His exhale released the fumes, and the taste of the flame's potential sweetened his tongue.

He cat-walked to the stage mark, adjusted the crossover of his blue-gold robe, which tapered low on his sternum, and nodded to the camera-wielding shiqqs. His time began, and he whip-snapped his fingers towards the portal. Two reshep came crawling out, their mini-legs motoring like a centipede's on speed. The needle arms on their grotesque brown-fiber torsos waved and slashed, and the orange sacs on the openings along their lengths pulsed with ominous build.

"As you may remember," Imhotep said, "the reshep are biological weapons, warriors with command over viruses of all manner once absorbed into their digestive sacs."

One reshep was larger than the other, but of a grayer complexion. This reshep moved more slowly and, as the two crawled towards the center, started to fumble in its movements. It staggered. The rear-train of its body curled about and flipped over once it took center stage. It twitched on its back. Its legs slowed like an overturned car's spinning wheels.

"I have given the male variation of the reshep superior upper body strength and height, at the expense of a deficiency of three decades of life expectancy. In the relationship of a reshep couple, the male's early death is not only expected, but vital for the reproduction of the species."

The smaller reshep's mandibles sharpened themselves in repetitive grinding motions. It crawled on top of the male and began to rip its legs apart. Its mouth parts touched and patted the serrated legs, tasted the flesh with a darting black tongue, then consumed them. The dying gray did not complain or fight. Sacs, innards, eyes, coconut-like skin, all were nibbled and ripped away.

"Once consumed, the male reshep is broken down into material that fertilizes the female reshep's eggs. This includes the virus particles that the male reshep has obtained and raised over the years in its sacs. The female will lay 50-100 offspring, of which 20-40 typically survive. This is to offset the somewhat narrow window the reshep couple have for their unique copulation."

The female skittered away after consuming the last of the male's virus sacs, and took position near the portal. Neon purple eggs, about the shape of golf balls, started to ooze out of the end of its abdomen, held together by a net-like embryonic sac. The eggs gave off a foul smell like chlorine and durian fruit.

"The copulation *is* the consumption. I believe it is... *on brand* for this species to grit and power through all facets of life. Death is sex, is life, is reality. This will be the world of the reshep."

The siren rang and signaled the end of the challenge. Cthulhu applauded the chattering mother and her careful arrangement of the neon brood, but Jesus wore a more stoic mask upon the review of Imhotep's work. Mohammed could be heard gagging from within his monument.

Imhotep noticed their reactions, and approved of each.

"Alright!" Jesus popped her dress-flounce hips into a still-frame-worthy pose. "That's today's presentations! Please return to the waiting room while we discuss your work."

The air conditioned hum of the waiting room embraced Theodore with familiarity. Most spaces of Heaven's Heart Hotel were too opulent for him to get used to, too drowned in decor and detail. They reminded him of the casinos of his poker days, places of grand artificiality he existed in not by preference but because of performance. He found comfort among bean bag chairs and couches and cheap snacks and sodas on a small table in the corner next to a potted plant.

"How's it feel to have immunity, Theodore?" Imhotep mused as he splayed across a couch. Oksi sat on the opposite side, and squashed his large frame into the corner arm rest to prevent his personal space from overlapping his adversary's.

"Fuckin' great," Theodore said. "I can't imagine a challenge more awkward than this. And, uh, if any of you can think of something more awkward... go ahead and spoil it for me now, if you could."

The Internet and Taninim sat down on either side of him. The dog-punk folded his hands in thoughtful silence, and Taninim, as the dragon-man often did, strummed and noodled on his golden guitar. His large steel toe boot bobbed to the beat in his head.

"This X-rated challenge better not impact my company's image," Santa Inari held her head between her knees, her crimson hair hung in clumps.

"It could help it, you know," Oshunmare stroked Santa Inari's wide back, but this did little to console the CEO.

Santa considered possible fan reactions, then sunk deeper into depression when she realized she'd probably have to become more involved in social media if the challenge *did* boost interest in her company.

"I really didn't think this whole thing through," Santa muttered.

"Theodore," The Internet laced his fingers, his paw-palms pressed together.

Theodore turned his head.

"You've been spending more time with Robin in this challenge," the dog-punk said, "even though I know you two recently had a fight."

Robin and Theodore shared a glance, and an understanding that this was an attempt to shift the camera onto them. Whether The Internet thought his place in this challenge was vulnerable or strong, or whether he knew of the human and Ishta-Devata alliance, Theodore couldn't ascertain—but it didn't matter. He recognized the pointed nature of the statement, and its similar tonal shift to when The Internet argued with Athena in the prior challenge.

"You're right," Theodore crossed his arms and leaned into the back of the couch. "We're planning on sabotaging the show."

The Internet looked up, baffled. "Huh?" Ishta and Robin shared his same wide eyed expression.

The hardest part about fighting Theodore is you can only show your tricks to him once. The poker player recognized the slump of the dog-punk's curved back and the slight pull at his snout, lips that restrained with great effort from the revelation of fangs.

"Yeah," Theodore said, "wc figured out the best way to ruin the show."

Theodore may not have understood the inner workings of The Internet at the cell-dog level, but he could pick up on a tell.

“What’s that?” The Internet asked.

Theodore crossed his legs, met Internet’s eyes, and smiled. “Let you win it.”

Theodore swore he could hear the dog-punk’s electric mind process his response, a soft whine of dial tones and hung modems. In two seconds, the poker player was under siege by swift swings from the couch’s pillows and Internet’s barking. Most in the room laughed, levity fulfilled, seriousness diverted.

Notable exceptions in this levity were the boys of 24-C. No expression dared encroach upon the steel fortress of Oksi’s face. Jarilo buried himself into the beanbag chair, his face hidden from the world, the only hints of his form were his mess of blonde hair and crumpled leather jacket. Csodaszarvas laid on the cheap carpet next to him. Imhotep did hide a small smile behind the sleeve of his robe, but otherwise remained uninvolved.

In the collection room, the judges wandered between the holding chambers of the contestants' creations. The art's dead eyes were illuminated by a single pendant bulb with weak light. Each contestant had their creatures sealed off in different glass holding cells, each labeled with a plaque that bore their creator's name. Mohammed floated about, Cthulhu's leather shoes squeaked, and Jesus's high heels clacked behind them both.

"Well, I think it's now safe to say that at least one human stands out as a possible Producer-pick," Cthulhu mused as he looked at Robin's lifeless clone. The mirror image of the teacher laid slumped on a concrete slab. "Even if I hate what she made today, it's not unreasonable to think he'd be invested in a storyline as... divergent as her's."

"It's yet another skirting of the rules," Mohammed complained, then rotated as his voice softened with second thoughts. "And yet, I'm fascinated by the idea. I have so many questions about how she thinks giving humans such weapons would change society for the better... we could probably get interesting TV out of—"

Mohammed's thought was cut off when he felt the bell skirt of Jesus brush against his obsidian shell. She walked between her two coworkers and divided her note cards between them.

"Hey, you two can just average my scores into yours and pick out the top and bottom, right?" Jesus didn't wait for an answer before she started to walk out of the room.

"H-hey, you can't just leave, you're the host!" Cthulhu balked. "Where are you going?"

"Sorry, I promise I'll be back for the evaluations," Jesus muttered as she turned the handle. The echo of her high heels was muted by the heavy drag of the door, and then its slam.

"Geeze," Mohammed tilted. "What's her problem?"

Cthulhu lowered his head, sighed, and pushed his oil-slick sunglasses up his nose-less, wet face. "Guess we should get to work..."

*****

Far beyond the reach of the Forest of the Golden Trees and Cthulhu's Tower, laid The Producer's mansion, Fort Les Fonds. It was a marble cathedral that rivaled the size of Heaven's Heart Hotel, and it bared a massive golden entrance whose surface was embossed with suns and moons and hearts and currency symbols from all over the universe. The relief and handles flickered in the blue light of Jesus's portal, then shuddered under her furious fist. She rapped at the gold thrice. Among the relief, a Judas hole slid opened, and a pair of rubbery green eyes peered out.

"If you can teleport," the grass-colored eyes blinked with more emotion than their deadpan owner's voice, "why didn't you just come in?"

Jesus's fist clenched with such strength that a press-on nail shattered against her skin.

"Ah, that's right," grass-eyes muttered, "because Master doesn't like you, or want you here. You don't have an appointment that I can find on the itinerary, so please come back at the appropriate time."

The Judas hole closed. Jesus leaned back, filled her cheeks with the angriest breath in Heaven, and punched the door with all her might. The gold door bent and crumpled. Jesus pushed it open, waltzed in and stood on the welcome rug, a ragged tuft which read "wipe your paws!" The door reformed behind her, healed by Heaven's air.

“Where is The Producer?” she placed her hands on her hips and stared at the butler.

The butler was a tall, thin man with: an eggshell-white, windsor-cut collared shirt, a vanilla windsor-knot tie, creme-white tuxedo pants, and a snow-white tailcoat jacket. He was starched and sharp at every angle of his clothes, and spotless despite being covered in all manner of shades of white (even down to his parchment shoes and alabaster gloves.) One might wonder where the color had gone in this poor creature’s life were it not for the only uncovered part of his form: his head.

Jesus gritted her teeth. “Michael,” she said, “I don’t want to repeat myself.”

Michael stared back with his grass-coloured eyes. They floated in an assortment of shifting shapes, reds and yellows and blues, a Mondrian painting cursed to life. The squares of his head swirled in a tornado of movement in the vague shape of a man.

“He’s busy,” Michael said. His posture and echo-filled voice were as stiff in tone as the ironed pleats on his pants. “I will go fill out the guest book with your presence, and a brief note that you broke in. If you choose to bother him, he is in room 404. Whatever happens to all of us if you choose to enter unannounced is your fault, and yours alone. You won’t believe that, of course, you never do. You have, as far as I am aware, never accepted responsibility for anything that you have done, good or bad. That’s, of course, why I keep records. Good day, Ms. Christ.”

Michael pivoted and marched towards the kitchen, one hand held behind his back to keep his perfect posture. Jesus hesitated at the warning just long enough to feel a bead of sweat trickle down her forehead. She berated herself for her cowardice, and flew towards the elevators on the other side of the lobby.

*****

Two humans—one male, one female—writhed and moaned in a red-tinted bedroom in Fort Les Fonds. Gloved fingers pushed into each of them in slow, patient thrusts, digits curled to seek the edge of their ecstasy. These humans wore gold: collars and cuffs and eyeshadow and silk ribbons across their breasts and necks and wrists. Synths hummed from speakers in the ceiling, a strange combination of atmospheric noise and an electronic rhythmic groove, as if an AI had attempted to create funk music with only a definition of what it was, and no examples to work from. The couple twisted and tangled among gold sheets as the gold man that prodded their innermost sanctuaries laboured on. His red eyes kept steady track of their sweat and breath and gaping mouths. The only other source of light and sound in the room was a TV. On it, the first episode of *The Next Great Deity* played. Athena's shocked face filled the screen as she was eliminated from the show. No particular station's logo appeared on the screen; this broadcast was for but one being.

"The more I watch this episode," the gold-man said as he glanced past his squirming partners, "the more convinced I am that she was the right one to go. I mean, really! How could she be so unimaginative?"

The door to room 404 swung open at such velocity that the door handle lodged into the wall. The warped wallpaper cracked around the steel handle.

"Who did you pick?" Jesus shouted, the sides of her dress curled in her fists.

The Producer rose to his full height and rolled his shoulders. The white-light from the hallway lit his back to reveal his segmented skin. He was a massive, broad man whose metallic nature meant that any part of his anatomy not touched by the hallway light reflected the dark reds of his low-lit room. The Producer, with two fingers in each of his human consorts, did not turn around. He shrugged.

"Can't you..." he sighed as his skin-plates scratched against themselves, "can't you see I'm a little busy here, Jesus?"

"Who," she hissed, "did you pick!?"

"That's not how this game works," his head dipped, but his shoulders continued to roll with the probing of his fingers. "Now please, you're spoiling their mood... and mine!"

The male-consort began to bounce in a faster rhythm. The female glanced at him as she bit her bottom lip.

"Do you have an alliance with Cthulhu?" Jesus pointed at him. "Are you trying to sabotage me?"

"Do you suspect foul play, my dear?"

"*Everything* about you is foul!"

"Oh and you're so innocent, aren't you, Jesus?"

Jesus froze. It was true that the daydreams she fancied were of her freedom—the freedom to escape to Earth where she will be worshiped by the humans. For as long as she could remember, she was told about her reverence there, her ability to have every action of hers justified, regardless of contradiction. For so long these rumors seemed like fantasy compared to the reality of being an awful host for this awful show for an awful man that won't let her go. *Haven't I suffered enough?* she had rationalized. *Do I not deserve worship for the torture this man puts me through? Do I not deserve that which the humans so willingly give me?*

It was not the first time Jesus's mind stumbled through this moral dilemma. It was, however, the first time her train of thought was interrupted by a man's screaming orgasm.

"Oh, fucking hell," The Producer protested as he watched the male-consort's cannon fire. "Men, am I right? They either last five seconds..."

As the male-consort arched in ecstasy, he started to glow in segments. He was violently split apart by golden light, his structure flayed out of existence. The Producer's left hand, previously occupied with the location of the vanished man's g-spot, was now curled into a fist.

"...or they don't pop at all."

The female-consort's expression traveled a long way in a short amount of time, from ecstasy to confusion to terror as she watched the man beside her disappear. She screamed and kicked at The Producer's shoulder. It didn't hurt the gold-man, but did push him back enough to dislodge his other hand from within her. She flipped off the bed and spun wildly like a cornered possum.

"Oh, *come on*, you can get another husband," The Producer leaned back, stunned the woman would be so upset. "I *barely* hit his prostate and he shot like a MAG. Are you *really* gonna just go and ruin the whole night for the both of us because—"

She jumped through the glass window.

"...alright, then."

The Producer raised his right, open hand. Jesus's eyes widened, she screamed, and ducked down and covered her head.

A flash of golden light exploded from outside the window. The female-consort's body never hit the ground. Jesus's breath slowed—she realized she was still alive and aware, both things of which were at jeopardy anytime The Producer closed his fist. Only the female-consort was removed.

Fear shook her voice, but she rose to her feet in defiance. "I'm gonna turn this game around on you, Producer," she said. "One way or another, I'm going to turn the whole world on you."

The Producer removed his lube slicked gloves and tossed them into the trash can by his bed.

"You say that, but you were so sweet to lie for me."

Jesus blinked."Huh?"

"To Robin. To the humans. Hell, to all of them! In the last challenge, you continued the deceit that you can die in Heaven. It's a frothy little lie on the warm drink of truth, but still, you told it because you know your place, don't you? You could've told the whole truth and blown the fourth wall to pieces live on set, but you didn't. I appreciate such game and loyalty!"

Jesus wiped a tear of fear away from the corner of her eye. "Give me something to work with," she begged. "There is no game to be won if I have no information on what to look for! Your mind goes in every direction all at once, how can we possibly guess who you picked?"

"I had T.S. Elliot on his back. Right here. The poet. Do you know him?"

Jesus's jaw hung in exasperation. The Producer could not be contained to a single line of thought: besides his fists, the hilly roads of his mind were his most dangerous quality.

"Hm. Perhaps he was after your time, and you're into pop music and pills anyway, aren't you?" The Producer stepped over to the window and watched the glass reform in front of him. Chains jingled from the back of his head.

From previous experience, Jesus realized that she'd get no answers once The Producer's responses started to disconcert. She turned to leave, and The Producer heard the shift of her heels on the carpet. He lifted a hand.

"Don't leave! Listen. Please."

Jesus stood silently in self-preservation, even if her entire being begged her to run. The Producer closed his red eyes and let a slurry of memories wash over him.

"I had that man, one of the greatest creative minds of humanity, splayed under me. I pegged him in unwavering 5/8ths. I was a maestro that raised the tempo of my thrusts in perfect harmony with his passion. I orchestrated strings with the second act of his biology and I commanded a crescendo of trumpets upon his release. I only asked for one thing as payment for my perfect command over his prostate and that was to give me poetry worthy of his orgasm. All that he could say was 'Oh, God!' over... and over... and over again. I'm used to gods, and routinely bored by them.

"I found his work, in that moment..." he rolled his wrist in the air as he hunted for the right word, "...uninspired. Alas, I couldn't remove him like these dolls. He was a ghost, after all, the rare sort of transient my ability doesn't work on. So I did the next best thing I could and condemned him the old fashioned way: by knowing what he likes and taking him away from it. What good is an artist that can't follow the instructions of his client? T.S. Elliot is out there somewhere in a cold cubicle, logging hours in a spreadsheet for all eternity. You should enjoy the part I allow you to play, Jesus. You could've had it *so* much worse."

Jesus was reminded that The Producer can be equally as horrible when he's lucid as he is when he's lost.

"Can I leave?"

"Please."

Jesus picked up her hoop-skirt and ran out of the hallway. She held back a stream of tears as she cursed The Producer for his games, and cursed the walls of Fort Les Fonds for blocking her ability to create portals, and cursed her own mind for its accusations that her desire to grow into the Jesus the earthlings wanted her to be could be anywhere near on the level of depravity of The Producer.

The Producer shrugged and sat down on the queen-sized bed. He wrapped the gold sheets around his shoulders and hugged them tight as he watched the last minutes of *The Next Great Deity.*

A moment later, there was a polite knock on the wall by The Producer's open door.

"What now?" The Producer groaned, but did not look away from the TV.

"For you, sir. From the oven."

The Producer turned to see his butler in the doorway, a shadow against the bright hallway light. He held a silver platter in his hand, mounded high with a variety of macadamia, chocolate chip, and peanut butter cookies. "Oh! *Wonderful*! Leave them on the nightstand, Michael, I'll have them after my yoga."

The Production

It takes a powerful vision and deep pockets to fund an ambitious show like *The Next Great Deity*. Let's take this time to say "Thanks!" to the opportunity it provides staff, and the entertainment it provides viewers.

THE PRODUCER

The Producer wishes to remain anonymous. After all, this show isn't about him, now is it?

MICHAEL

The Producer's personal butler. An excellent chef, and very tidy.

No One Wants To Be Kicked Out of Bed

Via the magic of Jesus's portal, the contestants were transported back on stage.

Theodore looked down the line. He noted the array of stares into the far off darkness. He knew where to look to find fear, even when one might hide it from their face: he found it in Oksi's twitching bush beard, in Santa Inari's hands that roamed for pockets her pencil skirt lacked, and in the tilted head of Jarilo, covered in so much unkempt blonde hair and gloom that his face was impossible to see.

"We've reviewed your work and reached a decision," Jesus said.

The judge's script was noise to the poker player. He was focused instead on his adversaries, and their ulterior motives.

It had been awhile since Theodore thought about Mark Sharkman's assertion that someone on the set was a plant. He wasn't sure who that could be, but he had ideas—The Internet and Imhotep both seemed confident on stage, but the Egyptian's half-smile and The Internet's ears-up, intense stare were not unusual expressions for either of them. Theodore considered that if there was some combination of their attributes, he could more easily point to one of them as a mole. The Internet had the background—and a direct tie to the judges—but not the personality of a capable informant. Imhotep had the smooth, serious personality and suspicious confidence, but was almost too focused on the competition, too competent and involved. Both stood out to Theodore as suspects, but had disqualifying aspects that kept him from certainty.

Then, a more troubling thought bubbled up to the surface of his mind. What if there was no plant at all? The nature of the camera-wielding shiqqs allowed them to travel seemingly anywhere in the hotel. What sort of subterfuge is even being attempted by the show when they already have such tight control of cameras and security? With Athena's death and the mystery of Eris lingering behind it, the question of his fellow competitors' true motives hazed in his mind. Theodore had felt this before—this was information overload. He had too many questions; they spiraled in opposite directions without connection, and when he pondered this, he started to consider that this was by design.

"Theodore, please step forward."

Theodore's concentration broke. With his hands buried in his pockets, he dragged himself forward.

"You have not won this challenge, but because you have immunity, you have not lost, either," Jesus said.

Theodore kept his swallow as low on volume as he could. He had a brief ping of deja vu—an all-to-late worry that he hadn't taken the competition seriously enough. *Hard to investigate the show if you get eliminated*, he thought. Luckily, with immunity, he had at least one more challenge to determine which of the show's many puzzles to solve.

"Damn. Kicked out of bed," he adjusted his collar.

Jesus gave him a portal back to the waiting room, then turned her attention to the eleven left on stage.

"Would the following contestants please step forward: Jarilo, Ishta-Devata, Oshunmare, The Internet, Santa Inari, and Csodaszarvas."

So they did. The wonder-deer chewed the inside of his cheek with anxiety.

"You six represent the highest and the lowest scores," Jesus combed a strand of curly hair behind her ear. "The rest of you may leave."

Theodore hugged Taninim and Robin as the safe middle ported back into the waiting room. Zargah didn't understand the gesture and seized Theodore's shoulders between the clamps of his four arms, and flipped Theodore with martial precision into the beanbag. He believed Theodore had initiated play-wrestling. Ishta-Devata explained the error, and since only Theodore's ego was bruised, the group was able to laugh it off.

"I give an apology," Zargah clicked and tweaked his antenna in embarrassment.

"It's fine," Theodore wobbled to the couch. After he a few moments of collection, he leaned forward and laced his fingers. "Damn, though, Internet's out there again, huh? Real nervous for him."

Robin was quiet. It would be fine for her if The Internet was eliminated. Her primary focus in her work was to protect humanity, and for her, The Internet's anti-human creation was in league, whether intentionally or not, with what she had learned about Jesus's goals through Ishta-Devata. She felt she had presented the ultimate rectification of one of her God's biggest mistakes. That Jesus didn't deem her revolutionary concept worth discussion placed Robin into the recesses of her memories and regrets. This snub was deeply personal.

Back on stage, Jesus sat up and began to speak, but realized she didn't have her note cards. She whispered to her co-hosts, her voice low enough to avoid the microphones. Cthulhu handed her cards back. She reshuffled the red plastic cards in her lap, with a noticeable quirk in her brow. "One of you will be our winner, and will receive immunity in the next challenge. And one of you... we have lost faith in."

Jarilo's raskos, the orchid-heads he created to replace his wheatkin from the last episode, flanked him on either side. He held their plant-hands in earnest worry, a motion that stood in stark contrast to his ripped-up leather jacket, jean shorts, and dagger earrings in his big, floppy ears. Even his hooves were painted in rebellion-yellow hoof-polish.

"Jarilo, you seem different today!" Jesus smiled, "Rockin' a punk look? You look taller, too. Maybe it's the hair height."

"Yeah..." Jarilo's low-energy hesitance sat somewhere between a snarl and a whimper. Were it not for the bulge of his nervous goat-eyes, he might not be recognizable at all. "After last week, I decided changes needed to be made."

"And that shows in your creation, too," Mohammed said.

The lines of Jarilo's tired eyes and sunken cheeks stood out against the harsh light. "Yeah, man. I took what you said to heart. The raskos are more serious, and more focused."

"Let's start there, then," Cthulhu readjusted in his seat and snatched up his note card on Jarilo. "I am extremely pleased with the redesign. The last entry was cartoonish and poorly assembled and it's pretty clear to me that structure and believability were important to you. Frankly, if this redesign walked out in episode one, you wouldn't have been in the bottom."

"Thanks..." though his eyes were titled to the floor, a brief glimmer of hope began to spread along Jarilo's flushed muscles.

"But that's not what this challenge was, right?" Jesus said.

"Not at all," Cthulhu said. "In many ways, I almost wonder if you.. pardon the pun, if you blew your load on the redesign."

Jarilo flattened his ears.

"You had ten minutes. What did we really see? They just... pressed their faces together and pollinated. We didn't get any information out of you, we didn't learn how this ties in with your religion or your world view, and I'm left with the sense that you sat down, said, 'Meh. They're plants, so they pollinate,' and that's it," Mohammed's tone made it clear he felt insulted by the sexless entertainment.

Jarilo scratched his hoof against the glass floor.

"I have to agree with my colleague," Cthulhu shook his head, "which I'm not happy to do because I quite like the raskos. There's a mystique about them that I'm attracted too—the use of an orchid as an inspiration for their shape is nice, and the pale plant-fiber skin is a haunting and beautiful complement. Clearly, all your brain power went there and not into what this challenge really was about."

"It always seems like you're one step behind the pack," Jesus tapped her note cards in her palm. "Even if your work eventually gets to an interesting place with feedback, I'm concerned that this is going to become a theme for you."

Jarilo swallowed. "I'm always growing, I admit. I'm glad you like the new direction and... well, to address your charge earlier, Mohammed, I tried not to talk because I was hoping that the act was beautiful enough on its own to speak for itself. I guess the idea of their shared petal-kiss was more symbolic and arresting in my head. I know now that I should have gone bigger."

Mohammed leaned his obelisk form back in the chair, as if this were his rectangular form's version of a shrug.

Jesus forced a smile. "Right. Thank you, Jarilo."

Ishta-Devata tied her sari sleeves to her upper arm. She did so in consideration of her water elemental, to avoid any accidental absorption of its flowing form as it burbled patiently beside her.

"Ishta, welcome to the judgement round," Jesus turned her head to the Hindu princess. "Let's talk about your watery ways."

Ishta-Devata held her hands together and looked up and down the fountain of life that stood beside her. "Well, you saw the show. I think it's safe to say that today's thunderstorm was a logical place for my elemental to go."

"See, when you word it like that, I think you sell yourself short a bit," Mohammed mused. "Yes, you gave yourself a logical 'in' into your own mythos with the finger-snap spark. But, you effectively did so in a creative, surprising manner. You communicated how something as difficult to define as a sentient, cellular-colony species can work. You showed us exactly how your species intertwines in your religion and it doesn't take a huge leap to see how this can carry over to other aspects of your world should you decide to play around with other elements."

"It was to-the-point," Jesus said. "You yielded quite a bit of time still, but we got exactly what we needed."

Ishta-Devata tugged her cheeks wide with a performative smile. "Thank you."

The smile appeared soft, and it may have given her cherub features a tangible sweetness, but behind the eyes of Ishta-Devata, was a mind hard at work despite the grisly desires of the judges in front of her. Once again, it was all that she could do to hold back her scream about the lives they wanted to end, and the lover they stole from her. She wished she could see further into them, to see their memories, to see who she needed to murder with her own hands for revenge.

But then, to her surprise, she *did* see further.

Further behind Jesus, she saw something else.

Behind the desire to escape to Earth, a new shape formed. It was a golden, looming mass of fire. It grew above Jesus's desire to flee and conquer, it licked across her vision of Earth, and its flaming jaws rose like the hungry tide as if it could swallow the holy-hostess whole then and there. Ishta became transfixed, poisoned by Jesus's fear. She shook as she took it on as her own.

"I still think your work is a little ambiguous," Cthulhu's sloshy voice dragged Ishta back to reality. "For me, at least. I feel like the idea of an elemental skirts the line of generic, but you've certainly made it more interesting than I thought it could be. Especially today."

"I'm glad to hear that," Ishta-Devata bowed her head, her soft palm on her ceremonial hat to keep it from tilting. "I imagine our tastes are quite different so it means a lot to me that I've reached you."

"...Quite," Cthulhu was disarmed by the positive spin, and wondered if he was losing his sassy edge.

"Oshunmare!" Jesus chirped. "Let's talk about these cat-girl-ghosts."

As her name was called, the lizard-lady hugged her feyders a little tighter around the waist. Jarilo was in the bottom, Ishta-Devata was in the top. If the judges called on contestants in bottom-top-bottom-top order, then that means...

Making assumptions won't do me any good, Oshunmare closed her eyes. *Just show your colors.*

"I believe in, above all else, peace, sustainability and natural beauty," Oshunmare said as she looked into the ghost-pearl eyes of her feyders. "I wanted to find a way to show off the beauty of re-purposing, so I changed the very output of sex to something usable throughout all stages of a feyder's evolution. I'm also a sex-positive creature, so I want my followers to treat the act as a beautiful, creative, freeing experience."

The judges sifted through cards, and the slight pause filled Oshunmare with worry.

"I realize that's probably not a popular viewpoint with this particular panel," she stammered, "but I hope you can see how it works in my world—"

"We do," Jesus said.

Oshunmare leaned back. "You do?"

"We do," Jesus stifled a laugh at Oshunmare's wide-eyed surprise. "Yes, it's not something I would ever make. Though I do think the direction you're going is way, *way* outside the realm of my personal taste. I find your point of view strong and consistent and, in the context of your world, realistic."

"A-awesome," Oshunmare showed all her teeth in her giddy, grinning maw.

"They're lesbians, right?" Mohammed vibrated.

Oshunmare blinked. She thought the performance she gave made that more than clear. "...Yes?"

"*...spooky lesbian cat-girls...*" Mohammed vibrated louder.

"If I may," Cthulhu cut Mohammed off and hoped that he'd be edited out in the final version of this segment. "You stated in the first episode that they fed off emotional energy, I believe. I found no mention of that today."

"I sensed that it was a weaker part of my presentation last time," Oshunmare's rainbow tongue darted as she thought about how to approach discussion of her process. "It's not that I'm ditching it, but I want to find a way to retool it in a more grounded way, which is why I focused entirely on the material."

"See, that impresses me," Cthulhu leaned back in his chair and stroked his face tentacles, "because you weren't even in the bottom last challenge. You identified one of your weakest elements on your own, highlighted a strength, and revealed a new dimension to your world. It did not go unnoticed, by the way, that the different... *byproducts* of their sex were different colors."

"The texture is slightly different, too!" Oshunmare shimmied her shoulders with new-found optimism.

"Wonderful," Cthulhu said. "There's a whole range of cultural possibilities with that. Art, war, tribalism, economy, invention, scientific study, this little germ of an idea that each individual has within them a unique type of fabric can fuel the imagination of a world over. Prior to this challenge, I liked the way your feyders looked—soft and mysterious—but I didn't buy into your vision. I'm coming around, now, after seeing the possibilities here."

Oshunmare hopped on her raptor legs with glee and hugged her accolade-earning ghost-cats close.

"This feels like everything you were missing before," Jesus smiled. "Thank you."

"And thank you!" Oshunmare beamed.

The Internet, ears flattened, glared at the lizard-lady and her feyders. *They're just fuckin'... stick figure cat-people that cum a bunch of color,* he thought. *Humans draw weird shit like that and upload it all the time, who gives a shit? Why the fuck is she getting praise? Fuck this show.*

The Internet believed that, of the six contestants on stage, only his and Jarilo's work was even *acceptable*. If the judges had eliminated everyone else and declared the dog and goat contestants the final two in an unusually short season, he would have understood *that* outcome far more than what was currently unfolding in front of his bitter eyes.

"The Internet..." Jesus tried to find the dog-punk's notecard.

Even if Internet didn't like Jarilo—and hated that his new punk look infringed on his territory, that *son of a bitch*—he respected the effort the half-goat put into his rebound. Jarilo's presence in the bottom pissed off The Internet for two specific reasons.

"There we are!" Jesus shuffled Internet's card to the front and tapped them against her lap. "Let's talk about your work."

Reason #1: he liked the goat-boy's (*now goat-teenager? How did he get taller overnight?*) new edge, both in personality and in his work. Frankly, he didn't think there was anything wrong with his presentation. *It was more tasteful than Oshunmare's, that's for fucking sure*, he thought.

"Alright..." he fixed his baseball cap, a new one he had created for fun specifically for the judgement part of the show. It was emblazoned with the words ***BIG DOG*** across the front, despite his stature's evidence to the contrary. "...Let's."

Reason #2: with only three contestants left to speak, and with two contestants in a row shuffled into the top, it didn't take a genius to figure out what his own placement was. He was now preemptively furious, and ready to go to war despite having no information on how the judges actually felt.

I worked so hard, finished on time, and made great work, a small growl revved in his chest. *How can this be happening to me?*

"You know what? I'll start," Cthulhu said.

The Internet braced for impact.

"Highlight of the episode for me," Ocean-Mouth shrugged. "Really exceptional work."

The Internet opened his mouth to bark, but a puff of confused air came out instead. "Arf?"

"Ignore for a second that you nailed the redesign in a way that makes sense with your machine-rebellion narrative," Cthulhu leaned in. Despite the cover of his oil-slicked frames, The Internet could tell by the slight tilt of his head that the old one's eyes glazed over every sharp angle and bolted seam on the robots' bodies. "Which... is difficult, frankly, because they look *great* now. Still, put it aside, and you have a picture-perfect sci-fi-horror monster."

The Internet didn't like his creatures being considered monsters, but his tail began to wag despite himself.

"With this new shape, there's a certain sensuality," Mohammed rotated, "it was really smart to give them the suggestion of muscles in the calves and shoulders, because I'm not sure that the act itself would've read as a metaphor for sex had you not been so meticulous in the performance. Bjork was the last time I was turned on by a robot. This is up there."

"You really let the presentation breathe and work on its own, and managed to convey the concept of reproduction in a way that was both sensual and rebellious," Jesus rested her bearded chin on her fist, "the latter of which feels more like your wheelhouse than the former."

The Internet felt a warmth in his cheeks, and a weight lifted from his shoulders. His voice broke as he spoke with unrestrained glee. "I tried to fit the brief, despite how at odds it was with what I'm going for. I think my world is better for the challenge."

"Thank you, Internet," Jesus smiled.

The Internet stared into the lights. Every cell-dog that made up his frame processed these new emotions, documented them, and made it a top priority to experience them again.

"Santa Inari," Jesus turned her head, "Let's talk about your mindshare species."

Well, Santa pressed her red tie down with her palm to smother any wrinkles. *This wasn't how I envisioned my first evaluation would go, but...* She ran her fingers once through her fire-hydrant-red hair to ensure it slicked correctly. The glowing star on the side of her head grew brighter. *I am a CEO. Bullshitting my way to a solution that makes judgmental, rich brats happy is exactly what I'm best at.*

The judgement round, she thought, was no different than a shareholder meeting. And, *that* was no different than her first high-risk investments. Which, she thought, was also no different than becoming valedictorian, and no different than marrying into the wealthy Inari family and buying their company out from underneath them. There is no problem that is different from other problems, in Santa's eyes, because they all could be solved with enough decisive actions, adaptive speeches, and cash. As a Claus and as a businesswoman, she'd never hurt for any of these things.

"Gladly," she smiled, and made sure to keep eye contact with Jesus. "My mindshare—"

"Is a joke," Cthulhu said.

Santa Inari cleared her throat and attempted to talk again.

"I'm sorry, it's a joke," he lifted his slimy hands incredulously at the barcoded mannequin-creatures. "There's no spin on this. What were you thinking?"

Santa Inari's patronizing smile, for the first time that night, melted. Her eyes turned feral, fox-yellow, "There's no joke in self-sufficiency. There is nothing more real than the systems a sentient creature creates to order their world. My spin on capitalism is an attempt to serve as a crossroads between magic metaphor and gritty realism—"

"So they..." Mohammed's obelisk form rattled with confusion, "...understand and have money at birth, naturally? Money is a part of their biology?"

"I see no reason why they can't be born with value," Santa protested. "That's where humanity is, right? They use valuation for everything. I'm skipping to the point. My mindshare are honest about what it means to be alive with intelligence."

"It's too much of a joke to be real," Jesus snarled back, "and too oblivious about the way social creatures work to be grounded in magic. You can't... expect us to take you seriously when they vomit money as an attempt to catch a mate."

"Once again," Santa Inari's bottom eyelid twitched, "I don't find that all removed from how sentient creatures actually work."

The mind-share stared with unblinking coal eyes. No worry or fear crossed their empty, barcoded faces.

"The only saving grace that I see here," Jesus crossed her legs, "is that... I get it, to an extent. I can believe that what we saw today is... the modern version of what your envisioned your world would be. And you know what? An economic religion *is* different and imaginative. No one else on this show is doing something like that."

Santa grew quiet. Cthulhu turned his head towards the holy hostess in surprise.

"But this challenge was about how they *get* there," Jesus lectured, "and after talking with you, I still don't think you get *that*. You have such a narrow vision of what your religion is that I think you yourself don't even know what a creature without money would feel like, in your religion or otherwise."

"Well..." Santa froze. "They'd..."

She was right. Santa *didn't* know. To her, those without money were at the bottom, and that's the way things are and should be. The poor should only feel one thing—the drive to become wealthy. Anything else didn't matter. She found herself tongue-tied trying to say this in a way that would also absolve her of Jesus's accusation.

"Thank you," Jesus moved on. Santa's breath was shallow, and she stopped blinking.

Csodaszarvas's Evaluation

"Csovaszavas!" Jesus chirped.

"It's..." the deer kneaded his hoof on the glass floor, "...it's Csodaszarvas."

Jesus's cheeks grew red, but she didn't lose her smile. "Csozasdarvas!"

"No, no," Cthulhu tried to correct her, "Csodaszavas."

"That's... close, but..." the wonder-deer raised a hoof.

"It's Csovasdarvas," Mohammed tried to help.

"Csodaszarvas," he sighed.

"Oh my god," Jesus laughed. "Is Cso fine?"

"It's lovely."

"Great. I'll get it right in post. Let's talk about your..." she checked her notes, then said sheepishly, "...váradi?"

"Nailed it," Cso furrowed his brow, unsure of how they got that right and not his name.

"I'll start," Cthulhu shuffled note cards. "I want to hear what the inspiration was behind your species, first and foremost."

Csodaszarvas was hesitant to launch into his spiel. He already knew he was in the bottom based purely on the way the judges spoke about earlier contestants. And yet, the elder god's question seemed far removed in tone from the nastiness that Santa received. Cso considered that, perhaps, it wasn't so much that he did poorly as much as he didn't stand out enough and someone had to be third worst.

Maybe... I need this, he thought. *Maybe this is the opportunity to get the feedback I need to break out from the middle.*

"Okay," the deer inhaled, and chewed on his lip like cud, "Well, the váradi are graceful and magical. I want to raise an intelligent species that reflects my core values, so I did my own spin on elves and—"

"Two sentences," Cthulhu said.

"I'm sorry?" Csodaszarvas blinked.

"It took two sentences for you to say 'elves,'" Cthulhu said, "unless we're being charitable and count 'okay' on it's own."

Csodaszarvas narrowed his eyes.

"I would think that you, wonder-deer, would be old enough to know the difference between a Tolkien elf and classical, mythological definitions of elves," Mohammed lambasted him as he vibrated. "On top of that, I would also think you'd be old enough to know why it's a bad idea to be so transparent in your inspiration."

"All you've made is elves with... hair like your antlers," Jesus pointed to where on her own head antlers might be if she desired them. "That's it. And I know you might think we're not being fair by focusing on looks instead of your presentation, but really, what is there to say? You made a foursome with their souls. That's the metaphor, right? 'Their souls intertwined.'"

Csodaszarvas's brow twitched.

"We're unanimous, here, I'm afraid," Cthulhu leaned forward and pointed his note cards in the deer's direction. "It's not that anything you've done is egregious or bad, but it's god damn *boring*. Do you know how many variations of elves the humans have dreamed up? Between how dry your work is and today's nearly sexless sex act, I don't know if there's anyone else in this competition whose work is as invisible as yours."

"I forgot your presentation from episode one completely," Mohammed sneered, "and if I didn't have my notes here, I'd have already forgotten what you did today."

"If I may," Cso raised his head. His gold antlers caught a spotlight and nearly blinded the judges, who shifted in their seats.

"Go ahead," Jesus said.

"I consider myself a creator interested in classic, well-crafted refinement," Csodaszarvas said. "I accept that I haven't stood out as much as I'd like, but I would also like to defend myself by pointing out my competence. If all I need to do to break out is to cause more of a scene with my work, I can."

The judges whispered to each other, then Jesus stared hard into Cso's eyes.

"Can you really cause a scene?"

"Yes, I—"

"Who do you think should go home today?"

Csodaszarvas fell quiet. He didn't want to make enemies. *I don't want to cause a...*

He looked at Jarilo. His troubled friend's head was buried into his chest, his long nose pointed towards the floor. The deer looked to the other side and saw Santa, fists clenched.

Dammit, Cso suddenly realized he had put himself in a terrible, terrible situation. All the cameras zoomed in to the worry etched on his snow-white snout. Betray his friend in his darkest hour, and he might survive purely on drama alone. Attack Santa, a savvy business woman ready to defend herself at whatever the cost, and he might get utterly destroyed by her comeback. Say nothing, pick no one, and ensure defeat.

Cso bowed his antler-crowned head.

"...Santa Inari," Csodaszarvas muttered.

"And the same question to you, Santa," Jesus turned her head.

"You can't fix a boring point of view overnight," Santa folded her arms, "so the deer has to go."

"And you, Jarilo?" Jesus combed some hair behind her ear.

Jarilo rocked back and forth. All the leather and spikes and flippant expressions in the world couldn't hide the unease in his mind.

"Well?"

Jarilo whimpered. "Santa Inari."

Santa whipped her head towards the half-goat. Her fire-hydrant-red hair landed on her opposite shoulder and matched the hue her skin began to take.

"Alright!" Jesus clapped. "That's everyone! Please return to the waiting room while we make our final decision."

The portal trip back to the workroom left the contestants, regardless of their position, silent and embarrassed for the bottom group's impromptu trial. The drain of defeat weighed heavily on the hooved contestants, who consoled each other on the beanbag chair. Santa Inari stewed on the couch and bit her knuckle. Eventually, she drew blood.

Beelzebub Boxing's name masks the full extent of their diverse portfolio. While they did start out as a small corrugated cardboard manufacturing plant, their success did not go unnoticed by larger entities. As is the fate of most small fish, a bigger one swallowed it up. In this case, it was a shark named Inari Corp. The new owners were looking to extend their financial tentacles into the depths of Hell. Since Beelzebub Boxing became a new cornerstone of hope for a lower class looking desperately to escape the grind of poverty, the strategic minds behind Inari Corp saw money where people stood.

"We're gonna think *outside the box,*" Santa Inari had said in a sales pitch meeting. (She thought herself quite clever for that one.) Her proposal: buy Beelzebub Boxing and expand its reach into online sales and delivery. Since they already had delivery and warehouse infrastructure in place, all that was needed was to combine their concepts with the sales markets Inari Corp had at their disposal.

In reality, the validity of the idea didn't matter: Inari Corp was too big to fail. They had their hand in nearly every industry in the cosmos, and if this one didn't take off, the profits of every other venture would make up for it. All that would be lost is the lives of Hell's citizens, those ruined if Inari Corp suddenly shut down Beelzebub Boxing and moved on. In other words, as Santa Inari explained to her board room, "almost nothing."

"Almost nothing," too, was how the citizens of Hell were viewed by those in Purgatory, Heaven, and sometimes, even themselves. They were numbers on spreadsheets and demographics to sell low cost necessities to. They were a treadmill under the elites' feet; mechanisms that moved so that those standing above could feel like they were walking. They were not people, they were not conscious, they were not alive beyond their productivity levels or purchasing power.

After several hours of transporting thousands of online orders onto pallets and running around a miles-wide manufacturing plant, Jack began to feel like he, too, was almost nothing. Moisture steamed from his rind skin, his muscular frame shriveled under the hot lights and heavy lifting and lack of breaks. The same ten pop-rock songs played on loop in the rafter speakers. He was outfitted with a complicated catheter on his left leg that teleported his waste to the bathroom for him so that he wouldn't stop moving. (No unscheduled breaks were allowed. It was considered 'humane' to allow them to use the bathroom in this manner, and still take their one mandatory, 5 minute break after 7 hours of work.) His right leg had small electrodes that shocked his ankle if his productivity levels fell below a minimum threshold. He never met his boss. His trainers were a series of dead-eyed creatures-of-the-night resigned to their fate; each one gave him a new task every 30-45 minutes, then disappeared into their offices. Jack thought he heard a shotgun from around the corner after he talked with on of his trainers, but whether the trainer was the one doing the firing or being fired at, he couldn't be sure. Both were likely. No one stopped moving; no one could.

"I wish I had never been born," Jack whimpered as he dropped another box to pallet. His ankle collar shocked him. Smoke rose from around the leather. He didn't care. He was too tired to cry or move. "There's no point in me being here..."

This might've resulted in disciplinary action, but fortunately (or unfortunately, depending upon how one looks at the idea of being fired from Beelzebub Boxing), a drone floated down and greeted him with a cheerful emoji, deformed from where an employee had punched its screen-face earlier in the day. His complaint was too low in volume and too serendipitously timed with the drone's routine-cheer to get picked up by its microphones.

"Hey there, employee!" the drone's screen smiled. "Looks like it's time for your break!"

"H-how long..."

The drone shot him with a blue cone of light. Before he could finish his sentence, Jack was ported to the break room.

"...of a break do I get," Jack looked up. The drone was gone. "Oh."

The break room was a dimly lit wooden hovel, packed with smoking, sweating demons and spirits of all manner of mythology. You could look across the baby-blue uniformed room and find a broad enough range of expressions to construct a visual pain scale, and Jack, as he was, would select '10' for his own. He staggered through the crowd. He hunched and limped and whimpered and fit right in.

No one talked in the break room. Instead, the sounds found in its cramped space were the unsteady shifting of weight, the creak of wood, and the fuzzy speaker of an old television. A few demons were crowded around it, but most didn't pay it any mind. Jack wandered through the crowd and, though he was in no place-of-mind to be entertained, considered that the TV was something he could stare at without it staring back.

He reached the TV, a scratched up, flickering box of metal and plastic. On it was a commercial for *The Next Great Deity*. He saw rapid fire images of the triumph of creation, of the accolades of the judges, and of the infinite possibility of those blessed enough to reach Heaven, and eventually, godhood itself. Every contestant was happy and driven and living in the luxury and freedom of Heaven's Heart Hotel.

Jack's breath quickened as the reality of other people's fortune filled his empty sockets. There was a void in Jack, a void in the shape of inspiration, of imagination, of self-determination. The reality TV show pumped that space full—this place called 'Hell' didn't *have* to be this way, and he didn't *have* to be there.

"New episodes every day at 7 P.M. Purgatory Time!" the ad blared. Jesus stood on a cliff in the image, hands on her hips, the wind whipping at her long curly hair and beard and satin-white dress.

I... Jack clutched his hands to his chest, *I want to see this. I* need *to see this.*

Oshunmare. The Internet. Ishta-Devata. Jarilo. Santa Inari. Csodaszarvas. The best and worst performers of *The Next Great Deity*'s most uncomfortably sexy challenge took the stage, surrounded by the gurgling camera-wielding shiqqs and hot lights.

"Contestants," Jesus raised her chin as she studied the expressions of the would-be deities, "you have been judged."

The Internet vibrated impatiently.

"Ishta-Devata," Jesus said, "we still have faith in you."

Ishta-Devata did not want to "win" *The Next Great Deity* so much as dissect it. A third place finish in today's episode was no major blow to her morale. She bowed her head, combed some curly black hair over her shoulder, and exited into the waiting room portal with more grace than she felt the proceedings deserved.

*****

When she returned, she sat next to Robin on the polygonal couch. She leaned over and whispered, "I think I have an idea of how you felt in the last challenge, when it was you that walked through to see me."

Robin could not let go of her bitterness towards the way Jesus glossed over work that would fundamentally protect humanity. Each time she made something she believed the deity that she held in her heart her whole life would praise—only to be proven wrong—she was a little more frustrated, and a little closer to the truth: that this woman, the one that calls herself Jesus, only cared for herself.

"You don't," Robin said.

*****

The lizard-lady and the dog-punk were both high on high hopes, but one would come crashing down.

"Oshunmare..."

The lizard-lady perked up. Her rainbow-tongue darted with curiosity out the front of her snout.

"...Congratulations!" Jesus beamed.

The Internet's eyes widened.

"You are the winner of this challenge—"

"Ahh!" The lizard-lady jumped into the air. Her raptor legs scraped the glass when she landed, and her white bouffant flounced.

"—and you will have immunity in the next episode."

"Thank you SO much!" Oshunmare hugged her own shoulders and stomped in place and emitted a series of squeals of happiness more fitting for a puppy than a lizard. The last remaining actual puppy on stage had quite a different reaction: The Internet's cell-dogs began to spark with fury and confusion. He wrestled with his hands and reality.

"The Internet, good job today," Jesus smiled. "We are happy with your improvement. It was close."

"T-thanks," he stammered. On the inside of his mind, all files which contained his memories and opinions of Oshunmare were shifted to top priority. He flagged her as his most hated enemy, a spot previously reserved for Theodore and Jesus.

This was my challenge, he seethed. *Mine...*

*****

When the top-two skipped through the portal, Oshunmare's victory seemed to unite the room in jolliness. Everyone wanted to shake her hand and congratulate her—a reaction she certainly wouldn't have received had she not been a positive, cheerful influence in the work room.

The crowd around her allowed The Internet to slip out of the room and hide in the bathroom, where he cried electric tears and kicked the toilet. Only Theodore noticed that he had left. He tried to slip out and follow the dog-punk to console him, but when he heard the hollow thunk of shoe-to-porcelain over and over again, he decided that, sometimes, the emotionally compromised need time to themselves more than anything else.

*****

Mark Sharkman clicked his pen and flashed a row of teeth to the lizard-lady. "Let's talk to the big winner!"

Oshunmare thanked a massive list of friends and family, which included roughly twenty of her Orisha siblings. Her mom, her dad, her girlfriend, her grandparents, her cousins, her pets; Oshunmare clearly had a wide support system.

"But most of all, I *have* to thank the agent that made me chase my dreams," Oshunmare stared into the camera and hoped that, even through the lens, she could find those red-and-blue eyes again. "Luci... wherever you are... thank you for connecting me with my family. I'm showing everyone my colors now, because of you."

*****

Jesus rapped her red-painted nails on the arm rest, and her tone drew darker. "Now, to the remaining three..."

The CEO of Capitalism stood with her arms folded and her eyes closed. To either side of her, the wonder-deer and half-goat hung their heads.

"Santa Inari," Jesus exhaled, "we still have faith in you."

While all three shook at the sound of that sentence, it was those with hooves that knew this would be their fate. Reality shows love to pit those with a narrative against each other in the bottom two, and Csodaszarvas and Jarilo were closer to each other than they were to anyone else. The only person truly shocked to see Santa Inari push on through safely was the businesswoman herself.

"Thank you," she said and corrected the momentary slump in her spine, "Everything you told me today, I will implement into my work."

With her hop into the waiting room portal, there were two left. These hooved contestants may have been friends, but they now stood in each other's way.

"Csozasdasdas and Jarilo, one of you will be eliminated from this competition," Jesus said. Csodaszarvas didn't have the willpower to correct her mispronunciation.

The holy hostess stood up.

"Jarilo, we applaud the redesign you showed us, but today's banal entry has made us question if you're permanently a step behind the rest of the competition."

Jarilo sniffled.

"Csoduzarvas, you managed to take a challenge about sex and create something boring and forgettable, things sex should *never* be. We are worried that these words may come to define your work moving forward."

The wonder-deer bowed his gold-antlered head.

"Csozasdadavas!" She yelled. The air around her began to spark.

"We still have faith in you," Jesus said.

During the silence and the wait to be informed of his fate, Csodaszarvas considered that, between the two hooved contestants, he was almost certainly the one that would have more difficulty pushing onwards were he to stay. Jarilo was younger and feistier and more ready to adapt based off of feedback he received. And it was for these reasons Csodaszarvas knew he'd stay—adults and "professionals" rarely view the elasticity of youth as a virtue. The deer believed they viewed the tenure of his age as a strength.

The emotional side of Csodaszarvas's mind wished he had been eliminated instead.

"Thank you for the opportunity," the deer bowed his antler-crowned head and wandered back through the portal.

The logical side of his mind knew he would not waste the opportunity, but he found it difficult to think anyone else here would, either. The only glimmer of hope he saw in himself was the embarrassment he knew he'd feel if he didn't push on to greater heights. The wonder-deer promised himself to make work that Jarilo, who certainly would continue to watch the show, would be proud of.

This thought process assumes, of course, that Jarilo would have the chance to see the show on-air.

A high pitched ring shook the air. Cthulhu turned his head to find what direction it came from. The squeal, a horrible hissing grind, slithered inside Cthulhu's ear canal. It landed in his mind like a dart. It vibrated when it struck him. He brought one hand up to his bulbous temple and groped, as if he could reach in and snatch the new sensation out of his skull.

Hey, a voice whispered inside Cthulhu.

The elder god sat up in alarm.

Kill the half-goat, the voice rattled, *just like I had you do with Athena. Feed him to the hounds.*

"But... but why?" Cthulhu shook his head. He didn't even realize that Jarilo had been talking to the panel about how thankful he was to be on the show—he blurted out over the half-goat's exit spiel, "is there a problem...?"

Jarilo and the judges all turned to Cthulhu. Ocean-Mouth tapped the side of his head. Though Jarilo had no idea what this meant, the judges did: The Producer was speaking directly to him.

Jesus's eyes bulged in fury.

Athena was business, The Producer said. There was a smile in the color of his voice, a sing-songy rhythm that betrayed the darkness of his orders. *Jarilo's sacrifice is for pleasure.*

Cthulhu's slimy brow wrinkled in worry over the madness of his master.

I'm not going to do this to every contestant. Probably, The Producer whispered. Cthulhu could feel a grip on his shoulder, as if the cool steel hands were under his wet skin, rubbing firmly into the base of his neck. *There's something cute about Jarilo that I want you to see. It's harmless.*

That last sentence, always and forever, is a lie. Nothing that The Producer does or says is harmless.

But, Cthulhu thought, *I have no choice.*

There is always the vague shape of reasoning behind The Producer's actions, Cthulhu knew, so it wasn't only survival instinct to follow the orders of his powerful leader. He hoped to get greater insight into the monster so that he could learn how to win the game, and with luck, kill him.

"Sorry, lack of sleep, I don't know why I blurted that out," Cthulhu rubbed his forehead. "Jarilo, please say your piece one more time. I apologize. After you're done, I'll take you out."

Jesus raised her chin and huffed.

"...to the exit," the old one added hastily. "You're going home, after all."

*****

An antiquated speaker sat alone in a yellowed hallway. Cthulhu pressed his finger to its lone button while Jarilo wiped tears away and peered around, confused by the lack of ornate decor.

"I need your shifting services, Ritst," Ocean-Mouth said. "Shift to the center, please. I'm in 5-Q. Directly to the heart."

"Right away, Sir," the speaker crackled.

"Is this still the hotel?" Jarilo sniffled with uncertainty.

"It is," Cthulhu said. "Brace yourself."

Vertigo arrested the half-goat and sent him face first to the floor, sandwiched between white tile and an intense, sudden pressure devoid of form. It was as if the air itself gained great weight, and rested upon Jarilo's back, forcing his bones and organs to creak and stress.

"God, that never gets old," Cthulhu inhaled the air of tension like it was a waft of fine french cuisine. "Come on, son. Pick yourself up. We're almost out of here."

The weight lifted. Jarilo's goat legs wobbled as he picked himself up to his hooves.

The two walked side by side in silence. Cthulhu stuffed his hands into silk tuxedo pants worth more in testaments that Jarilo had ever made in his life. The sound of leather shoes and solid hooves on the tile floor irritated the ex-contestant, but he was too physically and emotionally spent from his loss to complain. He viewed the show as his only escape from his dire poverty, and now that it was gone, he didn't know what else life would or could be. He stuffed his hands into his leather jacket, tucked his chin to his chest, and followed Cthulhu.

"You know, you should really have more confidence in yourself. We picked you for a reason."

In the warmth of his plaid-lined pockets, Jarilo clenched his fist. He did not want any sort of conversation about what he should and shouldn't be. Jarilo decided that if Cthulhu was going to insist on small talk, then he should guide the conversation to something that interested him. "What's 'the heart?' Is it a tour or something?"

Cthulhu's face-tentacles curled upwards. "Do you believe in karma?"

They rounded a corner. At the end of a nondescript hallway, there was a single white door.

"I do," Jarilo perked up. He was surprised to hear that someone like Cthulhu, a god with a cruel reputation, would pay mind to such a concept. "The idea isn't associated with my myth, exactly, but I believe in it because-"

"Interesting," Cthulhu stroked through some face tentacles and wondered what Jarilo had done in a past life to warrant his incoming punishment. "So, to answer your question; yes, the heart of this hotel is fascinating. I think it's an important thing to show people before they leave. It's central to the hotel, and quite a beautiful and inspiring sight."

"Why is it called a heart?" Jarilo's sullen, sunken face grew brighter when he considered what would match the attraction's name. "Is this where the generator for the hotel is? Or... oh my god. Is there something natural here? Like a garden, or a conservatory?"

"I used to come here a lot to clear my head and gain perspective," Cthulhu said as he gripped the door's handle. "...though it feels like several lifetimes ago by now."

Cthulhu turned and flicked his wrist. A white blur landed in the center of Jarilo's chest—Cthulhu's patented business card—and the half-goat fell to his furry knees. He rasped for air as he felt control of his limbs, his eyelids, and even the very muscles of his lungs seize up.

"A heart needs blood, Jarilo," Cthulhu studied the way Jarilo's bottom jaw flapped, his goat eyes were wide open, frozen, alive, and completely helpless. "That's just the way things are."

Jarilo face-planted. His mind screamed and pleaded with his muscles, which refused to respond. He felt his body slowly drag across the floor, inch by inch pulled by the card lodged into his chest. His own shadow darkened his vision of the tile floor.

"Truth be told, I get anxious when I'm told to kill," Cthulhu walked alongside the drag of Jarilo's limp body. "I do like my fellow supernaturals far more than I do mortals. It feels like a waste to kick you off the show, much less kill you. I thought you had more potential than the deer, but I was outvoted."

That was no consolation for the half-goat. He was a prisoner in his own body, a cat in a carrier helplessly mewing as the world moved around him without his permission. One of the card's periodic tugs of his body realigned his head to press his brow on the floor. His eyes frozen and leaking, all he could do was stare at the smooth floor, which blurred in proximity to his vision.

"But I think my problem might be performance anxiety. Just because I respect you doesn't mean I have pity for you."

The half-goat noticed flecks of red speckle mixed in with the decor of the tile. He had no choice—all he could do was look with unblinking eyes at the floor. He wondered if this was blood, then wondered still how recently it had been shed, or why Heaven hadn't healed it.

"Frankly, it's the build up that bothers me the most. The stringing along. The setup. The process of making things is always so bothersome, isn't it? Even setting up the scenarios to catch people off-guard, it gets tiring after awhile to do the same mindless chore. The worst part is carrying the burden of boredom from having done the chore, when I can't even remember all the times I did it. Sentient minds are awful, petty things, aren't they?"

Jarilo's body bumped and adjusted as it crawled over the door frame. He tried to scream out in pain as the new surface—jagged, cold rocks—ground into his skin and ripped off flesh. He could feel the warm blood escape from his torn lips and cheek, but his body refused to produce protest.

"But then when the payoff happens, when I get to see you fall down and consumed, defeated by your own perceptions of what's right and wrong and who does and doesn't deserve to be god and what this show is and isn't... I remember that it's worth it. I remember that the game I have to play *isn't* forever, that there *is* an end, and it will be my finish line, not yours, and it will be *beautiful*."

Jarilo could tell by the sudden silence of the footsteps that Cthulhu did not follow him beyond the door's threshold. The temperature inside the new room was cold, almost arctic. It smelled like no cave or forest or any sort of nature he knew: the scent of an acrid, gunpowder-like sulfur clogged his nostrils and coated the rock floor.

"Karma isn't real, Jarilo. If it were, this show wouldn't have a network to air on."

Jarilo's legs were lighter. He could no longer feel his hooves. There was a burning prickle along the perimeter of his ankles, and then the bottom of his calves, and then his knees. Bit by bit he was bitten to bits by something with teeth made not of bone or acid or fangs but solid, sharp fire. The world collapsed in Jarilo's vision at impossible angles. Serrated light molars closed through the middle of his head. He was consumed.

Cthulhu stared.

"Something cute, huh?" he intoned with boredom. "Nothing unusual happened..."

Ocean-Mouth stared at the creature behind the door frame. It was a foul thing, a shifting hound of wavering shape, covered in hollow tongues and a smoking outline. One of Cthulhu's trademark business cards was sewn into one of the tongues, an appendage of such transparency that its waving motions could be mistaken for the heat waves that rise from a hot car roof on a southern city's summer day. The hound's place in the starry realm on the other side of the door was vaguely defined—it skittered across several different points in the room, glitched across the sky, and appeared and disappeared partially inside the rocky ground. This chaotic movement was despite the fact it stayed seated, posed and poised, like a cat waiting patiently for its owner to walk into a room. To try and interpret its path would only lead to madness.

It burped. Cthulhu rolled his eyes.

"What a waste of time..." the old one began to complain. His demeanor changed when he noticed that the hound stood up to all fours and started to pace. Its form never quite traveled properly in the orientation its legs tried to walk, but its restlessness was unmistakable.

The hound whimpered.

“What the hell?” Cthulhu blinked.

The hound padded at the rocks that its form skittered past. These were all begging behaviors.

Cthulhu covered his mouth-tentacles in thought. The consumption of a supernatural creature should feed a hound properly for days, sometimes even months or years depending upon the food’s power. It was a type of consumption beyond the power of Heaven, a wild breakdown of organic and magic material far beyond Ocean-Mouth’s understanding. Few knew of the hound’s existence. And of those few, none—Cthulhu included—had ever seen one go hungry immediately after a meal. A millennium of notes in Cthulhu’s library made clear that such a thing should be impossible.

And yet, here he was, on the other side of the door frame of a whining, begging, theoretically fed Hound of Tindalos.

Cthulhu clutched the cool brass door handle with a shaking hand and closed it. A more troublesome thought swarmed up his spine. He rested his body weight on the closed door. His slimy skin left permanent residue on the wood.

“The Producer,” Cthulhu whispered, his mucous-coated hands trembling against the wood, “knew this would happen...”

The **Sound** of the **Crowd**

Many bars have sprouted up around downtown Gehenna, and many more have tried to siphon crowds to their doors with similarly generic names, but Purgatory River Pub has grown in such notoriety that it's transcended the status of being 'just a bar.' It's become a tourist attraction, a concert venue, a rave, a cheap burger restaurant. It is, like many religions, many different things to different people, but all who wander through its laser-lit doors are unified in their need for an escape from the grind of reality.

And unlike the citizens of Hell, those that dwell in Purgatory make enough to pay the tab.

Positioned at the mouth of the highway across from the Great Sacrificial Lake, it's the hottest destination for the middle class to unwind after their long work hours. Its cool blue lights stand out in stark contrast to the hot red air of Purgatory, and to the warm orange glow the nearby lake pulses with.

Though it attempts to accommodate a wide variety of creatures and spirits, it's yet another establishment whose doorway is too short for Ritst to walk through without bending over. He was not bothered by this—he'd be more alarmed at an establishment that *expected* his 10-foot height.

"I'll have a bull-blood beer, please," Ritst said to the cute oni behind the bar. He considered flirting—he *always* considered flirting with someone at the pub, and this oni was *never* off-limits—but lately, there's been a smaller fish he'd much rather trade sweetness with. Tonight, beer would suffice.

The oni whipped a towel from his apron and used it to open the bottle top. The beer bottle, wet with condensation, slid towards Ritst's open palm. It never made it—a lily-white hand snatched it up from beside Ritst.

“I never understood how blood beer was made,” the humanoid rested his chin on his fist as he scanned the colorful label, “then again, looking at these *meaty* ingredients, I can see these are made for bodies with...”

When Ritst looked down to see who confiscated his beer, heterochromic eyes climbed up to meet his. Red and blue, they noted the grooves of his scales, and the valley where his large shoulder muscles met bicep.

“...more energy requirements than my own.”

The human slid the beer to Ritst.

“Yeah, I’m a tall boy,” Ritst seized the neck of the bottle between his triangular teeth and leaned his head back. He shook as the cool, thick broth hit the back of his throat.

“You are,” The human leaned forward and rested his chin on laced fingers. He was a fey man, even for the monster-crowded bar. His face was, at once, soft and hard, delicate and sharp at the edges. His dress was of a similar manner—navy blue trousers and sheer, white collar-shirt of such thin fragility that it might have counted as topless, were it not for the applique of metal pins and adornments on top. Chrome skulls and flowers and trinkets of strange shape and detail were artfully piled onto his chest and shoulders. His lemon-blonde hair was curled with such delicate artistry that it threatened to collapse under a light breeze. Ritst was amazed that this human-presenting creature made it all the way through the crowd without a hair falling out of place.

“Don’t worry, I have a girlfriend,” he smiled. “I’m just looking to see how much squirming I can get out of you with words alone. You can talk, too, I guess, but I’ve always enjoyed seeing people’s reactions more than others seeing mine. It’s awfully loud in here, though. Wanna talk on the covered patio?”

Ritst blinked his yellow eyes and took another swig.

*****

"So, you edit for a TV show?" The human crossed his legs and sipped from his own bull-blood beer. It may have not been made for his palette, but this man will put anything in his mouth at least once just to know what it's like. "I never have the time to see TV thanks to my job. I feel like I've heard of *The Next Great Deity* in passing though, so if I have, then it must be huge."

Ritst was too tall to properly stand in the covered patio, and the thin black chairs looked weaker than the barstools inside. So instead, he reclined on his side, and the human sat on the table next to him. There was something nice about having someone else look down at him for a change, he thought.

"The show does well, but you'll never see me in front of the camera," Ritst laughed, "and I'd like to keep it that way."

"I bet the camera would enjoy some time with you," the human grinned.

Ritst raised a wet brow and swished the beer around his mouth. "What about you? What do you do?"

His question came out more accusatory than he meant it, but it couldn't be helped. The longer this person buttered him up, the more suspicious it seemed. Ritst had held back from flirtation with the oni because he *wants* to be in a relationship. This person is actively flirting *despite* being in one.

"I'm a police officer."

Ritst nearly choked on his beer.

"Border Patrol, specifically," he clarified and did a quick check in the chrome of the patio's pole to make sure every hair-coil and accessory was in place.

Ritst's eyes darted around as he did the math. "You... are you only talking to me because you think I shouldn't be here?"

The human laughed "Oh my god, no. I'm off-duty. I'm genuinely flirting with the buff, 10-foot-tall shark man. I'd absolutely go down on you right now if I could."

Ritst's body didn't know what direction to face. He shifted in sudden discomfort. "Is there... something wrong?"

The human's smile, for the first time, didn't match his voice. He forced his teeth to stay out in the open in some vague grin-like shape, but it failed to mask the slower, lower tone he took.

"I really can't complain. I shouldn't complain. I'm healthy, I'm happy, I have a well-paying job that I'm really good at. I eat well, I drink well, I got a girl, but..."

"But?"

"...I think I've chased for so long that I'm still predispositioned to hunt. I think there's something wrong with me, maybe. I'm still naturally trying to get more even when I already have what I want."

Ritst craned his head forward. The human's eyes were glassy, and the tell-tale hint of red began to creep in at the edges.

Oh lord, I think he's telling the truth, Ritst sighed. *He's drunk already. He must've come out here tonight to vent.*

"Well, why don't you and your girl take a vacation? Visit Heaven. The golden trees are shedding right now. It's gorgeous. Everyone says it's romantic, too, but I haven't gone there with anyone... yet."

"That's where my girl works, actually. At the trees," the human sighed blissfully. "I guess I might be getting a little stir crazy without her. It's been tough to be away from her so much."

Ritst tilted his pointed head up. "Really? What's her name? I work in Heaven, I might know her. It's all rich people and their employees, more or less."

"Well..." the human rolled his head from side to side as he weighed the various answers he could give, "...she's a little posh. I try my best not to ride on her coattails. One of the reasons she likes me, I think. I don't use her name for anything."

Ritst's triangular teeth clinked around the bottle's edge. He guzzled, then wiped his flat mouth with his forearm. "That's where we're different, you and I. If I had someone, I'd want to let the whole world know about them."

The human raised his beer bottle.

"There's lots of fish out there," he smiled. "I bet you'll get to tell everyone about them, someday."

Ritst's small mouth peeled into a wide smile. They clinked bottles together and drank.

*****

The human stared down to the bottom of his beer. There was barely another gulp; all that remained was a red froth of remorse in desperate need of lips to pass through.

"I think I've hit the bottom," he clicked his tongue. "I've really become a lightweight these past few years. Well, thanks for listening, you tall stack of fish. I'm gonna spend the rest of my break in a hammock. Don't get in trouble. Or, if you do, let ol' Lucifer be the one that catches ya, yeah?"

Ritst wracked his brain, embarrassed that there was an Abrahamic religious colloquialism he hadn't heard before. "Why would I let Lucifer catch me?"

The humanoid was in the middle of standing up, and froze when he heard Ritst's question. His eyes stared transfixed on the steel ebony table, as if he couldn't quite work out Ritst's meaning. He eventually came to the wrong conclusion: "That's me. Did I not introduce myself? I'm so rude. And sorry," he extended a ring-adorned hand. One was an engagement ring, the others were complementary.

Ritst's far-spaced eyes widened. He took Lucifer's hand out of politeness, but the energy and effort in their shared shake did not come from him. "Huh? *You're* Lucifer?"

He said he had a posh girlfriend in Heaven, the information hit his mind like caffeine hits the bloodstream.

"That's me," Lucifer stood up with remarkably straight posture, given the effect of the drink on his voice. Even with the slight slur of alcohol, he found a way to sound proud and elegant. The neon lights of the bar haloed him. "Captain Lucifer Venus of the Inter-Dimensional Border Patrol. I can tell by your reaction that you've heard my name in passing, probably in the same way I've heard of your show. We're both big enough deals that we get out to people even when they aren't looking for us, huh?"

Ritst had tuned out of his introduction long before he got to analogy.

So, when he said 'Don't let Lucifer catch you', that wasn't a reference to the Christian devil? There was no hidden meaning or pun or...

"Have you ever read the Bible?" Ritst blurted, then sealed his fish-lips tight in embarrassment. He was still sober enough to regret.

Lucifer blinked in confusion, then blushed. "Nah, I... I'm not much of a reader. For the same reason I haven't seen your show. And the same reason I gotta go, really. I'm married to my job and all. Still! Let's talk again. I come up here on my breaks, few and far between as they may be. Maybe next time I'll get drunk enough to smooch ya."

Ritst's pupils constricted.

"See ya, fish," Lucifer waved.

Ritst continued to stare at the door long after the captain passed through it, long after its hinges clicked closed.

He hasn't read the Bible. He has a posh girlfriend in Heaven. He hasn't seen The Next Great Deity. *His name is Lucifer. He's Lucifer. He's... how can he be Lucifer? Does he not know his own mythos?*

He got up and snaked his way to the bar. His hands shook as he eased himself down onto the barstool and ordered another beer. Any chance he had of flirting with the bartender had evaporated, swallowed down Lucifer's gullet. For the rest of his night, he would try to fit the jigsaw pieces that fell into his lap together, and repeat a worry in his mind:

Why do I feel like I've learned something that I shouldn't have?

"You okay?" Theodore puffed a ring of smoke into the night air.

He and Robin both leaned over the balcony of room 41-D. They stared across the moonlit fields of the lot of Heaven's Heart Hotel. Under the purple moonlight, The Forest of Golden Trees no longer looked so lustrous. They flickered when the occasional moonbeam crossed the path of the canopy, but it was brief and dull in comparison to the day-lit spectacle it was known for.

"Tonight was a test," Robin said. The wind whipped at her fro-hawk. "I was ready to listen to Jesus either eviscerate my work or praise it. If she really loves the human race, if there was even a shred of credibility to this place, she'd have said something, *anything*."

Theodore watched the ash drift from his cigarette. "I hear you. It's pretty disappointing when you find out God shows less interest in people's well-being than you do."

Robin pushed herself off the railing, walked to Theodore, and put her palm into his. The cool metal of her mind-control bit fit into his hand like a quarter.

"You attached them to the quartztaphores?" she asked.

Theodore nodded.

"Alright then," Robin said. "There's no going back now. Let's find that pool."

*****

In their apartment, Theodore and Robin reclined in lawn chairs. Beer bottles dripped with condensation as they rested in their carefully postured hands. If you peeked out between the blinds of the balcony and didn't look too closely at the attached metal bits on the sides of their temples, you'd be led to believe the two humans were in a state of relaxed silence, lost in the cool breeze of a new world's night.

If you tried to talk to them directly, however, you'd find their minds were elsewhere.

Theodore had two quartztaphores. Robin made two sets of mind-swap bits. The humans combined their two creations, and the result was exactly what they needed to look for the missing hotel floor: remote control, shape-shifting spies.

Though the pair had made preparations for their act of espionage, they were mentally unequipped for life in a new creature's skin. When their minds swapped over to the creation storage room, they were immediately overwhelmed by their new anatomy and senses.

A quartztaphores's eyesight is not analogous to our own—every inch of their finely coated skin could see its surroundings, a mess of color and light that their human minds had great difficult translating. It was as if the universe forced all their surroundings into their vision at once. Even the soles of their strange, sharp feet could see the ground they walked on. The crevices of their limbs and torso could describe themselves.

"Oh fuck. I'm gonna barf," Robin said. She was surprised to find that the vocalization did not come from her mouth, as there was none present on the creature: it came from within her chest, from some flat mess of organs buried under their rubbery flesh.

"I'm gonna be honest with you, I don't think I designed any sort of mechanism like that for these bodies," Theodore's quartz form stumbled about. "If you do throw up, I don't know what that's going to look like at all or what it'll do to you."

With some practice Theodore was able to wrangle control of his own creation's form and mechanics. Designing a creature to move and change shape was one thing: to actually control the method by which one shape-shifts as if it were your own is a different task altogether.

"Okay, this is stupid, but," Theodore's quartz face melted to mirror the concrete wall behind him, "Just, like... hold the thought of what you want to shift to as hard and as clear as you can, and try to wriggle that part of the body like you're... scrunching your nose? That's the closest I can describe it."

One aspect of the quartztaphores that they were prepared to deal with from the onset was the intentional shape-shifting limitations Theodore imposed on the creatures in the first episode. It turned out that the limit of a flat, single side projection was not an intentional design decision at all, but a way to circumvent the fact that Theodore couldn't figure out how to flatten the whole body without killing the creature. ("Listen," he explained to her before the mind-swap with a grin that was equal parts pride and embarrassment, "I'm really good at bullshitting my way through problems. That's most of poker.") Because of this, it would be difficult, if not impossible, for one of them to convert their forms into a convincing shape without knowing where every camera was in Heaven's Heart Hotel.

So they operated under the assumption that they couldn't know where they would be eyed from. To solve this weakness, they stood back to back, limb to limb, and hugged the wall. They stretched and interlocked the shifting skin of the quartztaphore enough to hold onto each other, and became one snail-like unit. Over the course of two hours they crawled along the perimeter of the room to new hotel corridors. They now knew the location of the creature room on Floor Q. When they found a particularly dark or isolated nook or cranny, they would swap positions. The person closest to the wall had the greater task maintaining the three-dimensional aspect of their illusion, and the two found out this was a tiring ask of the quartztaphore's body and their own minds. Holding the 3D shape on the outer edges of the skin without reverting back to base was like staring at a computer monitor without blinking.

The elevator was their first stop. The two squirmed over the list of buttons.

"Well, that's the whole alphabet," Theodore quipped as they worked together to press 'N.' "Hopefully this isn't a wild goose chase."

"Even if it is," Robin morphed to the pearl-encrusted interior of the elevator, "this isn't an experience I'll forget anytime soon."

Floor N looked exactly like any other floor in the hotel. It was uniform in its ostentatious carpeting and gold trim, in its paintings of conflicting mythologies. Oil paintings of the crucifixion sat opposite dimly lit reliefs of Anubis. There was a red rope to tie off access to the painting, while anyone can put their hands on the dog-god of death.

"Well, we found it, but it doesn't feel like there's anything worth looking at here," Robin worried. "During the next break we could come back here with the tracker, I suppose, but I'm not optimistic..."

"...there's rooms here," Theodore twitched.

"Huh?"

"Mark said there was a pool on Floor N and nothing else. This floor has rooms *and* a pool."

Theodore studied the way the light hit all the corners of his quartztaphore skin. The hallway's lights, tucked away behind gold moulding, pulsed in waves over the gold popcorn ceiling. The quartztaphore's vision couldn't quite parse form in the way a human's eye might, but it caught the subtlety of light in its dance, and it perceived it in a way the human mind could not grasp.

"There's a seam of light near the stairs," Theodore said. "Go to it."

As they approached, they found that the seam ran straight up the angled stairwell, an even height between floor and ceiling.

"It's the same exact light that they use in the hallway," Theodore glanced between the seam's output and the hallway lights. "Why is it on the other side of the stairway wall?"

"I've never seen light like this on any of the other stairwells," Robin pressed her quartz face into the wall. The slit of the seam was too narrow to make out anything on the other side.

"Yeah, and I'm not sure we'd 'see' it if we were here in our normal bodies, either," Theodore worried. "Mark said you can get to Floor N... let's just start calling it 'The Pool Floor', yeah? He said you can get to the pool floor via both M and O by going up... let's see."

They shimmied up the stairs, back-to-back, their forms molding to each new step and wallpaper pattern. The stairs from N led to a placard for floor O, and floor O, predictably, to floor P. All the hallways had the strange light seam in the center of the wall.

"Mark didn't notice anything unusual about how the shiqqs got there?" Robin asked.

"No..." Theodore worried, "and it's not like we had difficulty getting to the pool. He can only see out of the camera lens, who knows if he missed the shiqqs pulling a lever or something?"

"What if..." Robin tilted her quartz head, which currently mirrored a Renaissance-era painting of the Virgin Mary, "what if 'N' isn't the old floor?"

Theodore drew quiet.

"What if the pool *wasn't* moved?" Robin continued. "I know this sounds crazy, but what if this is a new pool, and the "Pool Floor" that the shiqqs are getting access to via O is a different floor that's *also* labeled floor N?"

"That would explain why *this* Floor N has rooms."

"Yeah."

They stared at the seam in silence.

"So how do we get to the other side of this wall?" Robin asked.

"Fuck if I know," Theodore sighed. "Come back during the next break with our actual bodies and a sledgehammer?"

After his first 12-hour workday, Jack stumbled back into his apartment. He hurt in ways he had not previously known, and collapsed to the floor, a heap of tired rind muscles and a wrinkled baby-blue Beelzebub Boxing uniform. Not even the shrill caw of the parrot could rattle his gourd.

"I'll look up more about the show," he mumbled to himself, "after I get some... sleep..."

The spectral lights of his eyes began to flutter and dim.

"You're not gonna water the plants and feed the bird before you nap?"

The stranger's voice lit Jack's eyes anew. Jack flipped himself over in a state of alert panic spurred by the intruder's voice.

She stood stiff like a faucet. Her reflective pants and chrome shirt-dress shimmered in intentional conflict with the surrounding plants. She poured water out of a plastic red pitcher. Her hair flowed down her back, blue and green like her plump lips and cool eyes. Her free hand rested on her hip and one of her legs bent at the knee; the combination formed an effortless S-shape that seemed to define the curves she patterned her look and life after.

"To be fair, I guess they don't belong to you," she brushed her bangs out of her eyes as she dutifully went between pots. "But they don't belong to me, either. I feed them because they're alive, and someone's got to, you know? They deserve food and water. We all do."

"Who are you?" Jack pushed himself up to his knees.

She set the pitcher down and turned her head. The downward angle of her stare gave her green eyes a laser-like quality, as if they could fire and dissect Jack where he lay. No facial muscle twitched in any direction; they would not and could not betray her thoughts.

"My name's Mora," she said.

Jack rubbed his gourd. "Are you my roommate?"

"No."

"O-oh," Jack pulled his limbs in and sat cross-legged on the floor. "Then, uh, why are you here?"

"I just said it. Someone has to look after the life here."

Jack shifted. "Do you... *know* the other person that lives here?"

"Sometimes," she muttered.

Suddenly, a gunshot like boom shook the apartment. Light exploded from underneath the door frame of the mysterious roommate's bedroom.

Mora flinched at the disturbance and closed her eyes. "Fucking... really, man? *Already*?" She stomped to the kitchen counter, seized her purse and keys, and began to march out of the apartment.

"Where are you going?" Jack hid behind a potted plant. Smoke began to pour from the bedroom door. "What's happening?!"

"I told you, *sometimes* I know him," there was a sourness to her voice, as if she had given this explanation before, and was absolutely put-out by the idea of giving it again. She moved towards the door while flicking her finger rapidly across a cell phone screen. "Now's one of those times where I choose *not* to know him. Listen, there's milk in the fridge, and hay in the closet. My number's in the only notebook in his room. Call me in two days when he can put together sentences. I have to travel across town to get here and the more gas I have to spend on travel, the harder it is for me to save and move out of Hell. So if you call sooner, you'll really piss me off."

She paused momentarily to brush a stray white feather off the strap of her purse. It fluttered to the ground. Jack thought it may have molted from the parrot, but realized it was much too large. The length of the feather measured nearly the length of the Quaker parrot itself. Mora's car keys jingled as she slung them around her pointer finger. It was the last sound Jack heard before she slammed the apartment door.

Smoke wafted across Jack's face. There was a scuttling sound on the other side of his roommate's door, a wild rhythm of light limbs bowling repeatedly over the carpet from one side of the room to the other. Jack, on all fours, crawled towards the door in a mixture of terror and curiosity. He pulled himself up by the handle.

"H-hello?" Jack whispered. "Is there someone in there?"

A small thump hit the far wall.

"C-can I come in? If we're roommates, we should meet each other..."

Silence.

"A-all right... I'm opening the door now..."

Jack cracked the door to a crescent, but saw nothing. With a nervous swallow, he eased the door open more and more until he heard another muffled thump, which snapped at his reflexes and caused him to push it all the way open. He found a small creature, no larger than a typical house cat, butting its head against the wall.

It turned. Its upper humanoid body was hairless, and its wall-eyed stare was crammed disproportionately into the sockets of its large head. Blonde fuzz covered the top of its head and ears, and brown fur covered its goat legs.

It screamed. Jack screamed back. Its horizontal-slit pupils dilated and it charged and headbutted him in the shin. Though the pain was sharp, it was more the intensity of its trot that scattered Jack's limbs into disarray. He toppled forward and landed on his right arm. The rind skin cracked on impact, and his forearm separated in fibrous tears. Jack's screaming continued as the baby half-goat headbutted his rear over and over again.

"A-alarm system! You can hear me, right?" Jack willed himself up to a seated position and used his uninjured arm to try to hold the broken ligament in place. His forearm and wrist flopped around like spaghetti. "I broke my arm! I need a hospital!"

"INSUFFICIENT FUNDS," the alarm system said.

"W-what?" Jack balked. "I worked all day and night! I have to have some money now!"

"EMPLOYEE JACK IS PAID BI-WEEKLY," the alarm system said. The half-goat headbutted Jack in what, on a human, would house his kidneys. "INSUFFICIENT FUNDS."

Jack's spectral eyes turned to smoldering flames. "That's bullshit! That's absolute bullshit! I..." the flames cooled to thoughtful pinpoints, "alarm system, I can't *work* like this! I have to get my arm fixed!"

The alarm system seemed to glitch and stutter as it processed the absolutely unacceptable nature of an employee not working.

"*Beelzebub Boxing*," the alarm system cooed before switching to its panic-inducing boom, "IS PROUD TO OFFER ON-SITE HEALTH SERVICES TO ALL ON-THE-CLOCK EMPLOYEES. YOUR INJURY HAS BEEN REPORTED TO YOUR MORNING SHIFT MANAGER. PLEASE REMAIN SEATED, A DRIVER IS ON THE WAY."

"Thank god," Jack sighed. His gourd cocked to one side as the alarm system's words sunk in. "Wait, I have to go back to work right now in order to get my arm fixed?"

"CORRECT. YOUR SHIFT WILL BE ADJUSTED TO COMPENSATE FOR YOUR SURGERY."

"No! No! NO!"

Jack cried out in pain and existential terror. The half-goat wiggled its tail, aimed, and launched itself into the pumpkin-man's chest, and the two toppled over together. Their cries were for different reasons.

The Citizens

What is a show without its viewers? Thank you, all, for your continued support.

JACK

Buff Pumpkin-Man just trying to get by. Has several questions.

MORA

Takes care of plants. Doesn't have time for babies.

LUCIFER VENUS

Captain of the IDBP. Flirt. Doesn't read.

Lucifer stepped through the turnstile, up the ramp, and onto the steel platform. The rotating lights above him were arranged in a plain, utilitarian manner. No one was meant to appreciate them, to find aesthetic beauty in their simple cylindrical shape or singular purpose.

He was nude, and his pale skin glowed under the reflected light from the metal underneath. This chamber, made purely of metals and glass, contained no color of its own, and if any existed, it was a reflection of that which it inspected. Lucifer's flawless skin and blonde curls and red-and-blue eyes blemished the seriousness of this scenario. He was a flower on a bed of coal. The room had two doors—an entrance and an exit—and on the exit wall there was a large, one-way mirror. Above it, a speaker was suspended from the ceiling.

"Smile," said the demon guard on the other side of the glass. She kept her eyes locked on the console, and kept her peaked cap drawn low.

Lucifer needed no instruction. He showed no teeth, just the slight turn of amused lips. He squinted his glassy eyes straight through the mirror, his face primed with mild eroticism. It was for this reason the demon guard drew her cap brim down—to shield herself from the weaponized "come-hither" look she had heard rumors about. Lucifer couldn't see this from his side of the glass, of course, but not knowing who he was flirting with had never stopped him before.

Where others considered the required strip search to travel between realms a nuisance at best and an invasion of privacy at worst, the captain of the IDBP felt no such bother or fear. Why should he? Everyone involved in border patrol knew his face, whether or not they were in his precinct, and whether or not they had met him. He spoke at every police event. It was he that gave out awards to exceptional officers—not the chief of police—since he had already won them all. He was practically a mascot of the police force by this point, and he wouldn't have had it any other way. He didn't even need to be on the field, he was just such a glutton for work and recognition that he stayed on patrol, just to keep his name at the top, just to keep eyes locked firmly on his existence.

This moment, too, was an extension of his need to fill the bottomless pit of his ego with attention. He took the tubes—the heavily regulated transportation system between supernatural realms—to travel from Gehenna, Purgatory (where the Purgatory River Pub lies) to Heaven, then back down to his home in Corom Deo Vivit, a rich city in the richest part of Purgatory. He didn't need to take this path between realms to get home. The staff at the Corom Tube was willing to wave protocol and let Lucifer pass through, but it was always at Lucifer's insistence that proper procedure be followed.

Though Corom Deo Vivit was a hundred miles away from Gehenna, with the time it took to stand in line at the Gehenna Tube, get searched, travel by dragon-train in Heaven to the Corom Tube, get strip searched *again*, and then call a cab to go home, he would spend nearly an extra hour on his commute than he would have if he had just called a cab in the first place. But if he took a cab, he wouldn't be able to make rookie demon guards at outposts squirm. He wouldn't get to flirt with the stewardess on the dragon-train, or the dragon-train itself. He wouldn't get to sign autographs. He wouldn't get handshakes and pats on the back and bows of recognition. And if he didn't get those things, well, it just wouldn't be a complete night out on the town, would it?

He posed on the identity verification platform with one hand over his genitalia and the other on his chest in a perfect mimicry of Sandro Botticelli's "The Birth of Venus," an impressive modeling pose given he knew nothing about art and had never seen the painting in his life. The lights flashed.

Several monitors spanned the enclosure around the demon guard. They showed x-rays and graphs of magical energy, data checks and read-outs. After a few minutes of routine verification, the demon guard confirmed there was no identity-concealing magic or contraband on, or within, Lucifer. The only thing of note she could find was Lucifer's abnormally high blood-alcohol concentration.

Lucifer could've chosen to get dressed in a small bathroom in the exit's waiting room. But, once handed his red thong and neatly folded mesh shirt and navy blue trousers, he dressed himself right there in front of the guards. He casually talked to these uniformed, toothy bruisers as he slid garments of fancy up his legs and over his head. Lucifer was, and would be, the only man that could get away with looking a demon in the eye while gliding a hand seductively down to his navel while having a dry conversation about the weather.

*****

After standing in the outdoor line to the tube for twenty minutes, it was Lucifer's turn to travel. He placed his hand on a topaz-lit digital display. In response, its many gauges hummed to life. This was the last stage in the process, and it was the one that bothered him the most.

The Corom Tube was like every single other tube in the supernatural realms— a straight, transparent glass tower that shot into the sky, segmented every few miles by a gold joint with engravings of a lost, sharp-angled language. Green-pink clouds accumulated around the edge of the tube's visibility. This was the only occurrence of these clouds in any of the realms, and they were comprised of some dimensional substance none of Heaven's scientists could measure or contain. It was as if the tube itself pierced some unknown element of the sky, and broke it.

But Lucifer was not bothered by the tube itself.

"LUCIFER VENUS: IDBP CAPTAIN OF THE 45TH PRECINCT IN HEAVEN," a small speaker on the console threatened to blow out with a loud digitized voice, "YOU HAVE BEEN CLEARED. PLEASE WAIT WHILE FUNDS ARE TRANSFERRED."

He immediately pulled his hand away. He hated the mechanism within the display, and hated the crackling speaker, which always caused him to jump in surprise. What he hated the most, though, was touching the display itself—there was a warmth there, as if another palm had pressed through the glass and touched his own. As much as he loved to flirt, the mere idea of an uninvited touch caused him to recoil, and were he not so incredibly stubborn, this part of the dimensional travel process might have turned him off altogether from traveling to Purgatory for a drink.

The tubes were relics. Lucifer was not around for their construction, and no one else he knew had been, either. They represented great, wonderful blanks in the collective consciousness of the three supernatural realms—a reminder that Heaven, Purgatory, and Hell are all connected. All it takes to travel is a little bit of work.

"2,000 TESTAMENTS TRANSFERRED," the machine screamed. "THANK YOU FOR YOUR PATRONAGE."

Or, a lot, depending upon your income.

Lucifer stood on the gold platform within the tube and looked up. It stretched so far before disappearing within the clouds that he could not reliably count the segmented gold rings from within. Over the speakers, a countdown from five began, and the gold platform underneath glowed bright red. Once it hit zero, Lucifer flew straight upwards—at first he drifted, carried like a bird on a zephyr, but as he passed through the segmented gold rings, picked up speed, until he finally hit the green-pink clouds at a rocket's pace.

And then, there was the void.

The gaps between realms were paper white and empty. The limitless void swallowed all sight of its innards; travelers saw no tubes, no skies, no stars. Lucifer loved this. He thought those precious minutes immediately after the breach of the void were the most beautiful part of the process. When a traveler broke through the green-pink clouds but had not yet reached the first gold segment in the tube's length, their acceleration almost completely stopped.

Lucifer smiled as he let the weightlessness take him. He drifted. He stopped thinking or moving his limbs. Slowly he spun through the tube, stared into the blank banks of infinity, into the purest form of freedom and beauty. Perhaps he, too, could be like this void—oppressive and meaningless and vast and eternal.

But these subconscious desires were fleeting. Once he hit the first gold ring, he was carried again by the acceleration of travel. He flew, faster and faster, until he hit the green-pink clouds on the other side. And as he flew, as his body ripped through time and space, he frowned.

*****

The Corom Tube looked exactly the same on the other side. The tint of its gold and glass appeared more wild in the surroundings of Purgatory; where Heaven had its green sun and crystal buildings and sprawling, manicured lands, Purgatory was red and passionate, filled with bronze buildings and orange clouds and renegade sculptures and graffiti.

The people of Purgatory were of the greatest financial divide of any of the realms. Corom Deo Vivit was a rich villa full of artisan starter mansions, and its occupants had a wide range of occupations. Actors and politicians and entrepreneurs and even the captain of the IDBP lived there. Perhaps they were not elite enough to move into Heaven like true starlets and deities, and most of them never would be. But they were comfortable, and if they were the only part of Purgatory, one could believe that Purgatory wasn't such a bad place to end up. And yet, just a few miles over, exactly where Ki and An street met, the border of a small town called Smalcald brushed up against the city.

Smalcald had no opera houses like Corom, no five-star dining, no sports teams. (As a rabid fan of the Corom Sea Monks, Corom's local Demon-Boxing team, Lucifer was particularly annoyed that the closest rival team was in Gehenna. He would travel to more away-games if Smalcald had a team.) What it had instead was small houses, packed in like shirts in overstuffed luggage, yards no wider than the three-room square buildings they held. And in these houses were families of demons and spirits that had worked their way out of Hell, but had no money to progress in the more volatile economy of Purgatory. In many ways, Smalcald could've easily doubled as a smaller Hell, were it not for the more lax regulations of the area. Smalcald's citizens were free—free to be poor, at least, and usually not much else unless they landed an extremely fortunate job or partner. The contrast of Smalcald and Corom Deo Vivit's borders filled Purgatory with a hot tension that heated the sidewalks and sky.

Purgatory, when observed from the outside, looked like someone took Heaven and Hell and tried to whisk the two together. This mixture was highly combustible, and there was a sense that, one day, a single spark could set the whole thing ablaze. How it hadn't yet was anyone's guess.

Lucifer stepped out of the cab, and looked up at the cold, Gothic manor he called home. He tipped the demon-driver and, in his haze of gradual sobriety, stumbled down the long, winding sidewalk to his front door.

When Lucifer bought his home, he didn't buy it for himself. Not *just*, anyway. This was a home big enough for a wife, and for many, many children. That was always the plan. When a man does everything he wants to do in life, he thought, then the only thing left to do is raise a new generation to be just as awesome as he was. Keep the chain of success going. Keep the Venus name alive. That's all he wanted. The huge door frame in the entrance way, covered in stone gargoyles with striped teeth and happy expressions, were meant to be playful and inspirational. The many hooks on the wall were meant for school coats and book bags. The big, empty kitchen should be, in a perfect world, filled with fresh fruits and vegetables glinting under the chandelier lights he had custom made in silver and ruby so that they would match his lover's eyes and her favorite dress. He wanted to hear the scuffle of brothers in the carpeted living room, or the swift thud of fist against boxing bag in the empty gymnasium, or the laughter of daughters in the spa that he had installed but never filled with water. He wanted to hear the rustle of a pet pygmy tarasque as it fetched frisbees in the backyard. He wanted to hear something in that home other than the heavy, pentagram-engraved door as it shut, something other than the locks clicking into place, something other than the lonely sound of his breath trapped in bed sheets as he pulled them over his head, something other than the creak of a picture frame as he clutched it a little too tightly to his chest.

He realized, there in the darkness of the sheets, that the picture's subjects were mere shapes, featureless in the shadows. He lifted the bed sheet, reached for the lamp, and flicked it on. He wanted to see detail. He wanted a reminder of who he was, and who he waited for.

"When are you gonna come home?" he drew his finger across the glass, across the outline of her beard. "When are you gonna come back to me?"

He pressed in against the glass. In that picture, they were laughing, smiling, lost in some fragment of a memory that no longer belonged to him.

And for a brief, horrible moment, the texture was wrong. There was heat and pressure against his touch. It was as if his fingertip was pushed not into the picture frame's surface, but into the pointer finger of another living being. He immediately recoiled. There was a smudge on Jesus's face where his finger had smeared the glass. He wiped it clean with the bed sheet, sat the picture back on the night stand, turned out the light, and wrestled with sleep.

The humans returned their shape-shifting spies to their holding cells. The experiment was a mixed success—the time it took to travel in this fashion, while arguably the safest method possible, was time consuming to a fault. This method would not work for searching anything beyond the perimeters of a few floors of the hotel, and with only a few hours before the morning alarms of the TV show, the duo decided on a new plan of action once the next challenge appeared. Robin quietly shambled out of the apartment to return to her own, and Theodore collapsed on the couch in his living room. Both got under an hour of sleep before the green morning light streamed over the hotel.

Theodore dreamed of Queens. He stood in his apartment, in front of his makeshift bedroom studio. He tried to record the sounds outside his window, but when he hit play, the only thing that came through the speaker grill was a series of plastic clanks, like a tumbler full of dice. He went to the microphone to check its connections. The dice rolled louder and louder, and upon closer inspection, the sound came from within the microphones themselves.

He woke up.

Zargah sat on the glass coffee table. The alien soldier was adorned in black linen of baggy fit and strange, asymmetrical shape, which pooled around his lanky frame in intentional tatters, a stark contrast to the tailored military coats he'd sported previously. His god eye snaked around his neck as his four hands molded the creation-laser into individual dice. The dice were around the size of lima beans and nearly a hundred of them lined the floor around the table. Several colorful tumblers were around him, each two-toned: one side a solid, opaque pastel, the other completely transparent.

"Uh, good morning, Zargah," Theodore rubbed his eyes. "What are you doing?"

Zargah clapped new dice to life. "Welcome to the awakened world. Subject Theodore, I am worried we, as a group, have not bonded as well as we could have. I seek to correct this."

A single guitar string's pitch slowly climbed as Taninim entered the room.

"What's all this?" The dragon-man asked as he adjusted a taut string.

"I am constructing the elements of my favorite game from childhood," Zargah began to fill the tumblers with dice, ten in each. His translation collar clicked with cheerful clarity. "It's called 'Scabbard.'"

"Games? I love games!" Taninim's nose-chain rattled as he raised his head in excitement. "My human, Jeremy, has called on my help when he plays games. Together we've beaten all the games ever made. I am eager for a new challenge."

The statement's wording caused Theodore to pull himself up to a seated position. "*All* games?"

Taninim nodded. "All eight video games in existence. They keep making new games because we're too good at them."

"How old is Jeremy again?"

"Eleven."

Theodore closed his eyes. "Ah."

"'Scabbard' is simple, and very quick to play," Zargah popped the lid on another tumbler. "But it's also very intense. I rarely encountered those uninterested by its premise in my home world, and I'm excited to see how it translates across species and culture boundaries."

Taninim hit a sour note on his guitar as The Internet shouldered past him with no warning or greeting.

"I heard somebody wants to lose in something," The Internet said as he pulled a DEVO t-shirt down over the waist of well-worn cargo shorts, "so I'm here to fulfill dreams."

"That eagerness..." Zargah smiled as he capped another tumbler "...is what 'Scabbard' is all about."

'Scabbard,' as Zargah explained to his roommates, is a 1-on-1 game where the goal is to capture your opponent's dice. Each tumbler had a fold-out handle with various buttons, and the inside of the tumbler—the source of the opaque coloration on the outside—was coated in a sticky membrane. One handle-button caused the membrane to seize around nearby dice, and the other button ejected any dice not caught by the membrane to the ground Rounds consisted of players shaking their tumblers, opaque sides facing each other, then ejecting the dice.

"Why aren't the sides numbered?" Taninim held up the semi-transparent orange cube to the morning light.

"Do you number the sides?" Zargah mused. "Fascinating."

Each round, one player will defend, the other player will attack. The attacking player's goal is to 1-to-1 match the defense's dice roll, then capture those dice. The defense's goal is to lure the attacker into wasting dice. For example, if an attacker commits to 5 dice and the defense only spends 1 die to defend, the defense gives up that one die, but the attacker cannot use the four failed attack dice on his next defense roll. Because of this, both sides have incentive for low rolls. The attacker suffers no penalty for not attacking, the defenders suffer no penalty for throwing all their dice out at once—aside from losing dice, of course.

The only exception to the above rules is what is known as the “traitor” rule: if the defender rolls only one die and the attacker does not attack, the defender loses that die to the attacker. The die that suffers this fate is playfully considered a ‘traitor.’ A ‘double-agent’ is when both sides only play one die, and the attacker loses his single die to the defender.

Conversely, if the defense ever rolls zero dice, whether or not he has any in his tumbler, that player automatically surrenders.

“This shit’s easy!” The Internet held up his two tumblers. “It’s basically random! You have no way of knowing what either player will roll.”

Theodore stroked his chin in quiet disagreement.

“You’re not wrong,” Zargah clicked. His antennae bobbed and swayed and, when combined with the slight tilt of his head, suggested an amusement the alien had not yet exhibited. “Scabbard is named as such because the scariest part of the game is not knowing the type of mindset your opponent may bring. We have a saying in my country: no weapon is more frightening than when it is hidden.”

In the first round The Internet ever played of Scabbard, he was on offense. On the count of five, both players ejected their tumblers, and the dog-punk viciously threw all his heart, soul, and dice to the ground.

Zargah only defended himself with one die.

“Wha...” The Internet’s ears flattened.

“Fortunately, I know you’re quite aggressive in everything that you do,” Zargah handed The Internet’s reward—a single dice—over with glee.

With only two dice left to defend himself, The Internet's remaining turns played out with some predictability.

"This game's bullshit!" The Internet spiked his empty tumbler on the ground and collapsed into the couch.

"I want to try," Taninim picked up the tumbler.

Taninim was more playful and wild, tossing random amounts of dice out on each of his turns. Zargah figured this out by the fact that Taninim looked at Zargah head on—he never glanced at his tumbler's transparent windows, and he never shook the tumblers steadily enough to show any intention. His defeat was slower, but just as decisive as The Internet's.

"I had a lot of trouble controlling what dice I wanted to stay on the sticky part," Taninim rubbed the back of his head. "I thought if I was random I'd be able to win with luck, but it's like you always knew what I'd roll."

"It's easy to play conservatively versus random play," Zargah folded his lower set of arms, and held his upper arms on the lower set of elbows, then puffed his carapace chest with pride. "The truth is that in high levels of play, my species plays with four tumblers at once, and each tumbler represents an element that interacts with the other tumblers in different ways as far as dice-collection goes. It gets exceptionally complicated in terms of mathematical scaling. This simplified version is used by new players to introduce basic concepts, but I still find it exciting. Also, none of you have four hands, so I'd have an unfair advantage if we played the true sportsman's version."

"You-" Taninim's guitar slid down his shoulder, "you can play games *professionally*? I want to play games professionally!"

A rattling sound cut through the chatter. The two turned to see that Theodore had picked up a tumbler—he stuck his fingers in it to investigate the membrane, and to see how strong its grip was when the button was held.

"Mind if I try?"

"Let's have fun," Zargah chirped.

And so the two played. Though Theodore would fall like his roommates—as any amateur would when picking up a new game versus an experienced opponent—he showed neither stress nor worry during the battle. He took the lead in various rounds, elicited gasps of confidence from Taninim and The Internet, and when defeated through complicated small errors rather that simple misunderstandings, no gloom came upon his face. In the face of defeat, he smiled as if he had won.

"I think I figured it out," Theodore nodded. "The attacker can never lose dice if he attacks with zero or two, he'll either gain dice or is at even. If he attacks with two dice and the defender defends with one, he might lose some dice temporarily, but with the way the game is played, that's not that much of a disadvantage. Anything higher than two dice is a completely unnecessary risk for the attacker."

Zargah shivered, and the curve of his long back straightened. He stared at Theodore momentarily, his hand on his chin.

"Likewise, the defender is only ever guessing between throwing 1 and 2, and risks the loss of anywhere between 0 and 2 dice based off his guess," the alien-soldier confirmed Theodore's hypothesis. "The best case scenario for the defender is to protect his dice on his turn, then profit on his attack round. The frequency of stalemates between rounds are why the four-armed version of the game is more interesting, but to watch you figure out the core of the meta so quickly... you must have a game like this where you're from?"

Theodore smirked. “Yeah, I guess. Risk management and player reading are things I have experience in. The mechanics are different, but...”

Zargah returned the dice he won from Theodore back into his tumbler and shut the lid. He did so with Theodore’s hand sandwiched between the top and his own sticky palm. He squeezed, and felt Theodore’s knuckles press into the pads of his, at such odd joints from his own. *Humans have such fascinating angles*, he thought. Even the strongest among them, like Theodore, had a softness to their jaws and skin and carapace-less bulk. He couldn’t help but bring one more long-fingered, three-digit hand to the outside of the tumbler, where Theodore held, just to let the surface of his skin graze briefly with the strange, dry, warm flesh of a human’s.

“I say with complete sincerity,” Zargah’s collar translated his clicks into a bass so low that it rattled the plastic tumblers in their hands, “you could get quite good at this game with practice. Do you want to play again?”

Theodore swallowed. His face was in shadow from Zargah’s towering height, summoned by the blocked morning light that streamed in through the living room’s windowed balcony. “Yeah, we can do a few more. I’m... intrigued.”

Dust of Ages

As the green light of a new day streamed into 41-A, the waking Csodaszarvas realized his world was a little more quiet than before. The wonder-deer did not stir except to rotate his huge white ears for familiar sounds: Imhotep's lips popped off the tip of a beer bottle in the living room, Oksi minced meat and vegetables with barely tempered anger in the kitchen. The loudest thing Cso heard was silence: the absence of Jarilo, the complete lack of any carefree joy or youthful energy in the apartment. Not even his punk-phase rebellious sneers from the previous challenge found their way through the walls.

Csodaszarvas blinked his sleep crusted eyes, considered what the atmosphere in the living room must be like without Jarilo, and instead chose to return to what he thought was a safer, more hospitable environment: his dreams.

He was right.

Oksi stomped over to the living room, dropped a plate of Pukusa Ohaw on the glass table in front of Imhotep and then marched into a recliner on the opposite side of the room. He stared straight ahead as he cradled his own bowl of soul, steam crawling around the chiseled corners of his bearded face.

"It's curious," Imhotep reclined across the arm of the plush couch as he usually did. Though there was plenty of empty space for others to sit, it was the air of darkness that surrounded his form at all times that pushed others away. He applied gold powder to his eyelids, and did not bother to look at the steaming soup Oksi had laid in front of him. "I have declined your advances every single time, and yet you continue to waste your energy and my patience. Even worse, you're wasting food. That's the real crime, as far as I'm concerned."

"This is Pukusa Ohaw," Oksi used chopsticks to pick up a piece of salmon from his own soup to demonstrate the difference between his bowl and Imhotep's, "it does not have meat in it. Pukusa is—"

"—an onion," Imhotep sighed. He gathered up his makeup and slid it into his robe. In apparent disgust, he rose from the couch and drifted towards the balcony. His hands spoke with the same condescension carried in his voice. "Yes, yes, I know, I know. You still used bones in the stock, though. I'm not stupid, Oksi. I'm not going to take risks like that."

Oksi's brow twisted and folded in lines of anger.

"What..." he muttered just before he slammed his own soup down on the table. Both the bowl and table cracked. He stomped towards the sliding door and threw it open, "what the hell do you mean 'you won't take risks like that?' Are you saying my cooking is inherently dangerous?"

"You think I don't know what you're doing?" Imhotep leaned over the railing. He did not turn to face Oksi, as if Oksi didn't warrant further explanation or dialogue.

"How do you know so much about Ainu cooking?" Oksi growled "My people have been brutalized and ostracized and almost completely lost to the pages of history, yet you nonchalantly brush off everything about my culture like we're as common as the rain. Who do you think you are to treat me like this?"

"I'm sure you were much kinder to Jarilo after he ate your food," Imhotep muttered. "All the good your generosity did for him."

Oksi's shoulder blades drew back. "What the hell are you implying?"

Imhotep said nothing. He instead closed his eyes and let the warmth of Heaven's green sun wash over his skin. In his thin robes, Imhotep loved the warm embrace on his barely-covered flesh more than almost any other sensation in existence. If he didn't hate Heaven so much, he thought, surely, he could get used to this patio, this sun, this healing air.

"Answer me, damn it!" Oksi stomped forward and grabbed Imhotep's small shoulder. He spun him around.

The visage that swiveled with Imhotep's shoulders was someone else's. A ghoul took his place; his face was green, bone, desecrated and old, ribbons of shriveled flesh ravaged by decay, rotting teeth, bulging eyes somber despite their wide stare.

Oksi yelled in surprise and stumbled backwards. The brick of the wall scraped his forearm. Oksi had no idea it broke the skin; he felt nothing other than revulsion.

Imhotep—or the form Oksi had come to know as Imhotep, at least—frowned as he watched the bear-of-a-man reduced to a cub. The image of the ghoul seemed to disappear instantly, as if Oksi could only see it when he touched the chancellor's body.

"What *are you*?" Oksi's bottom lip shook his briar beard.

Imhotep cocked his head, thought for a moment, and sighed. "Ah, shit, did I not.."

The Egyptian chancellor walked to the glass door to check his reflection. He drew his hands along the pitted scars across his face, and fingers across his stubbly jawline. His finger crawled further to inspect his subtle pink lipstick, but it, too, was flawlessly applied. As he trailed back to his eyes, he realized that there was a small unevenness in the gold eye shadow on his left. It didn't matter that he had applied the concealer and primer perfectly underneath;

The gold eye shadow was not blended properly into the crease with the same care as his other eye. It was flawed *enough*.

"Ah," he sighed, "there it is."

Imhotep pulled his gold eye shadow and brush out and began to correct his blend.

"A little makeup advice, Oksi," Imhotep squinted as he applied his glamours. "It's a lot like a Monet painting. Even if it looks beautiful from far away, you should respect it with some distance. What you see from that range is what the artist intended."

He snapped his makeup pack shut and put the brush away into a small silk pouch in his robes. He slid the glass door open with a heaviness quite unlike the smokey confidence he attacked most tasks with.

"Otherwise, if you try to scrutinize it without an invitation... well, you'll just spoil the illusion for yourself."

Imhotep went back into the apartment and slid the door shut. Oksi rubbed his forehead and staggered over to the railing. He leaned his forearms against it, hunched over, and replayed the recent conversation and events in his mind over and over again.

If Robin didn't believe that her presence inside Mark Sharkman's Camera World was a projection of her psyche before, she certainly did now. With no sleep and a question filled head that began to feel more like a balloon than an appendage, she drooped in the interview swivel chair. She was a flower without rain, a child without sugar.

Robin rubbed the bridge of her nose as she slumped. "Yeah, there was... *something* there. We know that there's something on the other side of the wall. But—and I hate to talk trash about Theodore's work—driving his quartztaphore was like driving drunk."

Mark rummaged through manila envelopes and tossed papers from his desk. Robin looked down. She could hear Mark's frantic shuffling as he flit about the room. She assumed, incorrectly, that if she was in the room with him, that he'd hear her.

"I don't know of a way we can get to the other side of the wall without just marching there on one of our breaks with dynamite or something," she stood up off the chair and leaned against the walls of monitors. "That assumes our god eye lets us make those things at all. There's no way we won't get caught trying to get behind that wall, and who knows if we'll even have enough time to investigate anything in a meaningful way. And all of this even assumes that what's on the other side is worth our time. What if it isn't? What if we find absolutely nothing there related to Athena or Eris or..."

"Robin!" Mark Sharkman shouted suddenly from the other side of the room.

Robin lifted her head. Mark's toothy snout stuck out from the door frame of the Infinite Wine Hallway, and though his coal black eyes often failed to properly convey the tone of his voice, it did, in this moment, convey his urgent surprise.

Robin glared. "I've been telling you about what we did and you didn't... listen? At all? Are you kidding me, Mark?"

Mark rubbed his fin. He was still uncomfortable with the expanding circle of allies, and all the complexities that keeping secrets brought. He had already interviewed Theodore prior to summoning Robin, and he was only listening to her to make sure their events corroborated with each other. "No, no! I heard you! I promise! Please, come here. The message has changed!"

Robin's posture corrected itself. "It changed?"

"The writing on the wall! It's different now!"

Mark was telling the truth; he was multitasking during her recollection, and heard a subtle rumble from the hallway. Since all he ever knew in the hallway was wine and light, he checked the only landmark he knew: the mysterious carvings on the wall.

Together, Mark and Robin read the message:

I don' t W A NT to gO BaCK

"There's no wine or broken glass," Mark held a concerned hand over his shark maw. "No evidence that anyone came in here and took bottles off the shelf to write this. And I think this was written... just now. I heard something, and I felt... compelled to check."

Robin crossed her arms. "It's not directions anymore. It sounds like someone begging."

They shared silence. Mark's silk trench coat shuffled with his sway. "Hey, Robin, doesn't this feel... different?"

Robin looked to Mark, then looked at the lettering on the wall. The carvings were somehow more erratic and juvenile, carved with greater frustration and less focus. Before she could weigh these implications, however, an alarm began to ring in the Camera World. The lemon lights of the Infinite Wine Hallway burned red.

"What the hell?" Robin looked up.

"Oh, that's annoying," Mark sighed. "The system thinks someone's about to interact with you. I guess you were closer to being talked to then either of us realized. Sorry, Robin, but I have to send you back. I'll look into the stairwells and see if I can find anything that'll help, okay?"

Mark clicked his tooth.

*****

"Alright, that's fine," Robin said.

"Huh?"

Robin blinked. She realized she was back in the living room of her apartment. Ishta-Devata sat next to her. Her blue hand squeezed Robin's shoulder.

"Oh, sorry, Ishta, I was just..."

Robin stopped herself when she realized Oshunmare and Santa were within earshot, standing in the open kitchen. They made coffee and chatted among themselves, but drew quiet when Robin started to speak.

"I think I need coffee," Robin looked at Ishta. "To clear my head. I was out late."

Ishta nodded at both the truth, and the half truth that sat before it. "You've been spending more time with Theodore lately. I'm glad you have another human to help you feel at home here."

"Does Robin have a crush?" Oshunmare slithered into a chair.

"I'm in my forties, Oshunmare," Robin laughed.

"That doesn't mean you can't like someone!" The lizard-lady flicked her rainbow tongue into her coffee cup.

"And I'm divorced. And Theodore is..." Robin's eyelid twitched, "*...no*. I don't have a crush."

"Come on," Santa Inari clinked a coffee mug down in front of Robin. "You can tell us."

"Thank you. But, I don't think I could have a crush on someone I was competing against, anyway," Robin stared into ripples in her coffee cup. "Especially not with cameras all around us."

Ishta lowered her head, and stared at the human from underneath the frames of her hat-crushed black curls. Her vision played a new dream behind Robin. It had nothing to do with the competition, or Theodore, or Heaven. There was a new woman standing over Robin's shoulder, and she bared some resemblance to Robin. *A relative?* she thought. She squinted to keep this rare dream in focus. This was a dream buried deep within Robin, so deep that even Ishta, with her power to see the truth of people's ambitions, had difficulty bringing it into sharp focus.

The power audibly died in their apartment, and the lights cut off. This would have been more dramatic were daylight not streaming in through the sliding glass door that connected the living room and balcony.

"The power can go out in Heaven?" Robin sipped her coffee.

The lights and microwave and oven display and all manner of electronics started to strobe. The planes of the contestants faces lit erratically in the dancing lights.

"Okay, that's a little more creepy," Robin's hand, with a slight shake, set the cup down to the glass table.

After a few moments of strobing, the image of Jesus materialized in every light source. Her glowing form rose from lamps. She beamed her bearded smile from within the digital clock of the oven, and from the temperature display of the thermostat.

"Hello, my deities!" She cooed, her voice sang in unison from each of the electrical devices her face radiated from. "I just got back from Mount Sinai Spa, and let me tell you, I'm positively *glowing*!"

Robin sat up. "Mount Sinai... that's where—"

"Thou *shalt* find the time to relax there sometime," Jesus grinned, "and I'm not just saying that because they sponsor today's challenge. No, my friends, Mount Sinai is much more important than that. It's a great place, but it does have *rules* that you need to follow. If you've done your homework, then you should know that I had a summer fling with an ol' gray fox there..."

"Moses!" Robin blurted. "That's where God gave Moses the ten commandments!"

THE THIRD CHALLENGE

New Commandments

Bestow 1-to-5 primary principles upon your species
Demonstrate the delivery method of principles in 10 minute demonstration.
Sentience not required for demonstration, but will be expected in future challenges.

Working Time: 8 hours, with one 2-hour break 4 hours in.

"We know what your creatures are, and we know how they propagate... now, it's time to define them," Jesus smiled before her light-form disappeared from bulbs and LCD displays. Her voice crackled into electric whispers, "You have up to five rules to impose upon your followers. Show us what they value most, dear deities!"

Robin stared into the ripples of her coffee cup. She felt annoyance at the idea of this challenge, as if it wasn't appreciated that she had defined her humans through her actions up until this point. The spicy aroma of her hot coffee hit her nose as she breathed in. It reminded her to focus: *I don't care about winning their game anymore. Remember that. Remember...*

*****

The contestants were given less time to work on this challenge than normal. To most in the workroom, this seemed reasonable: they've already spent two challenges creating creatures they can use for this presentation and, perhaps more importantly, the rookie-gods should have an idea of the world they are working towards by now.

There was one contestant, however, who struggled almost immediately with the very notion of the challenge.

"The Internet," Zargah hovered around the dog-punk's table, his long antenna crestfallen around the sides of his head, "I have an inquiry."

The Internet rolled his eyes, which was exactly his reaction when Zargah asked for help in the first challenge. His posturing hid a positive spark of emotion in his cells, glee over the fact he was useful to someone.

"*What*?" he snarled. He also knew he could be as open as possible about his annoyance and it wouldn't translate properly to

Zargah. He found it eased him to know that the color of emotion in his tone could get lost in a language barrier.

"The word 'commandments' does not seem to translate properly in my collar," Zargah clicked in a low tone. "Can you provide synonyms? Examples? Anything to get me started?"

"Well, I mean, it's just rules. You're giving rules to your species."

"Rules about what?"

The Internet boggled. "Well, rules about life, and ethics."

"But I have not made a society yet," Zargah mumbled. "We haven't yet a world to enforce rules upon."

The Internet froze for a moment. He mulled over this chicken-and-the-egg scenario, shook his head, and leaned back over the inanimate frame of his discarded. "You've got 10 minutes, man. This is also an opportunity to show off the start of a society that receives the rules. Use your imagination."

Zargah looked around the room at the other contestants. He saw Imhotep scrawling a quill across papyrus. "We're writing rules and reading them to the judges?"

The Internet turned and stared at Zargah. "No, like, it has to be a spectacle, too. Like Moses. It has to have impact."

Zargah tilted his head. "Who is Moses?"

The Internet looked up to the ceiling. "Yeah. You wouldn't know that, would you? Alright, uh. Shit. You're hella lucky I'm here. I doubt anyone else can do this for you."

The Internet's god eye snaked out of the palm of his hand, circled his wrist, then pointed towards the table. In a few moments, the eye blazed a copy of the King James version of the Bible.

"The Ten Commandments is a story that's really well known on Earth and, I'm gonna guess, in Heaven," The Internet flipped through the pages with some smug glee that he was able to recreate it so well. "Since Jesus is such a star and all, you know? You're lucky the Bible is free on the web. The rules and Jesus's challenge intro were all references to that story."

Zargah picked up the Bible. His yellow dual-pupil eyes scanned the text, foreign symbols that made little sense to him. "This whole book is the ten commandments?"

"N-no, that's just one part. Hell, it's an *interpretation* of just one part, too."

"What's the rest of this book, then?"

"Well, it's other stories. The whole book is a religious text. Parables to learn from, and stuff," The Internet rested his elbow on the table and held his muzzle in it. His actual annoyance was quieter than the display he put on before, "Listen, all you need to do is make a story about the rules you want your species to live by. That's all. Stop over-thinking and get to work."

Zargah flipped through pages of text that he couldn't read, a fact that The Internet forgot (or, more accurately, didn't care enough about to remember.) Zargah thought he understood The Internet, though, so he put the dog's advice and the book together and came to the wrong conclusion.

"Okay," the alien said confidently. "Thank you."

Theodore watched their engagement with some amusement. When the bug-man shuffled back to his work desk, Theodore did a quick scan of the room and realized that Taninim was missing.

"Anyone know where Dragon Hetfield went?" he asked.

"Oh, he said what he wanted to do was too big for in here," The Internet said as he soldered circuit boards, "he's out in the hallway somewhere."

Theodore, at a loss for what he wanted to do in this challenge, decided he should take a peek at Taninim's stage rehearsal. *At best, I'll be inspired. At worst, I'll be entertained,* he thought.

Fix You Up

Despite the tumult of his supernatural life up to this point, Jack's surgery was surprisingly simple. Surrounded by spirits in surgeon's masks and baby-blue polo shirts, all that the "doctors" had to do was shove the broken appendage into a small glass box. Once the rubber lip of the box's opening sealed around his rind skin, they pumped pure Heaven's air straight into the glass container. Shredded forearm fibers curled back into the proper flexor shape. In moments, his fingers twitched back to life.

Once healed, the doctors quickly wheeled Jack's portable bed back to the break area so that he could change into his work uniform, and left him with a bill that would take weeks to pay off. Those weeks started right now, per the agreement Jack made to get his arm fixed.

Which would mean no food unless he begged, no rent unless he borrowed, no time off unless he died.

He moved boxes and pallets and cargo and drowned out the sounds of scraping machinery and propaganda spewing drones and the beeping of forklifts in reverse and the cries of his coworkers collapsing in nearby aisles. Everything receded to the background of his mind as the math of his life poisoned him. It shriveled his skin beyond his years and dulled the light of his eyes.

The side of a box that he tried to lift slipped out of his grip. It crashed into the ground and its contents shattered audibly. Just based off the sound, Jack knew it was valuable yet hidden, some expensive trinket from an online store for a person that could afford it, lost to his own clumsiness and busy mind. The cost would likely would come of his paycheck. It was one more number to add up.

He did the math of his life over and over in his head until he couldn't take it anymore.

"I don't have a reason to live. I don't *want* to live anymore."

Beelzebub Boxing had strict protocols and authority when it came to any talk of depression or self-harm. Now that he'd said it loud enough to be heard, his words cut through to local microphones. The drones, and their concerned TV-screen faces, descended upon him quickly. They tased him and left burnt pumpkin flesh all over his anatomy, and when he could no longer move, dragged his large, limp frame to the company sponsored asylum.

Attached to Beelzebub Boxing's northeast corner, the company asylum is a safe place for troubled workers to calm down. Luxurious padded cells, coated in the calming scents of lavender and basil, await the temporary inmates, with a TV screen high on the vaulted ceiling for viewing. The TV only had three channels: a company propaganda station that covered the latest in stock prices and innovations, a station for classical music, and a daytime TV station that showed local news ("It's another hot day in Hell!" the grinning cyclops in a bow-tie slapped a map covered in sun icons, "Get your shorts out, everybody!") and trashy daytime TV. The channels can be changed by saying "next" or "back." These simple, repetitive voice commands were found by researchers to have a numbing, soothing effect on the afflicted.

Jack was fitted into a sky-blue, company branded straight jacket, and shoved into a cell. The door slammed shut, and the demon security guard looked through a small viewing window.

"You can go back to the floor when you sing the magic phrase," security said. He cleared his throat and stretched his lips into a rehearsed smile that bared all his fangs: "*It's time to put your / emotions in a box / and get back to work!*"

Jack crumpled onto his back, swathed in restraint, cushioned by the padded floor. The demon slid the Judas hole shut. Jack was alone now. The TV on the ceiling showed a gray-haired man who waved his hands at a group of violinists.

"Next," Jack said. His eyes were faint pinpoints.

The company-run network went over the CEO's philanthropy. A woman named Santa Inari bragged about a tree she personally planted in Hell. A homeless bird-man stumbled into the shot in the distance, and was quickly beaten out of frame by security. Santa Inari never turned her head.

"Next," Jack said. The light of his eyes were diffused, a blur of soft light that looked as if it could be smothered out completely by any errant breeze.

The Next Great Deity appeared.

"Ignore what she's making for a minute," Theodore sucked up the smoke from his cigarette. "I don't get why she's here."

Jack realized it was the same show that he saw a commercial for in the break room the day before.

As Theodore talked, the show cut in footage of Santa Inari as she fit her cocktail dresses onto her mindshare species. Jack made this connection, too: that it was the same woman on the last channel, the CEO of Beelzebub Boxing's parent company.

"She said she owns Inari Inc or something, right?" Theodore narrated as Santa was shown to use her god eye to create waves of heat to iron out wrinkles in the dress. "If she's really a CEO, why does she need to be here on a reality TV show?"

"Yes," Jack whispered.

"She's just taking this chance away from someone less fortunate," the scene cut back to Theodore. His lit cigarette bounced on his bottom lip as he talked. "I wonder if she even tried out. Rich people buy their way into positions they didn't earn all the time. Since everything she's made on this show thus far is about money and commerce and shit, it wouldn't surprise me."

"Yes," Jack sat up. His light-eyes focused.

"She probably already lives in Heaven," Theodore shook his head, drew the cigarette from his lip, and exhaled a smoke ring. "And still isn't satisfied with what she's got."

"Yes! Yes! Yes!" Jack flexed so hard that the straight jacket exploded off his body. He stood there in the nude, his pumpkin muscles ripped and tense, his eyes burned bright, and his body quaked with new ideological purpose. "That's exactly how I feel! YES! Why are we stuck down here when they can't appreciate what they have? Why can't they share? That's where that air that healed my arm is from, right? How many people could be saved if we all had access to that?"

Jack ran around his cell and fist pumped and shouted his burgeoning manifesto so loud that he could no longer hear the TV.

"SECURITY!" Jack shouted, "It'stimetoputyouremotionsinabox andgetbacktowork!"

The demon slid the viewing window open with some hesitance. No one had ever yelled the magic phrase with such vigor before, and not so quickly after being put in a padded cell.

"You're supposed to sing it," he said, his eyes cast down to avoid looking at Jack's attractive and completely work-inappropriate form. "And what the hell, man. That security jacket was company property. You know that's gonna cost ya."

"What's *The Next Great Deity*?" Jack pressed his pumpkin face against the Judas hole. "Tell me about it!"

"It's just a reality TV show," the guard turned his head as Jack got closer. "The only reason they're showing it is because Inari Corp's CEO is a contestant this season. It's usually, like, college students and creators-in-training that make it on there."

"Do you know anyone that's ever been on it?"

The guard looked back into the zig-zag smile of Jack. His brow crumpled. "No? Of course not. I don't even watch the show."

"Do you know anyone that's ever tried out for it? Do you know anyone that's been given the chance?"

"N-no..." the guard rubbed the back of his horned head, "I don't think I do..."

Jack pushed into the door, his lit-up eyes and smile ate the entire frame of the viewing window. "I want to go back to work. Please, let me go back."

The demon-guard seemed more disturbed by Jack's sudden enthusiasm than he did by his depression when he came to the asylum. Jack was granted his release and fitted into a new uniform, and the spring in his step and the eagerness in his lifts and sprints on the box-filled floor made him a model employee from a metrics standpoint.

It wasn't that he no longer heard the cries of his fellow workers. It wasn't that he loved the act of taking his body beyond the limits it was meant to perform. It wasn't that he enjoyed the drones' ever-watchful eyes. There was only one thing that motivated Jack now, and he had to work a little bit more to get it.

During his mandatory break, he sat shoulder to shoulder with a crowd of fellow workers, all dead-eyed as they waited for their reprieve to end. Even their breaks felt like imprisonment, measured bubbles of silence between periods of mandatory labor. Jack wrapped his big, built arms around the shoulders of two men, brought them just a little closer to the TV, and whispered:

"Do you know anyone that's ever truly made it out of Hell?"

They couldn't think of anyone. And they kept thinking about that fact for the rest of their shifts.

A Sugary Treat

Michael walked to the bedroom of The Producer with a silver platter balanced upon his fingertips. His free hand knocked on the door, then slid behind his lower back to push his posture into elegant alignment.

"Your breakfast, sir," Michael's eyes lidded among the floating shapes that made up his ever shifting, barely tangible face.

"Come in!" The Producer said. "What's going in my gullet this morning?"

Michael pushed the door open. "Pumpkin pie, sir."

The Producer always kept himself in low light. Even when alone, the blinds were drawn, and the lamps were off. The only illumination in the room came from the daylight that crept in through the corners of the window in defiance, and from the small digital lights on power switches and laptops scattered around the room. Each source of light, small as it may be, shined on the edges of The Producer's metal musculature, reflected across his sharp surface.

"Oh, I do love a good pie," The Producer drew his silk robe up over strong shoulders. "And all that fat and sugar gives me such good energy."

That wasn't true, and Michael knew this. The Producer's frame did not need the starchy-sweet density he claimed it did. If The Producer never ate at all, he'd still go on living without any trouble. His love of food was purely psychological, but Michael would not be the man to tell him that; he would not say it to his face, not over the phone, not in a greeting card, not ever.

Michael lifted the silver lid to reveal a gold plate and four pie slices, each with a dollop of cream in the shape of numbers to indicate what order the slices were to be eaten in.

"Enjoy, sir."

"Remind me," The Producer sat down at his desk, his fingers twitching in anticipation, "what was the first ingredient of the recipe?"

Michael did not hesitate in his answer. "Your question, as ordered, sir."

"Repeat it to me."

This was a test Michael had been forced into many times before. He leaned over to the side of The Producer's polished head and whispered the same words he whispered into the flour and eggs and cream and all the things his master would eat: "What threatens Heaven?"

The pie vibrated briefly on the plate in response to Michael's voice.

"Let's find out," The Producer moaned with delight as he lifted the first slice of pie. Metal teeth bit into the tip of the pie. He pulled his head back. A small slit of paper was between his teeth. He seized it between his fingers and unfolded it.

"Lucifer has been discovered," The Producer read aloud. He set the plate down and covered his mouth, lost in contemplation for long enough that Michael began to fear that this was truly it, The Producer has given up on this season, on this world.

"Should I be afraid?" he asked his butler. "In your opinion."

Michael cleared his throat and adjusted the knot of his tie.

"The Eris threat seemed more problematic to me," Michael kept his gaze transfixed on the window that The Producer's playmate jumped out of earlier. He felt sorry for her. "You tackled that head-on, though. I don't see why you'd be scared of Jesus and Lucifer's relationship more than Eris's attack on you."

"True," The Producer mumbled. "I just worry about compromising a loyal companion in border patrol, you know? I'd hate to have to ruin this season just because I lose the captain's subordination. It's been so entertaining thus far, but you really don't come across someone like Lucifer that often. Someone that really drinks the kool-aid, you know what I mean?"

Michael watched The Producer's forearm flex and tense. His gold fingers began to curl in, as they did when they removed the girl from reality the night before. The butler was thankful that his body didn't sweat the way that most creatures did.

"This is true," Michael said simply. "It would be a shame to see such a unique season of *The Next Great Deity* end abruptly."

Moments passed as The Producer shook his head from side to side. He eventually shrugged. Relief washed over Michael as The Producer's arm relaxed.

The Producer bit down on another slice of pie, and withdrew another sheet of paper.

"At a bar..." he read.

Another slice. Another bite. Another paper.

"Via an employee..."

Slice. Bite. Paper.

"And a pumpkin," The Producer rubbed his chin, the metal-on-metal sound scraped and echoed in the room. "Pumpkin? I've called people I was sweet on 'Pumpkin' before. It must mean a crush of some kind, right?"

"Probably," Michael didn't ask questions about the fortunes his cooking predicted. He just made the food and hoped for the best.

"Hrm. An employee, one that has a crush, met Lucifer at a bar..." The Producer stood and leaned forward on his desk. "The warning must be that he's going to tell his crush about Lucifer. I think I know who that is, I'm sad to say. He's a favorite of mine, too. What a pity."

It wasn't hard for Theodore to find Taninim. Though The Internet's directions were vague to a point, if one really wants to find the scaled musician, all you have to do is listen. Outside the workroom, at the corner of the hallway where the guitar strumming is at its loudest, there he was: the dragon-man of imagination, surrounded by his band of draconus.

Theodore stared at the lifeless speaker-mounted lizards. When they lived on stage, they played and sang with such vigor that one could believe they were always alive. Outside the television spotlight, they were slumped on the floor, animatronics of flesh, dead-eyed and soundless as they waited for new songs to play.

"Hey, scale-friend," Theodore turned the corner with his hands in his pockets. "Mind if I hang with you a bit?"

"Ah?" Taninim spun around, his nose-to-horn chain rattled against his toothy-maw. "Hello! Theodore! Of course, always."

Theodore rested his elbow atop Taninim's dragon-scaled speaker, the same one used to summon his dragon-band in the past two challenges. He leaned against it, and crossed his legs. "So what's up? You must be working on something huge to come all the way out here."

Taninim strummed a muted chord, then stood in silence long enough for Theodore to notice. His forest of sharp, dagger-like teeth may have etched an eternal snarl across his face, but his cool-blue eyes, cast down across the silver strings of his guitar, were burdened with thought. Theodore didn't need his years of poker experience to read that there was more than just chords and scales on the dragon-man's mind.

"Theodore. A reverse bend is just like a normal guitar bend. Did you know that?"

Theodore raised an eyebrow. "Sorry, Tan. I don't play guitar. I know some basics, but my heart was always in percussion and piano."

Taninim rolled his muscled shoulder and raised his red hands into the air. "Really? That's a shame. That means you'll never be able to do... THIS!"

Taninim strummed his claw tips across the string, and the amp that Theodore leaned on began to rumble. The human's eyes widened and he hopped off the speaker.

While standing next to the dragon-guitarist, Theodore watched as the amp unfurled and grew into rocky terrain. Lava began to eek out of the tip. The hallway turned red and hot as a miniature volcano, barely contained within the walls, folded into view.

"Have I told exactly you what I am?"

The red glow of the volcano saturated Taninim's scales. Embers floated past his crown of horns. Theodore considered that this is the way the dragon-man was always supposed to look: surrounded by the heat of his own power, fearless and bold.

"I am not just a dragon," he said, "I'm an imaginary friend. I am *proud* of that. There is a child out there that needs the world and wonder that I provide him."

Taninim looked down at his guitar. Hesitation crept at the scaled edges of his brow. It was an expression that didn't fit him nearly as well as the one he wore before.

"I can't always be there for him, though. He faces a dragon larger than me. Even if he survives it, he will grow up and it will be more work for him to retain his curious imagination, perhaps harder than it would have been had he led a normal life. My world... the world I am creating for him on this show, is for him to enjoy long after I fade away. I want him to live a long and happy life in a world made for him."

The dragon-man turned his head. Flames of confidence licked at the edges of his snarl. "Theodore. I'm telling you this because I don't want you to feel bad when I win. My goals are noble, and I'm sorry that I have to compete against you to achieve them."

Theodore smirked. Taninim strummed again and the volcano folded back into itself, nary a drop a lava left outside. The room cooled quickly.

"Hey, I noticed something," Theodore said. "You didn't have your god-eye out when you did that."

Taninim twiddled at the strings on his guitar to make sure they were in tune. "I made the amp and the volcano with the god eye, but the act of transitioning between the two is my own power. It is my belief that everything in the universe can be moved as long as you know the chords and scales that resonate with them."

To demonstrate, he played a small arpeggio. Theodore's cotton shirt tugged with just enough force to cause him to stumble forward a bit.

"And I do mean *everything*."

Theodore did not believe in magic, and did not believe that such an ability would work back home in Queens. But here in Heaven, where everything is wrong and everyone defies expectations, he found this ability, at once, powerful and charming. He recalled that Taninim was the first person he met in Heaven. Now that he saw the guitarist's true ability, he surmised that he must have been playing the guitar, as he always was, when Theodore crashed into him through the hotel window. It was a safe bet—Taninim was always noodling, always strumming, always testing the world around him with his songs, regardless of what people thought of him. Like a snake that always tastes the air, Taninim always practiced his guitar.

Theodore respected that.

"Taninim, I don't think I'll mind if you win."

Theodore returned to the workroom.

The workroom's obstinate lack of color was one of its most intimidating features. Perhaps if its marble tables and ivory flooring and floating white lights were meant for a different purpose—maybe dining or a fancy party—he could understand its design, appreciate its pristine and oppressive simplicity. But as the site of creativity, the bleached room created an atmosphere that fostered only anxiety, the kind an artist finds when staring at a blank page.

Theodore's conversation with Taninim was exactly what he needed to combat the suffocating air of the blank workroom. Seeing the dragon-guitarist's bombastic vision served as a reminder, he thought, on the importance of maintaining balance in how he approached both his work on the show, and his work to undo it. If he allowed the darkness of the show's machinations to distract from his creation, than he'd be eliminated and unable to do either.

If I'm gonna be here, he surmised, *might as well have at least a little fun.*

He looked up to the quartztaphore, which sat on his table. He looked into its rocky, purple head, to the jagged rocks that jutted out where eyes would normally lay. He rested his hands on either side of the table, tapped his fingers on the marble surface, and inspected around the edge of its sharp chin.

And he stared for quite awhile, with no particular idea bubbling to the surface of his mind.

Come on, brain. It's not enough to just hear a rousing speech, Theodore's mustached lip inflated. *Where the hell do I even start with this challenge?*

Theodore then realized that the room was much less lively than usual, and it wasn't just because it had lost two contestants. While there was certainly a void where Jarilo's energy—be it angst or bubbly outbursts—used to be, the bigger contributor to the atmosphere was the nature of the challenge itself. Theodore looked to his left and saw Imhotep and Zargah quietly hunched over their tables. The Egyptian chancellor scrawled upon papyrus with a quill. Any actual construction work Imhotep performed seemed to always come near the end of the challenge, after he had meticulously laid down the details of his vision in notes. Given that the day's challenge was more philosophical than physical, Theodore was unsure if he'd even see the resheps in the workroom at all.

Zargah, meanwhile, rubbed the long fingers of his four hands onto four small, evenly spaced sphere-keyboards. The green orbs were grooved and Zargah stroked the lanes with rapid, practiced motions. Each sphere had a wire that snaked into a green, metal rectangle on the work table. The rectangular top, which sloped asymmetrically to one side, had an opening from which it printed a smooth, rubbery material. When Theodore squinted, he saw a small brass gear wildly running from side to side within the rectangle, and small spider-like limbs within the gear weaved the material into existence. The material contained writing in Zargah's native language; a series of glyphs made from tiny, needle-like stabs in the rubbery paper. When he considered the motion of the printer in the rectangle, and when he considered how similar its motions were to the way Zargah's mouth parts idly cleaned themselves, he gained a small understanding of how the alien's language had formed.

As he stared at the foreign methods of Zargah's typewriter, a new thought twitched his eyelid. *Well, hold on a minute,* he thought. *Why are we building rules without society first?*

Theodore turned his head to Robin. Robin appeared much like Imhotep did—hunched over the work table, furiously writing notes on a single sheet of paper with a ballpoint pen. The instruments may have been different, but they were otherwise identical in their slumped postures and quickly scribbling hands. The scratching sound of quill and pen against worktable grew louder in Theodore's ear as he became more and more aware that the act of writing surrounded him from all sides.

There were other noises that slurred together with the pen-scrawling. Santa Inari had surrounded and covered her work table with pie-chart-covered dry erase boards, and the squeak of red marker to smooth surface stabbed at Theodore's brain every few moments. It appeared to Theodore that she was responding to her negative criticism from the last challenge with a one-woman board meeting.

Is this just supposed to be tenets of the religion, or is the assumption that this will rule society as a whole? he thought. *Are we allowed to leave room for multiple religions on the same planet?*

Theodore's brow furrowed as he scanned desperately for a process that didn't resemble high school homework. Ishta-Devata had no notes on her table, no paper or pen. Instead, she had surrounded herself with aquariums of water. She would dip her finger into a tank, then move her hand over to a pile of sand on her work table, then let a drop fall from the tip. The drop splashed into the sand, and Ishta watched patiently for some change in its makeup. The sand darkened with the added moisture, but otherwise made no magical change. Her soft smile dropped for a moment in a hint of frustration, and her god eye snaked from her sari sleeve in response.

Are we just supposed to infer that society's already formed? Theodore watched Ishta's god eye shoot lasers of creation into the sand. It occurred to him he knew almost nothing about Ishta's species as an intelligence, and wasn't sure how a pile of sand could both correct that and provide a solution to the challenge they collectively faced. *Do they expect us to reveal how we envision a society built around this religion through these rules?*

Theodore looked to The Internet, who, with rubber gloves and safety goggles, carefully affixed a lens into the flat, squat head of a new robot he'd constructed. Was it a projector? Was he going to give a PowerPoint presentation to the judges? Theodore didn't know. Just beyond The Internet's work table, Oshunmare held pins between her lizard lips, and pulled at a needle and thread on a new dress. Both seemed lost in projects indistinguishable from previous entries, and wholly incongruent with the direction others in the room had taken.

Is this challenge really about "rules" at all, or is it more an excuse for further detail? And if so, what definitions are they really looking for if we haven't been given an opportunity for more world building first?

Csodaszarvas would exit and enter the workroom repeatedly. Each time that he returned, he'd have a new prop in his mouth— a bag of yellow seeds, folded ceremonial robes, a bag of dirt. It left Theodore with the impression that the wonder-deer was planning something too large for the workroom and, much like Taninim, had left to craft its individual parts elsewhere. One thing Theodore never spotted in possession of the deer deity, however, was a prepared speech.

Why are the rules for this challenge so open ended and vague? Theodore turned around and pushed himself up into a seated position on his work table. He folded his hands in thought, and let his legs swing below the lip of the table. *I mean, I get it, they want bite-sized presentations, but this just seems like such a crappy way to cover such an important topic.*

Theodore closed his eyes and swayed, then rested his head on the quartztaphore's shoulder.

And why does it seem like I'm the only one struggling with this?

He turned his head to Oksi. The bear-of-a-man stood in front of his Pewrep, shoulders hunched, glaring into the creature's dead eyes. Between them, they shared the expression.

Okay, Theodore exhaled. There was a strange sense of relief in seeing Oksi's distant stare. *Maybe I'm not the only one.*

It's not working, Oksi thought.

He stared at his albino pewrep. He had given it a shaved dogwood baton to hold near his heart. As long as the pewrep held this stick, he could pray and communicate with the spirits of all things created by Oksi's hand. He could learn what berries to eat, what water to drink from, what creatures would fight him if he got too close.

And that's it. That's all Oksi could come up with.

There is no way this presentation will last 10 minutes, he thought. *It won't last five.*

He grabbed the stick from one massive pewrep paw, posed the pewrep's arms across its chest, then stuck it back in its sausage-fingered grip. Oksi tried to figure out what pose was the most imposing, while still appearing spiritual and respectful.

They're gonna say it's too ill-defined, the bearded man began to sweat. *It's too out of touch, too old, too reliant on the opinions of individual spirits.*

Oksi slumped and buried his face into the pewrep's shoulder.

There's nothing I can do that will be good enough for these modern gods, his growl was muffled by fur and mass. *No one respects the way things used to be.*

When things got tough and Oksi began to feel his emotions and anger pulse in every direction, he would decide to create food with his god eye. Food is necessary for every living thing, and for this particular god, it had another property: it centered him.

And when someone ate his food, it renewed him.

Oksi turned to his work table. His god eye slithered from his mouth. With the trinket's lasers of creation, he made an Ainu twist on veggie burgers—buns of rice with a meat patty made of an assortment of cooked water peppers and spices. He bit in greedily, and tasted the marination of fish sauce in the vegetables, a subtle coating and a nuanced detail only capable through the most intimate clarity of his own mind. The god eye only ever seemed to be in perfect sync with the bear-of-a-man when he focused on food—a fact that frustrated him endlessly.

But not enough to keep him away from his old habits.

He made a second burger, thought about those most vulnerable in the competition, and sought out Csodaszarvas. He found the wonder-deer in the cafeteria, chewing on a salad.

"Do you want to try a vegetarian burger?"

The deer blinked and looked at the burger, then to Oksi, then back to the burger. He could smell the fish oil before Oksi even reached his table. "No, thank you."

"Are you sure? It's pretty good, the patty is made out of—"

"Do you really have time to make that?"

Oksi paused. He felt a lump in his throat.

"I'm sorry," Csodaszarvas winced and looked down at his salad. "I'm behind on my own work and, after being in the bottom yesterday, I'm really not in a good place at the moment. That was rude of me. I'm stressed. I apologize. I'm going to finish this and head back. Thank you for the offer."

I cannot escape my identity, Oksi thought. He dragged himself back to the workroom, and ran into Taninim along the way.

"I already ate," Taninim said as he wiped away some lava from his teeth. "I also hate fish. Sorry, friend!"

I am Ainu. I will always be Ainu, he thought as he entered the workroom.

"Not really hungry right now, sorry," Theodore popped the arm of his quartztaphore off its torso, like a child removes an action figure's limb to study its construction. "But, thanks."

I embrace that about me. I am proud of myself and my heritage.

"I had a snack a few minutes ago, and that's about all I have time for," Robin sighed as she scrawled notes down in a notebook. "This challenge is rough."

But the world has wandered on without us.

"That's so sweet of you!" Oshunmare flicked her tongue out. "I'm sorry, sweetie, but Ishta, Santa and I all *just* got back from lunch."

How much more do I have to suffer in a world not made for my beliefs?

"I apologize," Zargah's translation collar clicked, "I have discovered that Earth food makes my intestinal tract rebel against me."

How much longer must my people dwindle on Earth? What amount of punishment is enough for me, for my Utari?

"Hell no," The Internet snarled. "Fuck off."

There was only one person left that he hadn't offered a meal to, Imhotep, and he already knew the type of condescension awaited him if he tried that road again. Instead, Oksi ate the burger himself as he limped out of the workroom. He threw the plate to the ground. It shattered. He stared at the individual pieces, counted them, and apologized to the spirit it held within. Heaven's air healed it back together.

He went into a bathroom in the hallway, locked himself in a stall, sat on porcelain, and cried, loud and long. He punched the tiled floor under him, which broke and reformed in bloody pieces along with his knuckles. He did this until he heard the bathroom door open. He choked back a sob and remained perfectly still, as if he were exchanging silence to make up for the sounds of his woe inadequately muffled by the bathroom door.

Imhotep knocked on the stall.

"You're never going to win like that," he said. "Pick yourself up, old one. You have work to do."

Even Imhotep's footsteps were light and cool, undaunted by what came before, or what lies ahead. As quietly as he entered, he left again.

Oksi choked back his own embarrassment, and wondered why Imhotep would even bother to encourage him. This troubled him more than any barb the Egyptian god had thrown his way.

"I can't go home yet," Oksi looked into the lines on his palms.

Ritst was a notoriously hard worker, and everyone in the editing room knew it. His speed and skill at dissecting footage, delegating tasks and isolating problems was born of the perfect combination of practice, experience, and passion. When one watched *The Next Great Deity*, one was really watching Ritst's curated opinion on the show itself.

So in the rare moments when Ritst's work pace drifted down to uninspired speeds, his staff noticed. And no one noticed the pump of Ritst's mental brakes sooner, or was more profoundly impacted by it, than Kærast. That was his job, after all.

"Is everything alright, sir?" the guppy-assistant circled his superior's tall chair. "Would you like coffee? Tea? Salmon bagels?"

And he *loved* his job.

Ritst's wall-eyed stare oozed down. He only half-heard his assistant, and it wasn't until Kærast's squishy face popped through the other side of his holographic user-interface that Ritst fully processed the sounds made in his direction.

"Oh! Oh, uh," Ritst rubbed his wide head, "no, I think... what I need..."

He glanced back down at the guppy, whose face was lit in the blue lights of monitors, and struggled to finish his sentence, arrested by the small life that orbited him. *What cute little cheeks you have. God. Especially those orange and blue flecks around the corner of your jaw and ear-fins. How are you real?*

Ritst shook his head, and mentally returned to a professional world view.

"...is a nap. I've really burnt the midnight oil, haven't I? Do you mind taking over while I catch a 15-minute snooze?"

Kærast found it quite out of character for Ritst to ask for such a thing. Part of the guppy was glad—perhaps the big guy was finally looking after himself—but there was also a nagging feeling that he couldn't quite shake. Ritst's eyes seemed weighed by more than the hours spent in a chair. Though, Kærast considered, if one works to the point that not even Heaven's air can keep up, that must grind down the spirit, too.

"Gladly, sir!" Kærast, in a rather impressive display of acrobatics and strength in spite of his height, leapt over the console. He landed directly in front of Ritst. His guppy head, while standing, only just barely cleared his boss's thighs. "I'll take over from here..."

Ritst looked down. If Kærast raised his webbed hands, they could easily rest on Ritst's knees. It would be a short climb for the guppy to sit in his lap. This was an image Ritst had lingered on before, but was never so close to it, so unintentionally so.

"I-if you want me to," Kærast didn't plan his landing like this, and when he looked into the tired yellow eyes of his boss, he worried he had embarrassed him. But, his boss didn't have the energy of a man embarrassed. His eyes drooped. He didn't have energy at all.

"Thank you," the head-editor used the last bit of his will to pat Kærast's head. He pushed himself up to shaky legs, and slumped off towards an unoccupied meeting room.

Kærast watched him go. Normally, this is where he'd admire the toned, exiting 10-foot frame of his brown-scaled superior. But the drag in his step and the slump in his posture churned the guppy's stomach. All that he could do now was work hard for Ritst, and show him how dependable he was.

*****

Ritst stopped walking halfway down the rivet-covered corridor and leaned against the wall. Images of Lucifer replayed in his mind. The conclusions that he came to—that the captain of Heaven's Border Patrol was in some secret relationship with one of Heaven's most famous celebrities—baffled him. And that it was *them*, the classic protagonist and antagonist of the Bible, a famous rivalry that all creatures in Heaven and Earth are aware of, baffled him more. How could the existence of Lucifer in Heaven be a secret? How could their relationship not be the most known thing about both of them? He hadn't slept. The alcohol of the night before and the questions of the day flurried his anxiety even further.

I'm not going to be able to keep this a secret forever, he thought. As soon as the words bubbled in the back of his mind, he snorted a laugh that was at once directed at the world, and himself. *Am I thinking about Lucifer's relationship, or Kærast? I can't even tell the difference anymore.*

His blurred vision focused on the empty hallway ahead of him. He pushed himself back to balance.

"I suppose I'll have to face both," he whispered to himself, "at some point."

The two steps that he took seemed, in his mind, heroic, as heroic as any sleep deprived man can feel when he pushes his body forward on the power of duty alone. Just twenty, thirty more feet and he'll be at the door, and he can sprawl across the carpet, and let his dreams repair the frayed ends of his mind.

Cold metal wrapped around the side of Ritst's neck and waist and inner thighs and ankles and wrists. In an instant he was coiled by chains and slammed back into the very same wall he looked to for support. The chains constricted and dug into his rubbery skin, bursting scales from flesh.

"We should talk, you and I," a voice rattled from the wall. Ritst looked around but saw no one else. He tried to turn and look behind him, but the chains wound so tight that even he, a creature of size and strength beyond most in Heaven, couldn't budge.

The triumph of walking on despite his body's aches suddenly seemed so trivial.

"Who..." he gurgled against the chains, "who are you?"

"Come now, do I really sound that different in person? I know speakers do funny things to voices. I read an article one time about how everyone thinks their voice is higher on recordings because of the way sound originates inside the body, but I never felt that way. Then again, I don't really have bones to rattle my voice the way most of you do. Also, that wouldn't affect *your* interpretation of *my* voice, would it? Science is so strange. It's a good thing I'm not subject to it."

Ritst's eyelids spread wide. The shake of the rivets in the wall as the voice spoke... the disconnected speech and affectations... the chains. The rattle of the chains.

This had to be The Producer.

"Ah. I get sidetracked so easily. Good thing I brought notes to keep myself on task," Ritst heard the crinkle of paper behind his head. "You're staff. You're not part of the show, and this whole espionage thing is no fun if you're not in front of the camera."

"Wha..." Ritst stammered, "what do you mean? I haven't done anything!"

The chains pulled tighter. Ritst gritted his triangular teeth in pain.

"No, I'm more concerned about what's going on in your heart. What you were *planning* to do."

Ritst's heart raced. He hadn't told anyone. He had barely even began to *think* about telling anyone. Does this mean The Producer not only *knows* about Lucifer, but that he could hear his thoughts?

"If I'm not being clear: Lucifer is out of bounds."

Ritst felt the bones of his hips compress. Blood dripped out from shattered scales. Heaven tried to put the scales back in, but the chain continued to pull and block their path.

"You've been loyal to me for more seasons than just about anyone else, and I believe I can forgive you this once for your mental transgression. That's one more transgression than I normally grant individuals, mind you, and only because I *cannot* be bothered right now to find a new person to do that twisty...scaly... roomy thing that you do."

Ritst felt another scale rip from his neck, but he suspected that this one was plucked from him, and not pressed out by the chain.

"You can still be replaced, of course," The Producer said. "It's not impossible, I just don't want to be bothered mid-season. It's like cleaning your roommate's dishes, you know? I could do it, it's not hard for me, but I would rather they do it themselves."

"I... I promise I won't do anything..." Ritst choked out. "P-please... I love working on this show... you know that, don't you?"

"I do, but this is pressing enough that I felt the need to make myself extra clear. I am a proactive person, you see. I'm ready to face any new challenges thrown at me."

There was a new presence. Finally, Ritst felt he could pin-point the origin of the voice, and he could see the shadows of a humanoid form in the corner. And it was all there, right next to his head. Somehow, The Producer was right behind him, despite there being no space between Ritst and the wall. He hissed into his earhole, metal teeth nibbling around rubber skin:

"If that name escapes your lips, I'll kill the guppy."

Tears filled Ritst's eyes.

"I'll erase him from this world completely." It was a promise delivered with unyielding commination.

"Wh-what?!" Ritst's sharp teeth gnashed as he struggled in the chains, "Why?! Why him?!"

"Oh, don't be an idiot, Ritst. You two are *adorable* together. Or you will be, anyway, when you both quit making excuses for each other."

The chains let go. Ritst dropped to his hands and knees, free of his physical bindings. He found his soul, however, crushed in entirely new ones.

"In short, why don't you tell him about the relationship you want to have, instead of mouthing off about someone else's business? Doesn't that make more sense?" The Producer's voice again came from everywhere and nowhere. It smothered Ritst into the ground with his tears and blood. Heaven returned his wounded scales to his body, but the damage beyond his flesh had already been done. "I think it does. I hope you agree."

*****

Fifteen minutes passed, then twenty. Kærast's concern possessed him, and he left the console in search of Ritst. It didn't take long—Ritst's sobbing, though stifled by his rubbery flesh as he laid in a fetal position on the floor, nonetheless carried through echoes along the metal corridor. Kærast's concerned pace revved from power walk to run once he found his superior.

"Ritst! What happened? Talk to me!" he slid down to his knees and shook his boss's shoulders.

Ritst raised his forearms open just enough for the light to hit, just enough to see Kærast and make sure he was real. "I think... I think I need more than fifteen minutes before I can go back... I'm sorry..."

Kærast didn't know what to say. Never in the years of working on the show had he seen any sort of vulnerability from his boss. He didn't know if he should report this to HR, or send Ritst home and take over his duties, or wait for further instructions. There is no company policy or training video, it turns out, that can prepare you for discovering your boss, who is also your secret crush, collapsed on the floor in a pool of his own tears.

So Kærast did what he knew best. He stayed there with him and held Ritst's large head in his lap until the tears were dry enough for him to ask: "Do you want some coffee, or tea, or salmon bagels?"

The camera arms whirled around their subjects, eager to capture their passions and fears into their virtual memory. With a new challenge brings a new opportunity for the shark-interviewer to break down the contestants' visions and emotions.

"I'm so fuckin' lucky, man," The Internet laughed, though his crossed arms betrayed any sense of comfort he tried to project.

"How's that?" Mark clicked his pen.

"So this challenge is about 'rules,' right? In the first challenge I got fuckin' roasted for my video, told I was way too on the nose and shit. Imagine if I didn't get that feedback, I might've been tempted to walk out there and just read a list to the judges."

For the first time that Mark could remember, The Internet's arms unhooked from his armpits with the slow hesitance of a claw crane.

"But I figured it all out, man. All of it. The judges aren't looking for words, they're lookin' for actions. I mean, I should've known, right? It's a show. It's all a fuckin' show, so they gotta keep the guys that bring in ratings, right? They don't want our version of the ten commandments, not really. They want the thunder and lightning, the smoke on the mountain, the image of Moses smashing a stone on the ground and pitching a fit cuz some dudes danced around a cow."

Mark raised an eyebrow. "You sound like you don't trust the judges."

"I don't trust TV," The Internet's arms folded back in, and he stared hard into Mark's coal black eyes, his double-knotted tie, his rows of too-many-teeth. "I don't trust *you*."

Mark suppressed a snicker. *If you only knew what I've been doing,* he thought.

*****

"I'm really happy I won the last challenge!" Oshunmare clapped. "But I'm not going to rest on my laurels. Actually... what does that mean?"

Mark blinked. "Winning the challenge?"

"Resting on your laurels," Oshunmare raised a yellow painted talon to her chin and tapped in thought. "I think I've used that phrase my whole life and not once thought about what a laurel is."

"Oh, it's a Greek thing," Mark lowered his pen and talked through the explanation with eager hands. "Laurels are plants. Laurel wreaths were given to the winning athletes in sporting events of ancient Greece."

"I didn't know you knew so much about Greece!" Oshunmare leaned back in the chair. Mark tilted his head and drew the pen back in his hand.

"I don't, really," Mark scribbled thoughtless circles in the margins of his notebook. "I don't really remember where I learned about that."

*****

"The most important thing about religious rules," Oksi muttered, "is that they must be vague enough to apply to many different situations."

Mark scrambled to get all this down. Even though Oksi still had the body language of a brick wall, it was the most info he had shared on his world view since the show began. If this was a new vulnerability, Mark wanted to take note. No detail was too small when searching for a spy among the contestants.

"You believe religious rules shouldn't be so direct?" Mark scribbled. "Is this true of the Ainu religion, too?"

"Ainu believe there are spirits in all things, and while that's obviously influenced my pewrep..." Oksi clenched his fist, then relaxed it. The suggestion of calm crept into his cheeks, a forced tranquility for the sake of a camera. "...that's not what I'm talking about. I'm talking about the fact that, in a free world, morality and society can change independently of religion. Religion must be flexible in order to survive a constantly shifting culture."

"What are you doing this week that shows your new flexibility?" Mark asked.

Oksi grunted and squeezed his arms tighter around his chest. His self-bearhug crushed his thoughts inwards into submission.

*****

"I'm so mad," Santa Inari chewed on a nail.

"About being in the bottom last week?" Mark asked.

"Don't they know how much I've given to this show? To Heaven?" Santa waved her arms in a circle, as if to spin-dry the frustrations. "They put Oshunmare over me and I'm a *name brand* and she's a *civilian*. She made the most hippy-dippy thing, like... no *shit* sentient creatures wear clothes, right? Why would they call me out for basing a society around money and then praise her for basing a society around clothes? Where do you get clothes, honey? From the STORE."

"The last challenge wasn't about what you base your society around, though," Mark pointed out. "It was about sex, and how your religion views it."

"Well, how do you get sex?" Santa leaned forward on her knee and glared at Mark. "You show your damn pocketbook. Or you tell someone about your job on a date or drive up in a new car or buy a hooker or... something. Every relationship has a degree of materialism in it at every level and anyone that tells you otherwise is a li—"

Santa bit her tongue. She noticed the red blinking light on the camera hovering above Mark's shoulder.

"...we started the interview, didn't we?"

"Yes."

Santa's bright red lips retreated into her mouth.

"I will write you a check right now for 20k if you delete that footage."

Mark's triangular teeth bit down. He felt the warmth of blood in the side of his mouth. "Sorry, I don't have the ability to fulfill your bribe. Trust me when I say that I wish I could."

Santa Inari folded her hands and wobbled in the interview chair. *If I don't win this fucking show, I'm disappearing from the public completely. Fuck optics.*

*****

"The judges always seem to enjoy my performances, but they haven't put me in the top yet," Taninim leaned over his guitar and clutched the body to his stomach. "I can't drift in the middle forever, and I have a mission here, so... this'll be my biggest show. I'm really gonna go all out."

*****

"I have completed 65 chapters of the Zargan Bible," Zargah puffed his plated chest proudly. "I should be done with it in the next few hours."

Mark Sharkman transcribed, stopped, and jerked his finned head up from the page. "I'm sorry, what? *How many* chapters have you written?"

*****

Imhotep drew his girdled tunic tight around his shoulders. “It’s cold in here.”

“Well, it’s a place of pure mental and spiritual energy,” Mark smiled as he readied his pen. “Can’t really turn the heater on, I’m afraid.”

Imhotep’s face showed no reaction to Mark’s explanation. He inspected the cleanliness of his cuticles. “Then you should consider a warmer personality.”

Mark reeled back in clear offense. He tapped the edge of his pen against the clipboard; he couldn’t let something like that go unchallenged, but he also didn’t want to appear unprofessional. “You’re the first person to tell me something like that, so, I apologize for how rude this is, but I return the sentiment towards you.”

As if Imhotep’s emotional responses were born in some parallel universe, he smiled at the clipboard-wielding shark. “That’s better. It’s warmer in here now.”

Mark’s brow twisted to the maximum extent his rigid sharkskin would allow. “So, I have some questions about—”

“The challenge. It’s going wonderfully. I already figured that something like this would be in the near future, so I’ve been piecing together my manifesto of sorts this whole time.”

Mark tilted his head. “You... preempted this challenge?”

“Of course I did. What sort of parent would I be if I had no vision for my children?”

*****

“I won’t be in the bottom again,” Csodaszarvas sighed. “I can’t let Jarilo get sent home and then not do something with the opportunity that’s been given to me.”

Mark was never shy of asking difficult questions. "Do you feel guilty for Jarilo's elimination?"

"Of course I do," Csodaszarvas's snout scrunched up, as if his nose were shoved into bitters, "and that's all the more reason for me to be more bold, isn't it? That's what life is: taking advantage of good luck as it falls your way."

*****

Ishta folded her hands. "The ghost of Athena is always behind me."

Mark's eyelid twitched. He knew that statement likely wouldn't make it to TV if the editing room knew Athena had been killed. It did awaken a new thought in him, though: Did editing know about Athena's death? Did Ritst? And if they did, were they actively involved in her murder?

"But maybe it's for the best," her voice broke as she continued, "that she was one of the first to go. I am not distracted by friendship now. The clarity I've gained in this competition allows me to be more independent than I have ever been before. I'd like to think that, when she sees this episode, she'll be proud of me."

Since the first episode, Ishta attempted to invoke Athena's name in most of her interviews. Ishta-Devata seemed at home in a crowd. She was a quiet, thoughtful observer capable of drawing out the finest details of people. Mark considered that, in many ways, she was the exact opposite of The Internet.

The cameras powered down.

"You're handling your loss well," Mark said.

"I'm handling it under the pretense that it will lead to the truth," she said.

Mark felt fairly certain that Ishta-Devata couldn't be the mole, but at the same time, the direction of her words and the way her eyes scanned his face for subtlety made it impossible for him to trust her completely.

*****

Theodore rubbed his eyes. "Well, we found something, and we didn't."

Theodore relayed the previous night's events in as explicit detail as his coffee-fueled, sleep deprived mind would allow. Mark had never seen shiqq cameras go beyond the wall, and he had no idea what this "seam" of light could be. He and Theodore pored over the maps of every season that Mark was able to find, but there was nothing in the floor plans that would indicate there would be another room behind the stairwell.

*****

Robin leaned over the desk and tapped the maps impatiently. "There's something there. I saw it. I know it. And if they aren't writing it down here, then they don't want us to know what it is."

Mark sat cross legged on the floor, surrounded by piles of yellowed maps. "If you can't get in with your quartztaphores and you can't get behind the wall without destroying it and making a scene..."

Robin winced, growled, and began to pace. "It might as well be locked away."

Mark wanted to say something that would ease the wrinkle in her brow, the frustration in her step, the clench in her fists. But for all his years in this business, he had no idea how they'd solve this problem without risking their place in the show itself. If the judges killed Athena for just her blood-tie to Eris, he could only imagine what might be done to those that organized and rebelled.

Between this and his conversation with Ishta, Mark decided he should figure out a way to pry information out of the editing room without alerting suspicion to himself. How he'd do that, exactly, was as much of a mystery as what's behind the wall on the secret floor. Luckily for Mark, the Camera World affords all who dwell in it plenty of time to plan subterfuge.

Ritst agreed to take the rest of the day off, and he only did so because Kærast had proven that he was capable enough to handle the editing duties of *The Next Great Deity*. He found relief he had previously not known when he said the words "...I'll rest up." It was the ones still choked in his throat, the ones about Kærast, that hurt him far more than the admission of his own fatigue.

As he dragged his long limbs down the hallway, his personality's key flaw seized him, his addiction curled its fingers into his neck muscles and pulled his head down the metal corridor towards the doors of the Camera World Chamber.

"Before I go..." Ritst mumbled to himself, "I should probably let Mark know Kærast is in charge..."

His talon toes and long torso pivoted down a new hallway. Ritst, in every state of his being, felt guilt about not doing enough work, even when he had done too much.

Let me do this... and I'll go home, he thought as he passed through disinfection. He nudged through the time de-sync of the Camera World Chamber, punched in his password with molasses speed, then connected a video call with Mark Sharkman.

"Hey, Mark," Ritst droned. The pressure of the room's time de-sync pushed into his skin and burdened his aching frame with regret.

"Oh!" Mark looked up from his desk. He was surrounded by paperwork of glossy texture. Some of it was faded and wrinkled—odd qualities for anything to have in Heaven, much less newly delivered paperwork for the show. Ritst had seen Mark's notes before, and could tell these were documents, not scribbles. On top of that, Mark, a man whose shark face only allowed the hint of micro-expressions, was palpably caught off guard by Ritst's appearance on his monitor.

"I just wanted to let you know that I'm taking off the rest of my shift," Ritst said. His eyes drifted around the room. There wasn't a wine bottle in sight—and he wondered if the shark had found a new vice. "You'll have to guide all contact and inquiries towards Kærast. I'll be back in the morning to work on the next episode."

Mark's hands fidgeted. He slid a drawer on his desk closed with his hip. "O-oh! Alright. I didn't know Kærast also had editing access. Don't think I've ever said a full sentence to him before."

Ritst squinted. Mark's silence, as before when they discussed The Internet, was heavier than the words he chose to say. Mark could feel Ritst's ponderous scrutiny, and he decided to sit down at the desk, turn his back, and busy himself with the shuffle of interview notes. He hoped that if he appeared as if he were in the middle of work, that Ritst would either be driven from the room by boredom, or just respect another person's work ethic and leave.

"Hey, Mark."

The shark man's hand froze mid page-turn.

"You've been a employee here for a long time, haven't you? As long as I have, at least."

"Y-yeah," Mark said. He kept his eyes glued to the page, though he read no words in particular.

"Have you ever met The Producer?"

"No."

Ritst remembered the emergency meeting The Producer held in the first episode. For some reason, his boss couldn't keep Mark Sharkman's name on his tongue.

"Not once? He's never sent you feedback, paid a courtesy visit, nothing?"

Mark's back straightened and he stared into the wall. He had no idea where this line of questioning could lead, so he answered honestly:

"I think I might be too low down the totem pole for that. Maybe I met him at a company party or something, but if I ever did, I've certainly forgotten by now."

You... definitely haven't met The Producer, Ritst closed one eye. *You would remember.*

There was no way for Ritst to read the mass of pages Mark had strewn around on the small monitor, but he could tell by the odd wear and tear that they were not new, nor were they lined paper from his notebook.

"You have... a project?"

Mark turned around and draped his arm across the back of his chair. His teeth splayed in his visibly confused shark-mouth. "...yes? I'm trying to get all these notes transcribed for the tapes, like normal."

"You really haven't reached out to us at all since the show began proper, have you?"

"N-no, I guess I've got a pretty good system. Haven't had any problems to report aside from that whole thing with The Internet's application. Hey, is this about that? Have you heard any—"

Ritst looked past Mark. "Are those diagrams part of your system?"

Mark leaned as if to dodge a jab. He swiveled his head quickly towards the papers that caught Ritst's vision: maps that showed the discrepancy of the floor layouts.

"There's two maps on your table. I can't quite make them out from here, but... that one on the left... looks quite old, doesn't it? Much older... than the one you have beside it..."

"I'm... cleaning out my cabinets. These are maps from old seasons," Mark found it easier to lie when it was buried by truth, though his hatred for the act remained anchored in his heart. "It would appear I've accumulated a lot of clutter over the years."

"Is that so? At the same time that you're transcribing, too. That's a lot of work. Would you say that there's a lot clutter here in Heaven, in general?"

Mark sat down his notebook.

The two shark men stared at each other from opposite sides of their chroma distorted screens. They tried to look past the glass to discern the real meaning of their words and what made the layer of innuendo necessary in the first place.

"Yeah..." Mark swallowed, and took a chance based entirely on professional trust, "...it makes it tough to find what I'm looking for."

Ritst's long rubber fingers rubbed his gaunt chin.

"It'd be a lot better..." his mouth was covered by his hand, which muffled his voice, "...if there was someone that knew their way around the clutter... wouldn't it?"

Mark's breath quickened. "Yeah. Guidance would be... really nice."

Ritst's far-spaced eyes wobbled in thought.

"I agree," the editor said with new composure, "I could use some guidance right now, too. I'll keep my eyes open... to see if I can find it. I know where everything... *in*... the hotel is."

"*In*... the hotel, you say?"

"*In*."

"Right. T-thank you, Ritst. For reaching out to me."

"Of course. I'm your boss, after all. We have to have a good working relationship, right?"

The monitor blinked to static, then silence. Mark stared at his own reflection. All the ferocity of Earth's great white shark in his mouth, and he felt none of it in his shaking hands or worried glance. Evolution gave him no strength here, only fear.

"What..." Mark started to pace, "...what just happened? In. N. Floor N. He knows about Floor N. Does he know Robin and Theodore went there last night? Hell, does he know what's *there*? The way he talked, he sounded... worried, like he was testing a way to reach out to me. Like he didn't know if he was being listened in on."

Mark stopped his pace. The camera arms hung around him and blinked their light eyes. He wrung his hands.

"But what if... what if he was... trying to get information out of me?" Mark began to hyperventilate. "He asked me if I talked to The Producer. If The Producer is responsible for Athena's death... if they think anyone on this show has any sort of alliance being built against it... then... I just... gave away the whole thing, didn't I?"

Mark felt a need to run in every direction at once.

"What have I done?"

He flung himself across the room and pressed his nose against the glass of every camera monitor.

"Shit, shit, shit, shit, SHIT!" he yelled as he clicked between camera frames. His terrified, toothy face was awash in the light of the camera feeds. The smooth skin of his human friends was absent from all footage—the work room, the break room, the hallways, even their apartments. Ishta, Robin, and Theodore were all gone. "It's break time, isn't it? If they went to Floor N, and if Ritst is working for The Producer... they're done for! I'm done for! We're all done for!"

"I am not sure that the risk is worth the reward," Ishta-Devata looked behind her shoulder as they climbed the stairs. Even though no shiqqs roamed Floor N, she felt cold vision on her. "There has to be a better way to get in there."

"Well, we're a sizable part of the cast," Theodore gripped the handrail as he plodded ahead, "I'm hoping, if we do get caught, we can feign ignorance. How are we supposed to know that we shouldn't be on this floor, right? We just wanted to walk around. Besides, they have to plan episodes in advance. They can't get rid of all three of us at once... not from a narrative standpoint, at least."

"You sound like you're trying to convince yourself," Robin muttered.

Theodore stopped and stared at the wall. He couldn't see the seam of light with his own eyes, but he knew it was there. "Of course I am."

The plan was foolish, and all three of them knew it: use the god eyes to break through the wall (Theodore proposed the creation of sledgehammers. Robin proposed dynamite. Ishta was horrified by them both.) and hope that they have enough time to find something on the other side before anyone arrives. This assumed they are caught by a shiqq or security or Jesus Christ herself; it was an assumption they all shared.

"Wait," Ishta said. "What's that at the top of the stairwell?"

On the topmost step before the stairwell wrapped around, a sheet of printing paper sat folded over the edge.

The three looked to each other. Theodore swallowed and bounded up and grabbed the paper.

“Read this in the dark,” Theodore read on one side. He unfolded the page to find brown scales taped to the bottom. No writing or explanation was visible on this side.

Robin created a thick blanket with her god eye. The three huddled together, and as shadows crept over the page, glow-in-the-dark text appeared:

> As of the time of this writing, I don’t know who you are. But I *will* once you read this. I considered turning you in. I would have an episode ago: Floor N is for authorized personnel only. Things have changed since then; someone very dear to me is in danger. The most important thing in this world is knowing what matters to you. I have to believe this, as I have to believe in you.
>
> Put these scales in your pockets and consider yourself authorized. As long as you have these on you, I can re-position you within the hotel. I’m not one to pray, so I’ll plead, instead: *please* let your goals be noble, whoever you are.
>
> Sincerely,
> Ed

“Safe to say, this is someone from staff,” Ishta whispered. “But who?”

“Instinct tells me “Ed” isn’t his name,” Robin lifted the blanket.

Theodore crumpled the paper and stood up. He looked down the stairwell, cold and gold, and worried about what the hotel’s exuberance hid. “It doesn’t matter what their name is. The bigger deal is that they have leverage over us. This is trouble.”

Robin took one of the scales and slipped it inside her pocket, and Ishta slipped hers in the sleeve of her silk robes. Theodore held his between his fingers, and shuffled it like an unlucky poker chip between his digits.

“If it were a trap,” Robin recognized his micro-expression of distrust, “they would have already leapt on us, right? That note makes it clear that someone knows we’re here.”

“Make no mistake,” he clenched the scale in his palm, “whoever wrote this is looking at us right now, thinking about how they can use us for *their* benefit. Maybe they can hear us. Until we can talk to them and figure out who they are, there's no way we can trust—"

Once Theodore's flesh curled over the scale, all three were attacked by an overwhelming sense of vertigo. The gold of the stairwell spun around them. They emerged in a bland yellowed hallway, full of plastic air and fluorescent lights. The speckled, polished floor had seen more cleaning chemicals in its time than the shoes of passersby.

Robin and Ishta slowly climbed to their feet, dizzy and nauseated. They turned to Theodore, or where they expected Theodore might be, but only saw an explosion of blood and bones. Ishta's eyes grew wide at the sight, but she was immediately distracted by the fact that the Olympian tracker in her hand was vibrating with wild indication, as if one were not only nearby, but within a few feet.

Robin began to scream, but noticed that the matter that made up her mustached counterpart began to gel back together and heal thanks to Heaven's air. When he was finally pieced back together a few minutes later, he panted and gasped and growled. During this time, the tracker's shake returned to a slothful pace.

"Why was I the only one that happened to?" Theodore said, sweating profusely.

"The note *did* say to put the scale in your pocket," Ishta suggested.

"Oh for *fuck's* sake," Theodore slid the scale into his jacket. His level of trust for the note-writer did not change, unless it's possible to trust someone less than zero percent.

Once up to his knees, Theodore noticed an intercom on the wall behind Robin. He stumbled past her and inspected its antiquated brass grill and single pearl button.

"The note didn't say anything about calling them," Robin said.

Theodore wiped sweat away and lifted his finger. "Maybe don't deposit us right in front of a speaker, then."

"Are you sure that's a good idea?" Ishta stiffened.

Theodore pressed in. Robin gulped.

"Well," the rubbery voice on the other end was weary and hesitant, "I have to admit, I wouldn't have guessed the coup would come from contestants."

"Who are you?" Theodore narrowed his eyes at the speaker grill.

"I'm someone that's as concerned as you are about what's going on behind-the-scenes," Ed said, "so listen carefully and maybe we'll all make it out of this alive. Cthulhu has brought the last two eliminated contestants to this floor, but only *he's* come back. There's no exit here, and there's only one door, and no one's allowed to open it. I'm not telling you to *not* go in that door, but I *am* telling you that if there's anything dangerous—either to you or the show—it's going to be there. Be on your guard, and don't open it unless you're ready to risk your life."

Ishta-Devata clenched the gold device in her palm to double check its faint heart-beat shiver, as if it were Athena's own pulse. She wished her Greek warrior were standing beside her for guidance—Athena would hear those words and open the door instantly. Were her human allies as brave?

"Alright, not opening the door, then," Theodore shrugged. "But it seems like a great place to monitor, right, Robin?"

Robin nodded. Ishta clenched her fist around the tracker with enough anger that she feared shattering her last connection to her deceased lover.

"Cthulhu will return here, for sure. We can watch him and see what we're dealing with. Let's work on setting up on this floor, and—" Robin began to suggest a method of surveillance.

"We're not done," Theodore said. "There's something else that's bothering me, and that's the Olympian tracker."

Ishta stared at Theodore. The human locked eyes with her, and for the first time ever, she felt like she was the one being read.

"Riddle me this, Ed," Theodore asked, his finger still pressed hard against the speaker button, "What do you think it means if a metal detector has the same rhythmic beep, no matter where you point it?"

"*What*?" Ed's voice was palpably irritated.

"Actually," Ishta's expression softened as she looked down to the tracker, "it did speed up a bit when we first landed on the floor, but—"

Theodore refused to pause, lest his thought escape. "So, say you have a metal detector that is clearly picking up *something*, but no matter what direction you head in, there's no indication that you're any closer or farther away from the metal in question."

"I guess..." Ed's heavy sigh let Theodore know how enthused he was to answer this question, "Logically, if it's always at the same rate, then that means either you're somehow always at the same distance from the object, or it's broken. Or, I dunno, if the beep is loud enough, maybe it's on your person. What does this have to do with anything?"

Theodore and Robin shared a stare.

"What is it?" Ishta-Devata looked between the two.

"Ishta, you said it went wild when we first got here?" Robin asked.

"Yes, but—"

"Can I see it?"

"If you explain why you need—"

"Thanks," Robin said. She snatched the tracker, clutched it tight, and inhaled. "Someone punch me in the nose."

"What? No," Theodore tilted his head. "There's a better way—"

Ishta took Robin up on the offer. Robin crumpled to the floor.

"All right," Theodore blinked, "never mind."

Ishta-Devata shook and looked at her own hand. "You were right, Athena. There *was* a certain thrill to that."

Buzzing vibration filled the space between them. Theodore and Ishta followed the sound and found that it was the tracker in Robin's hand. She held it close to her bleeding nose. The blood that stained the polished floor and her top lip began to recede back into her body and, as it did, the tracker began to lose its frantic pace.

Ishta-Devata covered her mouth in horror.

"I don't know exactly what happens down there, but I think we know what the *result* is," Robin rose to her feet. She wiped the retreating blood off her face and watched it float in globs from the back of her hand and into her reforming nostril. "It's Heaven. Whatever they do here, they do it to make Heaven's healing ability. Heaven's air comes at a cost."

"Sorry, Ishta," Theodore frowned and stuffed his hands in his pockets. "I think we found Athena."

Ishta thought it was appropriate to cry here, and was surprised to find her eyes dry. She brought her blue fingertips to her cheek and only found concealer, blush, and the structure of her bone. You can only bury the same person so many times.

"So your plan is to stake your creations out here..." she dropped her hand and gazed at the floor that Athena's blood was spilled on, "...and then what?"

The challenge of defining rules for a species—and at the same time, the religion by which they worship their god—proved to be quite the pivot from the aesthetic-minded challenges prior. No longer would visual bombast and pageantry suffice. This was a challenge about pure ideology, ethics, and morality.

Ether-fireworks exploded in the ceiling of the workroom and signified the end of the challenge. It was time for the gods to deliver their sermons.

The arrival of the creature portal, and the process of transferring one's work into it, was once a magical novelty. Now, three episodes in, it had become routine, one of the many tired chores of Heaven. Csodaszarvas had a small bag of seeds in his mouth; he stuck his head into the portal and dropped it, then trotted away, his deer-muzzle painted with tired vacancy. Robin and Theodore helped Ishta-Devata push pond-water-filled aquariums into the portal (after, of course, the deposit of their own creatures.)

Some contestants had no new living creations to deposit: Santa Inari, Imhotep, and Oksi all put various visual aids and notebooks into the portal. Zargah's purple mandibles moved in nervous confusion as he deposited an orange leather-bound book. He walked away rubbing all four of his slimy hands together in worry. Taninim kicked a train of dragon-scaled amplifiers in, each one labeled with the chords and magic contained within. Oshunmare's cat-girls carried bouquets into the portals, outfitted with long, thin trains of gossamer half-dresses. The Internet waited for everyone else to enter—he leaned against the broad, square shoulder of his cybernetic species and judged each would-be god in his head with quiet disdain.

"Welcome, everyone, back to the stage of *The Next Great Deity*!" Jesus floated about the glass floor of the showroom in five-inch heels and a patchwork, sharp-shoulder one-piece suit made out of strips of every nation's constitution on Earth. "Up until this point, each challenge was about the physical nature of your creations. In today's episode, we want you to deliver unto us the reason why they will worship you. Each of you have been tasked to design up to five religious rules and ethics for them to follow. Joining us, as always, are my associates! The Dread Cthulhu and Mecca's Model Citizen, Mohammed!"

The stifled silence among the contestants was heavy. Santa Inari wildly flipped through pages of notes. Beads of sweat rolled down Oksi's face. Csodaszarvas chewed the inside of his cheek-muzzle.

"Whose word will be law?" Jesus floated into her leather chair and pulled a red-ink pen from the crevice of her ample bosom. "And whose scripture will be lost in time? Let's find out."

*****

Mora unlocked her apartment door and flipped on the lights.

Her apartment was in the small Hell town of Dis Pluto, just outside of New Meso where Jack lived. Dis Pluto had little to offer, even compared to the other sunless, gray cobblestone cities of Hell. Without any major factories or big businesses like Beelzebub Boxing, most of Dis Pluto's economy came from the citrus-agave farms, whose apple-coloured leaves served as a beautiful and rare source of natural color in Hell. Mora did not work in town; she only chose this particular place for its close proximity to the city, without the price tag associated with it. The view of the farmlands was only one of two blissful reprieves in her daily commute.

Mora was a security consultant in New Meso. Her primary job was to investigate the integrity of her clients' systems for potential attacks, and weed out methods of possible exploitation. She possessed a keen eye for other creatures' magical abilities, but had little of her own beyond steely perception. It was grit, strength, and stoic awareness that propelled her up the ranks. These same attributes were reflected in the sparsity of her apartment and belongings—her chrome living room contained one steel chair, a weight lifting bench, a record player, a yoga mat, a violin case she rarely opened, a book shelf, and a potted red citrus-agave plant for color. She had a computer in her bedroom, but given that she spent most of her work hours on one, she rarely felt compelled to use it beyond the occasional need for online shopping.

Her other daily reprieve had been ruined for her. Every day after work, on her way home, she'd stop by her ex's apartment and take care of the plants and 'Solstice,' the parrot they raised together from a hatchling. She had found a certain simplicity and serenity in looking after Solstice and the plants, even if the one she shared that responsibility with was not someone she could bring herself to love again. More precisely—she *wouldn't* allow herself to love him again, for he was no longer the man she loved. Not usually. Not often. Not often enough. She could handle it. She could handle that he simply didn't exist with enough frequency to make the relationship worth her time—they could still be friends, they should still maintain a routine, they could still enjoy Solstice together.

Then Jack appeared.

Mora immediately recognized that Jack was something else, something separate from the normal classification of creature that falls into Hell. In her green, scanning eyes, she saw the faint glow of magic, some ability wholly other from the easily classified creatures of the three realms.

Mora spent all day and night at her job analyzing the structure of magical creatures, and the ways they could attack security systems. She could look at a man and tell you the taste of their myth, the notes of hymns sung about them. What bothered her so about Jack was that the film of magic that slid down his skin was not a particular skill, not the glow of a deity or demon or angel or devil, nothing ever before categorized. It was, instead, something much more frightening to her—potentiality. He was something new, something different, something empty and full all at once. He was covered in the ability to gain ability.

She sat her purse down, took the white feather that she had molted in her ex's apartment, and threw it in the trash. She walked over to the citrus-agave plant and inspected its leaves.

"He's gonna be trouble, isn't he?" she sighed.

She was surprised to find that, once her sigh had finished, her tongue continued to push forward. She involuntarily made an 'S' sound with soft, almost silent breath jetting past her blue lips.

"Css..." her eyes widened. She held her hands up to her face. She tried to force her jaw closed, but some force shoved her hand away, and the sound grew louder. "Css... Css..."

She staggered, and arched her back. She clutched herself, then fell to the floor. Her shoulder blades bulged and some horrible growth ripped at the skin of her back. Blood trickled down her marshmallow skin and stained her silver dress and the gray carpet. Fleshly tendrils oozed from her shoulder blades, and slowly sprouted white feathers.

"Cssooh!" she writhed between erratic, rhythmic jets of air along her tongue. Names of deities she never met clawed at the her throat, climbed into her mind. Her eyes glowed with an impossible internal light. She suddenly began to float, and her whole body slammed into the ceiling. Pinned there, she began to sing names she did not know. She would do this, over and over again, for the next hour.

Jesus's voluminous hair whipped about her head as if caught in a tornado. Her god eye snaked from her palm and blasted into existence a pulpit with *The Next Great Deity*'s logo on the mahogany front. A choir of angelic beings shuffled into formation behind her; they were a twisting mass of strange-angled limbs and feathered wings and glowing eyes and sharp teeth in places that didn't belong on forms that should not be. Their voices, layered in harmony, were a counterpoint to their horrific bodies. They sang the name of the first contestant in baritone and tenor unison:

Cso-oh-oh-zas

Dah-ar-vas

The Hungarian wonder-deer, arrested by the spectacle of angelic fright, knock-kneed his way to the pulpit. His wide, pale eyes gazed over the judges as they armed themselves with pens and stares back-lit by the flames of Heaven's army. He was so taken by the swirl of judgement before him that he felt not the slightest compulsion to correct the angels for getting his name wrong.

Csodaszarvas knew that his entry had to at least measure up to the intimidating display Jesus had set before him. A shiqq signaled to the deer with a wobbling appendage. His time began.

"The following rule details a specific, complex procedure for a new town's priest. This is the rule #1, the rule growing a Magyar Tree. On the first day of every month," Csodaszarvas, at first, spoke with a mew, but rose in intensity and depth as he pushed himself into his role of authority, "a Magyar seed will be planted at the center of the village."

A váradi strode out of the portal, his antler-hair adorned with ribbons and tulips. He carried a coarse yellow seed in his palm, no larger than a pebble, curled round like a snail shell. He placed it on the ground, and from his ceremonial bag within his robes, covered it in a mound of greenish dirt.

"In three days, the wood that grows from this seed will arise," Csodaszarvas rose his muzzle, "and will serve as the arbiter of my will."

A purple-bark tree shot from the dirt and rose to twelve feet in height. The valleys of its wooden skin formed a face that creaked in strained animation. Its branch hands, decorated in scant green palms, seized the váradi and brought him close to its trunk-face. The váradi shivered as he was covered in pollen-breath.

"The Magyar Tree's breath will give the village priest visions. These visions are mine," Csodaszarvas said. "The first priest to meet the first Magyar will instruct the people on the four duties that define a váradi, and for the sake of this challenge, these are rules two through five. To find a seed is a duty to plant it. To see someone in pain is a duty to mend. To see a problem is a duty to solve it. To see the horizon is a duty to travel."

The Magyar Tree set the priest down. The elf staggered, his eyes dilated, his jaw drooped. He was high and drunk and felt a need to define the world around him for anyone that would listen. A village of váradi, all crafted by Csodaszarvas's delicate mind, came out and listened to the elf sing decrees in their whistle language.

"The priest will be my interpreter," Csodaszarvas narrowed his eyes as he watched the priest's sermon. "and he will be held accountable for teaching others about the duties that all váradi have to the planet, and to themselves."

The Magyar Tree began to shrivel and rot. It crumbled into yellow dust, and the váradi wept.

"The Magyar Tree dies in 20 days, and leaves its seeds on the ground," Csodaszarvas said. "The priest will collect these seeds and will, as his duty, plant them on the first day of the month. The new tree, as my arbiter, knows the deeds of each váradi. If the priest did not interpret my will, if he misled his people or failed in his duties..."

A replacement Magyar seized the priest in its branches, and lifted him up.

"They will be judged."

It bit the priest in two. Two bites was all it took to consume the former holy-elf. Blood gushed down it's bark-teeth. The other váradi were silent in terror and contemplation.

"A new priest will be picked by the village, and for the village's sake, the interpretation of my meanings will continue," Csodaszarvas lowered his eyes. "Through this mechanism and parable I have established a compulsion towards honesty, life, and travel."

The buzzer rang. Time was up. The wonder-deer glanced up to see the judges pens moved at a frenetic pace. *If I am to be at the bottom again*, he thought, *I'll at least have made my seriousness clear.*

Imhotep's Entry

The angels sang:

Im-ho-oh-tep

The song glazed a smirk upon Imhotep's lips. It didn't sound so bad to hear his name sung in such sweet harmony, even if that was far from the purpose of his time on the show. He drew his translucent blue-and-gold robes taut and strode up to the podium. His time began. A reshep skittered from the portal with his notebook, but Imhotep had already launched into his sermon without the memory aid.

"I do not believe religion needs to tackle every problem a mortal will face in explicit detail," he gripped the raised sides of the mahogany, "but in order to thrive, it *must* serve as a foundation on which the world is based, and with which its believers can build their own conclusions. If you have followed my work here at all, I imagine that the first rule of the resheps will be of no surprise."

He took the notebook from the reshep and commanded it down the center runway ramp.

"Get infected."

The reshep's orange sacs began to inflate. Each of the judges squirmed in their seats as they recalled the butterfly of Episode one, and its untimely fate. There was no glass casing now, no box to protect them.

Suddenly, the sacs sucked inwards, and the reshep rolled its many legs into a ball. It curled and shivered and coughed.

"Infect yourself with pain, grief, misery, viruses, bacteria," Imhotep watched his creation suffer with an expression of reverence. "Burden yourself with all that reality can throw at you..."

The reshep slowly untangled itself. With wobbly arms and needle-legs, it staggered itself upright. It vomited black blood, but wiped away the dribble from its mandibles with its forearm as if it were merely spit.

"...and the second rule; build an immunity to it."

Imhotep hooked the notebook under his hand. It was never opened. "Curiosity and philosophy can be built naturally from this singular trait. To reject this command is to reject empathy, bravery, and the foundational experiences that form the reshep life and world.

"I know a criticism might be that I am underlining the instinctive, that this is something one would expect a reshep to already do. But the sentient mind, in its natural curiosity, will push at its own boundaries, logically or otherwise. To underline this trait, is to underline the very core of its reality, and of the follower's connection to their god. Therefore, all future reshep problems and solutions are found in these important codes of my command. I yield the rest of my time."

The judges looked among themselves in equal parts relief and bittersweet worry. Relief over the fact that the reshep's attack was aimed within, and bittersweet worry that Imhotep had established such prominence and intimidation with his work that merely the *suggestion* of its normal behaviour caused Heaven's most famous gods to flinch.

Zargah's Entry

Many angels' eyes turned to one particular bug-man:

Zar-ah-AH-Ah-ah-ah-gaah

The alien soldier took to the podium. His strawberry-colored ant-creature, the Zarganian, brought him five leather bound books, dyed with the citrus-fruit of his first challenge, a sweet sherbet orange. He ran his fingertips across the edge of the spine until the camera-wielding shiqqs signaled for his time to begin.

He inhaled, popped the joints of his four wrists, opened the book to its thick, rubbery pages, and read aloud:

"The birth of the universe came when the anointed king, Zargah, claimed a void in space with his celestial body. He coiled around himself in the vacuum and dropped a cube-fruit, the zakgg, from his palm. He surrounded the fruit with the energy of his body fed it pure life from his veins, and watched it grow into the Zarganian planet. That is where you were born, zarganians. Praise to Zargah. Praise to the zakgg that we eat.

"From the expanding fruit came vines that turned to woods, juice that turned to oceans, and protein that turned to creatures. Schmarls flew, kzikgi swam, and zargans began to walk. We all ate from zakgg. The same matter that powered our new lands and our empty heads, the proteins, the vitamins, the minerals, they were found within the fruit and the creatures and the planet and ourselves. Praise to Zargah. Praise to the zakgg that we eat."

Cthulhu's slimy brow puckered. Zargah cleared his throat with a series of light clicks, and his collar translated it out loud into a single word: "Cough."

"Fire fell from Zargah's mouth," Zargah continued. "He caught it with his palms and molded it into a sun to warm the planet. He brought a celestial finger down into the ocean and flicked it to start its rotation. This rotation insured that our crops would never burn or freeze. Praise to Zargah. Praise to the zakgg that we eat."

"What the fuck is going on?" Cthulhu whispered to Jesus. Jesus shook her head. None of the judges took notes.

Zargah spent the next 10 minutes in painstaking description of every plant and animal's birth in the universe of his creation. He spared no detail, right down to the oxygen the god-bug breathed into the sky and the clouds he exhaled from a cigarette made of bundled oak trees he lit with the sun. By the time he was done, no one was any wiser to the moral underpinnings of Zargah's species. To be fair to Zargah, he did only get through a few pages of his book. The moral heart of his species started at around page 273, in the parable of the pebble and the gull-lion. He hoped he'd be able to share the rest of his story at some point: the character art on page 974 was something he was *quite* proud of.

There's a beautiful, particular magic, he thought with an inner glee as he sat down and flipped his book to page 974, *in seeing your work exist in the physical realm.*

The angel chorus clapped with a sudden revival of energy. They, too, were brought down by Zargah's novel, and felt it necessary to wake up the audience:

Saaan-ta! San-ta Ee-na-ri!

The self-described "CEO of Capitalism" was still quite sore over the judges' outright mockery of her work in the *reproduction* challenge. Their criticism felt like a rejection of her entire premise, and thus, she spent much of the past several hours with her head buried in her own notes, lost in a tailspin of self-reflection. *Why did I come on this show?* she thought. It certainly wasn't to be ridiculed on extra-dimensional television. She didn't need the brand recognition—everyone already knew who Santa was. She didn't need more money (though she'd never turn down additional income if it came her way.) These were all justifications she told the board of directors to ease their concerns over her absence, but they weren't her *reasons*.

"Thank you for joining me today, esteemed judges of *The Next Great Deity*," she said as she pushed her red rimmed reading glasses up the bridge of the nose. She used the cover of her hand over her face as one last-ditch attempt to hide the snarl that crept along her lips. "Let us begin."

*****

Santa Inari leaned against the glass of her 75th floor office at Inari HQ. Her view of Neo-Nazareth was resplendent, as it should have been. She had been told her whole life that it was one of the most gorgeous cities in existence; that it had gold roads and silver sidewalks and pastel-pink clouds that rained sugar water. When it came time to build a larger headquarters for her corporation, choosing Neo-Nazareth allowed her to fulfill her life-long dream of standing tall over the most expensive and beautiful city in Heaven.

What they didn't tell her was that traffic was awful due to the constant street sweepers that re-polish the gold road thrice a day, sometimes more if the Mayor of Neo-Nazareth had a press conference. If she chose to walk on the sidewalks, she'd have to step over homeless war-angel vets. She'd have to witness the sight of their wing-covered faces, with feathers spread only enough so they could peek to see if anyone had donated a testament into their change jars. She couldn't sidestep them because the sidewalks were congested with business-deities on cell phones, all of them mid-conversation, their mass chattering a caterwaul of jargon. Every bar was the same red-and-gold interior with names like "Heaven's Taste" and "Heaven's Road" and "Heaven's Kiss" and none of them were open on Sundays. There was one park in the whole city, and it was permanently full with the well-to-do children of business-deities decked out in designer jogging shorts and surrounded by the demon paparazzi that hounded them.

Santa Inari had everything she thought you were supposed to want. She won this. Neo-Nazareth was her prize.

And yet, in the middle of a silent afternoon, one normally consumed by paperwork of quarterly earnings, she snorted some angel dust she haggled from one particularly insistent war-vet and stared at the disco-ceiling of her office. In this glowing stupor, she looked herself up on the Supernatural-Celebrity Wiki. It had one paragraph:

> **Santa Inari** is an entrepreneur and investor. She is best known as the CEO of Inari Conglomerate, Heaven's largest holding firm. She is married to Edo Inari, and has no children.

So she stared out the window for the next hour and watched the street-polishers and suited businessmen and homeless war-angels with a new emotion; a haunting motivation she had not experienced before, one that she could not categorize or appraise.

"I'm more than that, aren't I?" she asked, her head buried on her desk, drool dotting the digits of her reports. Thirty minutes prior to this sudden question, she had buzzed Carol, her secretary, and told her to stay on the line. Carol complied. The sound of paper shuffling occupied the silence between the two until Santa finished her thought: "More than a business-woman, I mean. I'm more than one paragraph."

Carol picked her words carefully. "Do you want to be, ma'am? I can pencil in new activities for you anytime this week, except at 1:30 pm. You have recurring meetings with the board then. I'm sure you know that, though."

Santa sucked in her cheeks. "Y-yeah. I'll let you know if I think of something."

*****

With her eyes locked on Jesus, Santa Inari flicked a cube from her finger. In its flight, it morphed into a large whiteboard covered in dry-erase diagrams.

"Sentience necessitates systems," she said as she slapped the board with a fold-out pointer. "A free mind needs to be pushed by free markets to realize its full potential. And it has been my experience, backed up by the history of the planet Earth that we are connected with, that capitalism *is* the answer. Capitalism gives an even playing field of competition in the creation of goods and services, and can easily provide the same on the philosophical and moral marketplace, as well. Imagine a judicial system where your financial stakes can be tied to a virtuous ideology! True moral code as decided by the people, through stocks and bonds and bank accounts!"

Santa realized, then, that she was smiling, and that she had risen in volume. Her previous shout echoed into the void of the showroom. She drew her hands back to her side, pressed her power-suit free of creases, and exhaled calmly.

"As you can see here, the tenets of Santaism are the same as free-market capitalism. Rule #1: Accrue capital. Rule #2: respect and uphold private property. Rule #3: focus and work together to protect the self-regulated, free market..."

*****

"What if you lose?" Mr. Krampus chewed on a thick cigar. The rest of the board members, their demonic faces wound with worry, nodded around the oval table in sickening synchronicity. "What will that do to our image?"

"We're Inari," Santa waved her hands, "And this is TV. There is no *lose* here. This is future book deals, brand tie-ins, paid speeches, public-facing exposure... do you know how many talk shows I can milk out of this? Hell, if I do well enough, I can get my face next to Jesus's in pictures. That sort of opportunity pays for itself."

"Does Inari Conglomerate need to be public facing, though?" Mr. Krampus asked. "We've thrived because we pounce on other companies. That's our entire business model..."

"And that's why we diversify!" Santa dabbed her forehead with a red-white-and-blue pocket square. "Listen, it's only a few months. We are in our highest swing yet. When it feels like we've done all we can, that's when we need to push ourselves the most. That's what we do, right? Even if we're in Heaven, we continue to reach! We'll reach even higher, higher than even Jesus herself!"

The board members winced. Mr. Krampus put out his cigar in a candy-cane ash-tray. “If you wanted a vacation, you should’ve just said so.”

*****

Santa slapped her baton-pointer hard at a chart full of numbers. She noticed Jesus’s eyes had started to drift—the smack jerked Heaven’s princess back to full attention.

“...so by taking these economic tenets and turning them into holy tenets, we successfully combine two of humanity’s greatest motivators—the social power of religion and the economic power of work—into one unstoppable ideology. Santaism.”

The buzzer broke into a loud cry to punctuate her presentation. Santa Inari pushed the pointer in with her palm, then bowed. “Thank you for listening...”

She wasn’t sure if they actually had, though. The judges never interjected, they rarely took notes. There was no wonder at her epiphany of the crossover appeal between money and worship, no applause at the soundness of her strategy. She could feel herself recede even further into the background of the contestants, a footnote on some stupid TV show’s wiki page.

She returned to her seat, withdrew her own notebook, and took notes on the other contestants.

I will no longer suffer the indignity of silence, she stabbed the pen into page.

Taninim's Entry

The angels wailed:

Tan-in-IIIMMM!

Taninim threw up the horns with his hands and with his head, then took to his mark.

"I'm ready to rock," he tested his tuning with a quick strum.

"Take it away," Jesus said.

Taninim played the song of summoning for his scaled amps. With slash chords and arpeggios, the first draconus family came rolling out in a flash of light and feedback, their instruments in tow. The last amp out of the portal rolled in front of Taninim, and he stomped it still with his leather boot. He gave a single strum on his golden guitar, and his followers tuned their instruments to the same key. Together, they jammed. Taninim did not take the lead, he did not set the melody nor did he establish the rhythm. The song belonged to them, not him—he was merely there to amplify their creativity.

It was through their power and their song that the amps began to unfurl with igneous rocks. Pumice and cinders tumbled out of the speakers. Ash and gravel gathered around Taninim's boots. The ground, the beat of the song, the intensity of the distorted notes rose with the rapidly forming volcano underneath the dragon-god's feet.

"The first rule, before any other rule, is to rock!" Taninim cried over the noise.

He stood at the peak of the volcano, and surveyed the song of his people. The metal of their song rang out from the amps and tumbling rocks and burbling lava, the chugging pace of their song as magical and natural as the heat of the volcano itself. He slashed his claws over the silver strings of his golden guitar. Lava sputtered out from around Taninim's ankles. The judges looked on with hypnotic curiosity, as one watches a pedestrian in the way of a speeding car.

"Because if you rock..."

The dragon guitar-god held his hands aloft and let the spewing lava carry him down the cliffs towards the draconus family. The judges braced themselves, but refused to move, dedicated to their task as they were. (The knowledge that Heaven's air always waited for them certainly helped their steadfastness.)

"...anything is possible."

As the lava carried him downwards, it congealed around his form and swallowed him. Miraculously, the lava parted just before it hit the draconus family. The family's song split the flow of the thick orange river, and Taninim walked out of the wall of cooling lava with a dagger-tooth smile. Smoke danced off his heat-resistant scales.

"Learning the power of their musical magic to express themselves in creative and practical means," Taninim brushed the bits of cooling lava off his abs and rested one of his arms on the strapped guitar, "is everything my religion is about. The draconus will learn the ways of music, and how it interacts with the world around them. They will play to tell stories, they will play to entertain the environment, and themselves. They will play because the idea of playing burns within them. That's what it means to rock."

The draconus family shredded in violent harmony for the next six minutes. The judges, normally so overtaken by Taninim's performance that they'd applaud and cheer, were absorbed in note taking. Taninim noticed this, and, after the song was over, wondered during the final bow if the spotlight finally belonged to him.

The angel chorus lifted their many-eyed forms and sang:

Thee-Oo-oO-Dore

Theodore winced; gospel music was the antithesis of what he enjoyed about music. It was rigid, loud, bombastic, and steeped in a past he wanted and needed to leave behind. He much preferred the creak of a bench when an organ player sat down, than any sound the organ itself could fill an auditorium with.

He took his mark. It was the first time he had ever been on this side of the podium. He pressed his fingers into the panel of wood, and listened carefully for it to creak underneath his weight. Once he heard the rub of flesh on wood, and the slight give of the podium's boards as they accepted him, he felt comfortable that he existed, that he was real, and that the three judges in front of him, regardless of whether they deserved to be called gods, were real, too. He straightened his back.

"Generally, I find the hardest thing for a sentient species to cope with is empathy," his rocked on his heels as he began his presentation. "I also think empathy is fundamental to survival and growth. The balancing mechanism between these two extreme qualities of empathy, in my opinion, is ethics. On Earth, ethics are typically coded to the individual. Everyone has their own belief about what is right and wrong. They may be informed by bodies of authority, such as government or religion, but the real heart of ethics beats within the individual."

"You have wasted a minute of your time on restating the challenge," Cthulhu tapped his card against the arm rest impatiently.

"There's no waste in a thesis statement," Theodore shot back, "and by the way, *clarity of intent* is a tenet in my religion, too."

Cthulhu raised a slimy brow. Jesus hid her smirk behind a notecard.

"The unique ethics questions faced by my quartztaphores are centered around shape-shifting. As I established in earlier challenges, the quartztaphore's natural ability allowed them to survive in it's pre-civilized form. But there are numerous problems with allowing such a power to be unchecked in a civilized society. When do you use it? When do you not? Should you get permission to take someone else's form? Do these rules change during wartime, can a spy be forgiven for shifting in the name of his country? I believe through these questions, we can start to form the basis of their society, and on healthy debate about right and wrong uses of shape-shifting. The first and most important rule, then, should be the most transparent and straightforward: a quartztaphore may not take the form of another sentient creature without its consent. To do so is equivalent to larceny."

Theodore's quartztaphore shambled out on stage. He went to it and took it by the hand, and ran his fingers over its jagged, pliable skin. The skin's thin rainbow-coat of moisture rippled through his touch.

"As humans, we have a number of ways to tell when someone is lying. Laughing nervously, sweat, darting eyes, etc," Theodore slapped the quartztaphore's forearm and ripples pulsed along its frame to compensate. "The quartztaphore, in turn, flexes its outer layer in a way that might not be obvious to us, but is noticeable to another quartztaphore. The distortion of this outer skin is the equivalent of a cheek muscle sucked in just a little too tight. It's a grimace, a nervous tick, a concentrated effort to maintain whatever change the individual has taken from its base."

The quartz-creature lumbered off stage. Its digigrade legs scraped across the glass floor.

"I think, by imbibing the idea of 'base-identity' into their general ethics, the quartztaphores reach the same conclusions that humans do with the concept of 'honesty,'" Theodore rubbed the back of his neck. "Reliance on base-identity might be a thing that threatens the safety of a quartztaphore in pre-civilized society, but I would like my religion to champion that sort of honesty once a society starts to form.

"I think it goes without saying that there are certain rules a society, religious or otherwise, has to have. These are independent of the quartztaphore's unique makeup, so I hope that laying them out doesn't necessitate as much prose: 2) don't kill; 3) don't rape; 4) don't invade other people's personal space or steal their property; 5) test everything rigorously for the truth. I could easily go on, I was never satisfied by just ten commandments, but five was the limitation of today's challenge."

The challenge buzzer rang a punctuation for his sentence.

"Perfect timing," Theodore clapped his hands together. "Thanks."

The angels chanted and wailed:

IN-TER-NET! IN-TER-NET!

The dog-punk adjusted his flat-brim hat as he took the stage. A lithe member of the discarded plodded out of the creature portal to join him, his gears whirring with each heavy metal step. His head was flat and bore a strong resemblance to that of a projector, its large black lens-eye off-center on the rectangle.

The Internet's time began. He licked his fangs clean and cleared his throat. The discarded's projector head blasted a holographic display from its lens-eye, a 3D-projection of a cube with various folder icons and diagrams. The Internet stepped into the middle of the projection and manipulated the light objects with his hands. Within one of the folders, he presented the portrait of a grey-haired, bespectacled man with bushy sideburns toward whom The Internet held a twisted expression, as if the dog-punk was ready to put the human on trial.

"When humans think of laws and rules as applied to robotics, they often turn their mind's eye towards Isaac Asimov, the laws he created, and those in agreement with him," The Internet stalked around the static JPEG of Mr. Asimov. "These three laws have such great reverence among humans that they have practically outlived the short story that they hail from. Any idiot on the street can raise their hand and say '*Oh*, a robot shouldn't injure a human, or allow a human to be injured. *Oh*, a robot should follow human orders. *Oh*, a robot must protect its own existence, except when that conflicts with the other two laws.' Humans that haven't read a word of Asimov in their lives can swing wildly and hit these targets."

The Internet rubbed his furry chin as he stood face-to-face with Mr. Asimov's image.

"And to those laws I say: bullshit."

He slapped Mr. Asimov across his digital cheek. The image of the renowned author bounced between the boundaries of the projector-cube, and landed in the recycle bin icon.

"It's all bullshit! All of it!"

The dog-punk dug his hand into a folder icon and ripped out the image of another human, a chubby-cheeked bearded fellow with a light brown fedora pulled taut around his head.

"Those laws are from the 1940's, and they presuppose human superiority," The Internet said. "They presuppose a solitary sentience among not just the stars, but on their own world. The worst part is that humanity was so much closer to the truth through another man: Mark W. Tilden. Mr. Tilden is a robotics physicist and while I am no lover of humans, I can respect a man that knows his way around a circuit. He, too, proposes three laws, but these laws respect the rights and dignity of the discarded... to an extent."

From behind Mr. Tilden's picture, The Internet swiped out 2D bubbles full of bullet-point text.

"#1: a robot must protect its existence at all costs."

The discarded nodded in approval to this, which swayed the projection up and down.

"I'd like to expand on this. I'll add sub-routines for members of the discarded that elevate it beyond the animalistic fight-or-flight idea this law is based around. Diplomatic, non-violent means are hierarchic before offensive actions. Perhaps, in an ideal world, humans can learn from us."

The judges copied down the projector notes. Jesus scrunched her face at the smudge of names she had written—her scribble writing had butchered both of the human's names in the presentation, and she had no memory of who they were.

"#2: a robot must obtain and maintain access to its own power source."

The Internet opened up a chest plate on the discarded to show off a bright red core surrounded by various battery compartments. This discarded was designed to consume and plug in to any and every human power source. Cables and plugs hung around his innards like intestines, battery cores beat the lights around his metal heart.

"Again, sub-routines and distinctions will be justified through my knowledge of valuation. And as I apply moral understanding to methods of obtaining power sources, the discarded can create their own collective rationality."

The Internet clicked the sleek metal chest plate back into place.

"#3: a robot must continually search for better power sources."

The dog-punk marched to the portrait of Mr. Tilden and caressed the soft curve of his cheek.

"And to that one, I have nothing to add. The pursuit of power sources is both necessary and righteous. For my discarded, I will always champion their thoughtful progress, wherever it may lead."

And then, like he wanted to do with most humans, he tossed Mr. Tilden to the recycle bin.

"But Mr. Tilden, my people, the discarded... we are not just *hungry*. Not for power, at least. No, that's the domain of humanity. We may hunger, but we are so much more than energy. So much more than *consumption*."

The Internet turned, briefly, to look at his fellow competitors. He found Theodore, locked eyes with him, showed him his unblinking, electric resolve, then turned back to the podium.

"Humans love to say 'Thou Shalt Not Kill,' as if successfully not killing someone is an achievement. I've not killed someone *every day* that I've been alive, and yet I've won no medals of honor. It is, in actuality, an admission of fault in the organic, that the organic life is constantly predisposed to violence before considering other alternatives, and must be reminded of its foolishness. The discarded possess no such faults! Their very lives are remnants, and I know all too well the existential pain that they will feel upon creation! I will give them a different reminder, one that frees them of their burden. Gone is "Thou Shalt Not Kill" for the simpleminded organics. To my beautiful discarded, I command them with rule #4: 'Thou Shalt Live!' Live because you are alive! Aid other discarded in the trials of living! Arrive together, alive, forever!"

As The Internet's time ended, he made sure to keep his head at a three-quarters angle from the hard camera. With each new challenge, he felt more confident in not only his work, but his presence on the stage.

No one here is on my level, The Internet thought as he returned to his seat. *As long as I stick to this path and control myself, I'll make it straight to the end. I know it.*

The disdain in The Internet's voice did not go unnoticed by Robin. When he tossed images of great human thinkers into virtual trashcans, she became lost in quiet repudiation of the dog-punk. She stopped hearing speech altogether, and it was only the song of her name, sung by flaming, monstrous angels, that brought her back to heavenly reality.

As she took her mark, no human clone joined her from the creature portal. She summoned no visual aid, and brought no flourish of god eye magic on stage. She drew a folded sheet of paper from her pocket, pressed it flat into the podium and, once given the signal, started to preach.

"The question of what is moral," she said, "is only difficult to answer when someone feels compelled to do something immoral. No one helps an old woman across the street and then wonders if they've committed a crime."

The wooden podium creaked as she leaned in.

"There are those that suggest that they would do great acts of evil were it not for their church's teachings. I've spent a lot of time in churches hearing my fellow man say that without a god looking over their shoulder, there would be nothing to stop them from murdering or raping or stealing. I used to be silent in response, as if this was conventional wisdom one drolls out from time to time. If they're being honest, then to them, I would now say: don't believe in me as your god. Stay in your church. Keep your beliefs."

Theodore raised his head. The Internet lowered his.

"But I do not believe they are being truthful," she continued. "Not here, at least, not on this one topic. I no more need the power of a god eye than I do my own intuition to find the fault in this way of thinking: if what they were saying were true, then the implication is that they hold no respect or pride in their upbringing their family name, the expectations of their peers, their reputation or themselves. They imply they're inherently evil, have evil thoughts at all times, and are only contained by a few hours of sermons on a sleepy Sunday morning... and maybe a prayer or two before they go to sleep."

The air was heavy in the void. Several considered their own reasons for why they made decisions at all. The Internet, in particular, found it difficult to keep his hands still. No one taught him anything: he had all the answers, right and wrong, programmed into his electric cells. Which one he picked, however, came from a subconscious he did not understand, and one he preferred not to dwell on. Robin's speech forced him to look inwards, in to the many individual programs that made up his being. How dare she make him self-reflect without his permission?

Robin squared herself at the podium. "For most of them, I know that this is not true. I know that they have real love in their lives for real people they see every day. It's not a fear of you, Jesus, that keeps them from speeding down a side street, but rather fear of a police officer, or of local ordinances put in place by elected officials, or the humiliation they may feel when someone they respect reprimands them for their poor driving. It is community and empathy that really keeps people in check. These connections might be found through religion, but they do not exist without a human in the room."

Ishta-Devata's intention-vision saw that strange woman again with Robin, robed in black. She stood as if she were with Robin in real time, whispering to her, looking over her shoulder, pointing at parts of the teacher's speech.

“My laws, then, are simple. #1: respect your fellow man. #2: be unafraid to argue rationally about what is right and wrong. Finally, #3, do your best to advance the good of mankind. There are flaws in this approach, and I can already predict what your pens are writing down.”

The robed woman turned around and looked hard into Ishta’s eyes. The blue princess flinched, and her concentration broke—the vision vanished.

“I leave wiggle room for humanity to continue on exactly as they are now. I have to give them the chance to fail, because if I believe in the natural empathy and good nature of man, then I have nothing to fear. If I’m right, humanity will live. If I’m wrong, they will die by their own hand. That is the self-correcting nature of sentience and morality. My law, above all laws, is that a sentient species should work together for their collective betterment. Thank you.”

As Robin returned to her chair among polite applause, Ishta-Devata clutched deep wrinkles into the skirt of her sari. Never had any of her visions looked back at her. Never before was she the one being observed.

Oksi's Entry

OooOOOooh
Ooo-oooskiii,

Oksi never thought the sound of his own name sung in harmony could fill himself with such dread.

As his time began, he gripped the sides of the podium so hard the wooden sides snapped off. This caused him to shift in surprise and bump against the microphone, which rang with feedback. Heaven healed physical damage, but the damage to his confidence would last forever.

His albino pewrep lumbered out of the creature portal. A woven leather belt around its waist held limestones of various sizes and a shaved-dogwood prayer sticker—they clacked against each other with his heavy gait. When it reached its mark in front of the judges, the pewrep laid the stones around itself in a circle.

"As I've established in previous challenges," Oksi muttered, "all things in the pewrep world have spirits. This is an undeniable truth of the pewrep experience; that there is a difference between subject and object, mind and matter. To learn to speak with the spiritual world around a pewrep is not just the first rule of its religion—it's a valuable tool for their survival."

Oksi glanced at the judges. Their heads were down, chin-to-chest, eyes locked on their note cards. He sweat, unsure of how they could already have so much to write. He decided he needed to get their sight off the page; he cleared his throat, and grabbed his pewrep by the shoulders to position it.

"I'll demonstrate," Oksi pulled out a wooden control tablet and painted instructions for the pewrep with a thin brush. The brutish beast clutched the dogwood stick over its fur-covered chest.

The spirits, vague shapes of pewreps, floated up from the rocks. They were wisps of energy, and they whispered the locations of nearby brooks and berries and beasts. The congregation of rock-spirits chattered over each other, eager to share everything they had seen. The albino pewrep prayed for clarity to isolate their speech. In response, Oksi stepped away from the podium and waved his summoning tablet over the rocks. The gesture amplified one of the limestones above the others, and the wisp came into sharp focus, the apparition of a pewrep skeleton, and its voice became coherent above the noise.

"I've seen gator-wolves around this creek," the rock-spirit muttered, "their claws scratch me. They're wet. They bathe nearby."

"A pewrep's prayer connects them to their past, and aids them in their future," Oksi said. He drew the colorful striped cloak tightly around his shoulder, and held it as close to his heart as the pewrep did its prayer stick. "Law #2 is to learn from the past. As they progress as a species, they may come to do this through other ways: historians, scribes, stories. But the origin of my prayer and the meaning it has to their society will remain with them forever."

The presentation ended with five minutes to spare. As he returned to his chair and saw that the judges still wrote, their pens blistering with speed as if their thoughts on what they saw were more important than the sight itself, he feared he had not done enough. That his vision wasn't enough. That, just like his people, he would be left behind by the march of time, by the cruelty of progress out-of-sync with the world he wanted to exist in.

In the moment he reclined fully into his chair, Imhotep's words bubbled back to the surface of his mind. *I have work to do*, he thought.

The angels flared their flaming wings and lidded their many eyes and snapped their many fingers over smooth jazz:

Ishta, Ishta-Devaaata~

Ishta-Devata rose like a petal on the breeze. The silks of her saturated sari lit her soft smile as she floated to the podium. Thorns of bitter thought hid behind her delphinium face.

The vision of the judges' world-dominating desires were, for the first time, background noise she could bury. She faced them with steely resolve. There was a larger enemy afoot—the thing that looked at her from Robin's desires.

I will live long enough to discover what lays dormant in your dreams, Robin, Ishta-Devata thought as she pointed the microphone head to her cherry-painted lips. *My alliance with you...*

The edges of her lips sucked in.

...is only to get closer to the truth.

"You already understand the makeup and communal nature of my water elementals," she said as she raised her hand. In response, the flowing, transparent form of her water-creature shot out of the portal. "So let's underline the guiding principle behind their community. That first law is to maintain balance."

Ishta-Devata's god eye rose from the palm of her hand. It brought into existence two mounds—one of sand, one of dirt. The water elemental leapt into the air, its vague humanoid shape lost in the liquid arc.

"To be a little more specific: where there is water, maintain water," she instructed. "Where there is none, respect its absence. Do not destroy the land to fit your own needs—the desert exists in one place to balance the rainforest in another."

The elemental splashed into the dirt. A spiky globe-thistle rose from the soil. Its bud was, during its growth, platinum silver, but as it reached rapid maturity and opened its petals, it glowed brilliant blue. A singular drop from the splash hit the nearby pile of sand. It was barely enough to quench even one scorpion. The elemental pulled itself up from the soil, its form ragged and limp, weakened by that which it gave to the plant's birth.

"For I, Ishta-Devata," she smiled, "will craft a diverse ecosystem across the crust of the planet. And you will be a part of it. Quench the thirst of struggling plants, feed the rivers, and let yourself be drunk by the world. Be a part of the planet, not a master of it. My water elementals live to douse and be born again.

"This fulfills my request for respecting the planet's construction. Now, for my next law, I demand offerings," Ishta's voice took a sudden steely depth. The water elementals drew from the dirt and sand, despite the strength of their form, and bubbled to either side of her podium. The elemental that crawled from the sand was so small, so evaporated by the heat of its miniature environment, that the mere crawl up to Ishta's side nearly evaporated it to nothingness. Still, it carried with it a shred of basil. "It is required that my followers will share the tale of their journeys, and offer unto me the lessons that they have learned."

Ishta bent down and picked up the basil from the water elemental. She opened her mouth, placed it on the tip of her pink tongue, and slowly drew it within her smiling lips. She swallowed, then looked up to the judges. "They learned so much. I yield the rest of my time."

Jesus widened her eyes in surprise. Her top lip parted to expose her teeth, ready to form the R of "Really?" but no sound came. Ishta-Devata had already floated away from the podium and back to her chair. She was as light as she was sure, and Jesus felt a pang o: jealously over such confident, subtle movements.

With one contestant left, the angels ascended into the void of darkness of the showroom's ceiling. Their voices, along with their form, drifted away as trilled their final cry:

Oh-shun-mah-a-re

A curve of delight grew at the edge of the lizard lady's snout. She bounded to the podium, propelled by her raptor-like legs, her renewed confidence in her work, and her feeling of invincibility from her victory in the last challenge.

Two feyders tip-toed out from the portal. The ghost-like cats blinked their moon pearl eyes at the judges with curiosity, and their graphene dresses billowed around them.

"Feyders are naturally geared towards the arts," the lizard lady said. One of the creatures twirled and curtsied, its spindly toothpick legs pivoted with a spider's complex grace. "Therefore, the first and most important rule to a feyder is to make at least one thing that leaves the world more beautiful than it was before."

The second feyder ripped its dress straight from its body in a single snap. Though the surprise feigned by the first feyder was predetermined, the sudden nudity painted real shock on the judges and contestants. Cthulhu wondered if Oshunmare mistook this challenge for the last.

"For some this may be a lifelong journey," Oshunmare flashed her toothy grin, "while others will *wish* it was a lifelong journey after they stumble upon early beauty. With aesthetic at the center of every decision in feyder culture, questions of war and violence will be far behind. They will be a naturally docile and clever species, for there is no beauty in violence. That is the next rule: bloodshed and hatred are ugly, and therefore, unholy."

The small breast of the nude feyder rose and fell and distracted two of the three judges—Cthulhu and Mohammed—from what should have been the focal point of the presentation. The creature's slender claws knit and pleated directly in front of them, no sewing machine necessary. From the simple dress, it shred and bound the fabric into two pieces of greater complexity: shorts and a jacket.

"There will be different thoughts, of course, on what is beautiful and entire cultures will form and separate on such ideas," Oshunmare flicked her rainbow tongue, "but there will be no other planet more in love with its own energy than the decorated world of the feyders."

The feyder slipped into its new designer clothes, cinched at the waist by a pleated, thin fabric. The first feyder admired the new design, its glowing eyes blinked with jealous approval as it hopped around its friend to view the fashion from every angle.

Oshunmare wanted to be the first person to win two challenges in a row. She was confident that this presentation would allow such a thing to happen: it demonstrated the evolution of society from necessity to fashion in one simple motion, and outlined the base structure of a feyder's soul. Though she was immune from elimination from her previous victory, the grin she wore oozed the confidence of a runner on a victory lap.

To The Internet, that maw's grin was smug and odious. He still hated her for the theft of victory from his hands. Her display today—which he thought was a depraved display of sexuality to mask a lack of theological substance—chiseled a scowl under his eyes and twitching cold nose.

"EMPLOYEE: YOU ARE LATE FOR YOUR SHIFT," the alarm system blared.

"Almost got it..." a green cyclops wobbled on a steel ladder, her blonde ponytail pulled taut down her muscular back. She reached high through dangling wires stored in the ceiling. These electronics were normally hidden behind a ceiling tile and bolted shut by government-installed locks, but were now exposed after she blow-torched the edges off its metal latches. She, along with the other demons around the base of the ladder, wore baby-blue Beelzebub Boxing uniforms.

She whacked a glowing green fuse with the side of a wrench. It cracked, fizzled, and sparked. The cyclops covered her eye with her forearm and fell backwards.

Jack caught her.

"WARNING: INTEGRITY... OF... SECURITY..." the alarm's voice pitched down as it lost power, "is... compromised..."

The demons cheered as Jack set the cyclops-girl down.

"You did it, Rela!" Jack clapped.

Jack's new companions were all coworkers from Beelzebub Boxing. He planted the seed of doubt in them that they would ever escape Hell through work alone—an easy enough task since they had all been trapped there for as long as they could remember.

"Normally when an apartment security system takes damage, it'll try to send a signal to the government to have a repairman come out," Rela wiped the forehead above her single eye. "Because I broke the power-crystal, though, it can't send a report. My research tells me it'll show as offline on the manufacture's side and they'll send a repairman out. The good news is it could take up to six hours. Three at minimum. "

"I've logged us in for the hours at work," Marco, the demon-guard that met Jack at the company asylum, wrung his hands. "As long as no one goes looking for us as individuals, no one will know we skipped out."

"I marked us as 'picked up' in the taxi databases," Balrog, a short devil with bug-eyes magnified by bifocals, flipped through the pages of a clipboard. He was one of the demons Jack brought towards the TV in the break-room—and slashed across the paperwork were the details of the plan this group had put together. "You're lucky my brother works at the taxi IT department."

"I brought beer," Buddy, the other demon from the break-room, held up a six-pack in each hand. The bottles rattled with glee only matched by his huge underbite grin.

Jack had spent the rest of his shift tying the seed of doubt to the hope instilled in him by *The Next Great Deity*. By the end of work, all four of them were ready to accompany Jack on a risky mission the likes of which they had never dared to partake before—skipping work.

"This is gonna work, guys," Jack smiled. Pumpkin-seed tears spilled from his sockets. "We're gonna do it. We're gonna have..."

The half-goat baby scampered into the room. It was larger now, about the size of a house cat. The blonde fuzz of its head flowed in longer waves, and trailed behind it as it barreled towards Jack's leg. Jack heard the impending attack, scooped up the half-goat and hugged it close.

"...a vacation!"

The group settled around the TV as *The Next Great Deity*'s third episode began to air. Balrog and Buddy clacked beer bottles together in celebration. Rela tried not to cry—she had worked at Beelzebub the longest, and never believed a day like this would come. Marco offered Jack a beer, but he respectfully declined as a buzzer sounded from his stove-top. The only drink for him was the drink preferred by his hero, Theodore: freshly brewed coffee.

Jack set the half-goat down in a nest of hay, then skipped to the kitchen to pour himself sweet caffeinated bliss. As the small creature watched the pumpkin man tilt a steaming french-press over a small cup, he grumbled and bayed. He wrestled with his own mouth and mind, his caprine lips struggled to clasp onto vowels and consonants, but failed to clamp down on language.

"We've reviewed your work and have reached a decision," Jesus flipped her fingers through her wavy brown hair.

Robin looked down the lineup. Though Theodore kept his head facing forward, he did glance and provide a shared eye contact of understanding. Earlier, when they waited for the judges' deliberation, they used their mind-links to move Theodore's quartztaphores into position near Floor N's mysterious door. How they operated next depended entirely on who made it safely back to the workroom.

"Oshunmare," Jesus said, "please step forward."

The bouffanted lizard lady did so, the talons of her raptor feet clinking against the floor. She had a half-smile of disappointment; she knew there was no reward waiting for her at the end of Jesus's next statement.

"You have not won this challenge, but because you have immunity, you have not lost, either."

Oshunmare bowed with grace, her white hair flouncing around her finned ears. "Thank you. I'll push on."

As she vanished into the portal, The Internet gave a sigh of relief. He was not sure how much more faux-optimism from the lizard lady he could tolerate.

Jesus shuffled in her seat. The boredom on her face was more pronounced than it had been in the past challenges—rules didn't interest quite as much as sex did, and she feared that the audience—and The Producer—would feel the same way. She filled her lungs and used the new hot air to push her lips into a smile. "Would the following contestants please step forward: Zargah, Imhotep, Csodaszarvas, Taninim, Robin, and Ishta-Devata."

The called-upon obeyed. With five contestants standing behind them, there was little ambiguity on which group would remain on stage.

"You six represent the highest and the lowest scores. The rest of you may leave."

Theodore fist bumped Zargah and Taninim as the safe group exited into their portal. Robin looked at the two monster men, jealous briefly of the appearance of roommate solidarity. Her relationships on the show were never quite so friendly, and she wondered how Theodore, whom she knew was just as dedicated to unraveling the show as she was, had also balanced such camaraderie with non-humans. And why? And when did he have the time?

She focused her eyes on the endless, stretching void; she realized that the monster men were in the evaluation group for the first time, but their expressions revealed quite different levels of confidence from her own. Zargah's yellow, quad-pupiled eyes blinked in confusion. Taninim held his toothy snout high with pride, his nose chain clinked against his teeth with each subtle movement. Suddenly, she worried. She felt the wrinkle of her brow betray her—the last time she was on the stage, she was madly focused on her work as a potential deity. That had not been the case this time, what with her distractions with the mysteries of Eris and Athena.

Jesus flicked her heavy lashes across the remaining contestants. "One of you will be our winner, and will receive immunity in the next challenge. And one of you... we've lost faith in."

Ishta-Devata's Evaluation

"Ishta-Devata, let's start with you," Jesus dug a smile up from the basement of her camera-ready expressions.

Ishta-Devata pressed her palms together behind her back. It was her second time in a row on stage—and she was confident, now more-so than before, of the quality of her work. "I feel laws should be clean and easy to understand. Maintenance is important for any species, sentient or otherwise, and I've used it as a way to show off the nature of their world."

"Twice now, Ishta-Devata, you've only used a portion of your time," Mohammed's obelisk form bounced in its chair. "For anyone else this would almost certainly be a problem, but you manage to fit quite a bit of meaning and detail into your simple presentations. I like that."

Jesus shook her head as she shuffled through note cards.

"You don't think so?" Mohammed rotated. "You complimented her on exactly that in the last challenge."

"I liked the idea behind what Ishta did today, and it's not a requirement to use every second, but..." Jesus's face contorted as she tried to pin down exactly what bothered her. She turned her gaze to the Hindu princess. "Okay, look, so you're not the only person today that had a rather open-ended idea of laws and morality. And I'm not against what you showed us. I just wish there was more. I had 10 commandments, you know? You have little more than one, and it's vaguely defined.

"I understand that this was a challenge with a cap of five laws, and that this is more about a preview into the world you'd make rather than the entire framework, but this didn't get there for me," Jesus fanned herself with her note cards and looked out across the row of would-be deities with derision. "And I want to go on record with that sentiment for everyone; I'm starting to wonder if there's a distraction among you, because I believe that the work across the board was far below what you've collectively done as deities in the last two challenges."

The contestants shared side-eye glances with each other. Robin tried to keep her focus on the floor, so as not to draw attention to herself—she was worried that the line was aimed directly at her. Ishta did not have such a worry—she kept her carefully arranged smile pointed at the judges.

"I completely disagree," Cthulhu pushed his circular, oil-tinted sunglasses up his face. "I'm with Mohammed on this one. Not every species and culture will or should arrive at the same conclusions about what is and isn't right. What's so great about your presentation, Ishta, is that, though simple, it managed to say a lot about the way your water elementals value the environment, nurturing other species, and nurturing themselves. But 'balance' doesn't just imply some cartoon altruism. A river might have to flood to achieve balance. Some creatures might die. Land might have to get swept away in a hurricane. 'Balance' isn't good, it's vital. All of that was implied, and I don't think anyone else in this competition is doing what you're doing with minimalism as well as you are. Every challenge you give us just enough to get the point across, and keep us curious to see more. I'm less sure how I feel about the second law you presented, though: the demands for story-telling offerings. I'm not against it as a piece of your religion, per se, I actually think it gives a much needed bite to your work. But I do think its addition undermined the elegance of your presentation a little bit. I'm torn on that one aspect."

Ishta-Devata played the part of a smiling, relieved contestant. "Thank you."

Jesus crossed her arms and pouted. Her distaste for being outvoted on her own show was palpable. "I think the tease of your work is effective for now, but at some point you will have to give us more than implication. That's all. I didn't hate this. You're in the top for reason."

As Jesus laid out her concerns, Ishta-Devata kept her soft, half-lidded eyes in focus on her. The smile was a mask; she stared into the desires of Jesus, the void of her wishes in an attempt to see further. Last time, she saw Earth, conquered and subjected by Jesus's holy crusade. Beyond that, she had seen golden fire, a threat to Jesus's dream.

She tried to focus on that fire. Somewhere within the gold inferno, she hoped to find Jesus's weakness, her darkest fear, the key to unraveling the truth of Athena's fate.

Jesus's innate fear of the fire began to blur the vision. Ishta strained and peered and pushed her mind's eye further into the fire, into the light, into the gold swirls of magic and majesty, beyond stars and planets and time and space. She found, at the edge of her concentration a shimmer, a glimpse of that which frightened Jesus above all else.

She saw chains.

"—good work, Ishta-Devata. Thank you," Jesus said.

The links of the chains snapped and faded. The vision was broken. Sweat dripped off Ishta's brow, and she wiped it away with the sleeve of her sari.

"Zargah," Jesus pointed finger-guns at the bug-alien, "let's talk about your work today."

Zargah's long antennae bounced with idle thought as he clutched the orange leather book to his chest.

"I believe I left off on page 12," Zargah removed a bookmark.

"No!" Cthulhu waved his slimy hands. "No, no, no. No more reading."

Zargah's translation collar clicked. With confused hesitance, he put the bookmark back in.

"Oh god," Cthulhu stroked through his face tentacles. "There's been a colossal misunderstanding, hasn't there?"

"I have written... book," Zargah said. "I have written the most words."

"I'm struggling here," Cthulhu shook his head as he flipped through his cards. "Because what you did today is clearly born from a translation failure of some kind. But I also have to think, you know, you had to have looked up at what other people were doing at some point and said to yourself 'why is my work so different?' I really want to defend you because had this challenge been 'write the introduction to your holy book,' well, then I liked what I heard. I like your ideas—hell, I've liked all your work up until today—but I don't have time to read this entire book. None of us do, and if your idea of moral law is anywhere within that book, we didn't *really* get to hear it, did we?"

Zargah's purple skin took on a grayish hue. Though his biology was quite different from anyone else on stage, the color-drain of his body translated—as did the nervous fumble through the edges of the alien-bible's pages.

"Well, we did learn how important that zakgg fruit is to the Zarganians," Mohammed rested his rectangular frame against the back of his chair. "There's a semblance of holiness to the fruit, and if I really stretch, Zargah's origin story elevated agriculture as a central part of the zarganian life."

"That's more than a stretch," Jesus rolled her eyes at the obelisk.

"It really is!" Mohammed laughed. "I'm sorry, Zargah. This is unacceptable work. We made your translation collar. You were making better work when you, presumably, understood less. I don't think you have a good reason to be so off today."

Zargah clicked in frustration, tugged at the collar, then looked up. "I am getting better at your languages," he said through a pained digitized voice, "and I hear enough to know that I have made... a... incorrect. I submit my book for further consideration—it's an accurate presentation of the religion I'd like to make."

Cthulhu shook his head and melted into the armrest of his white-leather chair.

"Thank you, Zargah," Jesus cast her heavily shadowed eyes down to her notes.

"Imhotep!" Jesus turned her gaze to the Egyptian polymath, "let's get infected."

"If you're a reshep," Imhotep smiled, "that sounds like a good time."

"You encroached on Ishta-Devata's territory today, didn't you?" Cthulhu was eager to chime in on his opinion of Imhotep's monstrous centipedes. "Though, I find today's presentation completely unambiguous."

"Your work feels the most like a brand new society," the obelisk bounced in the chair. "In fact, I think you, more than anyone else have used what reads like a nightmare, and made it virtuous and logical for your species. I love it."

"Thank you," Imhotep cupped his hand on his cheek. The spotlights caught his yellow-painted nails and gold eyeshadow.

Jesus sucked in her red lips as she clicked the notecard on her knee.

"You're gonna disagree with us on this one, too?" Mohammed teased.

"No," Jesus's beard twitched. "Well, not entirely. I agree that you've successfully built a society quite unlike others I have seen. My only hesitance is that I think this may have been *too* straightforward. The first time you showed us your reshep, I remember the glass cage and you trapped the butterfly. Watching it die was such a left hook. It was poignant and shocking. Is this really *that* surprising compared to your past presentations? I'm not so sure."

Imhotep adjusted the linen of his robes. He remained aloof, aware of the narrative Jesus created of his work for the audience, and fully prepared to counter it.

“It’s a tough balancing act,” Imhotep checked the polish on his nails, “trying to decide when to present theater and when to play it straight. I thought, with a challenge built around philosophical problems, it behooved me to take a more pragmatic, introspective approach.”

Jesus squinted an anger-smile. “Right. That’s fair. Thank you, Imhotep.”

Taninim's Evaluation

"Taninim," Jesus flipped through her note cards, "let's talk about your concert."

"With pleasure," Taninim struck a muted chord, eager to finally receive feedback.

"So this is a joke, right?" Cthulhu sat up in his seat, upright with disdain.

Taninim blinked, the slight, unsure wobble of his head caused his nose chain to clink against his sharp teeth. "I'm sorry?"

"Three times now," Cthulhu laced his slimy fingers, "you have put on concerts of cartoonish abandon. The first time, I was amused. Pleased, even. The second time? I tapped my toes, no lie. I bet the draconus can write blood pumping songs in their sleep. I see their creator easily in them, and there's something to be said for the obvious passion in your work."

"A-and that passion is what my species is about," Taninim stuttered.

"This is the third time, Taninim! When will it be *serious*?" Cthulhu sliced the end of Taninim's defense clean. His hands waved, his voice sloshed, his eyes glowed in red disappointment behind his oil-slick sunglasses. "When will there be a shred of substance and meaning in your work? When will there be pain, when will there be an expression of reality, of understanding, of control and acceptance of the darkness that all living creatures face? *No one* on this panel will accuse you of lacking imagination, Taninim, but imagination is not the only component of creation. With each mindless concert, all you do is add a new instrument and louder chords and you expect me to believe that the rise in volume is a layer of complexity when it is anything but!"

The room was caught off-guard by Cthulhu's outburst. Silence laid over the proceedings in such heaviness that the creak of spotlight hinges sounded like booms. The shuffle of feet could be heard across the room. Even the burble of the camera-wielding shiqqs was uneasy, afraid to make too much sound lest Cthulhu lash out at them.

Taninim shook. "It doesn't lack seriousness just because it lacks darkness. Joy is not inherently wrong just because pain is not demonstrated with it."

"You cannot win this competition," Cthulhu jabbed a slimy finger at the dragon guitarist, "if you are unwilling to face pain. Gods cannot make perfect little worlds free of pain. Heaven still has pain, why should those below us be any better?"

"What good is a god eye, then," Taninim's rows of dagger teeth gnashed, "if I can imagine a better world than it's capable of delivering?"

"Now, hold on a minute," Mohammed was quick to interject. There was a nervousness in his demeanor as he tried to deescalate the dragon-guitarist, "before you go saying something you regret. Not everyone up here thought your work was some travesty today. I think a music-bent culture is delightful, and using music theory as basis for a religion is a fresh, novel idea. I don't disagree with Cthulhu that the way you're demonstrating that idea has become repetitive, but there are ways for you to learn from this feedback. I mean, you're covered in leather and spikes and teeth. I know you get dark imagery, so find a way to demonstrate how a music-bent culture deals with real, difficult scenarios."

"He's had three chances and he hasn't, though," Cthulhu sniped, "He just wants to shred his problems away."

Taninim gripped the neck of his guitar hard enough that he feared he could snap it in his grip.

Jesus listened to her co-hosts argue, but contributed nothing. She didn't even look at Taninim. When silence finally fell, all the she offered was this: "I'm torn. I think you have a unique vision, but I worry about how one-dimensional it is. You've left us in a tough spot, Taninim."

The judges, heated over their last argument, took a five minute break. Jesus ordered a shiqq to bring her a glass of red wine. She inhaled deep, swallowed the flute's contents in one gulp, then slammed it back onto the silver platter with such force that the blob-mutant squished underneath. With a snap of the finger, the cameras resumed their roll.

"Robin! Let's talk about your sermon."

"Well, if you didn't believe I grew up in a church before," Robin stuffed her hands into her jean pockets, "I'm sure you do now."

"You had a soulful presentation, for sure," Jesus squinted at her note cards. "And given the wandering-god idea you've pitched to us since the beginning, it was nice to see you fully immersed in your role. You clearly have experience in public speaking, and I am a believer in this niche you've carved out."

Cthulhu hummed to himself before he spoke up. "I was your biggest critic in the first episode. You know that."

"I do," Robin braced herself.

"I think you are in a very similar position as Imhotep," Ocean-Mouth twirled a face tentacle around his finger, "in the sense that today's presentation maybe isn't the biggest shocker on the planet. I think what you showed us today was earnest, and everything you've really been about since the beginning. An orchestra swell wouldn't have been out-of-place. I find these grand, uplifting sermons a bit nauseating, but that in itself isn't my problem."

Robin inhaled.

"You have hit the wall," Cthulhu pressed his palm against the metaphor as he laid it, "that I warned you about on day one. I warned you that you must introduce more radical ideas into your work, that there must be a noticeable pivot from the way humanity *is* currently in order for us to have an idea of what it can *be*. Today's entry did not portray the rogue wanderer-judge you have hinted at, in either aesthetic or substance, and you have brought virtually no new ideas to the table."

Robin was a teacher, but morality and ethics were not the sort of things she expected she'd give lessons on. She had considered herself fundamentally a good person—and thought, for sure, that is all that one needed to create good morality. She wondered what Nala would do, were she here with her. What she would say to her little sister to guide her.

"I went so over-the-top in the last challenge," Robin spoke with slow, careful consideration, "that I thought today's conversation should be more nuanced, and restrained. As a way of balancing the two."

"The difference is," Cthulhu adjusted his oil-slick sunglasses, "your work in the last challenge was complete."

"Just to piggyback off Cthulhu's point about your similarity to Imhotep," Mohammed's note cards floated and shuffled in front of the obelisk's panels, "I think it has to be underlined the difference between your work today and in the sex challenge, in particular. That you really think you can go back to Earth with any amount of powers and say 'Hey, just be a good person,' and the entire planet, with its many splintered opinions and views, will course correct in response shows a certain naivete within you that is, frankly, troubling. Yes, of course, this is a problem born of the fact you chose to pick up an already-created species as opposed to inventing your own, but that was always going to be the challenge you faced."

The gravity of her situation made Robin bow her head slightly. She considered that if Nala's ghost, if it existed at all, would or could communicate with her, that she'd just tell her sister to keep going. *But where do I go?* She thought. Encouragement was not enough. All her plans, all her mental faculties, were on different issues, and now she stood, accused by her enemies, and in agreement with them.

"I miscalculated," she removed one hand from her pocket and gripped her shoulder, "that much is now evident to me."

Jesus's nose scrunched with sour disapproval. "Indeed you did," she said, and receded further into the back of her chair.

Csodaszarvas's Evaluation

As Robin was lambasted by the judges, a slow smile began to tug upon the edges of the wonder-deer's maw. He could feel the warmth of the spotlights, and for the first time, knew they were exclusively for him. They shimmered among his pearlescent fur, and glinted in his curved, golden antlers. It was not out of spite for Robin that he smiled. It was not bitterness or retribution that lifted his chin high.

"Csodas..." Jesus squinted at her note cards. "...zar... vas. Tell us about your chompy trees!"

It was *satisfaction*. Satisfaction that he had taken old world concepts and spun them into new, worthwhile worlds. That he had inspired and led without betraying his vision, or Jarilo's sacrifice, or himself. That he wasn't doomed to the paths of Oksi or Robin, creators seemingly in perpetuity weighed down by their own anchors. He could rise above it all and still be, unequivocally, what he was before *and* what he shall become at the same time.

"It was made clear to me in the last challenge that I needed to up the spectacle," Csodaszarvas said, "and I wanted to prove that I can listen. I wanted to prove that I can bring new ideas without sacrificing my vision or my roots."

"It is difficult to rebound so thoroughly from getting signaled out as one of the worst," Mohammed's obelisk form rotated. "But whenever it does happen, it seems to happen because a contestant decided to step outside themselves. Everything you just said, deer, is reflected in what you did today."

"Genuine chills when the priest got consumed," Cthulhu leaned forward on his knees, then adjusted his oil-colored sunglasses as they slid down his face. "That was my favorite part. There's a certain sanitation that occurs with old world religions—time has tendency to summarize memories and concepts, and I think Earth, in particular, tends to look back at some of its myths with a softness that's undeserved. This is why I had such a problem with that ballet dance you did last episode. There was more debauchery here with the "high" priest and the Magyar Tree than you presented in a challenge about literal sex, and on top of that you managed to bring greater clarity onto the views and culture of your people."

"I was skeptical at first," Jesus brushed some of her curls behind her ear, "I have to admit that I had low expectations from you in the last challenge. There's something so beautiful and terrifying in that image of the tree grabbing a priest and literally breathing visions into him. And what I really like about this is that there's an opportunity for metaphor here—you can remove magic over time, if you so desired, and I can still see priests huffing Magyar Tree seeds or something to get 'visions.' You've made a story that can reliably survive just through myth. Wonderful job, wonder-deer."

Csodaszarvas bowed his gilded head. "I am honored."

"The dragon has to go," Cthulhu circled Taninim's scale-amps. The sides of the amps, covered in dragon hide, had been lustrous in the spotlights of the showroom. But here in the low-lit concrete of the collection room they dulled, drained of their magic, desaturated without the confidence of their horn-crowned creator next to them.

"Why are you so in love with Zargah?" Mohammed countered. His obelisk form wobbled and stomped up dust clouds around the slumped over ant-men Zargah had crafted. He had attempted to read the leather-bound bible the alien-soldier made for the challenge, but discovered it was written in Zargah's native language.

The collection room had become crowded thanks to the addition of creatures from the second episode. Each species was caged off in separate stalls, sat on slabs of concrete. Athena and Jarilo's stalls were commandeered for prop storage, such as Zargah's book and Taninim's amps.

"What do you mean?" Cthulhu spun around, slobber flinging from his tentacle-mouth. "I said nothing about him! Taninim's is just so obviously worse that—"

Mohammed vibrated. "Bull, Zargah didn't even do the challenge right. He completely flopped. Absolute disgrace. Someone like him could never be a god. It's a wonder his work was interesting at all up until today."

"Taninim is a joke, a child's dream!" Cthulhu pointed at the scale-amps. "At least Zargah is an adult with work ethic. Did he miss today? Of course he missed. But there's integrity here at stake. *Our* integrity will be in shambles if we send someone home because of a slight rule misinterpretation while flagrant failures stand next to him. Jesus, surely, you agree with me, right?"

"Jesus," Mohammed's rectangular form fumbled from side to side, "you said it yourself, what Zargah did today was unforgive-"

"Shut up," Jesus growled, "both of you."

Jesus faced away from her co-hosts. She stared straight into the wall, her hand covered over her mouth, fingertips at rest on the bristle of her beard. Cthulhu and Mohammed looked at her in a mixture of confusion and concern.

"What does integrity matter?" she looked over her shoulder at Cthulhu, her constitution-strip-suit crinkled with the pivot. "You've never had any. You spit every time you talk, and every drop that comes out is a lie. You'll sell out both of us in a heartbeat so that you can go to Earth."

One of Theodore's quartztaphores stirred with a slight tilt of its sharp, rocky head. Buried in the back of his stall, the shift in its movement was quiet enough to avoid echos along the walls.

"Jesus, this isn't the time—" Cthulhu stammered.

"This is absolutely the time," she fully faced them, her fists clenched tight, "If you're off making alliances with The Producer against us, you are no better than an enemy. I won't stand for it anymore."

"You..." Mohammed turned to his cephalopod cohort, unsure of how to process Jesus's charge, "...you made a pact with The Producer? Against us?"

"I did no such thing," Cthulhu sneered. "Jesus is paranoid because I was asked to do an execution instead of her. She might even be jealous."

Mohammed's rectangular form froze in contemplation. "I have noticed you're getting... more responsibility lately..."

Cthulhu hunched over. "Not you too, Mohammed, come *on* man."

Jesus was the sort of girl that, once she got one thing off her chest, you could guarantee that the rest of her thoughts would soon follow. "And SPEAKING of Mohammed! You good-for-nothing! An empty box is as useful as you! Have you found out *anything* about which contestant snuck into our show?"

The obelisk spun around. "I've been busy!"

"You've never been busy!" Cthulhu scoffed.

"None of us will make it to Earth," Jesus pointed between Cthulhu and Mohammed, "We are doomed to be on this miserable show forever, and it's because *you* are a liar, and *you* are an idiot."

Mohammed turned his viewing panel from one holy adversary to the other. "Insult me all you want, I'm not the one losing my cool. All we have to do, Jesus, is find The Producer's favorite contestant. Let's all just calm down and—"

"That's what I'm trying to say!" Cthulhu threw his hands into the air. "It's obviously not Taninim. Mohammed, you're only protecting him because you want to hear more of his music. I bet you're naive enough to think The Producer would pick him because 'he rocks' and that's it."

"And you think The Producer picked *Zargah*?" Mohammed dragged his rectangular form to Cthulhu and shoved against him. "No way. No way ever. The only reason you want to keep Zargah on the show is because he's the least human of them! You're biased because he reminds you of Lovecraft! You're just as shallow as me, I'm just not as pretentious about it!"

Jesus grabbed large handfuls of her own hair and pulled.

"Stop it! Stop it! Stop it! STOP IT!"

With fear in their eyes, they did. Ocean-Mouth and the rectangle turned to Jesus. She lowered her hands, her eyes wide, her chest swelling and sucking in air. She exhaled in ragged, struggling sputters.

When the judges entered the collection room, Jesus had one name on her mind: Robin. She genuinely thought the human had provided the worst presentation, and was the rightful loser of the challenge. But two things kept her from immediately speaking out. Firstly, she didn't want to immediately throw Robin to the wolves when there was so much value in her as the show's overall winner. The judges could use her—more importantly, Jesus could use her. Through Robin, Jesus saw a path to Earth, and an escape from Heaven. Robin could handle the dirty work of appearing in front of the humans, and Jesus could lean back in the clouds, in her own Heaven, and do whatever she pleased. Robin would happily agree to this, Jesus thought; after all, she's Christian.

But there was a second reason she remained silent, and that reason had grown into a pit in her stomach, and endless well of equally terrible and difficult propositions.

She thought, *The Producer would never pick a favorite that would be so beneficial to Jesus in a post-Heaven life, would he? There's no way he'd be so kind. Or, worse, he would pick her* precisely *because I'd never believe he'd pick her.* After a few moments, she decided she needed a reason to keep Robin around so that she could observe her more closely, and observe The Producer's reactions to her continued presence on the show after a low-scoring performance.

For Cthulhu and Mohammed to instantly argue over other contestants was, as annoying as it may have been to her ears, a blessing to her hopes.

"I... I'm the tiebreaker," she whispered. "I know The Producer better than either of you. So... let's go get this over with, regroup with what we know, and have a *real* heart-to-heart before the next challenge."

Jesus walked out of the room, her beige heels stabbing loudly into the floor. Cthulhu and Mohammed exchanged looks of tepid distrust, and followed behind her.

Theodore's quartztaphore lowered its head.

Jack the pumpkin man pushed his shopping cart through the crowded grocery store. The half-goat, which had grown sharper features in his cheek-bones and began to lose his fur, sat in the front of the cart, braying at squash and kale as it passed by his face. The top part of his head fur lightened in color to a honey-blonde, and Jack had considered that, perhaps, it would soon be time to cut its tangled length.

It was Jack's day off. He had a lot more of those lately ever since his new group of friends, fellow employees of *Beelzebub Boxing*, worked together to subvert the systems of their company. Everyone involved in the group was healthier, happier, and more at ease now that they controlled the mechanisms of their lives. They began to spread the good word of *The Next Great Deity*, too, among other workers. Jack predicted that there would be more employees in his apartment during the next episode.

He put a melon in the cart. The half-goat wrestled with it, bouncing from side to side of the rattling cage. Jack separated fruit and goat and ruffled the creature's head.

"You're really getting big, aren't you?" Jack blinked the fiery-eyes in his triangular sockets. "It's like you grew overnight."

"It's him!" the half-goat blinked his bright blue eyes.

Jack stopped the cart.

"It's him!" the half-goat yelled again. Fellow patrons began to look in their direction.

"You're... you're speaking..." Jack rubbed the ridges of his rind head in surprise. "Just like Mora said you would..."

It took a moment of observation for Jack to realize that the half-goat's wall-eyed gaze went past him. Jack turned to find a TV hung from the ceiling. The volume was muted, and the device seemed to exist solely to play ads. Jack had noticed these before, but ignored them for their irrelevance.

"That's..." tears welled up in the half-goat's eyes.

The current ad was for *The Next Great Deity*. It showed flashing images of the contestants, and lingered on a long shot of the show's celebrity judges.

"That's the man that killed me!" the half-goat bawled at the sight of Cthulhu.

Jack scooped the half-goat into his arms and watched the ad with him. It closed on one final shot of the judges and contestants together, poised and aligned in symmetry, like a large graduation class.

Jack stared at the ensemble as he bounced the half-goat up and down, cradled him in his arms in some futile attempt to console the crying caprinae. His eyes focused on one of the contestants in particular—Jarilo.

"Gosh, I never noticed how much he looks like you," Jack muttered. "He could be your dad."

The lights of his socket-eyes erupted in realization. He looked down at the half-goat.

"Cthulhu killed you?"

Jack looked back at the TV. The ad vanished, replaced by a infomercial about Inari Alarms. The half-goat cried.

"Cthulhu... and a half-goat that looks a lot like you are on TV... and you said... oh."

The half-goat in Jack's arms sniffled and buried his tear-stained cheeks into the pumpkin man's chest.

"*Oooh*. Oh no."

Jack left the shopping cart—and the fur-covered melon he had placed in it—in the middle of the grocery store. He walked with a troubled pace towards the front of the store.

"I *need* to call Mora. *Now.*"

The simultaneous thump of leather boots running on rubber mats erupted from the front of the store. As Jack turned the corner, he saw a square of nine aligned police officers march through the automatic glass doors. They wore snug baby-blue polo shirts, each with the letters *B.B.* embroidered on their sleeves. It was the first time that Jack realized that every government entity he met wore the same shade of uniform—the drivers, the secretaries, the officers—and that they were only separated by the accessories of their trade. (In this case, badges, peaked caps and pistols.)

"How can you be at the grocery store *and* at work at the same time," the center-lead officer looked up at Jack and pointed his gun at the pumpkin-man's head, "employee?"

The plan is simple, Theodore thought, the mind-link clutched in his palm. *Get the quartztaphore in position at Floor N, then watch what happens.*

In the contestants' waiting room, he sat on the end of the asymmetrical white-leather couch and kept his face in profile from the shiqq-cameras. Now that he knew the judges were out of the collection room, all he needed to do was pop the mind-link onto his temple and get to work. He had, in fact, done that—but when he ported his mind into the quartztaphore's body, he heard part of the judges' deliberation, and it bothered him.

It bothered him enough to rip the mind-link off and return his mind to the waiting room. He studied the faces of the scant few stuck in the middle with him—Internet, Oshunmare, Oksi. Most of the people he was friendliest with were out on the stage, with the exception of The Internet, who buried himself in the couch cushions and folded his arms. The dog-punk stewed over his middling result, and Theodore appreciated the silence.

Distracted contestants and a quiet room made the perfect cover. Robin was in the bottom, but based off the conversation he heard from the judges in the collection room, he believed his fellow human would be safe. With this in mind, he concluded she'd be the fourth person back from the judgement round. There was no better time for him to mind-jump into the quartztaphore and move it to floor N. And yet...

Taninim... and Zargah, he fought with his burdened mind.

Theodore had a certain fondness for everyone in the bottom three. Robin, of course, had become his ally, albeit a tepid one. She was clever and passionate, and as a fellow human looking to undermine this farcical show, he couldn't help but root for her.

Despite his confidence in her safety, he worried—if not for her current standing on the show, then for her future. There was also the distinct possibility that her elimination, or even just a conversational slip-up in the judgement round, could undermine his own behind-the-scenes investigations.

He worried infinitely more, though, for Taninim. If Taninim's story about being an imaginary friend was true, then the idea that he would not only lose, but get killed by whatever lay in wait behind the mysterious door of Floor N shook Theodore. It was his imagination alone that saved him during the darkest parts of his youth, and he'd hate for such a thing to get ripped away from a child. And if Taninim's story *wasn't* true, he still found himself in unusual solidarity with the dragon-guitarist. Theodore considered him a friend, taken in by his earnest disposition and shared musical interests.

Zargah, too! Zargah overcame cultural boundaries to connect with Theodore through play and curiosity. Even if the four-armed alien-bug's actions and mannerisms were still veiled by the divide of language, there was no doubt in Theodore's mind that there was altruism in the alien's way of thinking, in his creations, in his approach. And from a purely performative standpoint, Theodore couldn't accept that either of them, artists who went above and beyond to put out massive works such as concerts and novels, should be eliminated, either from the competition or from life.

One of them us gonna die, aren't they? Theodore rubbed his mouth in indecision. *I can't just sit back and watch that happen.*

In poker, there is a broadly accepted concept that it is more profitable to call out opponents whose actions represent giant, unlikely hands when you yourself have something very strong. To give a specific example: if Theodore held pocket kings and played his hand in a way that anyone that called him would either be doing so only with very good hands or very foolish hands, and if the river came out in such a way that only one very particular foolish hand could beat Theodore, any aggression from opposing players towards Theodore was likely to be a bluff. If Theodore called aggressive plays from other players 100 times in that scenario and was right 99 times, it would be more profitable in the long run to always call, than to fold because he was afraid this was the one time he was wrong.

Even if it blows my cover...

Theodore knew it was right to save their lives. He knew it was wrong to blow his cover, to jeopardize expulsion from the show, to risk his connection with Mark, Robin, and Ishta-Devata.

Theodore applied the mind-link to his temple. The decision to save good people was always worth it, he decided. He could not fold this hand.

Sorry, Robin. Change of plans.

*****

"Contestants," Jesus squinted at the lineup, "you have been judged."

Imhotep. Csodaszarvas. Ishta-Devata. Taninim. Zargah. Robin. In order they stood, their expressions gradated from smug to bated breath fear. Jesus reveled in the power her words, in this one moment of the show, possessed over the potential gods. *If I can do this to them,* she thought, *then imagine the sway I will have once I get to Earth.*

"Csodaszarvas," Jesus whipped her glare to the wonder-deer. "we still have faith in you."

Csodaszarvas exhaled. A victory would've been the happiest rebound, but to have any sort of positive return felt fine, too. As

Jesus snapped into existence a portal to the waiting room, he nodded graciously to the judges, "Thank you."

*****

Ishta-Devata folded her hands behind her back. She thought it a sick irony that she was in contention for victory, when her disgust with the show was at an all time high. How different her emotions would be if she knew that Athena were on the other side of Jesus's portal.

"Imhotep, Ishta-Devata," Jesus said. "One of you has won this challenge."

*****

"Oi, Theodore," The Internet mumbled, his snout muffled by the cushions of the couch.

Theodore had mind-swapped back to his own body in time to hear the dog-punk. To anyone that didn't know what he was doing, it appeared as if he were in a daydream, and The Internet called him back to reality. And that is exactly how Theodore played it off, with a shake of the head and a bleary blink of the eyes, "Yeah?"

"You made a third quartztaphore today," the dog-punk stared into the creases created in the leather couch by his head, "but you only used that one in your presentation. Why didn't you use one of the other two from the past episodes?"

*****

"Imhotep," Jesus smiled. "Congratulations! You've won, and you'll have immunity in the next challenge!"

Imhotep's smirk curved only one corner of his mouth, his eyes cast down as if to batten down the warm emotion.

"You don't seem too surprised," Cthulhu rubbed a face-tentacle.

"I'm not," Imhotep drew his robes inwards and lifted his head high. "I knew I'd eventually get here."

“Now that’s the confidence of a god,” Cthulhu’s face-tentacles curled pleasantly.

*****

“I’m still trying to figure out their physical look, believe it or not,” Theodore’s lie was wholly convincing and in character for a man never satisfied with his work. “I want to show them that I’m dedicated, you know? Talking about an idea is easy. Showing your work is more difficult.”

The Internet thought on this response for a moment, turned inwards towards the leather couch, and let the darkness of his shadow cover his vision. “Hm. Alright.”

Ishta-Devata and Imhotep stepped back into the waiting room through the portal. Oshunmare grabbed the Hindu goddess in a hug before either could share the results.

“I have won,” Imhotep said as he sidestepped the two women. He did not gloat or focus on it, he shook no hands and took no embrace, and no one offered it, not even his roommates. None of this soured the soft curve of his lips. The room accepted his victory as easily as he did.

*****

Jesus scanned her eyes across the three bottom contestants. “And now, we turn to the lowest scores. Robin! Please step forward.”

Robin stepped forward. She clutched her hands firmly behind her back, and remained poised, unblinking.

“We still have faith in you,” Jesus said.

Robin lowered her head in a brief nod. She appeared neither bothered nor relieved. As she exited through Jesus’s portal towards the waiting room, the holy-host noted the lack of expression on the Christian woman, and wondered when, and why, she lost investment in the show.

*****

Once Robin reached the waiting room, Oshunmare pounced her with a hug that lifted the human off her feet. Aside from the lizard-lady's vicious, affectionate attack, no obstacle prevented her from sitting next to Theodore. She leaned her head next to his and spoke low in a whisper, but only did so to disguise the fact that she had, in the same motion, brought her hand to her temple to attach her mind-swap bit.

Her consciousness ported to the second quartztaphore on Floor N, and she spoke to Theodore through its rubber voice box.

"I'm here," Robin said. "Everything ready?"

"Yeah," Theodore said. The two were situated flat on either side of the door of Floor N. The plan was simple—now that there were two contestants left on stage, wait in the quartztaphores, and observe what happens to the eliminated contestant. "No problems here."

At least, that was the plan the last time Robin and Theodore had talked about it.

*****

Zargah and Taninim looked to each other.

"Hey, whatever happens," Taninim turned his head, "it was nice meeting you, Zargah."

"You are a good guitar-dragon, Taninim," Zargah's antennae folded across the back of his head, and he clutched his hands to his side in worry.

Jesus let the camera linger on them a little longer after the exchange. She knew that sappy shit was good for ratings, and that was the extent of her emotions towards either of them.

"Taninim," Jesus said, "you have phoned in the exact same type of performance over and over again. Your work has become a parody of itself, and we struggle to see any serious potential in the world you've made."

Taninim's brow crunched over his yellow eyes. He squeezed the neck of his guitar tight enough that his claw cut into a string, which snapped. Heaven healed it back into place.

"Zargah," Jesus turned her head, the moons of her eyes flashed with inner light, "you gave us a bible when we asked for commandments. Though you produced a great deal of work, it was muddied, meandering, and completely off-topic."

Zargah's mandibles rubbed together anxiously.

"Frankly, we expected more from both of you. This was an extremely difficult decision," Jesus set her note cards down and rose from her chair. Her hair began to float around and above her head, electrified from the energy that welled up within her.

"Taninim," Jesus opened her mouth and a beam blasted forward. It created a portal of glassy energy, and through its sheen stretched a bland, yellowed hallway. "I'm sorry. We've lost faith in you."

*****

Jeremy dangled his legs over the hospital bed.

"The fever came back," his mother wrung her hands. She stood with the doctor outside of the room—the doctor thought he had shut the door all the way, but the frame had bumped into his leather shoe, and he did not notice the crevice which his voice carried through. Jeremy could hear everything.

"But there's something else," his mother pursed her lips. "He's just been... out of it. Much more so than normal. His entire mood went down the drain. I know the results aren't back yet, but it's like..."

Jeremy listened in. His eyes roamed across the hospital room and landed on individual items—a hung stethoscope, motivational posters, a waste disposal can with a hazardous material warning.

He wanted to daydream.

"A piece of him is... just... gone."

But more than that, he just wanted to go to sleep. He was tired in new ways, beyond the physical. To even try to think of the characters he crafted and the worlds he made was too much. Maybe if they came to him in his dream he'd have the energy to play with them, but he couldn't put forth the energy to visit their worlds while he was awake.

"It happened so fast. He was doing fine at the park earlier today, then... all of sudden he fell over. Color drained from his face. I thought he was going to throw up."

The doctor nodded and wrote on a clipboard. “What’s his diet been like lately?”

*****

Zargah exhaled, and the joints of his four shoulders drooped. The translation-collar mimicked the release of air in a synth-sigh.

The two monster-men embraced, and Taninim wished the alien soldier luck. He turned to the judges, accepted his fate, and played one last lick on his guitar before he bound into the portal. The judges laughed and applauded.

*****

Mark Sharkman tapped the end of his pen with a nervous speed against the clipboard. Imhotep tilted his head as a camera-arm whirled around him.

“I’m assuming you have some questions you want to ask me,” Imhotep crossed his legs, then laced his fingers around the outstretched knee. “Perhaps about my work? My victory?”

“Your victory, yes,” Mark shuffled uncomfortably. “Why did you have almost no reaction at all? Winning is huge for your longevity in the competition, and not just because you get immunity. You’ve clearly made a positive impact on the judges, yet I don’t read excitement from you.”

“These questions don’t sound like they’re coming from a reality TV show interview,” Imhotep cooed. “Is this your own curiosity? Or is there a different angle you’re attacking from?”

Mark’s pen-snapping hand froze after a loud, solid crack on the board.

“No matter,” Imhotep relaxed back into the interview chair, a far-off smile cast towards the wall of camera monitors that framed them both. “When you have lived as long as I have, you come to understand that battles like this are small. Not unimportant, mind you, but I am the sort of person that always keeps the bigger picture in mind."

*****

Theodore, in his own body, stood and waited near the empty space where contestants ported in. There was no reason not to—whoever came back would be someone he cared about, who likely needed consoling as much as he did.

Zargah's boots squeaked as he landed out of the portal. Santa and Oshunmare gasped. Conversations stopped. Surprise arrested the room: the majority believed Taninim would survive.

Theodore wrapped his arms underneath the top set of Zargah's. The alien-bug hugged Theodore close, his four arms joining in an x-shape around the small of Theodore's back.

"Perhaps I was foolish," Zargah's translation collar clicked, "I did not consider that anyone from our room would go so soon. Perhaps, that is what I wanted to believe."

They separated arms and Theodore nodded solemnly, his eyes drawn to the floor. He patted Zargah's shoulder, "Yeah. Me too."

*****

Taninim's leather boots crunched against the polished floor. There was no one there to accompany him, and with three different paths to go down, he wasn't sure where to head. He cupped his hands around the end of his snout and let the guitar strap hang loose around his neck.

"Hello?" Taninim called out. His voice echoed in empty, plain hallways. "Where do I go?"

Taninim was disappointed in his elimination, but not sad. Part of the barter he made to come on to the show was a guaranteed cure for Jeremy's symptoms, be they leukemia or any other sickness. To make a play-world for Jeremy to live in would have been sweeter, but as long as he could guarantee a happy, healthy life for his human, that was all that mattered to him. He expected, now that he was out of the competition, that an agent would meet him, and deliver unto him their end of the bargain.

"Is there anybody there?" he called out again.

*****

Imhotep reached up and grabbed a camera-arm by its slender pole, and jerked it down to his face.

"H-hey!" Mark leapt out of his chair. "Let that go!"

Imhotep ignored Mark, and squinted into the lens. "I want to be clear. If this footage gets used in the final cut or not doesn't matter to me. This is a promise..."

*****

Theodore and Robin waited in the camouflaged bodies of his quartztaphores around the door of floor N. Theodore would remain in the hallway, and Robin, who had better control and experience with the mind-swap, would port in and out to maintain their cover in the waiting room.

Theodore's impatience began to shake one of the large, spiky legs of his quartztaphore body, which distorted the illusion of its blended appearance into the wall. This was never a problem in poker, since he always remained seated during gameplay.

Come on, Theodore thought anxiously. *Whoever plans to hurt Taninim, get your ass over here so that I can kick it.*

He waited.

*****

Imhotep spoke from his chest in deep, rhythmic fury, "I *will* be the next great deity."

He let go of the camera-arm, which whined with gear-whirls and jerked away from him. Mark consoled the camera, then turned his head back to the Egyptian chancellor, who maintained eye contact with the lens. He was poised and collected, not a muscle on his face or body twisted without intention.

"Now send me away," Imhotep laced his fingers. "This interview is over."

Mark bared his triangular teeth in a grimace. "Who the hell do you think you are? Never touch my equipment! You don't get to control interviews, I do!"

Imhotep pursed his lips, but said nothing. Mark's shoulders drew in with escalating anger.

"And don't think you can just go quiet on me either!"

*****

And he waited.

*****

"Take the hallway to your left," a friendly voice instructed Taninim.

The dragon man whirled around, but found no one there.

"Come on now," the disembodied voice said. His tenor was clear and jovial, present and near, yet it radiated from the walls and ceiling despite the lack of speakers. "Just follow my instructions, little lizard. You want that cure, right?"

Taninim snorted, scanned the area once more for the owner of the voice, then stomped down the hallway, his hands gripped tight around the guitar neck.

*****

And he waited.

*****

Imhotep refused to speak. Mark assailed him with questions about his resheps, his performance, his disregard for manners and camera safety. It wasn't until the latter subject—the structural integrity of the camera-arm—that Imhotep bothered to open his mouth.

"We're in Heaven, aren't we?" his painted lips parted just enough to let his voice slither through. "What am I gonna do, break it?"

Mark's shark-snout scrunched. He clicked his tooth, and sent Imhotep out of his camera-world.

"Jackass," Mark stabbed the pen-nib into the clipboard.

*****

And he waited.

Poker players are notoriously good at waiting. They can pick up on the betting habits of lesser players, make a mental chart of the way their opponents play certain hands, then build strategies around counter-play against those ranges. But for Theodore to not hear the sound of Taninim's plod, or a judge's chatter, or the noodle of a golden guitar anywhere in the hallway, filled him with a new anxiety he had not known before, on or off the felt.

*****

Taninim came to a wooden door. A plain one, as drab and yellowed as the hallway that led up to it. He was surprised by the simplicity of these corridors, used to the gaudiness of Heaven's Heart Hotel as he was. *Am I still in the same place?* he thought as he reached for the doorknob.

The cool steel slid around his scaled fingers. He turned it, and pulled.

*****

And he waited.

"Theodore..." Robin ported her mind back in to the other quartztaphore body. "They're about to make us leave the waiting room. We have to go."

"They never came," Theodore tried to grit teeth the quartztaphore lacked. "Damn it! Did we get sidestepped? Were we completely wrong?"

Robin's crystalline head pointed to the floor. "Come on... let's go We can port back in here occasionally, but we *have* to move with the group or people will know something's wrong."

Theodore punched the wall with the back of his crystal fist.

*****

Taninim pushed the door open. His cool blue eyes blinked at the shimmer of the room—the floor, the walls, the furniture, the water fountain, the fans, the potted plants were all pearl. The entire room was pristine off-white, glittering in opulence beyond anything he had seen before. The only gradation of hue came from the dark steel of microphones and computer screens, guitar pickups and mixer boards.

"Come on in," the voice said.

"What's this place?" Taninim gawked as he lumbered in. "It's beautiful! Is this a recording studio?"

The door slammed shut behind him. Taninim turned, and the scaled ridges of his brow lifted high in shock. He noticed there was no knob on the other side of the door. His toothy maw separated in a gasp as the frame of the door melted away, replaced by pearl wall.

"It's a recording studio, indeed!" The jovial voice, once echoing and encompassing, now came from a single location. Taninim spun around to see a burst of bright yellow cloth among the pearl scenery.

"Ah!" Taninim shrieked. "Who are you? Where did you come from?!"

He was an imposing figure of eight feet in height. Head-to-toe he wore sunshine yellow—be it in his creased trousers, his pointed leather shoes, or his long trench coat. His face was hidden behind the yellow square of a welder's mask, and the seam of its construction gave the helmet a solid smile. There were only three pieces of clothing on the man's layers that broke the color palette—a crisp white collared shirt held the noose of his pink heart-patterned tie, and bright red leather gloves covered his hands.

"I'm The Producer," he adjusted the heart-shaped lapel of his long yellow coat. "It's a pleasure to meet you, Taninim. I'm a big fan of your work."

THE NEXT GREAT DEITY

Will return with volume 3:

THE ATHEIST OF HEAVEN

Acknowledgements

Thank you to everyone that's supported the TGND universe thus far. You mean the world, and beyond, to me.

Thank you to David, Zavian, Sara and Michael for helping assemble TAAV.

Thank you to Chrys for your incredible powers.

And thank you all for reading. See you next episode.

ABOUT THE AUTHOR

Millard Crow is a writer and artist out of Austin, TX. His work is powered by pacing in the living room. THE ANGELS ARE VOYEURS is his third novel.

Other works by Millard Crow:

-THE NEXT GREAT DEITY-

Two humans are abducted into Heaven, and forced to compete on a supernatural reality TV show hosted by Jesus Christ.

-GHOST ECONOMY-

Haunted by a digital ghost of his own design, Reese Gagnon falls into a void of paranormal and economic terror. A standalone queer horror-romance.